The McCarron's Destiny

Charlie's Story

Sharon K. Middleton

Black Rose Writing | Texas

ISBN: 978-1-68433-796-5
PUBLISHED BY BLACK ROSE WRITING
www.blackrosewriting.com

Printed in the United States of America
Suggested Retail Price (SRP) $19.95

The McCarron's Destiny is printed in Adobe Caslon

*As a planet-friendly publisher, Black Rose Writing does its best to eliminate unnecessary waste to reduce paper usage and energy costs, while never compromising the reading experience. As a result, the final word count vs. page count may not meet common expectations.

Praise for
The McCarron's Corner Series

"A tale with an intriguing historical setting and time-travel premise…"
–*Kirkus Reviews*

"…weaves vivid descriptions of the Revolutionary War era."
–*IndieReader*

"A richly imaginative series."
–Bruce Logan, author of *Finding Lien*

"Middleton writes different historical eras with ease."
–John Hazen, award-winning author of *Fava*

McCarron's Corner has won multiple awards for Historical Romance.

Acknowledgments

This novel is dedicated to all the animals and humans who have entered our lives and made our lives richer and fuller as a result of their presence with the love you only find once in your lifetime.

This has been a tough year. Stay healthy. Visit your family and friends. If you can't visit, then call. Tomorrow may be too late. No one knows for whom the bell tolls. It will toll for each of us some day.

Last, this is a work of fiction. While I try to be historically accurate, it is a novel, and not a history book.

The McCarron's Destiny

Charlie's Story

Cast of Characters

Charles Ranscome Hobbs Winslow – Hero of our story. Charles was born of the marriage of Charles Hobbs and Fancy Selk. His father died before his birth at the Battle of Yorktown. We met Charles first in *The McCarron's Daughter*. He traveled forward in time in *Diary of the Reluctant Duchess*, and saw him as a teen in *Path of the Guiding Light*.

Kelly Nguyen – Heroine of our story, Kelly is a second generation Vietnamese-American. Kelly loves Charlie enough to follow him to the ends of the earth. She is new to the *McCarron's Corner* series.

Francesca 'Fancy' Winslow – Charles' mom. We met her first at age 4 in *Home to McCarron's Corner*, and as a young woman in *Beyond McCarron's Corner*. Fancy is the story teller in the books since *Diary of the Reluctant Duchess*, where she wrote the story of the Duchess and changed her life.

Kirk O'Malley – Kirk was married to Fancy in the past. He is Charlie's stepfather. Kirk was presumed dead at sea. Kirk showed up years later and is now married to Melanie Henson O'Malley. We met him first in *The McCarron's Daughter*.

Bella Winslow Vargas – Charlie's sister, daughter of Fancy and her first husband, Calvin Hobbs. Calvin has long been dead. Bella was later adopted by Richard Winslow. We met her in *Beyond McCarron's Corner*, as an infant.

Dr. Miguel Vargas – We met Miguel in *Path of the Guiding Light*. Bella and he met at Trinity University. They marry in *The McCarron's Destiny*. They will appear again in future *McCarron's Corner* novels.

Tamsin Fitz Simmons – Fancy's mother and Charlie's grandmother. We met her first in *Home to McCarron's Corner*.

Sara 'Sassy' Selk – Richard's mother – We met her first in *Beyond McCarron's Corner*. Sassy was a historian in the future. She considered herself to be a Conservative. Richard correctly advised her she was a conservative in the future, but she is a progressive in the 1700's. She was one of Washington's spies, and convinced her husband, William, to free his slaves. She is pro-women's rights. She also helps craft the new constitution behind the scenes.

William Selk – we met Will in *Beyond McCarron's Corner*. He is married to Sassy, and he was also one of Washington's spies. He is a ship captain and owns plantations in Virginia and Puerto Rico.

Marcus McCarron Fitz Simmons – we first met introverted Marcus in *Beyond McCarron's Corner*. Tall, blonde, and always thinking. He fought in the French and Indian War and went west before the end of the war to establish McCarron's Corner. Fancy says he should have been a writer like her.

Lily McCarron Fitz Simmons – we first met extroverted Lily in *Beyond McCarron's Corner*. She then yelled at me until I wrote *Home to McCarron's Corner*, which is Marc and her story. She trained as a Cherokee shaman when she first arrived at McCarron's Corner as a young doctor. Tall, slim as a reed, with dark auburn hair and intriguing eyes, she is tough as nails.

Winston Fitz Simmons – Fancy's half-brother, son of Tamsin Fitz Simmons and Jay Fitz Simmons. We first met him in *The McCarron's Daughter*. Winston is tall, dark and handsome.

Annabelle 'Anne' Hays – daughter of Lord Hays who owns the Meadow Glen estate next over from Spring Haven in the Cotswolds. Petite, blonde, blue-eyed Anne looks like the perfect wife for an English nobleman. Anne is a new character.

Banastre Tarleton – we first met him in *The McCarron's Daughter*. Tarleton was a British Colonel in the Revolutionary War. He later wrote a memoir of his 'adventures' in the New World, in which he claimed to have had sexual relations with 20,000 women in the Colonies. He is considered a hero in Great Britain. He remains our 'bad guy' in *The McCarron's Destiny*. I cannot respect any man who bragged he had sex with 20,000 women!

Brice Darlington – Darlington is Tarleton's 'identical cousin.' He is often involved in Tarleton's bad acts.

Chapter 1
Bella's Wedding
Last Year

"Mom, is he here yet?" Our daughter, Bella, fretted as she peaked around me into the crowded cathedral.

I sighed and shook my head as I hugged her. "Sweetheart, Miguel is here. He is who matters most. He's your groom. Everyone is here except your brother. Charlie texted me that he is about twenty miles away now. The roads are icy coming in from College Station, and he is taking it very slow. Don't worry. Dad explained the delay. No one thinks Miguel or you chickened out … or eloped." I slapped her hands. "Don't bite your nails. You will ruin your pretty manicure. Everything will be fine. I promise."

Bella dropped her hands and took a deep breath. "Okay. I sure don't want to mess up my hands tonight. If you're sure he'll show up."

I hugged my beautiful daughter close to me again. It was three days before Christmas. I couldn't believe she was all grown up and about to get married. She looked incredibly beautiful in the exquisite fifties vintage wedding gown. The fitted bodice was made of pale silver silk with a matching fabric sash at the waist. Delicate silk orchids accented the neckline of the vintage gown. The skirt belled out gracefully into a full white tulle skirt perfect for my diminutive daughter. Her auburn hair was done in a soft updo that beautifully showed off her elegant, swan-like neck.

Selection of the gown had been a two-year ordeal. Bella first wanted a tea-length gown like Audrey Hepburn wore in Breakfast at Tiffany's. Her bridesmaids were going to wear tea-length 50's gowns in varying pastel shades. We looked for vintage gowns across the country. Bella had just tried on a beautiful dress that looked identical to the original Audrey Hepburn wedding gown when her eyes landed on the exquisite Ceil Chapman creation. In an instant, her plans changed from tea-length youthfulness to understated sophistication which still looked youthful but would be perfect for the cathedral wedding.

Bella still chose vintage fifties ball gowns for her attendants. She allowed each to select their favorite color. Bella chose Elizabeth as her maid of honor, and Liz glowed in the lavender tulle ball gown. I privately wished all the girls had chosen the lavender because it looked beautiful next to Bella's gown. Our Liz glows in any shade of purple. The other girls decided they would all wear periwinkle blue gowns made in a complimentary style that looked like they were also made by the renowned designer. The girls would all wear little white faux fur shrugs to help ward off the winter cold in the cavernous cathedral.

Faith Wolf, the adorable flower girl, was clad in a white gown with a full tulle skirt and a pale silver sash that matched the fabric in Bella's gown. It had a heart-shaped cutout on the back, but we had it specially made with long sleeves. She had a faux fur shrug to wear before and after the ceremony. Faith is the daughter of our friends, Baylie Smith-Wolf and Shadow Wolf, who goes by 'Max' here. She is 'differently abled,' as her mother puts it, and has a genetic disorder called partial trisomy 21. Baylie pulled Faith's straight black hair into a high ponytail which we managed to somehow style in curls. The flower petals the child carried were shades of blue, pink and white.

I wore a beautiful rose-colored mother of the bride outfit, with a jacket, a fitted waist and a 'fit 'n' flare' skirt. The guys wore James Bond style tuxedos like they wore at Bella's senior prom, white jackets, black trousers, white dress shirts, and black bow ties. They looked very debonair.

I still wasn't completely convinced Charlie was late getting here due to the weather. It was complicated. He met Kelly Nguyen a few months after we moved to San Antonio. They began as friends through animal rescue and quickly became an item. They went to each other's proms and continued to date in college.

It shocked us to learn that it was Kelly's brother who had been killed crossing McCullough Avenue one afternoon on his way home and that Chico, the dog Charlie rescued, had been her brother's dog, but her parents were always very polite with us. We always made sure Chico was put away in

Charlie's room when the Nguyen's came over. I didn't want to upset Kelly's mother.

We could see love blossoming between the young couple. Richard and I thought Kelly was perfect for him. I could see her dad wasn't thrilled she was dating Charles, but Col. Nguyen never uttered a word of criticism in our presence. He was always a bit guarded with us. I thought it was simply him trying to protect his wife since Charlie adopted their son's dog.

At Thanksgiving, everyone including Miguel and his family along with Kelly and her family came to our house for dinner. We have had big dinners like this with them several times. Afterwards, Charlie went down on one knee and asked Kelly to marry him. He pulled out the antique jade and diamond ring his father gave me long ago. Stricken, tears began to slide down her cheeks as Kelly stammered that she thought Charlie knew her parents expected her to marry a young man of Vietnamese American descent. I had never seen Kelly so submissive, so scared of her father before. She kept glancing at her dad as if she was terrified how he might react. Charlie paled and apologized to Col. Nguyen. Charlie then turned and left to return to Texas A&M without another word to anyone.

He had not had much to say to any of us since that fateful afternoon.

I thought he would come home for Christmas break when classes ended. Charlie called last Friday, and claimed he had assignments in the university vet clinic through the end of this week. I bit my tongue but let it go. He might have had clinic assignments. Not likely, but possible. I became worried when he didn't appear for the wedding rehearsal. The main things to practice were six-year-old Faith learning how to serve as flower girl, and for Bella's old Skye terrier, Mimi Munchkin, to get the routine down to carry the pillow with the rings attached, so she would give the pillow to Miguel at the appropriate time. Originally, it was planned that Bella's Mimi would give the pillow holding the rings to Charlie, who would untie the rings and hand them to Miguel. When Charlie failed to appear last night, we modified the plan.

Still, it would have been nice for Miguel's best man to show up. After all, doesn't the best man usually throw a bachelor's party for the groom? Fortunately, Miguel's dad stepped up to the plate and offered to fill in as best man if necessary. "After all, *m'hijo*, I'll already be there, and I have a tux for the wedding." Manny took the guys downtown for drinks at the revolving restaurant at the top of Tower of the Americas where they all told their favorite stories about Miguel.

Richard called Charlie and told him in blunt language that he expected Charlie to be here tonight for Bella and Miguel's wedding and 'to pull his head out of his butt asap.' I choked when Richard uttered those words. He isn't usually so blunt. That's more my style.

Miguel phoned him, too, and told Charlie that he was counting on Charlie to be here. It would break Bella's heart if her brother did not come, and it would cause a serious rift with Miguel and his family. I knew he dreaded seeing Kelly, but if he intended to back out, he should have told everyone weeks ago. He damned sure shouldn't have waited until literally the last minute.

"Don't worry, honey. Daddy says if your brother is not here by 8 that Dr. Vargas will be Miguel's best man and we will go ahead and start. In the meantime, Mrs. Manfort is playing Christmas songs and the audience seems to be having a great time in a singalong."

Bella rolled her eyes at me. "Oh, great. Just what I always dreamed my big cathedral wedding would be: singalong with Freda Manfort!"

Elizabeth giggled, insouciant as ever. "Chill, sis. It will be fine. They are singing Christmas carols. It's quite lovely. Listen."

Richard hurried in and hugged Bella. "Charlie's here, Bella Boo. Let's get a move on."

Her eyes lit up and she bounced on her toes with excitement. "Thank you, Daddy."

Miguel's brother, Matteo, began playing his guitar and singing the words to one of the Christmas versions of Leonard Cohen's Hallelujah.

"I've read about this baby boy

Who came to earth to bring us joy.

I just want to sing this song to you."

The groomsmen silently moved into place next to Miguel, as the bridesmaids began entering the cathedral. Dara would be the last bridesmaid to enter, and as the other girls began down the aisle, Dara began singing, also. We all smiled as Dara's lilting soprano voice began singing her part of the song selected to be the prelude as Bella would make her grand entrance.

"It goes like this, the fourth, the fifth, the minor fall, the major lift, with every breath I'm singing Hallelujah…"

"Gosh, I wish I could sing like she can." Bella sounded wistful.

"We all wish we could sing like Dara. You ready?" I whispered as I smoothed a stray hair into place.

Bella nodded as her beautiful blue eyes began to sparkle with excitement. As Matteo and Dara sang the Hallelujah refrain, Dara started down the aisle. Bella took a deep breath and then placed one hand on her father's arm and the other on mine so we could both walk our girl down the aisle.

I struggled to control my emotions. I did not want to cry. I was happy and excited for Bella, even though this new phase of her life would take my eldest child further away from me than we had been in years.

This was real. My baby girl was getting married.

The bridesmaids slowly walked down the aisle and then sweet little Faith started down the aisle as well. Faith blinked, her shoulders sagging, as if stunned the church had transformed since the previous night with the myriad blue and silver flowers, candles, and hundreds of people. Even the Christmas tree was decorated with blue and silver ornaments. The child stood pale and trembling until Baylie bent over, kissed Faith's forehead and whispered something to her child. Faith beamed up at her mom before she straightened her shoulders and started down the aisle exactly as she had practiced. After she walked a few steps, she began gently dropping the flower petals in front of the bride. We practiced that, because at first Faith wanted to gleefully throw handfuls of petals while shouting, "Here comes Bella! Here comes the bride!" As cute as that might have been, I am pretty sure both Bella and the Bishop were relieved to see Faith was able to contain her enthusiasm, so the focus remained on the wedding.

Just before we started down the aisle, Bella smiled at me. She pursed her lips in a kiss and whispered, "Thank you for everything, Mommy. I love you."

We've done that air kiss thing since she was little bitty. I dropped my hold on her arm and grabbed the air kiss with my right hand. I pressed it to my heart before I sent an air kiss back to her. I held my head up a little higher, retook her arm, and smiled, even more determined not to cry. "I love you more, my darling."

We began down the aisle with our daughter as Matteo's and Dara's beautiful voices soared again in the beloved chorus.

Then Matteo sang, "A couple came to Bethlehem.

Expecting child, they searched the inns,

To find a place where you'd be born soon."

Dara sang the next verse.

"There was no room for them to stay

So, in a stable filled with hay,

God's only Son was born,

Oh, Hallelujah!"

The bridesmaids reached the cathedral front, and turned to face the audience and the approaching bride, as the bridesmaids and groomsmen all joined in to sing the Hallelujah chorus.

They continued with the beautiful lyrics as Bella slowly processed through the exquisite cathedral to the front, where everyone joined in for the final refrain of hallelujahs.

Bella's eyes were bright with unshed tears as the song ended. When Bishop Garcia asked who gave this woman in holy matrimony, I struggled to hold back my own tears, but I held up my head proudly and said in unison with Richard, "We both do."

Bishop Garcia beamed at us. "I love it when both parents join together to give the bride away."

We placed Bella's hands in Miguel's, kissed them both, and went to our seats on the front pew. I glanced over at Marta Vargas, and realized she had tears running down her cheeks. She smiled and gave me a 'thumbs up' as she struggled to control her flood of emotions.

I nodded and struggled to smile, my lips trembling with emotions. Richard put an arm around me, pulling me close to him. He held my hands close to his heart and bent to kiss my cheek.

"I am sure everyone enjoyed that beautiful rendition of the Christmas version of Hallelujah as the bride's processional. We are gathered here this evening in the sight of God to unite this couple in Holy Matrimony. Marriage is a mysterious holy sacrament. It creates an indissoluble bond which unites the spouses, just as in one love, Jesus and the Church are united. Your mission as a married couple will be a service of love. Love is the reality in this mysterious sacrament. You see, God created mankind in his own likeness. He called humans into being through His love. After all, God IS love. That is why marriage is considered a holy sacrament."

Suddenly, a flood of memories swept me away. I remembered the day I learned I was pregnant with my sweet Bella. I was only seventeen and unwed.

I remembered when Calvin rescued me from Simon Le Grande and we fled to Mount Vernon, where my darling girl was born. I smiled as I remembered when Will took us west so Bella and I could live with his future wife, Sassy. More memories flooded me as I remembered our return to Belle Rose the next year, when Calvin and I married two years later in Bermuda, and how much he adored Bella.

I swiped at a tear sliding down my cheek as I recalled that awful day when Calvin died in my arms at Yorktown.

I smiled as I recalled falling in love with Richard, and how Bella gave me permission to marry him. When she told Richard, he was the 'very best daddy in the whole wide world.'

The memories continued to flood me as I could no longer contain my tears.

Richard hugged me closer. "You okay?"

Wordless, I nodded as I tried to smile up at my husband. "Yeah, but he better be good to her."

"He will be. He's a good man. He loves her with all his heart." He raised my hands to kiss them.

The San Fernando Cathedral was built in the 1700s by the original fifteen families of San Antonio settlers who immigrated from the Canary Islands. Richard proudly tells me that Sassy's family were among those original fifteen families. A statue dedicated to the original settlers is in front of the San Antonio Courthouse, across the street from the Cathedral. It is the oldest church in Texas, and it has a rich history in Texas of responding to the needs of the people in the community around the church.

It wasn't far from the cathedral to the Gunther Pavilion at the Briscoe, where the toney reception would be held. As we entered, I felt myself begin to relax for the first time in months. Everything was presented perfectly with just the right Hispanic and Texan features, or what Bella and Miguel termed "Texican Uber Chic." The guests milled about, sipping margaritas and mojitos as they waited for everyone to arrive. Soon, people were seated and being served dinner as the toasts began.

Everyone expected Charlie to give a toast as best man. He tapped a knife to his champagne glass, and as the crowd quieted, he began. "I met Miguel six years ago when we came to San Antonio so Bella could tour Trinity University. He was selected to be our tour guide because he was a biochem major who had a strong interest in music. He had been accepted to begin medical school at UTMB San Antonio the following fall. With that unusual combination, he seemed a perfect fit to escort our family on the tour of the campus. It didn't take long to spot the sparks flying between this pair. It didn't take much longer to figure out they were madly in love."

He clicked a button and the lights dimmed as a video began to play on the screen behind him. "Six years ago, at Bella's senior prom, Miguel asked my sister to marry him. He loved her then. He loves her now. You only find a love like this once. You only find it then if you are meant to be together. Miguel, Bella, I love you guys. May your love endure through all eternity."

I think a few people were surprised his toast was so short. I was impressed he showed up for the wedding and somehow managed to make a toast at the reception. The video of Miguel's proposal was a clever touch that added sweetness and poignancy to the moment and enabled Charlie to make a great toast with a minimum of words.

As the toasts ended, I noticed Charlie edging towards the exit. Mental alarms began to sound when Kelly quietly arose and followed him. Silent, I slipped from my seat to follow them outside. I wanted to see whatever was about to transpire between those two.

"Charles, wait!"

Charlie leaned his head against the door as he let out a long sigh. "Not now, Kelly. Not tonight. I am not up to any more drama tonight."

She grabbed his sleeve. "Please, Charles, we need to talk-"

"About what? Your answer was 'no.' Your dad wants you to marry some Vietnamese American guy. God forbid you should marry an 'evil white man'. Believe me, I got it the first time."

"That's not fair." She struggled not to cry.

He shrugged. "Life isn't fair. You want to talk? Not tonight. You are not going to ruin my sister's wedding."

She snorted angrily. "Well, you sure sound righteous. You nearly ruined the whole damned thing."

He rolled his eyes as he sighed, exasperated. "And this is exactly why I did not want to come, but I did. The wedding was beautiful. So is the reception. Now, I'm leaving. Don't start this tonight."

He pulled his sleeve from her grasp as tears welled up in her beautiful dark eyes again.

"But Charlie, we need to talk-" she began, her voice quivering.

He shook his head. "No, not tonight. I already told you I want to marry you. You said no. I am not going to reopen this conversation at my sister's wedding reception."

"Charlie, you know I love you…"

At that point, I felt like an interloper in a private moment. I cringed as I observed tears slide down her cheeks.

My son shut his eyes again, trying to blot out the sight. "Not tonight, Kelly, please. Make up your mind whether you are going to remain Daddy's little girl or whether you are a woman who wants your own once-in-a-blue-moon love. But rest assured: I am damned sure not begging you to marry me tonight at my sister's wedding." He pushed the door open and then turned back to her. "You know where I will be."

"But Charlie…" Her voice became even more tremulous as she struggled to contain her sobbing.

He shook his head again. "Not. Tonight."

Charlie quickly strode over to his Ford F-250 pickup. As he opened the door, Kelly caught up to him. As she grabbed his arm again, he laid his head against the door. "Oh, God, not tonight, Kelly. You're killing me. Not here. Please, don't make a scene here in the parking lot of the ritziest hotel in town. Please, babe, not tonight."

"But Charlie-"

He gently eased her clutching fingers from his arm. "You're killing me, Kell. We can talk tomorrow. I can't deal with this tonight outside my sister's wedding reception." He looked into her tear-filled eyes. "And if your answer is still no, then we really have no need to talk at all."

He climbed into the truck, started the ignition, and carefully eased it away from the beautiful girl standing by herself crying in the parking lot. I slipped back into the pavilion, letting the door quietly shut as Kelly stood weeping as she watched Charlie's truck drive down the street.

Chapter 2
Duke and Darby

It wasn't always so melodramatic in the Winslow home. Everything changed when our son's old dog died.

Darby was a puppy when Charlie found him. The dog had been an integral part of our lives ever since. Charlie told us many times that Darby rescued him over the years. It became his mantra.

Charlie was a timid child when we first moved to Georgia. My shy boy had a hard time fitting in with the new gang in the new town. The Irish accent didn't help. At least, he seemed to have a hard time fitting in until he found that ragged, little puppy outside the local Dairy Queen right after his fourth birthday. Richard said there was a Blue Moon that night. That meant it was the second full moon of the month. Darby made a miraculous change in Charlie. Our shy, introvert became outgoing and confident with the help of a little red mutt.

A few years later, the Blue Ridge Animal Shelter did a commercial about Duke and Darby they called 'Rescued by His Rescuer.' That one-time commercial evolved into occasional infomercials, and finally into a weekly television show. There is a lot of difference between occasional five-minute infomercials and a weekly thirty-minute show. Charlie had to feature at least two animals per segment. He interviewed veterinarians as well as pet groomers and trainers. They included special tips about the animals featured that day, including any unusual vet and dietary needs, grooming, or training needs the featured animals might have. Charlie began drawing the featured Rescuer of the Week. Charlie got the idea from his art teacher, who encouraged Charlie to incorporate drawings into the show. The illustration of the animal was then presented to the person who adopted the animal the week after the show aired, in a segment of the show called 'Duke's Doodles.' Charlie progressed from colored pencils to watercolors and finally to working in oils by his sophomore year in high school. That year, the Atlanta paper ran a full-page spread about our talented teen. When he was a sophomore, Charlie received an award from the Governor for his Duke and Darby program, which helped re-home 1500 animals since it began as a commercial years before. The governor showed vignettes of the animals placed through Charlie's efforts over the years. He also showed the drawings of many of the animals Charlie had drawn, although the governor focused on the ones created since the television show began the segment called 'Duke's Doodles.'

Darby received an award as well. Charlie always insisted Darby was the real Rescuer, and he just helped. Darby 'sat pretty' as the Governor placed the ribbon around Darby's neck, and slurped a big kiss across the Governor's face when presented with a new squeaky toy.

But then, tragedy struck.

Around the time of the Governor's Award, Darby began having some health issues. He started wheezing and coughing. The vet told us Darby suffered from congestive heart failure and his heart was giving out. The vet put Darby on medication to help control his heart condition. It worked for a few months, but soon, the drug no longer proved to be of much help. Richard and I figured the dog knew his time was drawing near and he was preparing to cross the Rainbow Bridge. Charlie could not accept that his beloved companion was on a downward spiral.

Despite all Charlie's efforts, the day finally came when Darby crossed the Rainbow Bridge. Darby waited patiently by Charlie's bed until Charlie came home from school that afternoon, just like he did every day. Charlie gently lifted Darby onto his bed, and Darby crawled into his master's lap. I smiled as I heard the old dog sigh. I figured he laid his head on Charlie's knee as Charlie began to tell Darby about his day at school.

But then, Charlie's voice faltered, and he called out, "Mom, please come here. I need you."

I didn't like the tremor in my son's voice. I frowned and tossed the dish towel down to hurry to his room. "What's up?"

But, as soon as my eyes landed on my son, I knew. Tears filled my eyes. My fifteen-year-old son sat on his bed, hugging the body of his best friend as he rocked back and forth with tears streaming down his cheeks.

"Why, Mom? Why did he have to die? Dad's a cardiovascular surgeon. Why couldn't anyone save my dog?"

I cringed at the pain in Charlie's voice. Wordless, I rushed to his bed and sat down beside my son and pulled him into my arms. "He waited for you to come home. He died in your arms. This little dog knew he was loved every single day he lived with you. He waited for you to come home so he could tell you goodbye."

My voice broke off. It can be hard to talk while you cry. Charlie and I sat there, crying, hugging the still, lifeless body of the little red dog who meant so much to all of us for all those years.

The Duke and Darby show did not air that week. The following week, the show was somber. It was short one of the featured players.

"My name is Charles Winslow. My friends call me 'Duke.' My best friend died last week. I would like to tell you about Darby and how he rescued me all those years ago."

Charlie told his audience about his dog. How, in Charlie's mind, God sent Darby to rescue Charlie after we moved to the mountains of North Georgia, which is vastly different from where we lived on the southern coast of Ireland. The life my children had in Georgia was wonderful, but it was quite different to grow up in a log home on five acres in the Cashes Valley than to grow up in an Elizabethan manor house overlooking the bay, outside of Cork. Charlie told how he felt so lost, so dreadfully foreign and alone when we first settled in Ellijay years ago. And then, how a little red dog named Darby rescued him.

Charlie explained how Darby became the 'spokes-dog' for the regional shelters, to help other families find their Rescuer as he found in Darby. Charlie showed numerous photos of Darby taken over the years by my husband as well as from the commercials and the television show throughout the episode. At the end, Charlie showed a painting of Darby in the meadow by our home. I remembered Darby jumped high into the air that day to catch the ball Charlie tossed to him. My husband managed to capture the moment on film, and Charlie painted it. Charlie then read an essay he wrote in tribute to his dog.

My old dog died today.

He was my heart dog, my best friend.

My old dog died today.

He lived with me for eleven years and ten months.

My old dog died today.

He rescued me when I needed a friend the most.

My old dog died today.

He could heel, sit, come, and stay when just a pup.

My old dog died today.

He laid beside me when I was sick. He gave me the will to live.

My old dog died today.

He helped me to survive by the magic of his love.

My old dog died today.

He loved me and slept beside me on my bed every night.

My old dog died today.

He waited until I came home to cross the Bridge.

My old dog died today.

His old heart, so filled with love, finally gave out.

My old dog died today.

He was my once-in-a-blue-moon friend.

My old dog died today.

What will I do without him?

My old dog died today.

And part of me died today as well.

"Run brave and free, Darbs. I'll meet you at the Rainbow Bridge, I promise. I love you."

Richard pulled me close to his chest and murmured words of love as I sobbed in the wings as the screen faded to black. A small note at the end stated the show would be off the air while Duke tried to adjust to the loss of Darby, but that Duke wanted everyone to remember that second hand-pets made first-hand friends. Duke and Darby wanted them to come on out to their local shelters and find their rescuers like Duke found with Darby.

Bittersweet.

We all cried as the director called it a wrap.

The following Monday afternoon, Charlie surprised me by coming to the clinic after school. "My English teacher is raving about the poem, " Charlie announced, his voice somber.

I glanced up from the chart I was working on and smiled at my handsome son. "I didn't expect to see you at the clinic today. Hmm. Is it a poem? What did he say?"

He shrugged. "Mr. Carlton said he really liked it. He gave me an A on it for my junior writing project. I think he felt sorry for me since my dog died. He wants to send it into some poetry competition with the AWP, whatever that is."

"The American Writing Program? That's a big deal, Charlie."

He nodded as he twisted a packet of papers in his hands. I noticed he couldn't quite look me in the eye, a sure sign the situation troubled him. "Yeah, that's what Mr. Carlton said. Here's the information he gave me about this contest. Heck, I didn't even know it was a poem until he told me. He laughed when I said that. He said if I win, I will have to go to their awards ceremony."

I tilted my head as I studied Charlie's face. Hmm. Maybe that was the source of his agitation and conflict. He sounded excited, but his brow furrowed into worry lines I didn't usually see on my teen's face. As I began looking over the papers, he began gnawing on his thumbnail, always a sure sign he felt anxious. My usually straightforward teen was sending very mixed messages through his body language. "Where will the conference be held?"

He laughed, but the sound was joyless, brittle, like a boot crushing an autumn leaf. "San Antonio."

"Oh." No wonder his face showed such ambivalence. We planned to move there at the end of the school term, and Charlie was less than thrilled. "Heck, you wouldn't even get a nice trip out of that deal."

"Yeah. Not the chocolate I would have chosen for myself."

I took a big breath before I tackled The Subject. "You know, son, there will be shelters there where you can work —"

"No. It won't be the same, Mom. I won't have Darby to help me." He rubbed his forehead as if trying to rub away the pain eating at him from the death of his best friend. His voice choked up, and he turned towards the door as if he were about to leave.

"Charlie, your dog would not want you to give up," I coaxed. "And maybe you would find-"

"Don't say it, Mom, I won't find another Darby. There isn't another Darby. He was one of a kind. Remember? He was my 'once-in-a-blue-moon' dog. They don't come along every day." His voice cracked as he spoke.

I shook my head. "No, but maybe you could help some other kids find their Darby, their once-in-a-blue-moon dog. After all, second-hand pets make—"

"First-hand friends. Yeah, I know, Mom. I'm the one who came up with that slogan. Remember?" He tried to smile.

My heart ached for my son. The poor kid was taking the death of his dog damned hard, and I didn't have a clue how to help him with his overwhelming grief. This went way beyond 'bittersweet.' That little red mutt helped my kid adjust to North Georgia years ago. What would help Charlie adjust to all the changes facing him now?

Charlie did not resume the show. They produced one additional episode in the spring, as a summary of Duke and Darby over the years. Charlie called it a tribute to Darbs. At the end of the show, Charlie stated we would be moving to Texas soon and the show would not resume production. Once again, he reminded people that shelter dogs, cats, and other animals would continue to need homes. "I appreciate all you have done for the animals in our community over the years. After all, second-hand pets make first-hand friends. Please don't forget them when I move. Come on out and find your new best friend. Thank you for all your years of encouragement and support, and goodbye from all of us with the Duke and Darby Show."

Everyone was in tears as we left the set.

We moved to San Antonio a month to the day after the semester ended. It thrilled my husband to be back in San Antonio. He spent the first ten years of his life here while his dad taught history at Trinity University. Richard always considered San Antonio to be 'home.' It delighted him to purchase the historic Del Monte mansion he dreamed of owning since he was a kid riding his bike through the elegant, high-priced neighborhood near Trinity.

Charlie appeared anything but thrilled to be in San Antonio. Sullen and despondent, he managed a nod at the pool, but not much more. It was as if his ability to laugh, joke, and smile vanished as we crossed the Georgia state line while we drove to Texas. With each passing mile, Charlie seemed more morose, withdrawn and reticent. An introverted, sad boy replaced the outgoing and confident young man Charlie had become over the past twelve years.

Richard and I hoped Charlie's mood would change once we settled into life in San Antonio. It did, but not for the better. As his depression and anxiety escalated, Charlie complained about the Texas heat, which I loved. He often wistfully commented about how much he missed the mountains, rivers, and lakes back home. We took the kids to the Texas Hill Country, hoping Charlie would fall in love with the wide-ranging beauty of the state. He remained unimpressed. My son who always wore a smile and had a happy outlook on life in Georgia saw nothing positive about Texas. His unspoken grief broke our hearts.

Charlie moped a lot that summer. He swam in the pool in the backyard and worried about his fall classes. Charlie would be a senior. He also enrolled for the second year in dual credit courses that counted for both his senior high courses and for college credits. He already earned a year's worth of college credits his junior year in Ellijay.

Charlie often walked the three blocks to Trinity, where he became a common sight in the expansive Chapman Library. Charlie spent many hours there researching colleges with pre-vet programs and applying on-line for admission the following year.

Charlie also did a lot of running once he realized how easy it was to get to Breckenridge Park from our new home. The wooded trails of the park snake along part of the San Antonio River, providing a quiet refuge in the busy city which my son desperately needed. He would go on long runs from our house, across the Trinity campus, through the low water crossing in Breckenridge Park, hanging a left at the Witte Museum, and continuing down Broadway to Richard's new offices near Central Market. After a rest and a drink of water, Charlie would head back to the house, often going by the Japanese Tea Garden or the zoo, both also located in the Park. By fall, he lost any residual baby fat as his muscles tempered into a lean, mean, running machine. Richard joined Charlie several times a week for the five-mile run, with new definition to his already well-honed abs. They also found a local branch of the Fight Club, a mixed martial arts studio Richard and Charlie used to attend in Georgia, so they could continue their workouts. The guys insist MMA is a fabulous stress reliever. God knew they both needed stress relief and it kept them in great physical shape.

But nothing we did could get Charlie to visit the animal shelter located in the park. Each time I suggested he stop by there on his run and see if they could use another volunteer, his eyes clouded with unshed tears. He could try to smile and would shrug when no words would come out. I knew what he meant. Not yet, Mom. I'm nowhere near ready.

Classes soon began, and the new high school kept him busier than ever before. Charlie loved and hated St. Anthony's. He had never attended a private school before, but he always excelled in his studies. Charlie quickly realized this school was far more stringent than his old high school in Ellijay. He was busy with his studies, working hard to maintain his excellent grades in his dual credit classes. He wanted that perfect 6.0 grade point average from his new high school and college classes like he earned in Georgia. He knew that would make a big impact on future vet school admission.

One afternoon, he came in cussing up a storm. I didn't even attempt to correct him about the profanity. I just grabbed his arm. "What happened? What upset you so much?"

He jerked away from me. "I won that damned poetry contest. The dean read the blasted poem out loud at an assembly today and showed a clip from our last show. My dog died. It just about kills me every time I see that blasted video or hear that damned poem. I ... I ..."

And then he collapsed. Literally. I caught him as he went down, and he laid in my arms, crying for the loss of the little red dog who owned his heart for so many years.

"It's okay, honey. Everything will be okay. You don't have to go to the awards ceremony. You can skip it. I know the loss of your dog is still eating at you—"

"No, Mom, it's killing me. I swear, I think I'm losing my mind. I can't find myself here. I'm so lost."

I cringed as his voice broke with emotion.

"You need a new rescuer, Charlie, but you're afraid to open up enough to allow another animal into your heart to rescue you." I sat, rubbing his back, struggling to find the right words.

His head jerked up to stare at me. At first, he started to protest, but then, the tears began again. "I just can't, Mom. I'm not ready for another pet. I'm still grieving for Darby. How do I ever replace my best friend?"

I hugged him close, secretly thrilled as his hands clung to me like he did when he was a little boy. "You don't. You can never replace Darbs. But at some point, you may want another animal in your life. After all, don't you want to be a vet someday? That's what you've told me for years. Your college applications are all for colleges with outstanding veterinary medicine programs. Look, I don't care where you go or what you study. I want you to feel fulfilled. Heck, you can go to Oxford, or skip college and go straight to London to the House of Lords if that is what you want."

He groaned. "I doubt my future lies there, Mom. Can you imagine the way those snooty lords would react to my southern drawl?"

I laughed at the thought. "They would probably mock you every bit as much as the boys did in Ellijay about your Irish accent when we moved there. But the bigger issue right now is how are you going to deal with your grief? What can we do to help you?"

My tall, gangly son arose from the floor in a smooth, languid movement that foreshadowed the graceful man he would someday become. His tall, handsome, and elegant father was quite a bit older than me. I never knew him when he was Charlie's age. I suspect Charlie looks a lot like his dad looked when Calvin was a teen. I see a lot of his dad in Charlie's features although Charlie is much sweeter than his dad. Calvin could be the most charming man on the face of the earth one minute and a total ass the next. But I digress. Besides, I shouldn't talk poorly about the dead.

Charlie sighed as he walked over to his desk, where he picked up a photo of Darby and him. He gently caressed the edge of the sleek, stainless steel frame as a smile teased his lips. Finally, he sat the photo back on his desk, rubbed his forehead and took a deep breath. "I think I need a counselor here, like I had back home."

I nodded, excited to hear him ask for help. "I'll find one, son. I'll call Dr. Tanakawa and get him to refer us to someone. I promise."

He nodded and tried to smile. "Thank you, Mom."

Chapter 3
The New Beginning

The next day, I began searching for a counselor to work with my sixteen-year-old son. I started by calling our old counselor in Blue Ridge. Dr. T gave me the names of psychologists and licensed professional therapists in San Antonio. It took me a week to find the one I thought would be the best fit for Charlie and another week to manage to schedule a session for Charlie to meet with her. After the first appointment, Charlie had little to say to me, but he seemed less grief-stricken. Inch by inch, day by day, the hold his grief held on Charlie seemed to lessen.

Finally, the weather turned a bit cooler. What would have felt like crisp, cool autumn in North Georgia was winter in South Texas. Charlie often ran the half mile from school to the house after his classes. He would sling down his backpack before changing out of his school uniform and then would run on to his therapist's office. If he had therapy on a day when he had classes at the university, he went straight to the therapy session after those classes. Either way, I usually picked him up after his weekly therapy session.

I was late to pick him up that day. I showed the pre-surgical video to a group of heart patients, and afterward, as usual, they had heaps of questions. As I finished, I texted Charlie I was on my way to get him. He texted back he was walking home through the park, that he was fine, and I didn't need to hurry. I texted him a little later to see if he changed his mind. It surprised me when my phone rang almost immediately.

"Mom? Would you mind coming after me? I'd like to talk to you about an idea I have." He sounded excited for the first time in months.

I smiled, thrilled to hear a note of excitement in his voice again. "Sure. Where are you?"

He gave me the address and directions. My heart lurched as I realized it was right across the street from the zoo. "I'll be there in a few minutes."

I blinked back tears as I pulled up to the Paul Jolley Center for Pet Adoptions. I took a deep breath, squared my shoulders, put on my best smile, and walked in, still wearing my surgical scrubs from the clinic. *Oh, dear God, let this work for my son.* "Hi, I'm Mrs. Winslow. I'm here to pick up my son, Charles. I hear he dropped by today."

The jovial, older lady sitting at the desk smiled. "Oh, yes, ma'am. What a sweet young man you have raised. Charles really impresses us. He seems very mature and has such a love for animals. He's chatting with the director right now and visiting some of the dogs."

That sounded good. Really good. My heart in my throat, I forced another smile. "Would it be alright if I went in? I'd love to see the facility, too."

Her face lit up with a big smile as she jumped up from her seat. "Oh, of course, Mrs. Winslow. Please follow me."

I walked up behind the director and Charlie. My son knelt by a little, scruffy brown dog, a good bit smaller than Darby. The dog's suspicion of the strange boy was evident. The little dog growled and backed away from the beef jerky in Charlie's extended hand. Charlie kept talking, soft and low, and after a few minutes, the little dog's tail wagged. Then, the little fellow crept over to Charlie and snatched the jerky out of his extended hand.

Charlie grinned at the director. "Beef jerky wins them over every time."

The director beamed at Charlie. "That's amazing, son. He hasn't wanted any human contact since the family returned him two weeks ago."

"They weren't the right match for him." Charlie reached over and scratched the little dog between his ears. The little dog's head whipped up, and for a minute, I feared the dog would bite my son. Instead, after a moment's pause, the little dog licked Charlie's hand. The little dog sighed and seemed to relax to the comforting touch of the human boy knelt beside him.

"Good boy. What a good boy." As Charlie glanced up at the director I noticed a smile played on his lips and a new light shone in his eyes. "I worked with several dogs like him in Georgia, Mr. Jones. He's been badly hurt, first, when his boy died, and he wound up here, and a second time when the adoptive family returned him. He lost his trust, but he can learn to trust again."

Mr. Jones grinned. "Yes, I believe he can, Charles."

I cleared my throat, and the slender, silver-haired man whirled around. "Oh, I didn't know you were there, ma'am. May I help you?"

I held out my hand. "It looks like you already have, Mr. Jones. I'm Mrs. Winslow, Charles' mother. I'm so glad he decided to drop by to see you."

Mr. Jones pushed up his glasses as he grabbed my hand to shake it vigorously. "Oh, yes, indeed, I'm thrilled Charles dropped by and asked to see me. Once he gets to know the dogs, he's going to start doing some commercials for us."

I struggled to contain my excitement. "Well, he has a real knack to convince people to open their hearts to second-hand pets."

"That's what I understand. So, you'll be coming back on Saturday, Charles? May I advertise that you will be here?"

I gasped as the little dog crawled into Charlie's lap.

My son slowly stroked the little dog. As the dog sighed, Charlie smiled. "Yes, sir. But no one will know who Charles Winslow is. The old show was called 'The Duke and Darby Show.' You might get one of the old commercials from Blue Ridge and say Duke will be here to interview prospective new team members. Although I must tell you, Mr. Jones, this little guy has my vote right now."

He smiled again. I thought my heart might burst as Charlie's smile spread across his face and into his beautiful, chocolate brown eyes. I had not seen him look so animated, so downright happy, much less a smile to reach his eyes, since Darby died.

"What's his name?" I asked, as Charlie and the little dog began playing on the floor.

"His name is Chico," said Mr. Jones. "He's four years old. It's a tragic situation. The young man who owned him was killed in an auto-pedestrian accident."

"Oh, my God, how horrible!" I cringed.

"Mr. Jones, could I come back before Saturday to see him again? Maybe I could take him out in the fenced yard," Charlie said. "We could play some fetch."

Mr. Jones smiled. "Charles Winslow, you are welcome to come by anytime we are open."

Charlie patted Chico on the head again and arose from the floor to walk out with me. As he started towards the kennel gate, Chico whined and put his front paws on Charlie's leg, his tongue lolling out of his mouth beguilingly. Charlie bent back down to the little dog. "Aw, it'll be okay, Chico. I'll be back tomorrow. But we gotta take this slow, little fellow. We have to know this is right for both of us."

I pulled Mr. Jones aside. "Don't let that dog go with anyone else. Please, let Charlie and the dog see if they are a match."

Mr. Jones patted my hand. "Believe me, Chico won't go to anyone unless I think it is the right placement. Let's keep our fingers crossed."

I nodded as I held up my crossed fingers to Mr. Jones before I headed out the door after my son. I struggled to keep a bland face as we started for the car. Finally, I could hold it in no longer. "I'm so proud of you, son."

He chuckled, obviously embarrassed. "Well, don't be, just yet. Let's see how this works out. But, Mom, I had a dream that it was time. What is it you say about dreams? If you dream it three times, it's an omen? Well, last night was the third time I dreamed that Darby was scolding me for not helping pets find their furever homes. I managed to go by there a couple of times, and Mrs. Adler – that's the secretary at the front desk – showed me around. I finally managed to make myself talk to Mr. Jones today. I resisted talking to him the first couple of times I went by, but my therapist urged me to give it a go. Today, I summoned up my courage and walked to the shelter. Mr. Jones seems like a nice guy. He thinks it's wonderful I want to become a vet."

"Good for you, son. Darby would be so proud of you."

I regretted saying it as soon as the words left my lips. I watched the happy teen turn somber again in a flash. Nostrils pinched tight, and with anxiety clear on his face.

"Would he, Mom? Or would he be upset?"

Oh, gosh, think fast, Fancy. "No, honey, I think Darby would be happy for you, and for all the animals that you will help to find their furever homes. That's why he keeps appearing in your dreams."

"I sure hope you're right."

But the smile was gone. Charlie rode the rest of the way home in silence as he gnawed on his thumbnail. He doesn't usually bite his nails, but he will give that thumbnail 'what for' when he is anxious. He headed straight to his room when we got to the house.

Richard came in a little later, carrying a bouquet of blue irises and a bottle of my favorite Chardonnay. He drew me into a kiss that swept me off my feet.

Richard kissed me again quickly as he raised me to my feet. "How did you persuade him to go?"

I shook my head. "I didn't. It was his decision. He says he had a dream three times which motivated him to go. He and his therapist agreed Charlie needed to go check it out. He walked there after therapy today. Our sly young fox already went over there a couple of times to scope out the place. Today, he talked with the manager. They worked on a deal for Charlie to do commercials for the shelter. But, Richard, that's not the best part. He found a dog!"

Richard laughed, his amber eyes glowing with mischief. "Well, sweetie, it's an animal shelter. I'm sure he found lots of dogs – oh! You mean, a dog for him?"

I nodded. "I think so. Charlie and the dog are going to see each other a couple of times before Charlie says 'yes,' for sure, but I saw that look on his face like he had the first day when he found Darby. I think this dog will win his heart."

My husband beamed at me. "That's wonderful. We'll keep our fingers crossed. After all, Saturday is going to be a blue moon."

My heart leapt. "Just like when he found Darbs."

Richard nodded. "Exactly."

Charlie went over to the Center every afternoon the rest of the week. He visited with other dogs as well, but by Friday, Charlie confirmed the one who stole his heart was the little brown wire-haired dachshund called Chico. And on Saturday, they recorded the infomercial, highlighting several of the dogs.

"Hi, my name is Charles Winslow. I used to do "The Duke and Darby Show" in the Atlanta area. Darby was my dog, and we used to work with rescue groups in North Georgia to help second-hand pets find new homes. You see, second-hand pets can make first-hand friends. I know that because when I discovered my Darby, he had been thrown away. Literally. A woman tossed him out of a car onto the side of a busy street. I was just a little kid then, but I jumped up and ran to rescue the terrified puppy. My dad says things like that rarely happen. He says they only happen 'once in a blue moon.' They are meant to be. And later, Darby became my rescuer."

At that point, they began showing pictures from the Duke and Darby Show.

"Oh, you folks thought I rescued Darby. Well, I guess that in a way, I did. But, you see, Darby then rescued my family and me several times. Darby was more than a second-hand pet who became my first-hand friend. He was my best friend. My confidant. My biggest supporter. He was truly my once in a lifetime bestie. Together, Darbs and I helped over 1500 second-hand pets find brand new, loving, furever homes where they could be first-hand friends to their humans.

"But then, my best friend died. And to top it off, my family moved from the mountains of North Georgia to San Antonio. I love San Antonio, don't get me wrong, but it has been rough adjusting for me. I miss the mountains. I miss my friends. But most of all, I miss my dog.

"Then, this past week, I had a dream. My Darby came to talk to me. We played frisbee in the meadow beside our home in Georgia before we sat down beneath a giant pine tree there, just like we used to do. As we sat cooling off in the shade, my dog told me he was disappointed I stopped helping other animals find their furever homes where they, too, could be rescuers. He said it was high time for me to get up from my pity party and to start helping others again.

"He told me something else, too. He told me to go find myself a new rescuer because I needed to be rescued all over again. It was time for me to find a new Blue Moon friend."

At that point, Charlie struggled to maintain his composure. I stood in the wings, crying my eyes out, as I watched my son. I pressed my hand against my lips, hoping it would help muffle the sounds of my crying. Richard sniffed and placed his arm around my shoulders. I glanced up at him and tried to smile. Richard leaned over and kissed my cheek as Charlie began to speak again.

"I love you," Richard whispered.

"I love you, more," I choked out the words and gave him a tremulous smile.

Charlie cleared his throat and began talking again. "So, I came down here and spoke to the folks. They showed me around and introduced me to some of the dogs. You see, I'm a dog man. I knew my rescuer would be a dog.

"I saw some great dogs that day. And, then I met Chico, a funny little brown dog. Mr. Jones says Chico is a registered wire-haired dachshund. I didn't know there was such a thing as a wire-haired dachshund. Chico seemed very sad when I first met him. His owner died a few months ago in an auto-pedestrian accident. He was about my age. A car hit the young man crossing McCullough after school one day. The odd thing is the young man attended my school. His mom couldn't bear to look at Chico after her son died. So, Chico went to another family, but he never quite bonded with them. After a month, the family returned him. Mr. Jones tells me Chico became more depressed after he was returned to the shelter. It was as if the little guy gave up all hope.

"When I visited Chico, he held back at first. I knew how he felt. Was this too good to be true? Would he be hurt again? But over the next few days, we began to bond. We have already become pretty good friends. Chico will come home with me today. And by the way, tonight is a blue moon, just like it was when I found my Darby.

"Do you know why they call it a 'blue moon'? A blue moon occurs when you have a second full moon in a month. Blue moons are rare, about as rare as finding the ideal pet for yourself. That's what I call finding your blue moon friend, the one so rare and perfect a match for you that you would swear you found him -or her – during a blue moon.

"No, I understand Chico cannot replace Darby. No one dog can. But I realize there is room in my heart for another friend. I need another dog, and Chico needs me. We will work together to rescue each other and to become a team. We will work with the Paul Jolley Center for Pet Adoptions to help other second-hand pets find their first-hand friends and furever homes as well. I'll come to the shelter and we will feature a dog of the week. Today's dog is Chico. Don't call for him. He already claimed me. Blue moon, remember? But Chico and I hope you will call or come by to visit the other great dogs and cats at the Adoption Center. We also hope you will come back to see us in this new adventure we are about to begin together.

"I'm Charles Winslow. This is my new dog, Chico. We will be looking for a name for our show. Please email your suggestions to the Center. And please, always remember, second-hand pets make first-class friends."

"That's a wrap! That was fabulous, young man. Your show is going to be fantastic. You're a natural," gushed the director.

The sound man nodded in agreement. "I never saw a kid own the camera the way Charles does. Well done, young man."

"So, you're calling yourself 'Charles' now? Do I have to call you Charles, too?" I teased.

Charlie's eyes crinkled with mischief as he laughed. "Mom, you know the house rule. You can call me anything you want as long as you don't call me late for supper."

I beamed at my son. "You should call the show Chico and the Man."

Everyone started laughing. Charlie tilted his head at me and grinned as he lifted his hands, questioning the suggestion. "Why?"

Mr. Jones laughed so hard I thought he might fall. He took off his glasses to wipe his face. "It was an old television show. Chico was a teenager. Your mom is comparing your show to that one, except now you would be the man. Your Chico would have top billing."

Charlie grinned and shook his head. "Leave it to my Mom. We'll see what names come in, and then we can all decide."

We finished the adoption paperwork, and Charlie slipped the new collar and tags onto Chico. Chico jumped up and danced on his hind legs, barking with excitement as we started for the exit. Charlie laughed, clearly thrilled by his new friend. I wasn't sure who was more excited, Charlie, Chico, Mr. Jones, Richard, or me.

As we started to leave, Charlie looked back toward Mr. Jones and me and laughed. "Chico and the Man, hmm? Mom, that's clever. Thank you again, Mr. Jones. I am crazy about this boy. Chico and I will be back later in the week."

As he turned to head out the door, a pretty, young girl rushed in it. She was petite, with shoulder-length, straight, black hair held back with a pink headband that matched her outfit. If we were in North Georgia, I would think her dark, almond-shaped eyes indicated Cherokee heritage. In San Antonio, I suspected she might be Asian American rather than Native American. She barreled right into Charlie as they both rounded the corner at the same time. Charlie caught her as she crashed into him.

"I'm so sorry!" She began babbling, obviously rattled.

As she regained her balance and her breath, Charlie flashed her a big smile. "Oh, no, it was my fault. I wasn't watching where I was going. Are you okay?"

Her eyes grew wide. I couldn't tell if it was shock, surprise, or both. 'You-you're him! You're Duke! I used to watch your show all the time. I read you were going to be here today, and I had to come down and try to meet you. And here you are! Oh, I'm babbling like a fool. I'm sorry."

"You used to watch my show? But it didn't come on here in Texas. How did you see it?" Charlie appeared intrigued by the pretty teen.

Her cheeks flushed red with embarrassment. "Oh, I knew I would mess this up. We used to live in Augusta, Ga., south of Atlanta. My dad is a Major in the Army, and he was the base commander. We moved back to San Antonio last spring. I felt horrible for you when Darby died. He was such a super dog. Anyway, when I saw you would be here today, I had to come. I heard you were looking for a new sidekick."

Charlie's cheeks were pink, too, but from excitement. He patted her arm, and then, as if he were suddenly self-conscious, he looked down to Chico. "Well, I found one."

She bent down and extended her hand to Chico. "Oh, that's great! What's his name? Huh. He looks just like the dog my brother had."

Chico sniffed her hand and wagged his tail. After she scratched behind his ears, he licked her hand, and then the little dog turned back to Charlie with a big dog grin across his face.

"His name is Chico," Charlie said.

She sank to the floor, and Chico climbed into her lap. I was surprised to see tears well up in her eyes. "I should have known. Hey, baby. So, you finally found your new boy, huh?"

I felt surprise to see tears well up in her dark brown eyes as her lips trembled with emotion.

Charlie smiled. "Yes, he's going home with us today. Hey, I think he likes you. So, I guess it will be the Charlie and Chico Show."

She shook her head, blinked the tears back from her eyes, and smiled at Charlie. "No, it should be the Chuck and Chico Show. Better alliteration. Although Chico and the Man would be a fun title, too."

She looked up at Charlie, her brown eyes twinkling again, and winked.

He laughed. "Oh, you must have heard my Mom. That was her idea. Hmm. Chuck and Chico. I kinda like that."

She beamed with excitement. "Well, I figured you would be getting another animal to help, like Darby used to help you. Believe me, I think it's great Chico will be your new sidekick. You have no idea how great an idea I think this is. But I also remembered you had a human friend who helped you, too. I think his name was Kevin. I seem to remember you have a cat allergy, and Kevin handled the cats. I thought maybe you could use a new human friend, too, since we both just moved here not long ago."

Charlie's eyes grew wide with excitement. "I love cats, but they make me swell up like a toad, as my Mom says. And, yes, you're right. I haven't made many new friends since we moved to Texas."

She looked up at him, her eyes narrowing. "It's hard to make good friends. You know, real friends."

He gulped. He blushed and glanced down at the dog at his feet. "Yeah, it's been tough. It's hard for me to make new friends."

She giggled. "Oh, yeah, I can tell you are very shy from the shows."

He shook his head. "That's just a character I portrayed on a show. I can be hard to get to know. And I miss home."

Her eyes softened. "I know that feeling. Dad moved around so much it seemed like we just made friends and we had to move again. After a while, I quit trying to make friends for a long time. And, I'm not allergic to cats. I have a cat I rescued in Augusta."

She blanched as she suddenly threw her hands up over her face. "Oh, my heavens, I can be such a goof. My name is Kelly Nguyen."

She held out her hand. Charlie took it into his, bowed, and kissed her hand. "I'm Charles Winslow, Kelly. I'm delighted to make your acquaintance."

She smiled, her dark eyes dancing with excitement. "No wonder they used to call you 'Duke.' With manners like that, anyone would think you were royalty or something. That must be the most sophisticated thing I ever saw a guy do."

He chuckled, embarrassed as his cheeks turned red. "Well, you see, when we first moved to Ellijay, I sounded kind of weird. We had just moved back to the States from Ireland. I was little then. I learned to talk in Ireland. I sounded more Irish than American. The guys used to make fun of my funny accent, so I told them I was going to be a Duke when I grew up."

She laughed, clearly enchanted by my handsome son. "That was clever. I just sounded like a Texan when we moved to Georgia."

He tilted his head as he studied her. "Oh? Where's your family from?"

"My Mom is from here. My Dad came from Ft. Worth. They met at A&M. My Dad was in the Corps."

Charlie tilted his head as he studied her face. "They met at Texas A&M? Wow, what a coincidence. That's my top pick for where I want to go to college next year."

"You do? Cool. Yes, they met in the Sbisa Dining Hall over something Dad calls a Burrito Surprise. I was born in Killeen, and we lived on base there when I was little. Then we lived in Germany for four years, San Antonio for four, and Augusta for the past four. We were all thrilled Dad managed to get transferred back here, with a promotion to colonel hopefully coming through soon. We love San Antonio, and we want to live here after Dad retires."

As the two teens continued talking, I stepped back quietly and smiled at Mr. Jones and Richard. "I think he's going to be okay."

Mr. Jones beamed with excitement. "Do you realize that dog came from her family? The boy who was killed was her brother."

Richard hugged me. "Wow. How's that for coincidence?"

I shook my head. "There's no such thing as coincidence. It was meant to happen. Just like he was meant to meet her today."

Richard grinned. "But who would have dreamed he would find a dog and a girl the same day?"

I leaned my head against my husband's chest. "Well, it's the blue moon tonight. Miracles happen during the full moon, especially when it is blue."

In the years since that magical day, Charlie and Kelly grew to be best friends before they fell in love. I was sure they would marry and 'live happily ever after.' It seemed like a match made in heaven until that fateful Thanksgiving Day when my son's heart broke over Kelly's 'no.' Fortunately, he still had Chico. I don't know how he would have survived losing Kelly without that dog.

Chapter 4
The Following April

"Hey, Mom, you got some mail sent over from Suarez House!" Ronan yelled.

I dried my hands on the dish towel and then hurried over to my youngest child. Ronan grinned as he handed me the thick missive. I grinned back and quickly snatched the letter from the only teen still living in the house. I scampered to the couch to settle down to read my letter.

Years ago, Richard's mother, Sassy, fell through a hole in time and met and married my brother, Will. Will subsequently figured out how she could write her son, Richard, by sending letters to her relatives here in San Antonio, to be held until future dates. We never figured out how the letters still appear, but they show up fairly regularly. The old family house from the 1700s was fondly known as Suarez House, having been donated to Trinity University some years ago by Sassy's brother, Jim Suarez.

"It's from my Daddy," I announced with a big grin as my younger son, Ronan, settled onto the couch beside me. I quickly scanned the letter with Ronan reading over my shoulder.

"Daughter, we have been visiting your brother, Fitz, in London where he is currently attending the House of Lords. Last week, I had the opportunity to talk with Prince George. I learned how Calvin convinced King George to name you the Duchess of Ranscome. Calvin convinced King George to allow the two of ye, Calvin and you, to hold the title of Duke and Duchess Regent until you gave birth to a male child born of your marriage. If anything happened to Calvin and no son was born, you would remain the Duchess Regent, and you could remarry. If a son were born of your marriage to Calvin or a subsequent marriage, your first-born son would become the prospective Duke. You could not name one of the girls to follow according to the deal

Calvin cut with King George, even though the original title from Queen Elizabeth was given to a female. Of course, she was naught but a baroness then. Lily was quite disappointed to learn that the girls could not inherit the title. King George may have been sinking into madness back then, but he was no one's fool, at least in 1781 when he worked out the deal with Calvin. So, this means Charles is already the Duke of Ranscome and has been since birth."

Ronan laughed. "It looks like Charlie was telling the truth when he called himself Duke for all those years, Mom."

My eyes widened in surprise. "Wow! It sure does. The amazing thing is that Calvin never referred to himself as the Duke. As vain as he was – heck, as narcissistic as he was - I can't believe he didn't flaunt that tidbit to Will and everyone else. He would have thought it would hurt William; ironically, my big brother would have laughed. There must be more to that story than Daddy is telling me here. Oh, well, I guess it is nonessential information if Daddy didn't put it in this letter."

I continued reading about Marc, Lily, Tamsin, and my half-brother, Winston Fitz Simmons, the Earl of Waterside. "Fitz has been covering for Charles at the House of Lords for years, but he insists it is past time for Charles to return to Great Britain and assume his responsibilities to the crown. Prinny is hinting Charles' failure to do so could jeopardize both of his titles. As such, I must urge Charles to return, if it is his desire to assume the onerous duties associated with the titles. Fitz says to tell Charles that there are many beautiful and eligible young ladies here. They would be thrilled to meet a young, handsome and eligible Duke."

I stopped reading as I pondered Marc's words. Hmm. Charlie still grieved over Kelly's rejection. He would graduate from A&M with his DVM soon. If he were going to return to claim his rightful place in British society, this could be a good time for him to make a change. As much as I would hate to lose my son if he returned to the past, I had to accept that this was his destiny. He was born to be the Duke of Ranscome and the Earl of Spring Haven.

I sighed. Miguel and Bella would move to Boston after he completed his residency at UTMB Galveston next month. Miguel had accepted a position with one of the premiere medical research facilities in the country, Biozyme Boston. His mentor was a Vice President there and offered him the job after he returned to UTMB in the fall semester. One reason they married at

Christmas was so they could move straight to Boston once he finished his residency. Bella already had their things half packed. We had planned a family vacation at the cabin at McCarron's Corner for a week after both graduations. Come June 1st, Bella and Miguel would head north to Boston. I wondered whether Charlie might head north as well, on horseback through Indian Territory to catch a Ranscome ship on to Great Britain.

While Miguel and Bella were both excited about winters filled with snow, Richard felt sure that thrill would diminish after their first winter in Boston. He had vivid and unpleasant memories of shoveling snow when Owen, Sassy and he lived in Framingham just outside of Boston when he was young. Miguel and Bella flew to Boston over spring break to house hunt, and had a contract pending on a beautiful Victorian home built around the turn of the last century in Marlborough. We knew they were approved for the loan but there appeared to be some snag in the process, perhaps because Miguel had not started working at Biozyme yet. I wasn't sure why they needed a 3000 square foot Victorian Painted Lady for their first home, but they could afford it and they were both delighted with the beautiful old house, even though it meant it should take him about 40 minutes each way to commute to work via the Mass Turnpike.

To add to my sense of forthcoming loss, Bella and Miguel told us last week that they are expecting a baby in late October. While we teased them about a Halloween baby, I felt grief stricken that she would be so far from me when my first grandchild was born. I already knew where I would be for at least a week or two when her baby arrived. I intended to be part of that baby's life. It would know its Gramma.

I had fretted for months about their move halfway across the country. Suddenly, Boston did not seem so far. Bella and Miguel would be on the northeast coast, approximately 2000 miles away, but we could still visit, call and write. If Charlie went back in time to assume his titular responsibilities, he could send us letters, but we could not visit, call or write him. I would never meet his wife, or his children and grandchildren. How could I endure that loss and never see my son again?

Suddenly heavy hearted, I sighed. It was Charlie's life, Charlie's future, Charlie's decision. Not mine. I folded the letter and replaced it into the envelope before I placed it on the table. He was coming home for the weekend and we could talk about the letter from his Papa.

Charlie came in about an hour later. After the usual hugs and inquiries about how school was going, I said, "I got a letter from your Papa McCarron today."

I handed it to him. He frowned, but after only a moment's hesitation, he took the folded parchment from my hand. I watched as he quickly read Marc's scrawled words. Finally, he looked at me, stunned. "I'm already the Duke?"

I nodded. "Yes, so he says."

"Hmm. So, I can go back and assume those responsibilities, or remain here?"

I nodded, as my stomach clenched. He sounded thoughtful, pensive. He was clearly considering this option. "It's up to you. Your life and your choice."

"But I need to decide what I will do pretty soon." He stood up. "I'll be back later, Mom."

I frowned. "Will you be back here in time for dinner?"

He stopped and turned back towards me. "I'm not sure. I'll let you know, but don't hold supper for me when it is ready."

"But Charlie-" I began.

He bent to kiss my cheek. "I have some thinking to do. I'll let you know if I won't be on time for dinner."

Chapter 5
Kelly
April

Charlie quickly kissed Kelly before they both slid into the booth at the diner. He pulled her hands into his own. "What did you decide?"

Tears welled up in her eyes. "Charles, you know my Dad. If we run off and elope, he will find us and make our lives a living hell."

"What if we could go someplace where he cannot find us? Could you be happy if you knew you would never see your family again? And I really mean 'never'."

Her smile was bittersweet as she reached over to stroke his cheek. "Of course, I would go with you. But my Dad is a Colonel in the United States Army. He worked Spec Ops for years. He will find us. Believe me, he has his ways."

"Babe, I might know a way we could go far, far away. So far he will never find us." Charlie struggled to bite back the grin playing on his lips.

Her laugh sounded dry as fall leaves. "Where, Mars? Charles, face the facts. It's not like we can go live on another planet or in another universe. It's not like time travel really exists–"

"But it does."

She sighed. Such a prospect was too good to even remotely consider. She sighed as she shook her head, and then gently caressed his cheek. "I know you have said that before, but no one has ever done it. Time travel is a fantasy. It isn't–"

"Kelly, I was born on December 25, 1781 at the Belle Rose Plantation in the Commonwealth of Virginia. I am the Duke of Ranscome. I'm going back to assume my titular duties, to fulfill my destiny. Will you go with me?"

Her eyes widened in shock as she pulled her hand back from his. "Charles, don't joke. This is not funny."

Charlie reached over and took her hand into his again. "I'm not joking. Will you go with me?"

She gulped as she glanced around the restaurant nervously as her hands began to shake. "Are you serious?"

He nodded as he inched closer to her in the booth. "Yes. Bella was born at Mount Vernon in 1778. Martha Washington is her godmother. Mom was born in 1760 at Belle Rose. We can go back. We can live in Ireland or England. I'll have to spend some time every year in London to fulfill my duties at the House of Lords-"

"Charlie, this is crazy. This can't be a real possibility." Her eyes were large as dinner plates.

"Would you believe my Mom?" His voice was soft, but calm, assured, confident.

She stared at him, her mouth dry, her heart beating like crazy. She wanted to believe him. But could this be true? Could they really run away to make a new life in the past? "Yes."

He picked up the ticket and stood up, still holding her hand. "Come on. Let's go talk to Mom."

She hesitated. "Charlie, you're not teasing me, are you? Because that would be mean."

He leaned over and kissed her again. "I've never been more serious in all my life. Come on. Let's go."

Charlie paid the bill, and they each drove over to the Winslow house. Charlie opened the gate so Kelly could drive her car inside out of sight. "Hey, Mom, Kelly and I need to talk to you."

Kelly could feel her heart pounding like crazy as they entered the Winslow home. She had not been there since Charlie asked her to marry him in November. She wasn't sure how his family would react to her showing up like this. She pulled back as they stepped inside the door. "She's not mad at me, is she?"

Charlie dipped down to give her a quick kiss. "Don't be silly. Come on. Let's go to the library so I can get Mom to come in there with us."

Kelly gulped and glanced back towards the street. "And you're sure my Dad can't see the car behind the fence?"

He chuckled and squeezed her hand. "I promise. He cannot see the car behind that fence unless he stands on a ladder. You're safe. He can't get to you here, Kell. I swear."

She clutched his hand. "No, you don't understand. If he's out hunting for me, he might see me come back out."

Charlie frowned. "Are you having second thoughts?"

She gulped, trembling. "Charlie, you know what he can be like…"

He saw her wince as her voice wavered from nervousness. "He damned sure better not lay a hand on you. I swear, if he ever hits you again, I'll kill him."

She gulped again. "Don't talk like that. You scare me when you say things like that."

His lips narrowed. "Well, I mean it. He hit you too many times. I told you months ago--"

"I -- I know. Okay. Let's talk to your mom. Just understand that if he figures out I'm over here, you guys are gonna have to hide me."

She saw the tension in Charlie's neck begin to relax as his lips curved into a smile again. "Okay. Come on."

He tucked her into the office and shut the door before he stepped into the hallway. "Hey, Mom, could I see you a minute in here?"

Ronan's head popped up. "What's up, dude?"

"None of your business. Where's Mom?"

Ronan shrugged. "I think she's sitting outside writing. Why?"

Charlie shook his head. "Like I said, man, not your business."

He strode over to the back door and smiled at his Mom. "Could you come in for a few minutes? I need to talk to you about, you know, what we talked about earlier."

Fancy glanced up from her laptop at her son and smiled as she patted the seat beside her. "Sure, handsome. Want to sit down?"

He shook his head. "No. Let's go inside."

"Hmm. This sounds serious. Where do you want to talk?"

He grabbed her hand. "Library."

Fancy Winslow's eyes widened in surprise as they entered the library to discover Kelly cowering inside. She rushed over to the girl and gathered her into her arms. "Honey, are you okay?"

Kelly struggled to smile. "I'm fine. Mrs. Winslow, Charlie says he, uh, he is going away and he wants me to go with him."

Fancy's eyes widened in surprise. "Did you tell her?"

Charlie nodded. "Yes, ma'am."

Fancy paled. "You told her everything?"

He nodded again. "Everything."

Kelly started trembling again. "It can't be real, can it, Mrs. Winslow? I mean, he wasn't really born in 1871, was he?"

"No, he wasn't."

Kelly cut her eyes at Charlie, but before he could respond, Fancy said, "He was born in 1781. It's all real, Kelly. So, was this where you went, son? To talk to Kelly?"

"Yes, ma'am. I'm hoping she'll go with me."

Fancy stared at them both. "Okay. There's a lot to tell, but first, you have to promise to to never tell another living person what I am about to say."

Kelly clutched to Charlie's hand. "I promise, Mrs. Winslow. I won't say a word."

They talked for hours. Finally, Kelly's phone rang. She held it up to show Charlie before she answered it, and held a finger to her mouth for them to keep quiet.

It was her dad. "Where are you?"

"I went to the mall and did some shopping. I ate some supper. I'm heading home now."

He paused a minute "Good. Don't delay."

She couldn't believe her hands shook so badly as she disconnected the call. "I have to go home. He's upset."

Charlie frowned. "Kelly, I'm telling you, if he lays a finger on you--"

She shook her head. "No, I'll be okay. He hasn't hit me in a ... a long time. Charlie, I love you, but this is a lot to absorb. You are asking me to leave my Mom, my sister, even leave my cat."

"Bring the cat with you."

"You're allergic, you silly goose. I realize worrying about Mom and the cat sounds foolish, but I don't know what Dad would do to them if I disappeared. Let me think about it for a day or two."

"Kelly--" he began.

Fancy laid a hand on his shoulder. "Give her the time, son. She needs to come to terms with what you are asking. It's not an easy adjustment. Believe me, I know."

Kelly flashed a hint of a smile at Fancy. "I guess you would know, considering you came here without the kids at first."

Fancy smiled. "I will be eternally grateful that my father and step-mother brought my children to me. And it's a lot easier coming here than going there. You should talk to Richard about going there."

Kelly paled as the door opened and Dr. Winslow peeked inside. "Hey, what's going on, guys? Hey, Kelly, I wondered whose car was in my spot. Are you okay?"

She nodded, overwhelmed by the information she had received that evening. "Uh, I'm a little rattled, Doc."

"Charlie told her about going home," Fancy said.

"Okay. Hey, wait." He glared at Charlie. "You told her?"

"Yes, sir." Charlie glared right back at Dr. Winslow as he pulled Kelly closer to him.

Richard Winslow shook his head. "And may I ask why?"

"That's simple. I want her to go with me."

Richard looked quickly over to Kelly. "And?"

"I'm thinking about it." She glanced down at her phone. "Look I need to go home. My dad is already upset because I'm late. Could we talk again tomorrow?"

Richard stared at her before answering. "Sure. But do not say a word about this to your family. It could have disastrous repercussions. Do you understand?"

She nodded as she still clung to Charlie's hand. "Yes, sir, I understand. I just need a little more time. There's a lot involved here."

Richard shook his head. "Not a word, Kelly. Not one damned word. You could endanger Charlie if you said anything. Heck, you could disrupt the entire time - space continuum."

She looked up at him, shocked by his words. "I promise, Dr. Winslow. I won't say a word. That's part of what makes this so hard. As much as I love Charlie, I also love my Mom. I could manage to leave my sister. Sophie and I are not that close. But Mom... and Fluff..."

"It'll be okay, babe. I promise." Charlie looked over to his dad. "She's afraid he'll take it out on her Mom or the cat if she disappears."

Richard flexed his shoulders. "Is that it?"

She nodded, unable to utter another word.

"Okay. We'll see you tomorrow."

The next day, Kelly came rushing back in the Winslow house. "Dad's at the base, and Mom let me escape for a little bit. Can we talk now?"

Richard looked up from the surgical file he was reviewing. "Sure, kiddo. Come on in. Ask away."

"What's it really like back then?"

"Dirty. Stinky. Disease ridden. No electricity. No gas heat. And yet, it is so beautiful that it will make you ache. I often thought if you could combine the best of now with the best of then, it would be a wonderful place to live. It's tough, but you could do it. I'd be lying if I told you it won't be tough. Believe me, it's an adjustment, but love can make it work."

She tried to smile. "You really think so?"

He nodded. "I know so. You have survived twenty-one years with your dad. I know he can be rough on you. If you could survive that, you can survive time travel."

She shook her head. "No, Dad's okay, Dr. Winslow. As long as he doesn't find out."

Richard frowned. "Then what's the problem?"

A tear slid down her cheek. "It's... leaving my Mom. And leaving that silly cat. Those are the hard parts."

Richard reached over to pull her into a hug. "It'll be okay, baby girl. Your mom will survive. We will get word to her if and when you ever want us to tell her about where you are. We can get you all your inoculations before you go. Those would include smallpox, malaria, polio, all the exotic diseases in addition to updating your shots you had as a kid."

She nodded. *This could really happen. Charlie and I could escape Dad and make a life of our own.*

Dr. Winslow continued. "We can send you with supplies you will need along the way. Food, medicine, sanitary supplies, soap, toilet paper, period correct clothing, water purification straws and tablets. Firestarters, matches. I can even send you with guns and ammo if you want. We will make sure you have all the things you need to go."

She blinked as his words sank in. "Wow. Toilet paper and sanitary supplies. Water purification supplies. Guns and ammo. I hadn't even thought about those things. Well, thank heaven that Dad taught us all how to shoot. Army base commanders are big on their kids knowing how to handle firearms properly. But even so, this is going to be tough. You know, I wouldn't do this for anyone but Charlie."

He nodded as he patted her hands. "I know, baby girl. So, what will it be? Are you ready for the grand adventure of your lifetime?"

She gulped and then looked up at Dr. Winslow. "How can I not go with him, Dr. Winslow? He's all I ever wanted. He is the love of my life. Just promise me my dad won't find us."

He chuckled and hugged her. "Don't worry, Kelly. He won't learn it from us, and if he doesn't learn it from us, he won't learn it at all."

Charlie walked into the office where they were talking, and sat on the arm of the chair where Kelly sat. He bent over and kissed her cheek. "You decide?"

She nodded and smiled. "Yes. Let's go."

Charlie beamed with excitement. "So, when do we do this, Dad?"

"How about Memorial Day weekend? We're supposed to go to the cabin then anyway. Mike and Bella will meet us there for the weekend."

"Hmm. That's only three weeks from now."

Richard smiled. "I guess we better get busy."

•　　•　　•

Three weeks later, Kelly stood mentally checking if she had everything she needed. Dr. Winslow got her the vaccination for smallpox, polio, and other exotic diseases, and she updated her other vaccinations at college. She told the nurse there she was hoping to go overseas during the summer and wanted to be sure she was safe to go. The Winslows would have everything else for her when she got to their house. The time had flown by quickly since she agreed to meet Charlie in Georgia so they could travel to the past to their new lives.

She sighed and smiled. Yes, she was to leave for the airport for her grand adventure, as Dr. Winslow called it.

"Kelly!"

Kelly jumped at the sound of anger in her father's voice. Her dad was not supposed to be home that afternoon. She had hoped to slip out of the house and be gone to the airport to fly to Georgia before he came home and realized she had run away to be with Charlie. Uber should be coming to pick her up any time now. She had just finished sliding the exquisite silk wedding *Ao Dai* into her backpack when his angry shout shattered her hope. Hands trembling, she quickly slid the backpack into a corner in her closet and then hurried downstairs.

Her heart sank as she realized her father held her phone. He refused to allow her to put a security code on her phone so no one could access it without her knowledge and permission. She gulped and stood up a little straighter, if that was possible. If he had her phone, he knew her plans.

"Where were you planning to go?" His voice was cold, gruff, professional. She imagined his soldiers hated to hear him use this tone.

She squared her shoulders before she answered. "Atlanta."

His lips narrowed. "I am aware of that. The ticket has been cancelled. Where were you going once you arrived in Atlanta?"

I was going to marry Charles. We were going to the Belle Rose Plantation and then on to London in the early nineteenth century where my husband, the Fourth Earl of Spring Haven and Fourth Duke of Ranscome, would fulfill his destiny in the House of Lords. She wet her lips. No, she couldn't tell her dad all that. He might knock her across the room thinking she was being a smart mouthed kid. "I was going to meet Charles. We were … um … we were going hiking with Bella and Miguel this weekend. They will be moving to Boston soon. It was supposed to be a last get-together."

"I told you that you are not to see that boy again. Why do you disrespect me like this? You will have a life filled with heartache if you marry that boy. Don't you remember I have told you how this country disrespected Asian Americans for years? Asians could immigrate here but could not even become citizens until the 1940s. Your grandparents, your mother and I faced significant racism when we all first immigrated here. There is still significant racism towards Asian Americans. You are aware of that. That is why we only dated Vietnamese people when your mother and I were young, and it is why we always discouraged you from dating Charles. When I learned you had been sneaking off to see him, I put my foot down. No more dating that boy. He is not right for you. You are going to marry a nice, respectable Vietnamese young man. We are having dinner with the Tran family tonight to finalize the arrangements for John and you to marry. Now, go to your room. You need to get dressed. Go upstairs, take a bath, put on some makeup and fix your hair. Those silly Princess Leia buns won't work tonight. And put on your new *Ao Dai*. Your mother made it specially for tonight. I want you to look like a proper prospective Vietnamese wife, not some crazy manga girl. The Tran family will be here within the hour."

Kelly's mouth went dry. She felt the color drain from her face. "The wedding *Ao Dai*?"

Col. Nguyen frowned. "Of course not, you idiot. The pink one for the betrothal ceremony. Now, hurry up. You must not be late."

She hesitated only for a moment. "May I call Charles and tell him I am not coming?"

Col. Nguyen laughed. "No. I think he will figure that out soon enough when you don't show up."

Kelly nodded. She turned to go to her room, trembling so much she could barely walk and wiped the tears from her cheeks. *How could I have been so foolish as to leave my phone charging downstairs? If only I had left earlier this afternoon. I thought about walking to the CVS Pharmacy and calling for Uber from there. I could have charged the phone at the airport. I never dreamed Dad would come home early. He never comes home early – but then, we don't usually have a betrothal ceremony either. Now everything is ruined.*

Kelly struggled to control her crying as she pulled her buns down and began to brush her thick, lustrous black hair despite the shaking of her hands. Charlie loved her hair worn in the Princess Leia buns. She managed to bathe and to put on her makeup the traditional way her mother had taught her. She pulled out the betrothal *Ao Dai* her mother presented her earlier that week and began to dress. At least now it made sense why Mom made the beautiful pink dress for her. She had to admit it was the prettiest betrothal *Ao Dai* she ever saw. My God, they were about to perform the *an hoi*, the betrothal ceremony. At least they did not plan the engagement party and the wedding for the same night. She knew the wedding could be anywhere from a day to a year after the official betrothal ceremony, although many young couples now held the betrothal, engagement party, and wedding all the same day.

Her parents never said a word to her about the betrothal ceremony being tonight, other than they mentioned that they arranged she would marry Johnny Tran. She only met Johnny two or three times in her life for a total of maybe a half hour. He seemed like a nice young man, but he wasn't Charles. Why did her parents have to be so old fashioned? She fought back a new deluge of tears as she slipped delicate white jade earrings into her earlobes. Her beloved grandmother gave them to her for her twelfth birthday. Kelly sat on the edge of her bed to await her mother, who she knew would come to fetch her for the betrothal ceremony.

It was a shame the dress was not white. White was the color most Asians wore for funerals. She felt like she was preparing for a funeral.

She was twenty-one. She knew Vietnamese believed it was bad luck to marry in your twenty-second year. Her birthday would be just before New Year's. That meant they intended the wedding to proceed before her birthday. She rolled her eyes, as she figured her parents had been to the fortune teller to see what day and time in the next few months would be most propitious for the wedding.

Thank heaven the wedding wasn't tonight.

Kelly pressed her hands together as the doorbell rang. She knew the Trans and Johnny were downstairs, beginning the ceremony. His parents would have brought round lacquered boxes filled with Areca nuts, betel leaves, tea cakes, fruit, wine, and other delicacies. She could tell from the noise downstairs that a good number of people came with them. It also sounded like the Tran family brought a lot of gifts, too. Her dad was laughing loudly and bragging about what a great catch John was to Mr. Tran. Well, that was what people did to show off their wealth. John's parents were decent people but were most definitely *nouveaux riches*. Mr. Tran loved to gloat over their money.

Kelly knew she was expected to remain in her room until her mother fetched her. It would demonstrate poor upbringing if she went downstairs before her mother came for her. She was tempted, but she did not want the beating her father would inflict upon her afterwards if she trotted downstairs on her own volition. He was already angry enough at her. But this was so old fashioned. She could not believe her parents were forcing her into a marriage to a near-stranger, here in the United States of America!

She pressed her hand against her brow. *Calm down, Kelly. Everything will still work out, somehow. It must.*

One thing was certain. Kelly knew she would *not* marry Johnny Tran.

Chapter 6
Fancy
Now

We waited by the telephone on Friday, eager for the call from Kelly that she was en route to Atlanta. Finally, Charlie grew impatient, and drove into Atlanta, to await her arrival at the airport.

Charlie called us two hours later, his voice thick with frustration and anxiety. "She didn't get off the plane, and I can't get her on the phone, Mom. What do I do?"

"Check with the airlines and see if she missed her plane. She's probably on another flight, and just running late. Everything will be fine. Just hang in there."

Four hours later, Charlie dragged back into the house. Without another word, he grabbed his bags. "Come on. Let's go to the cabin."

I frowned. "But Charlie-"

He shook his head. "I can't get her on the phone. She never showed up at the airport. I need to be realistic, Mom. She isn't coming. She caved in to her dad. Let's go to the cabin. Full moon is tomorrow night. The portal just opens right before full moon. Wolf, Baylie and Faith are going then. The plan is I go with them. They will get someone to guide me to the coast. Come on, let's go. Destiny calls."

"But son-" I began.

He shook his head, his face tight with emotion. "Nope. I must have called her over a hundred times this afternoon. I'm all done, Mom. She's not coming. Let's go."

I looked at Richard and shook my head as I held my hand up in the air. "What do we do?"

He looked grim. "You heard the man. Let's go. Destiny awaits."

We went on to the cabin. I kept telling Charlie that Kelly would call or show up at any minute, but we got no call on the way to the cabin or after we arrived there. All day Saturday, Charlie paced back and forth with frequent glimpses out the windows towards the trail.

Finally, he sighed. "I tell you, Mom, she's not coming."

"She still might make it, son. Be patient." I tried to be optimistic although I feared he was correct.

He raked his hands through his hair as he sighed again in frustration. "I've been patient, Mom. She knows we must go just before the full moon tonight. She was supposed to get to Atlanta yesterday. I waited at Hartsfield International for hours. No call, nothing. Then, the one text from her sister that said Kelly got held up and would come today. She still isn't here. If she's not here soon, I have to face the facts. She's not coming."

I cast a nervous glance at Richard. He reached over and patted Charlie on the back. "Then it's not the right time, son."

"To go or to stay?"

Richard shrugged. "You have to decide that. But if you are going, the time is coming soon or you will miss your window of opportunity, at least for this month."

Wolf cleared his throat. "If you are meant to be together, Charlie, you will be reunited. But as your father said, we must go soon. We must leave before the full moon rises."

Shadow Wolf was a Cherokee chieftain from the past who came forward in time to find Baylie, the woman he loved. In the past, Baylie Smith was known as Guider, short for her Cherokee name, Path of the Guiding Light. Now they would return home with their daughter, Faith, to the Cohutta Cherokees in the early nineteenth century to help their people move westward before the Trail of Tears.

Faith has a condition called mosaicism, a mild form of Down Syndrome. Fortunately, her deficits are minor although she comes across as developmentally delayed, especially in her speech. Bella could communicate with the child from the beginning, and taught Faith sign language when her speech development was delayed.

Charlie rubbed his hand over his face. His shoulders sagged as he slowly nodded. "I know. Let's make a final check of our supplies and make sure we have everything loaded, Wolf. If she is not here by then... well, then we can leave."

Richard helped Charlie and Wolf double check their supplies as I sat with Baylie, Faith and Bella at the table. Bella held Faith close, telling her again how much 'Aunt Bella' loved her. I could tell it would be hard on my daughter as well as Baylie's child to be separated. Bella and Faith had an incredible bond. "I may not get to see you again, but always remember your Aunt Bella loves you dearly, little one."

Faith blinked back unshed tears. "I want you to come, too."

Bella hugged her tightly. "Me, too, my little angel. But you have a great adventure ahead of you with your Mommy and Daddy. If I went with you, then Tio Mike and my Mommy and Daddy would miss me. And my destiny lies here, just as yours lies Before."

Faith nodded. We could see she was unsure exactly what this thing called 'destiny' was, although her parents had spoken to the child of the prophecy and her role in the destiny of their people virtually every day of her life.

Faith and her family were returning to guide the Cohutta Cherokee westward towards 'the new promised land,' which would be in the mountains of Oklahoma. They would also see to it that Cherokee guides helped Charlie get at least as far to the east as Augusta, if not all the way to the coast. That was why it was essential that Charlie went with them at this time. They might not be there a month later, if he waited. After all, as Wolf said, time does not flow in a straight line. What is a month here might be many years there. As it was, he had been here in the present for five years.

Based on the letter from my father, we figured they had been gone from the past seventeen years.

Finally, with all the equipment and supplies loaded on the pack horses, we said our last goodbyes. I realized it might be the last time I would ever see my son. I blinked back my tears, determined not to let them spill before he left. I struggled not to visibly tremble. I didn't want him to remember me crying and shaking the last time he saw me "You don't want to wait? Something must have happened to keep her from–"

"She's not coming, Mom. She would be here by now. I'll be okay. It … it wasn't meant to be." He pulled me close for another hug and then kissed my forehead again.

"I love you," I whispered as I clung to my son.

"I love you more, Mom. I'll write." He kissed my cheek.

"Not possible. You can't possibly love me more than I love you. You better write to me. Be sure to keep that journal. I may not be able to find another one from the Duchess of Ranscome, but the Duke needs to let his Mom know what happens." I kissed him again. My fingers smoothed his silky, curly hair and his just-shaved cheek. I clutched his shirt, rubbing the linen fabric back and forth one last time. Old habits die hard. I needed to imprint the feel of his hair, skin and his shirt into my memory. I kissed him once more and then forced myself back so the others could bid him farewell.

Bella could not hold her tears back as she hugged Charlie close. "My baby brother. I remember the day you were born. We had been playing in the snow outside Belle Rose when Mom went into labor. How can I let you go? My baby will need his uncle."

Charlie whispered words of consolation to her which helped her stop crying. As he continued to talk to her, his voice soft and controlled, she gave him a tremulous smile and nodded.

"I promise. I'll take good care of her," she said with another nod as he kissed her cheek.

Richard hugged Charlie and bid him farewell and then slipped his arms around me as Wolf, Baylie, Faith, and Charlie mounted up and rode through the portal.

It looked so easy. But the portal in time would not open unless you were meant to pass through it to another time. It opened for me years ago when I came here to be with my beloved Richard. I never regretted coming, although I often miss my family who remain behind. My heart lurched and I began trembling again as my son disappeared as he traveled more than 200 years into the past to fulfill his own destiny, to create his own legacy.

I still don't know how I managed to hold up. I was sure I would burst into tears at any moment and would commence begging my son not to go. But Charlie was right. Going to the House of Lords was as much his destiny as forging westward to the mountains of Oklahoma was the destiny of the Cohutta Cherokees. Charles Ranscome Hobbs, as he would be known

Before, would not only be Earl of Spring Haven; he would also be Duke of Ranscome over all the many Ranscome holdings throughout Great Britain. Even so, I felt as though my heart was ripping apart. I would probably never see my eldest son again.

Richard hugged me tightly as Charlie disappeared from our sight. "He'll be fine."

My throat was too tight to utter a single word. I laid my head against Richard as I gently rubbed his sleeve back and forth. Even now, that repetitive movement can help me hold my stuff together during difficult moments. This definitely ranked as one of my life's most difficult moments.

I frowned. Where the hell was Kelly?

Chapter 7
Kelly
Now

Kelly's mother finally came to lead her downstairs, to officially meet Mr. and Mrs. Tran and Johnny. Kelly knew it would mean she was not well-educated or well-raised if she waltzed downstairs on her own. Such imprudent behavior would probably result in the betrothal being broken before even completed. As tempted as she was to cause that, she could not make herself tempt the fates and earn the beating of her lifetime she knew she would receive from her father. Of course, worse yet would be if her father ordered John to beat her in front of everyone, so they could see he would be the man in the household once John and she married. Her dad would probably do that, too.

As they entered the dining room, Kelly was astounded at the large number of red trays filled with gifts the Tran family brought. The table was heavily laden with presents and a wide assortment of Vietnamese foods. Wow, they even brought a whole roasted suckling pig!

Just as Kelly wore the traditional pink *Ao Dai* for the betrothal ceremony, John wore the traditional blue which men usually wore to these ceremonies. She noticed he looked every bit as uncomfortable as she felt.

"Hey, John." Kelly sounded quiet and subdued.

"Hey, Kelly. Pretty dress. Pink is your color. You okay?" He frowned as he studied her face.

She nodded and looked away as her eyes filled with tears. "Yeah, I guess. And you?"

"About the same."

Her mother brought her the teapot, and Kelly began to carefully fill the cups for the various people in attendance, beginning first with John's grandparents. *Be careful not to spill a drop*, she thought. *It's supposed to be bad luck.* She bit back a giggle as she wondered if it would comprise enough bad luck to cancel the betrothal if she 'accidentally' dumped the teapot. John glanced at her quizzically, and then flashed her a quick grin and a wink. *Hmmm. He must be thinking the same thing.*

She managed somehow to pour the tea for everyone without a mishap. John spoke to her throughout the ceremony in a low, calm voice in soothing terms. She smiled at him, grateful he was being so kind and thoughtful.

"It'll be okay, Kelly. I promise."

She struggled not to cry as her mind went blank at his words. She blinked back tears as she tried to smile. They sat quietly, as their parents completed the betrothal ceremony.

As everyone was leaving, John approached her father. "Col. Nguyen, sir, Kelly and I don't know each other very well. Would you allow me to take her out tomorrow? I thought we could go to the Japanese Tea Garden, since that is where our wedding ceremony will be held."

Kelly's heart began pounding in her chest ninety to nothing. Her husband-to-be knew more about their forthcoming nuptials than she did. She gulped and nodded as she forced a smile upon her face. "That would be wonderful, Father. We could decide where we want our photos taken."

John nodded. "My thoughts exactly. I figured we would want some in front of the waterfall, but beyond that, I thought Kelly would like to have a voice in the photographic locations."

Father's eyes narrowed and then he smiled. "Of course, John. Why don't you pick her up around noon? You two can have lunch while you are out."

"Thank you, Col. Nguyen. I promise to take good care of her."

John surprised her when he pulled her close for a kiss before he left. Their families clapped and murmured approval. Her heart began to clamor in alarm as he pulled her outside into her father's rose garden and pulled her close again.

"Uh, John-"

He held a finger up to her lips and playfully kissed the tip of her nose. "Play along with this. Listen, your sister says you were going to meet Winslow this weekend."

Kelly's eyes widened in surprise. "Yeah, but–"

"She called Charlie and left a message for him that you were delayed. Bring some extra clothes in your backpack tomorrow. And your prettiest dress."

She frowned. "Why? What do you have planned?"

He grinned and waved to the crowd peering out the window at them and pulled her into another embrace. "Just act like you are going along with this, Kelly. Bring your wedding dress. You might want it when you reconnect with Winslow."

She threw her arms around his neck. "Are you serious? Oh, Johnny!"

He grinned at the window and then kissed her again.

Her father looked quite pleased when they returned into the house. "I told you he was the right man, Kelly."

She nodded, trying not to let him see just how excited she was. 'Yes, Father. You made a very good choice. John is a pleasant surprise."

John picked Kelly up the next morning a little before noon. She was almost out of her room when she turned back and grabbed her backpack from her closet. She swung it over her shoulder to use it like a purse. She double checked to make sure she had packed underwear, socks, a change of jeans, an extra t-shirt, as well as the wedding gown and matching overcoat. Fortunately, the silk garments rolled down small. They would wrinkle, but they could be ironed. As a last thought, she added the exquisite antique white jade jewelry her grandmother gave her over the years. She pulled out the cash she had hidden in her pillow and shoved it into her wallet before she ran down the stairs.

As John's car pulled away from the curb, he grinned and dropped an old-fashioned flip phone to her hands. "I kind of figured your dad took your phone away from you. Need to call him?"

Her heart leapt. "Oh, John, you're a lifesaver. You have no idea…" She punched in Charlie's number and then frowned. No answer. Oh, well, she could leave a message. "Charlie? This is Kelly. My Dad took my phone and locked me in my room when he realized I was coming to Georgia. Um … a friend helped me get out awhile today and gave me another phone to use. Listen, please wait for me. I'm coming. I promise, I'm coming, somehow. Please wait for me. Call me at this number if you get this call. I love you."

She looked over at John, embarrassment all over her face. "Uh, let me explain-"

He grinned as he shook his head. "No need, Kelly. I'm in the same boat. My parents are opposed to my seeing Sandra, too. So, what gives with you and Winslow?"

She struggled to contain my tears. "We were going to elope this weekend. My dad apparently got wind of it and wouldn't let me out of his sight. Oh, John, you seem like a nice guy, but-"

He reached over and patted her hands. "It's okay, Kelly. I love Sandy. I intend to marry her. Let's see about getting you to the airport, okay? Hey, how about we drive to Austin? I can put you on a plane there. It will be one helluva lot harder for your dad to track you down that way after you 'slip away from me and disappear'. If push comes to shove, I'll tell your dad that you wanted to see the UT campus since I'm in law school there, and we wanted to check out apartments. You slipped away from me at a restaurant."

She nodded as she felt the first surge of hope since her dad confronted her. "Oh, that would be wonderful, John. We probably need to go by the Gardens first. I would bet my Dad has someone watching for us there. Afterwards, I would love a ride to the airport, any airport, if you aren't concerned my Dad will give you Billy Hell."

He laughed. "Heck, I'll just lie to him. I'm studying to be a lawyer, remember? It will be good practice. I'll tell him that when we went to lunch, you said you were going to the restroom and the next thing I knew you disappeared. I went looking for you, and the hostess told me that she thought someone picked you up."

She laughed. "And you hunted for me, and couldn't find me?"

He smiled. "Exactly. Come on. Let's go."

She leaned over to give him a quick peck on the cheek. "Thank you, John. I will never forget this."

John texted some photos to her Dad from the Japanese Tea Gardens of the places they claimed they wanted photos at the wedding. Afterwards, they headed north to Austin, where her new best friend let Kelly out at the airport entrance. Fortunately, her Dad had not found her stash in the pillow so she had money to buy another ticket. She told John she would fly to Atlanta and waved to him as she entered the airport. She did not want her Dad to figure out where she went if he managed to force John to spill the beans. Charlie had told her the way to the cabin was about four miles south of the Beech Bottom trailhead, on the way to the Jacks River Falls. She figured out the trailhead was closer to Chattanooga than Atlanta, so she planned to buy a ticket to Chattanooga.

Once inside the airport, she went to the Delta desk instead of the Southwest Airlines desk and obtained a ticket. Since she could not get Charlie on the phone, she figured the best thing would be for her to head to Chattanooga, call for Uber, and go to the Beech Bottom Trail in the Cohutta Wilderness. Kelly bought a flashlight and an Uber card, so she would have enough money to pay for her ride without relying on a credit card. She knew her Dad would be watching her credit cards once he realized she had slipped out of his clutches. As she passed the checkpoint to go to her plane, her heart finally filled with excitement again.

Chapter 8
Fancy
Now

I still felt numb when we got back to our home at Cashes Valley late that night. The next morning, I sat on the porch sipping my coffee as I looked out over the beautiful mountain vista towards McCarron's Corner. One reason we bought this home was because I felt closer to my family here where I could see Cohutta Mountain. My shoulders slumped as I finally gave in to the deluge of tears I had held back since Charlie left the preceding evening.

I didn't hear her approach. Her voice startled me, bringing me back to the reality of the twenty-first century. "Mrs. Winslow? Where's Charles? I hiked to the cabin last night, but it was empty."

I blinked, stunned by both her unexpected appearance and the near-hysterical tone of her voice. I scrambled up from the swing to gather her into my arms. "Kelly, honey, he left yesterday evening. He waited until just before sundown, but he had to leave then if he went with Wolf and Baylie. Where were you? We thought you would get here Friday."

Kelly began sobbing as she sank onto the glider beside me. "My Dad figured out I was coming to see Charlie. He locked me in my room. Can you imagine a man doing such a thing to a girl my age? I managed to get out yesterday, but I had to buy another plane ticket. It had a connecting flight in Oklahoma City and another in Nashville en route to Chattanooga. I know it sounds crazy, but it was the first flight I could get out of Austin to Chattanooga. That flight was delayed for hours. Heck, we sat on the tarmac in Oklahoma City nearly two hours. I must have tried to call a dozen times from there alone. The delay in Oklahoma City made me miss my connecting flight in Nashville. I had to wait three more hours for another flight to Chattanooga. I thought it would be better not to try to get to Atlanta again. Dad would figure for sure that was where I headed. I kept calling and calling but Charlie didn't answer. I finally found the cabin about midnight last night. You guys had already left."

Rivulets of tears streamed down her face. She gasped as she tried to catch her breath. As her sobbing slowed, I figured I could ask her some more questions. I cleared my throat.

"Honey, we have no cell phone reception in the Cohutta Wilderness. Why didn't you call the landline number at the cabin yesterday?"

Kelly looked shocked and she began to cry. "The number for the cabin is on my cell phone my Dad confiscated Friday. He refused to let me call Charles. I didn't have the cabin number written down anywhere else. Dammit, I should have had it in my wallet or my backpack. Dad still has my cell. I left Charles text messages, emails, phone messages from the phone my friend gave me. I thought Charles would get the messages. I thought he would wait for me. When I got to the cabin, you guys had already left. I knew it was late, but I never dreamed he would leave without me. I told myself all day long he would wait for me. I hiked back to the trailhead, and I waited there until morning. It was kind of freaky sleeping in a chair in front of that cabin. When cars started coming in, I woke up. I couldn't get Uber to send anyone to pick me up to bring me here to your house until about 6 this morning. It took the guy a couple of hours to get there, and then two more to get here. I didn't have your phone number. Charlie told me it was unlisted, so I didn't even try to call you. I finally got Bella on the phone about thirty minutes ago. She gave me the address just before their plane left. I should have got the phone number from her, too, but the steward was saying she had to turn off her phone. I guess I wasn't thinking by then. I'm so exhausted. Oh, Mrs. Winslow, what do I do now? How can I get to Charles?"

She sank into my arms and we cried together for the young man we both had lost.

Just then, Richard returned from taking Miguel and Bella to the airport in Atlanta. "Kelly, we thought you weren't coming. What happened?"

I quickly explained as Kelly lay huddled against me, pale and trembling from shock.

"The trail guides who work at the trailhead have our number." Richard kept his voice low and calm, but he could not hide the shock he felt.

I nodded. "They have the number for the cabin, too. But she didn't get there until late last night. They were closed and we had already left."

Richard's eyes narrowed as he tapped a finger against his temple. "Hmm. Well, we can try to send her just before the next full moon."

Kelly looked horror-stricken. "No one was at the ranger's cabin when I arrived last night. I didn't even think to ask them for the phone number this morning while I waited for the driver. I am too tired to think straight. Dr. Winslow, what will I do until the next full moon? Dad will find me."

"He won't find you at the cabin. Most people don't even know it exists." Richard smirked as he winked at me.

"But some people know it exists, darling. They know about it at the trailhead, and she went there hunting for us. What if she stays at Wolf and Baylie's house? It's in the Cohutta Wilderness, close to the Jacks River Trail, but he would have no reason to look for her there. Plus, their cabin is primitive enough that it will give Kelly a chance to see if she really wants to go back in time or not." I smiled as I envisioned the modern girl in a house with limited electricity, no phone connection, and no Wi-Fi. It did have running water and flushing toilets, which she would not have in the past. I realized I would have to teach her how to cook on the wood stove.

"I definitely want to go, Mrs. Winslow. I can't believe this is so messed up." Tears welled up in her beautiful eyes again.

Richard tilted his head. "Well, sweetie, if you can't go at the next full moon-"

"But I *must* go, Dr. Winslow. He'll be so u-u-upset with me. He'll never understand. I have to find him and explain."

My heart lurched. The poor girl cried so hard she could barely get the words out.

Richard smiled and patted her shoulder. "Well, here's the deal, honey. Sometimes you can't go because the time isn't right. I had to try a couple of times before I managed to go years ago. But if you can't go next month-"

"I'll keep trying until I can," she blurted, her lips trembling as a new deluge of tears spilled from her eyes.

He beamed at her and pulled the tearful girl into his arms. "That's our girl. Hmm... The next month has two full moons. The second full moon is called a blue moon."

Kelly blinked and grabbed Richard's hand. "Charlie was always talking about blue moons. I thought it was just an expression."

Richard shook his head. "Oh, no, Kelly. Blue moons occur, but they are rare. A blue moon is the second full moon in a month."

I nodded. "Yes, indeed they do occur. I came here long ago on the eve of the blue moon. It was my destiny."

She took a deep breath and stood up straighter as her eyes filled with resolve and determination. "Charles used to talk about a once-in-a-blue-moon love. I understood it meant something special, but I never knew exactly what he meant. Now I get it. I intend to claim my own once-in-a-blue-moon-destiny. It was your destiny, Mrs. Winslow, and now it will be mine."

Chapter 9
Charlie
1802

Charlie rode with Baylie, Wolf, and little Faith through the portal in time and into the Cohutta Cherokee village. He felt a flood of emotions as they entered the village which he last entered eighteen years earlier as a small child. He struggled to shove his feelings of rejection that Kelly had not arrived to come with him out of his mind and to focus on the moment. As they entered the village, dogs began yipping at their heels, alerting villagers of their arrival.

As they pulled up near the village meeting hall and began to dismount from their steeds, Charlie heard a woman let out a squeal of excitement and run up to them. "Father, you finally returned! Guider, it is wonderful to see you again. And who are you, little one?"

Faith hung back hiding behind her parents. Wolf chuckled and pulled his youngest child before him. "This is our Faithful Angel. We call her Faith. Faith, this is your big sister, Hope."

Faith's eyes lit up. "My father spoke of you often."

Hope looked puzzled. The child's words were difficult to understand. Hope leaned forward to her father and spoke softly so the child would not hear her words. "What did she say?"

Guider smiled and pulled her child close for a hug. "Faith is what we call 'differently abled' Beyond. She said her father spoke of you often. Faith does many things the same way you and I do. She has a speech impediment, and words can be difficult for her to clearly pronounce. However, she knows sign language."

Faith nodded, eager to please her parents and her sister. She signed to Hope, "I am happy to meet you. Our father told me much about you."

Hope beamed and signed back to her little sister. "We are happy you came home. And who is this handsome fellow?"

Charlie chuckled as his cheeks reddened from embarrassment. "Charles Ranscome Hobbs, ma'am. My family call me Charlie."

"By the Great Spirit above, Charlie, you were a little boy the last time we saw you when your grandparents took you forward in time to find your mother. I'm Hope. My people call me the Bright Star of Hope." Hope appeared astonished.

Charlie chuckled, suddenly self-conscious. "I should have known. You have those blue eyes my Mom calls 'Selk blue eyes.'"

She nodded. "Yes, I inherited them from my mother. Of course, she was your mother's Aunt Ginny."

Just then, a Cherokee warrior bounded over to Charlie to grab him into a bear hug. "You're my sister Fancy's lad! How is your mother? How are they all doing?"

Charlie thought fast. Michael McCarron was his mother's half brother. He had lived with the Cherokees since he married Hope in 1779. "Uncle Michael? Oh, you are called Red Wolf here, right?"

Michael nodded as he grinned at the young man. "Aye. It has been many moons indeed since I heard anyone call me Michael."

Charlie smiled as he began to relax. This was the welcome he dreamed they would receive. "Mother is very well. They are all doing very well. Mother sends you her love."

"Charlie has returned to go to Great Britain where he will assume his responsibilities there. He will head eastward to Augusta soon in the first leg of his long journey," Wolf said. "I assured him there will be braves eager to guide him."

Hope laughed, her blue eyes twinkling with excitement. "Absolutely, Father. I can think of one right now who will jump at the opportunity."

It was 1802. That meant Charlie was the same age here that he had been back home in the future. He hoped some of the clothes he brought would be reasonably stylish for the Regency era. Oh well, if not, he could buy a new wardrobe at Williamsburg or in London when he finally arrived there. In the meantime, he wore button front jeans and a homespun shirt with a vest like his Papa Marc used to wear long ago when Charlie was a kid. He carried a light-weight linen jacket and a cravat in his saddlebags in case they went into towns. Dad warned him to be sure to wear a cravat and jacket if they went into towns. The jeans might not be period correct, but by damn, they would do for now.

His heart lurched as he watched Wolf hug Baylie and Michael and Hope hold each other's hands. Gosh, he missed Kelly something awful.

It was hotter than the blazes that summer on the way to the coast. Charlie was glad he brought Chico. The little fellow helped him through a damned rough patch in the desolate weeks after Kelly did not show up to come with him. The dog was a Godsend. He no longer thought constantly about poor Darbs. Chico was a different dog, but he helped Charlie heal after the loss of his old friend. The little dog seemed to know Charlie was grieving once again for the loss of his family as well as the girl he left behind. Chico snuggled up close to him while they rode and laid beside him at night on his bedroll.

Charlie shrugged as he scratched Chico's ears. He should have known not to expect Kelly to buck her dad. He always knew she was afraid of Col. Nguyen. He never understood why she feared him so much, but he always knew her father scared the daylights out of her. Mom warned him once that people have their own demons and not to question Kelly unless she wanted to discuss her relationship with her dad. Even then, Mom warned, Kelly might not open up to him right away. She reminded Charlie that it was hard for her to tell Richard about the traumas she endured as a child. Charlie wasn't sure why Mom said that because he was sure Kelly's childhood had to be infinitely better than Mom's childhood had been.

Charlie wasn't even sure anymore why he asked Kelly to come with him, even though he still loved her. *I just set myself up for more heartache. Oh, well, this trip would be god awful rough for a woman accustomed to the 21st century luxuries with little to no camping experience.*

The trip was tough enough for Charlie. Camping out, always cooking over an open fire, days of riding, sleeping in a hammock strung between two trees or on a bed roll on the hard ground at night. Now he understood why Baylie said she missed her bed so much. Not to mention the blasted bugs. He brought insect repellant with him, but it barely affected these little buggers.

He sighed, disgusted with himself and struggled to shrug off the depression enveloping him. At least he brought the water purification system. *Stop it, Winslow, You don't have time for this pity party. Quit it. Now.*

Charlie's cousin, Black Wolf, was the son of Hope and Michael. Black Wolf eagerly agreed to lead him to Augusta. They agreed the southern route to Savannah would be easier than through the mountains, even though it was more miles. Heading straight to Charleston would keep them in the mountains longer and the mountains would get higher along the way. They agreed the smarter route would be to head south to Augusta and then on to Savannah.

Charlie thought Joe McCarron, as Black Wolf now called himself, would turn back towards the mountains at Augusta. Instead, the young man who was almost the same age as Charlie, continued with him to the coast. "I told my parents I would go on with you awhile. I want to see the rest of the world. I want to see Belle Rose, where my grandmother was born. I want to see Ireland, where my grandfather was born, and where he still lives."

Charlie smiled. "I was born at Belle Rose, too. So was my Mom. I really look forward to seeing Ireland and our grandfather again. And who knows? Maybe you will accompany me all the way to London."

Joe grinned. "And maybe on to Europe."

Charlie laughed. "Now you're talking about a grand adventure."

"Yes. Why are you so sad, cousin?"

Charlie was silent for a few minutes before he answered. "I have to admit that I miss my family."

Joe shook his head. "No, this is more than the loss of your family. You miss the girl you left behind."

Charlie blinked back tears. He nodded and rubbed his forehead. "Yeah."

Joe did not ask anything else. They rode along in uncomfortable silence.

They continued through beautiful, old growth hemlocks, conifers, pines, and younger deciduous trees. What was that about 'the forest primeval?' Oh, yeah, now he remembered. Mom taught him the passage from the poem when he was a kid. She often recited the part describing the old growth forests of the 18th century.

Charlie recited the words from memory of Longfellow's description of a primeval forest from *Evangeline*. "This is the forest primeval. The murmuring pines and the hemlocks. Bearded with moss, and in garments green, indistinct in the twilight. Stand like Druids of old, with voices sad and prophetic. Stand like harper's hoar, with beards that rest on their bosoms."

Yes, the description fit. This must be the forest primeval in all its beauty and glory.

"What did you say?" His cousin looked puzzled.

Charlie shrugged, as if embarrassed. "It's part of a poem my Mom used to recite to me. She said it describes the forests of this era."

Joe nodded. "Yes, it did. You must teach it to me."

Yet despite the beauty and glory of the forest primeval, they still had to deal with biting gnats, mosquitoes, and more than one venomous snake along the way to Augusta. They killed another rattlesnake just last night. Thank heaven he spotted it before it got to Chico. *Exactly why did I decide to do this?* Charlie thought again as he shook his head.

Chico rode on the saddle with Charlie most of the time. The feisty little dachshund was too small to keep up with the horses for very long. It terrified Charlie to think a rattler or a water moccasin would get the dog if he gave Chico too much freedom.

He lost enough. Home. Family. The woman he loved. By damn, he was not going to lose his dog on this trip, too. He realized Chico was not a young dog, but he was not ready to let the little fellow go. Not yet. Not here.

Joe cut his warrior's braids and covered the shaved portion of his head with a neckerchief and a hat to help disguise that he was Cherokee. Once he donned European-styled clothing, he almost looked civilized, with his Selk blue eyes. Almost. A second glance at the young man revealed something Charlie identified as feral, for lack of a better word. It wasn't just his sun-darkened skin. There was something in his cousin as primeval as the forests they traversed. *Like Druids of old, sad and prophetic. Hmm. Maybe not sad, that would be me, but solemn and most definitely like a prophet of old even without the hoary beard – or maybe like someone called to help fulfill part of an ancient prophecy.*

Feral or not, Charlie was glad to have Joe's company. Joe could lighten his mood and make him laugh when Charlie had thought no one could. Joe was a damned good scout and could find a trail where Charlie would swear none existed. Joe was an excellent shot and kept the two of them in meat on the trip, even if some of it was snake. And like their grandfather, Joe had an affinity for languages which Charlie greatly appreciated and admired. While they camped out some nights, other nights Joe's ability with Native languages enabled him to negotiate sleeping quarters with local Indians, who were happy to help Joe guide the white man out of Indian Territory.

"But you speak many languages, too, Charlie. Don't put yourself down," Joe demurred one afternoon.

Charlie shrugged with a wry smile. "I speak English, Cherokee, Spanish, French, and some Irish Gaelic. But you speak Creek, Chickasaw, and Choctaw in addition to English, Cherokee, and some French. Your languages are handier on much of this trip than most of mine."

Joe's eyes narrowed as he considered Charlie's words. "Hmm. Perhaps so. But you can read and write all your languages. Most of the ones I speak have no written language."

Charlie looked over at Joe, startled by his words. "You can't read or write English?"

Joe blushed. "Not well. Neither was considered necessary while I was growing up with the Cherokees in the Cohutta Wilderness. My grandparents and my father taught me some, but reading always proved difficult for me. My grandparents left when I was only seven years old."

Charlie's eyes narrowed. "Hmm… Want me to teach you?"

Joe's eyes widened in surprise. "Would you? Yes, I would like that."

"Then it's settled. I'll be happy to help you improve your reading and writing. And maybe you will help me learn Creek. Or maybe we can practice Irish together, for when we get to Ireland."

Joe smiled as he nodded, excited by the proposal. "I would like that as well. It is good we can trade our skills. It means we both have worth and merit to the other."

"Oh, really, Joe? How could you doubt I value you? You are guiding me through the wilderness." Charlie bit back the grin teasing his mouth as he shook his head.

As the men rode on and they talked about their hopes and dreams, Charlie's mood continued to lighten. They talked about the land they both loved and about their hopes for loving marriages and children.

Charlie chuckled, suddenly self-conscious. "Well, I used to think I would marry the woman I loved, and we would have a big family, like Mom and Dad. But now? I don't know. Maybe I'm just supposed to marry the young woman who will be the best match for a damned duke."

"Don't give up on love, Charlie. Life is not worth living without love. I have seen that with my parents as well as our grandparents." Joe's eyes burned with unexpected passion.

"I thought Kelly was the love of my life. I thought she was going to be my forever love." Charlie looked pensive.

"If it is meant to be, it will be. But you must search for the other half of your heart. For your destiny. If Kelly comes someday, you have your answer. It was meant to be. But if Kelly never comes, you are meant to meet another woman here. Otherwise, you could not have come from Beyond."

Charlie's eyes narrowed as he studied his cousin. "You really think so?"

Joe looked up from the hoof he was paring. "I know so. No one can pass through time unless their destiny is here. You will find your mate here, Charlie."

Charlie nodded, suddenly rendered speechless by the taciturn young man's poetic words. *Wow. He sounds like Dad says Wolf sounded all those years ago when Dad went back to the future without Mom.* And then he remembered Wolf was Joe's other grandfather. *Huh. How about that? Nearly twenty years later, and Joe is giving me the same advice his grandfather gave my dad back then.* He cleared his throat. "Well, I was able to come through the opening in time. I know my destiny is here."

Joe finished paring the hoof on the mare, and then swung up into the saddle. "There. Let's go."

Charlie mounted his horse as well, and the two young men rode on the last few miles through the area known as the Piedmont into Augusta in silence, each still deep in thought about their futures.

They knew they were halfway to the coast when they reached Augusta. They had made pretty good time in the mountains, although they only averaged about 10 to 20 miles a day through them. They reached Augusta in ten days. It amazed Charlie they managed the trip so much faster than his family did years ago in the Conestoga wagon. He admitted it must have been rough traversing the mountains with four rambunctious kids, a man with a broken leg, multiple horses, and the cumbersome wagon. It was hard enough on nimble footed horses accustomed to the rugged mountainous terrain.

They decided to recoup in Augusta, rest a few days and replenish their supplies before tackling the next leg of their journey. Three days later, they headed out for Savannah. They crossed the fall line into the coastal plain, where they passed the fertile farmlands full of cotton as well as food products.

Charlie warned Joe they should be on the lookout for alligators as well as poisonous snakes. No such giant lizards lived in the Cohutta Wilderness. Joe laughed, thinking Charlie fabricated the story about the prehistoric reptiles until he saw his first. At that point, Joe paled, kicked his horse to hurry up, and made no more jokes about the giant lizards of which Charlie had warned.

Charlie made sure to carry Chico. "You are not going to be gator bait, little buddy."

As they approached the coastline, the thriving farms became less frequent as they encountered the wetter, poorly drained, swampy territory known to the settlers as the Pine Barrens. They both kept a close eye out for snakes and gators. Finally, they reached the Savannah River, and followed it into the town of Savannah. Charlie located Ranscome Shipping and arranged transportation for them north to the Belle Rose Plantation. Two days later, the two young men boarded the Belle Rive, which would carry them north.

Joe was speechless, his blue eyes shining bright with excitement, as the ship pulled out onto the open waters of the Atlantic Ocean.

Charlie laughed. "If this impresses you, wait until we head out to Ireland. All we will see for days will be water and sky."

Joe grinned, his dark eyes sparkling in the sun. Charlie had to smile at Joe's enthusiasm. He could almost feel Joe's excitement about the adventure ahead of them.

Charlie laughed, thinking how much fun he would be having if he could see Kelly's reaction to the open waters. *Not meant to be,* he thought. His throat went dry and he quit laughing.

He grimaced as he glanced down and realized he had scratched gnat bites on his wrist raw and bleeding. It amazed him that insect repellent from the future did nothing to stop these little demons. Chico tilted his head and gave him a puzzled look before the little fellow bent over to lick the wound. Charlie could not believe the blasted gnat bites itched so badly. Of course, it didn't help that now he had a heat rash on top of the gnat bites, or that several looked infected. Triple antibiotic ointment helped, as did Benadryl and Calamine lotion, but sheesh! This was ridiculous. Was it worth all this to claim his rightful place as the Duke of Ranscome?

At least it was a bit cooler on the open sea. He enjoyed the trip up the coast from Charleston to Belle Rose. He figured the ship could not go all the way to Belle Rose on the Potomac, but it would get him close. They could ride their horses the rest of the way if necessary.

The ship and all things nautical enthralled Joe. He listened attentively to Captain Chisholm and the men as they talked about sailing not merely across the Atlantic but circumnavigating the globe. Soon, the men were teaching the nimble and fearless young Cherokee how to climb high in the rigging to adjust sails and lines. Charlie could see Joe might be hard pressed to return to live in Indian Territory again now that he had discovered the deep blue seas.

Charlie caught himself scratching his gnat-bitten arm again. His hand stopped mid-scratch and he expelled a long sigh. Neither Mom nor Dad had shared the little gems of knowledge about insects and insect bites of the 18th century to him before he left. *Oh, well, so long as I don't contract malaria.*

His dog was nowhere to be seen. Probably hunting for rats, he thought. Chico had proven to be a fine ratter on the voyage, more than earning his keep by killing vermin.

Charlie's Journal

I promised Mom I would keep a journal before I left. I forgot all about that until now. Oh, well, better late than that I never begin it.

I was way past doggone tired by the time the sailing vessel docked alongside the Belle Rose Plantation this afternoon. I could tell for the last few miles that the property appeared to be beautifully maintained. My heart leapt into my throat in shocked surprise at the sight of blacks working the fields. I then blinked, even more surprised to see whites working side by side with the blacks who I thought were probably slaves.

"White people live in houses like this?" Joe looked stunned as he pointed to the Belle Rose mansion.

I shrugged. "Some do. Others live in the little houses like those along the river. I think our grandfather used to live in one of those little houses when he was a young man. Why?"

Joe gaped in stunned surprise. "I thought our Grandfather's cabin at McCarron's Corner was big, but this is … this is…"

"Enormous," I interjected. "And Mom says Ranscome Manor will make this house look small."

Joe 'tsked, and shook his head. "Why?"

I chuckled. "I have no idea. It seems the British believe in showing off their wealth. The bigger the house, the more important they think the man is."

Joe frowned. "But a man's true wealth is not found in material goods. It is in his peace of mind, in finding his own true flame, in seeing his children born and grow to maturity. It is in his knowledge he is fulfilling his destiny."

My head jerked over to Joe. "My God, and they call the Cherokees savages. You have a better understanding of what is truly valuable in life than I ever heard a white man explain. Well, except for our Grandfather. I remember he talked like that."

Joe looked pleased by my words. "He lived with the Cherokee for many years. Lone Eagle is a very wise man."

I chuckled again. "And he had Red Moon Woman to help guide him on his path. Hey, look, we're pulling up to the dock now."

Once the Belle Rive docked, Joe and I swung our bags over our shoulders and bid our farewells to the Captain and crew. I sat Chico on the ground, and Joe and I laughed as the little dog began barking as he raced up the steps towards the beautiful mansion. He seemed glad to be back on solid ground. As we started leading our horses up the steps towards the veranda which overlooked the river, a young woman came bounding down the stairs.

"Did you gentlemen intend to get off at Belle Rose?" she inquired as she bent over to pet Chico.

I laughed. I was sure this was my cousin, Rosa Linda. She looked enough like a photo Dad kept on his desk of his mom – Sassy – that I would have thought it was her if I hadn't known Aunt Sassy must be in her fifties by now. "Yes, indeed, miss. My name is Charles Ranscome Hobbs Winslow. I'm-"

As soon as he said his name, her eyes brightened. "Cousin Charlie! Mother and Daddy will be so excited you are here. Cousin Fitz has been writing, most concerned you had not arrived yet. Mother, you'll never guess who has arrived!"

I glanced over at Joe, laughing. "If they are this excited to see me, wait until they learn who you are."

Rosa Linda stopped to turn and peer into Joe's eyes. "Oh, my land, he looks like an Indian, but those eyes... Mother says those are Selk blue eyes. Daddy, a man is here who must be related to Aunt Ginny!"

Joe and I chuckled as we followed the young lady on up the steps to the veranda. Just as they stepped into the shade, Aunt Sassy and Uncle Will burst out of the house to stop dead in their tracks as they stared at us. Aunt Sassy was still trim, with beautiful brown hair just beginning to grey a bit. She had managed to retain the slim figure he vaguely remembered from long ago. Uncle Will must be at least seventy by now, but his blue eyes still shown bright. He still had all his hair, but it was what Dad calls 'salt and pepper' now instead of pure black. I blinked as I glanced from him to a portrait of Grandpa Jo hanging over the fireplace. *My God*, I thought, *he could be a double for his dad. No wonder Grandma always said Uncle Will would be a really handsome man when he got old.*

"*Ai, Dios mio*, you look just like your father. Well, at least how I imagine what Calvin looked like when he was a young man." The pretty, brown haired woman pulled me into her arms for a hug before she pushed me back to better inspect me. "Let me look at you. Oh, Charlie, you're all grown up, and so handsome. We're so relieved you decided to come."

"Let me see that young fellow, Sassy. My land a 'mercy, you're right, Little Bit. He looks just like his daddy when Calvin was a young fellow. It's like looking into the past." Uncle Will sounded dumbfounded.

I chuckled, suddenly embarrassed. "Thank you both. Mom says she thinks I look like my Dad probably looked when he was young. I've never even seen a painting of him. Anyway, I could never have made it without Joe's help. Joe is Hope and Michael's son."

Sassy gasped. Will beamed as he pulled Joe into his arms. "I haven't seen you in years, Black Wolf."

Joe's tanned cheeks reddened at the unexpected display of emotion. "I am Joe McCarron on this trip, Uncle Will. I figured I should use my English name."

"Well, Josiah McCarron, it is a pleasure to see you at the Belle Rose Plantation. I have to admit I never expected you to turn up here."

My eyes narrowed. "Dang, it never occurred to me that you are named after Grampa Jo. I should have realized it."

Joe laughed and patted Charlie on the shoulder. "It is not important. What matters is that we arrived at last, safe and sound."

We visited with Aunt Sassy, Uncle Will and their family at Belle Rose for two weeks. The last evening as Joe and I packed to leave aboard a Ranscome ship a few days later, Aunt Sassy came running up the stairs to us, waving a letter at us.

She panted from exertion, holding her side as she gasped out her message to us. "Boys, you're going to board the Ranscome Revenge tonight. Uncle Will says you will leave bright and early tomorrow morning."

Joe frowned. "Why, Aunt Sassy? What's wrong?"

I could feel the blood thrumming through my ears. *Oh, God, please don't let my Papa be dead. Please –*

Her eyes darted from Joe to me as tears welled up in her eyes. "It's Tammy. She's had a stroke. They wrote to Fitz to come back to Cork from London, if possible. Lily thinks you need to get there as soon as possible. I would go, too, but..."

I blinked. All I could think was, *my lord, Micah died from a stroke, and now Tamsin had a stroke. That's my maternal grandmother and my paternal great-grandfather.*

I took a deep breath. "How is my Papa?"

It shocked me to hear my voice quaver as I asked the question.

She shook her head as she handed me the letter. "He's okay. Tammy had the stroke while arguing with Marc. They always argued a lot. Those two are very different. They have never been good together. I don't know why Marc insists on living at Waterside when they would be quite welcome to move over to Ranscome Manor. Lily says that Tamsin is partially paralyzed. She still could not speak when Lily wrote. Marc is frantic for you to get there. Fitz is expected back from London any day now. Finish your packing. You need to board the ship tonight. Will says the ship will leave at high tide. That should be around 4 a.m."

We stopped at Boston to let Rosa Linda depart. She had been visiting her family at Belle Rose for the past month, but she lived on the Mystic River near Boston with Elijiah Curtis, her husband. It did not surprise me to learn they met because the young man was a shipbuilder, who built ships for the Ranscome shipping line.

Huh, my shipping line now, I realized with a start. I gave myself a good shake.

We spent the night with Rosa Linda and Elijiah before we headed out into the Atlantic the next day. I will never forget the look of delight on Joe's face as we entered the wide, open expanse of the Atlantic Ocean, the winds beating down on our faces like a hard rain. Of course, we had been traveling on open waters since Savannah, but it is different when there is no land in sight in any direction.

For me, it was a bit forbidding. And with each passing mile, I felt sadder and more alone. I missed Kelly so much I swear my heart ached. My dog must have sensed my mood. He whined and licked my hands more than once.

For Joe? It seemed like a dream come true. He stood there grinning like a possum, as Dad would say.

Joe and I were lucky. We did not suffer from seasickness. That was especially fortuitous considering that it took a good forty days to cross the ocean and to arrive at Cork. And let me tell you, Mom, Waterside is every bit as beautiful as you described it.

Chico had a ball hunting for rats on the ship. He found one occasionally, just often enough to keep his interest. The men all loved the feisty little dachshund. I had to watch them, or they would feed him way too many scraps.

"If he gets too fat, he won't hunt for rats," I warned them. The crew laugh when I tell them that, but it slows down their feeding of treats to Chico for a day or two.

At night, my little dog jumps up on the bed, circles around, and then lies down beside me with a sigh. Most nights, I fall asleep as he licks my fingers. He makes it clear that I am obliged to scratch his head while he licks. He will stop licking to nudge my other hand up to the top of his head. God only knows how I manage to find sleep scratching my dog's head, but I do somehow, night after night. Usually, my last thought is, thank heaven I have my dog. What would I do without him?

Joe says I smile in my sleep with Chico curled up beside me.

Chapter 10
Fancy
In the Present

Kelly appeared disappointed twenty-eight days later when the portal refused to open for her. She bit back her tears, swallowed hard, and then straightened her back. "So it will be the blue moon then. That makes sense. If my dad doesn't find me in the meantime, everything will be fine."

I patted her on the back. "That's right, sweetie. And yes, he called about you a couple of times, but he certainly hasn't come around. Don't worry. Everything will work out just fine."

Richard remained silent. I didn't miss the look of concern in his eyes.

The truth was her dad called virtually every day since Kelly arrived on our doorstep. We kept insisting we knew nothing about her whereabouts, but I could tell he didn't believe me. He was suspicious because we were spending the summer in Georgia. I hadn't told him we had personal reasons to do so. It wasn't his blasted business, and the reasons for our stay did not originally involve Kelly.

We took Kelly out to the cabin bright and early the next morning after she arrived, loaded with enough food for a month. The electricity was still on because the house was going to be listed on Airbnb, so Kelly could use the refrigerator. She would have to adjust to doing without air conditioning, television, the internet and wifi. Now was as good a time as any. I would leave the electricity on but urged her to try to use the lights as little as possible since she would not have the luxury of electricity when she traveled to the past. I warned her there would be no gas stoves or electric refrigerators in the past and she needed to try to get used to doing without modern conveniences. She would cook most of her meals on the grill outside, to get accustomed to cooking over an open fire. It was fueled with charcoal, not gas. At least she did not have to wash clothes in an iron pot over a hot fire outside. However, she would wash her clothes in a big sink in the basement, and hang them out to dry on the clothesline behind the cabin.

We were careful not to go out to Wolf and Baylie's cabin very often. I only called Kelly when I left our house from 'burn phones' Richard picked up on a trip to Atlanta. There was no land line at the cabin. Kelly knew to only call us in case of an emergency. This was also part of her getting used to doing without a phone, and those simple parameters proved hard enough for the girl. Besides, the phone connections to the Cohutta Wilderness were sketchy at best. She still called a couple of times when she felt overwhelmed by loneliness at the isolated cabin.

I began working on a pile of Sassy's old reenactment dresses so Kelly would have appropriate clothing to wear when – if - she managed to go back in time. She was just about the same size Sassy had been when she went back in time. Richard kept Sassy's old gowns. Sassy had some exquisite Regency era gowns I thought would work beautifully for Kelly. I also made a couple of trips into Atlanta to purchase Asian-influenced fabrics to make her a couple of dresses which looked appropriate for a 'Chinese' girl to wear in the early 1800's upon arriving in Great Britain. We had agreed she would pose as a girl from an upper-class 'Chinese' family who immigrated to 'the Colonies.' Kelly did not think the 'Chinese' pose would work because her feet were unbound, but I figured most people would have no idea where Vietnam was located. Kelly told me the Nguyen Lords had ruled most of Vietnam for about sixty years, and that the Nguyen Dynasty would begin in 1802. We all knew the British would still refer to the United States as 'the Colonies' even though Great Britain granted the United States its freedom in 1783. I found patterns for both Regency and Vietnamese clothing on Pinterest, Etsy and eBay. Combined with the traditional Regency attire I remade for her, I felt sure she would be well-dressed, whether she chose to go as a 'Chinese immigrant' or not.

I ran out to the cabin twice that month to do fittings for Kelly. I made both trips under the pretense that I needed to check on Wolf and Baylie's cabin, which was listed for rental on Airbnb. Kelly was thrilled with the gowns. I showed her how to style her hair in popular Regency styles. We both enjoyed playing with hairstyles to find the best ones for our 'Chinese Princess.' I laughed as she pirouetted around the room showing off a pretty, pink and white striped gown in the Regency style, with her dark hair braided and coiled into a high bun. "My Dad would hate my hair like this."

"Too bad. That is a popular style in the early 1800s, and it looks wonderful on you," I retorted with a patient smile. "Here, let me show you how a genteel young lady of that era would have enhanced her beauty with just a dab of makeup."

She beamed at me as she perched on a tall stool for me to deftly make her face look straight out of the Regency period. "Ooh, I love it, Mrs. Winslow! I look so pretty."

I shook my head. "You are pretty, Kelly, and don't you ever forget it. You are a beautiful young woman. That was one of the things Charlie said about you the day he met you. 'Wow, Mom, a new dog, and I met a drop-dead gorgeous girl today, too – and she seems to like me!'"

She blushed. "He didn't say that."

"I cross my heart. He did say it. He met you on a blue moon, and you enchanted him from the beginning, sweetheart."

She beamed at me. "I love him so much, Mrs. Winslow. I never dreamed it would hurt so badly to be apart from him. Oh well, as long as I can find him again."

I bit back the thought that I hoped she loved him enough to cope with the different life she would encounter in the early nineteenth century. Even with my preparations, she would find life in the early 1800s vastly different from life in the twenty-first century.

We also packed a variety of medicines we knew she could use in the past, as well as foodstuffs and 'necessities' like toilet paper, soap, sanitary napkins, and tampons to take on her journey. She had enough disposable sanitary products to meet her needs for six months. That should get her to Great Britain. Once there, she would use homemade pads made of cloth and an old-fashioned sanitary belt. I cringed as I remembered the days long ago when I used those. I made her two dozen cloth pads and sent her with a couple of old-fashioned sanitary belts I found on eBay. The toilet paper, modern meds and sanitary needs would all be loaded onto the pack horses along with her beautiful clothing for her to take with her 'Before'. She also had two dozen rolls of camera film and a camera so she could take photos to send to us, and some presents from us to Charles for Christmas and his birthday. She would take the burn phones, too. She could make recordings and take additional photos with those to send us. She knew how to use the fire starter and had a box of matches for emergencies. She had a sharp knife in a sheath as well as a firearm for personal protection. I prayed she would not need them, but I knew from experience she might need those items as much as anything she was taking with her.

She also had some prepackaged meals to take 'just in case'. She laughed at the dehydrated, instant meals, but agreed it might be better than starvation. We would send her with a water purification straw and a water purification system they could use along the way. It would hold three liters of water and could hang from a saddle horn under a saddle blanket. She also would take a hammock, a foil blanket, and a sleeping bag. I doubted she would need the blanket or the sleeping bag, but the weather csn be unpredictable in the mountains in the summer. We practiced putting up the hammock so she would be able to use it, and would know how to get in it to sleep at nights above the ground. This was a super light hammock, but it still had a mosquito net and tree straps with carabiners for easy use. Of course, I made sure she had a sewing kit and scissors for any sewing emergencies along the way. At the last minute, I remembered to bring her several cans of insect repellent as well as sunblock. I didn't want her to arrive at her destination sunburned and covered in bug bites. Hopefully, we covered everything the girl would need along the difficult trail to the coast.

Finally, it was two days before the blue moon. We were all getting pretty antsy and Richard figured it was time we headed to the Cohutta Wilderness. We hitched the horse trailer to the Land Rover and loaded up everything to drive over and get Kelly. Just as we started out of the drive, a car pulled up behind us, blocking us in the driveway.

Richard shook his head in disgust. "Oh, shit, I knew this was going too easy to be true."

I suddenly felt far colder than was possible in the summer heat of Georgia. I tried to paste a nonchalant smile on my face. "Why, hello, Col. Nguyen. How are you? What on earth brought you to Blue Ridge this fine summer day?"

He just stared at me for a minute. "Where is she?"

I frowned, as if I didn't understand who he meant. "Who?"

He rolled his eyes. "Don't play coy with me, Mrs. Winslow. Kelly. Where is my daughter? Where has your son taken her?"

I laughed. "My son? Charlie hasn't seen Kelly in months. He certainly hasn't taken her anyplace. Why? Can't you keep up with your own family?"

He muttered something in Vietnamese with a scowl. "Madam, I want to know where my daughter is. I expect you to tell me right now."

I laughed again.

Richard chortled. "Oh, you must be kidding. You really think your 'big Colonel in the Army' voice will intimidate my wife? Nguyen, she has chewed up and spit out better men than you. Many times. My god, there isn't a doctor who has ever been around her that dares to talk to her like that, at least more than once. Including me."

I laid a hand on his arm. "Now, Richard, be nice. Colonel Nguyen, if we knew where she was, don't you think we would tell you? But I guarantee you, she is not with Charles."

His eyes narrowed. "How do you know that?"

I pasted my most innocuous smile on my face. "We sent him off to Europe before you started calling to hunt for Kelly. If she didn't have a passport when she left your home, she could not possibly be in Europe now."

He studied me, as if trying to decide whether to believe me. "You have been here a long time this summer."

I nodded. "Yes, we have. My husband has been doing surgeries with his partner in Atlanta for the past month. Dr. Smith's wife is very ill, and I have spent a lot of time with her."

His eyes narrowed in distrust. "What is wrong with her?"

I sighed in frustration. "Well, not that it is any of your damned business, but she has stage 4 cancer."

That was the unfortunate truth. Dee was in chemo for cancer. She had been treated for lung cancer five years earlier, and we all thought she beat the disease. Five years is supposed to be the magic marker in lung cancer cases. There is only a 19% survival rate for making that five-year mark, well below the survival rate for other cancers. We had all begun to relax when the damned disease reared its ugly head again. It metastasized and spread to her brain. We didn't know if she would conquer the disease again, but if anyone could, it was Dee. She was as tough and tenacious as anyone I would ever know. She had undergone additional surgeries, and now was coping with the hideous side effects of chemotherapy once more with some help from medicinal marijuana. Dee was one of my dearest friends, and I stayed in North Georgia that summer to be able to spend time with her... just in case. To be honest, I was not sure she could do it again.

I didn't bother to explain all that to Col. Nguyen. It wasn't his damned business.

Even so, he looked horrified. "I am sorry. I did not realize..."

"Since we have answered your questions, I think it is time you move your car," Richard's suggestion sounded cordial yet firm.

"Where are you going?" asked the Colonel.

Richard let out a snort of exasperation. "Oh, for... look, man, not that it is any of your business, we are going to pick up friends and go camping. You are not invited. Now, get the hell out of my driveway before I call the sheriff's office and a tow truck and have you forcibly removed from my property."

Col. Nguyen looked shocked at Richard's tone. "You would not dare to do that."

"Really? You want to bet?" Richard started punching in numbers on his cell phone as if to call the Gilmer County Sheriff's Office.

I could tell Col. Nguyen was not accustomed to hearing anyone speak to him in that manner. His lips thinned, but he moved the car.

"So now what?" I asked as we pulled out. "He's going to follow us."

Richard shrugged and he rolled his eyes. "He can try. He won't get very far in that little Miata."

It was a good fifteen miles out to Baylie and Wolf's house on the Jacks River Road. As we turned off Highway 2 onto the Jacks River Road, Richard snickered. "He won't last much longer."

We both began to laugh as the Colonel's rental car slowed to a crawl on the one lane dirt road. Richard hurried on down the road in our sleek and comfortable four-wheel drive Land Rover. I began laughing uncontrollably as the Land Rover covered the Colonel's rental car with red dust. As we rounded a bend, we heard the pop of a tire behind us. I beamed at my husband. "Sounds like you were right."

"Yeah, but that also means we probably need to park the car and horse trailer behind the cabin in Wolf's barn. We'll have to ride into the wilderness on the horses from this direction. It's further, but it should guarantee the ass can't follow us. Plus, he won't see Kelly with us. Military drones won't help him either in the dense forest with no idea where we were headed." Richard flashed me a sexy grin.

A few minutes later, we pulled across the wooden bridge across the Jacks River at the entrance to the cabin. I quickly jumped out to shut the gate and to lock it behind us as Richard pulled past me to go around the house and into the barn. I grabbed a broom out of the back of the Land Rover and quickly swept away the evidence the Land Rover had pulled on the property with the horse trailer. Kelly ran out to hug us as we came up the back steps into the cabin. She looked shocked at first as we explained what happened, but then burst into laughter as Richard explained we would go cross-country on horseback the rest of the way.

"It will kill him if he ever figures I slipped right through his fingers. I would love to see his face when he realizes it, but the fact that I'll be long gone, and he won't be able to find me will be even sweeter. You will never know how much I appreciate all your help and support."

I hugged her close. "Just find Charlie. And love him."

"Always," she promised as she reached over to hug me. "Gosh, you would be the best mother-in-law a girl could ever have. I hate to lose you."

I stifled back tears at her words. "Just send photos from time to time. And take care of our boy."

Within an hour, we loaded the supplies onto the horses, and Kelly, Richard and I headed across the back of the property into the vastness of the Cohutta Wilderness. By the next morning, we reached the cabin. That evening, Kelly managed to access the portal. She was still blowing us kisses as she disappeared into the past, guiding two pack horses laden down with her belongings behind her as she headed out to find her once-in-a-blue-moon destiny.

I smiled. Colonel Nguyen would be hard pressed to find Kelly now.

Chapter 11
Kelly
1802

Kelly had to admit it was scary to travel through Cohutta Wilderness by herself. It excited Kelly to reach the Cherokee Village that evening. Baylie ran to her and grabbed her into an enormous hug. "We didn't think you were coming."

"Dad did everything in his power to keep me from coming, but I'm tenacious. My destiny is here with Charlie. Listen, Bay, I really need to use the restroom. Where is it?"

Baylie looked funny. "Uh, honey, there is no restroom like you are accustomed to using back home. There is a latrine a little down from the village."

Kelly looked confused. "What is a latrine?"

Baylie chuckled. "Well, it's kind of a toilet. We use a pit latrine, which is a simple and inexpensive toilet built over a hole in the ground. We dig it four feet long and four feet wide. A wooden base is over it, with seats. It's kind of an outhouse, without the walls, although there are four poles at the corners covered with a roof so we can use the facilities when it is raining or snowing."

Kelly paled. "Are you serious?"

Baylie nodded as she struggled not to laugh. Poor Kelly looked horrified. "Yes. We put lime down to hold down smell and to form a layer between poop and the air. When lime is mixed with moisture, it forms a kind of plaster."

Kelly felt sick to her stomach and held up a hand. "That is way more information than I needed tonight, Baylie."

Baylie couldn't hold back her laughter any longer. "I tell you what, kiddo. You use the chamber pot tonight, and I will take you to the latrine tomorrow morning."

A wave of revulsion washed over her face. "Oh, wonderful. Where do I go to use it?"

"Over here in the corner. I can stand in front of you and spread my skirt to give you a little privacy."

Kelly felt sick to her stomach. "Oh, that sounds just fabulous. Maybe I can just hold."

Baylie laughed. "Until when? I hear there is a fancy bathroom at Belle Rose with a big tub and a commode, but nothing like that until there. You are going to be using a lot of primitive resources along the way."

Kelly took a deep breath. "Okay. I can do this. I must do it. I'm going to find my Charlie."

Two days later, she set out for the coast with two Cherokee scouts and an older Cherokee lady, Rose, to act as her 'Abigail', or chaperone. She decided the fancy latrine at the Cherokee Village was pretty nice after she had to 'pop a squat' in the woods the first time. It grossed her out to have to bury her waste. Thank heaven Baylie gave her a little spade and showed her how to do that before they began their journey. She might have died of embarrassment if one of the guides had to demonstrate it for her.

"My lord, I had no idea mosquitoes could grow so large." Kelly swatted at another humongous mosquito.

Rose chuckled. "Oh, child, you have no idea. Just wait until we reach the swamps near the coast. We will be covered with hordes of mosquitoes, all eager for the taste of human blood."

Kelly cringed. Rose's verbiage brought imagery to her mind of tiny vampiric entities attacking them from all directions. Her delicate skin already itched from the myriad bites covering her exposed flesh and ached from the worst sunburn of her life. Her thighs were rubbed raw, and her butt was saddle sore. Thank heaven the Winslow's encouraged her to ride every day on the Smith – Wolf property while she was at their cabin or she would be suffering more. Her exhaustion seemed insurmountable, and they had only been on the road a half a day.

Thank God Dr. Winslow managed to get her a smallpox vaccination and a dose of oral polio vaccine in addition to a malaria inoculation before she came back in time. She had already seen people scarred from smallpox on their trip. All her other inoculations were updated, 'just in case.' Dr. Winslow even gave her a new flu shot and pneumonia shot before she left. At least she did not have to worry about catching some awful disease like polio or smallpox and dying before she found Charles.

Well, Charles warned her this trip would not be easy. He did not lie. Heck, he didn't even exaggerate. Of course, the trip would have been much more palatable with him by her side, joking and flirting along the way. Charles could distract her from the worst of circumstances and make her ignore all adversities. She thought Charles could have distracted her from having to use the latrine. After all, he managed to distract her for five years from her Dad.

She felt fortunate the Cherokees sent the two guides and Rose to escort her safely to Belle Rose Plantation, but the travel was painfully slow. They only made a hundred miles or so by the time they had been on the road a week. Travel was beyond tough in the mountains, with no roads, in the old-growth forests. They had to get off the horses and lead them at times because the mountains were so steep. It shocked her to see European settlers continued to migrate westward through the steep mountains. Were they that desperate for a new home of their own?

She had a hard time understanding the Cherokees, but no more than they did with her. She spoke very little Cherokee. They had little experience speaking English with outsiders. She already understood why everyone had warned her that she would have to adjust to language differences. She struggled every day not to use language from the future, because phrases she used at home brought looks of confusion here. The Cherokees figured out 'OMG!' was an expression of great surprise, and that 'no way, Jose!' meant she did not want to do something at all. God knew she had a new appreciation for hot and cold running water and flushing toilets. She understood now why Fancy told her she would miss hot baths and flushing toilets most of all when she traveled back in time.

They finally reached Augusta. It felt so good to strip off her filthy clothes and sink into a hot bath and a real bed again, even if the innkeeper did look askance at them and made the 'Damned Redskin men' sleep in the loft in the barn. She cringed when he used the racially charged pejorative, 'Redskins,' to describe gentle Rose and their stalwart, loyal guides, Winter Hawk and Running Bear, but Kelly wisely bit her tongue. The innkeeper finally relented and allowed Rose to sleep inside with her with the proviso that the Cherokee woman would sleep on the floor. It galled Kelly that they were not allowed to eat in the tavern, although the innkeeper permitted her to obtain plates of food for everyone to eat outside beneath an ancient oak tree.

Rose and the men were fine with that. They did not want to be in the smelly, hot tavern.

Rose was not accustomed to sleeping on a feather mattress and deemed it unfit for sleep. She preferred to sleep on the floor on her bedroll. Kelly did not know why the innkeeper allowed Rose to stay inside the inn. It tickled her that the man bought the story she was Princess Nguyen Keiu Linh from the Gulf of Tonkin. Kelly claimed to be on her way from the Far East to visit the Congress of the United States of America and Rose was her chaperone. She wore an *Ao Dai* with a split skirt and loose-fitting pants. She wore boots, and slid her knife into the boot for easy access if needed. She covered her head with a conical-shaped straw hat with a fine gauze veil over it to protect her skin from the brutal summer sun and the biting insects. She appeared foreign enough that the innkeeper realized she was not Native American.

Kelly laughed. Her name was Nguyen Keiu Linh in Vietnamese. Keiu meant 'graceful or pretty', and Linh meant 'gentle spirit or soul'. Her dad would not think she was very gentle-spirited if he could see her right now. Her parents called her Kelly because most Americans had trouble pronouncing Keiu Linh. Her parents could just as easily have called her Kay Lynn.

There were two saving graces to this god awful trip from hell. First, at the end of her arduous journey, she would be reunited with Charlie. She missed him horribly. She never imagined it was possible to miss a person so much. She missed Bobby after he died, but this was at least a hundred times worse. She dreamed about a happy reunion with Charles, where she would rush into his arms, where he would pull her to him and ravish her with kisses as he told her, 'oh, my darling, I missed you so much. I am so thrilled you managed to come!'

She prayed he would not find another love in the meantime. She had nightmares that he would find a 'suitable English bride' when he thought she refused to come back in time with him. After all, he was handsome, charming, well educated, rich, and held two titles. Any woman would be lucky to catch his attention. Surely that would not happen if she was meant to be his once-in-a-blue-moon love. Kelly struggled to push those worrisome thoughts out of her head as they trudged mile after exhausting mile across the Appalachian Mountains.

Second, she would in all probability never see her father again. She shook her head as she thought for the thousandth time that if she ever saw her father again, she might be compelled to kill him. Assuming, of course, that he did not kill his 'pretty daughter with a gentle spirit' first. Dad must be livid. She slipped through his fingers. She hoped he did not take his anger out on Johnny Tran or the Winslow's. Without Johnny's help, she could never have escaped the clutches of her controlling father. Without the Winslow's, she could never have come back in time to follow Charles.

Her college roommate took Fluff and promised to give him a good home for the rest of his life. She told her parents the elderly cat died while she was at college. She had decided the trip would be impossibly difficult for a cat to make. She struggled not to think about how much she missed the cat.

She already missed her Mother more than she ever dreamed possible. She often found herself wishing she could see or talk to her Mom. Yesterday, she got tossed off her horse when it spooked over the 'kakking' of a northern goshawk overhead just before the predatory bird swooped towards them. As her tears of pain and frustration began to fall, she lamented, "I want my Mom!"

It shocked her as soon as the words passed her lips. No, she would have to stifle such thoughts. There was no room for them on this trip. She wiped the tears from her face, smearing a little dirt across her cheek in the process, arose, and mounted her horse again. *No turning back, Kelly*, she kept telling herself. *No turning back. Your future is before you. Nothing but sadness lies behind you.*

But what if he found someone else? What would I do? How would I survive?

Kelly sighed as she sank into the soft feather mattress. What was it that Scarlett always said? Oh, yes. 'Tomorrow is another day.' Besides Baylie swore she could not have come back in time if her destiny did not lie here.

That night, she tossed and turned as she tried to fall asleep. Sleep did not come quickly. She continued to worry whether Charlie would be happy to see her upon her arrival. *Push those negative thoughts out of your mind and go to sleep*, she told herself. She intended to enjoy the comfort of the clean room and the soft bed for the night. They still had another week or so until they reached the coastline, and they would pass through hellacious swampy lands on the way, again sleeping on the hard, rocky ground.

She also knew she would have to face the shocked expressions of many people along the way who had never seen an Asian woman before and who would resent the Cherokees accompanying her. She had expected racism, but never dreamed it would be so overt, much less directed at her. She expected it towards the Native Americans and Blacks but she was the Princess. Between the obscenities muttered at them, the poor treatment of the Cherokees, and the shocking refusal to allow any of them to eat in the tavern portion of the inn, Kelly felt rattled to the max. At least the innkeeper brute allowed her to purchase plates of food for Rose, the men and for herself.

No one had ever refused her access to a place before based on her race. It shook her up. Would this be happening if she accompanied Charles? Would they both have been forbidden access to the tavern? She sighed. Maybe she was lucky the innkeeper believed she was a foreign princess and allowed Rose and her to stay in a room overnight.

The next morning, she felt refreshed and ready to take on the next portion of the trip, no matter what kind of racist nonsense they might encounter. She already counted the days until they could find a ship at Savannah to take them to the Belle Rose Plantation. She carried letters with her to give to Aunt Sassy and Uncle Will when she arrived there. She hoped and prayed Charles would still be in Virginia with his family. Hopefully, he would be delighted to see her, and they would marry while there. If he was still in Virginia, she doubted Charles would have found another love yet. Rose could return to her village. Kelly's need for a chaperone would end when she reunited with Charles. If he no longer visited Belle Rose, Kelly would locate another ship to carry her across the Atlantic Ocean to find Charles in Ireland or England. Poor Rose would accompany her to Britain if need be. Time would tell.

She did not want to dwell upon the possibility that Charles was no longer at Belle Rose. Things would be so much simpler if he was still there. Things would be even simpler if he still wanted to marry her. *Please, dear God, let him still want to marry me.*

They headed to Savannah the next morning after they managed to obtain additional needed supplies from vendors willing to sell to 'that damned Chinese girl and them stinking Redskins.' And Dad thought the racism was bad towards Asian Americans in the future? Kelly cringed with each new expletive but somehow managed to hold her head high like the princess she claimed to be while she bit her tongue. *Don't cause trouble. A princess would ignore their stupidity,* she reminded herself. *This too shall pass.*

At least, she hoped and prayed the overt racism would end when she found Charlie. She now had serious doubts.

She had traveled across Georgia and the Carolinas at least a half dozen times while her family lived in Georgia. Savannah was a favorite vacation spot of her parents as were the beaches at Tybee Island. The dirt trail they traversed was not the beautiful highway of the future. It was little more than the trail she followed from the Beech Bottom trailhead to the Winslow cabin. Fortunately, the trail was not the sodden, muddy mess as Charles had described it when his family traveled to McCarron's Corner after the hurricane when he was a child.

Ironically, she had never paid close attention to the way the terrain changed from mountains to rolling hills to flat, coastal plains and then the barren swamps when they lived in Georgia. With the coastal plains came more plantations, and with plantations came the shock of slaves working in the fields under the often-hostile eyes of whip wielding overseers. Kelly stared in shocked disbelief the first time she saw slaves working in a cotton field. She blanched and cringed each time she saw a whip lash out at the humans working in the fields. She bit her tongue in increasing fury as she observed new injuries atop old scars laid onto the backs of people with no other 'sin' than darker skin than the men wielding the whips. Good lord, did these people have no heart? Did the owners and overseers have no souls? How could they treat other human beings like this? They treated their livestock better than they treated their slaves.

And then it hit her like a load of lead bricks. *They think the slaves are no more than livestock,* she realized in dismay.

As darkness approached one evening, they prepared to make camp on the edge of a large plantation they had ridden past during most of the day. As they began to hobble and unsaddle the horses, an irate, overweight, red-faced Anglo man rode up.

"What the hell do you damned Redskins think you're doin'?"

Kelly arose slowly, her anger rising like bile. She fought it down and forced a smile upon her lips. "I am not a 'Redskin', sir. I am Chinese. My guides are taking me to Savannah. We thought we could spend the night here-"

"No. You ain't gonna spend the night on my property, you damned foreign trash. Now, get back up on your horse and head on down that road."

He leveled his long rifle in her direction. The Cherokees bent to pick up the saddles.

Kelly's lips thinned in anger. "No. You are being unreasonable, sir, in addition to downright un-Christian. We only want to spend the night. We will leave at dawn."

"Gal, I done told you once. I'll tell you one more time since you appear to be touched in the head. Get off my land."

Suddenly, the weeks of overt racism bubbled over and Kelly exploded. "You're a sorry excuse for an American. This is supposed to be the land of golden opportunity for all immigrants. How dare you treat a fellow immigrant like this? Your family probably came to Georgia when it was a penal colony. You're the trash. My family are kings and queens in our country. I asked you, as a Christian, to allow us, as fellow Christians, to spend one paltry night, and you respond with a raised firearm-"

Winter Hawk reached out and grabbed her, slapping his hand across her mouth. "I am sorry, sir. She does not understand. She is a princess in her country. She has come far to talk to Congress, and she has no knowledge of the customs of this country. We will move on. I am sorry. The Princess meant no offense. Her understanding of your language is sometimes, how do you say it? Ah, yes. It is sometimes inadequate."

The property owner nodded. "You fellows had best explain it to the little *princess* that folks don't take kindly to such foolish talk around these parts. Now, head on out."

Winter Hawk dragged Kelly to her horse. As she struggled to talk, he shook her. "Stop it, before you get us all killed, you stupid girl. Come on. We need to go. Now."

"But-" she began.

He shook his head. "No 'but's,' Princess Kieu Linh. This white man owns this land. He does not want us here. I don't plan to die tonight, for you or anyone else. We must ride on."

He threw her up on the horse, mounting after her, gathered the reins into one hand as he held her with the other. "Let's go."

Rose and Running Bear were already mounted, with Running Bear holding the leads to Kelly's horse and the pack horses. They kicked their horses and rode into the encroaching darkness of the oncoming night. They rode in silence for an hour before they stopped again. Finally, as they unpacked gear needed for the night, Kelly spoke. "He pointed a gun at me."

Rose looked at Running Bear, who shrugged.

Winter Hawk frowned. "You're lucky that is all he did. It won't be the last time a white man points a gun at you with your mouth. That man would have shot you, too, if I had not stopped your foolish tirade. You cannot talk to a white man like that. We are lucky he did not kill us all. We did not agree to bring you on this journey for you to get us killed."

Winter Hawk's quiet voice shook with unspent fury.

Kelly frowned. "But-"

He shook his head. "There are no 'but's', Princess. You came from a different world where I imagine people treat each other with more respect. You have not yet realized that this is not the same world you left behind. Times are dangerous for all of us who are not white. You must tread a narrow path. Can you do it?"

She was silent while she pondered his words. "I … I don't know."

"Well, you better decide pretty damned quick because I don't intend to get my ass killed over some stupid woman from the future who lacks common sense."

"That is enough, Winter Hawk. Kelly did not realize the full extent of the differences from her world to this one. Now, hopefully she does." Rose placed a protective arm around Kelly's shoulders.

Kelly pressed her hand to her mouth and struggled not to cry. Her throat tightened with unspent emotions. It would help nothing if she wept in front of the others. It would make her look even more inept and foolish than she had already managed to make herself look. They sat in the camp in silence. As Kelly settled into her sleeping bag brought from home, she finally allowed her tears to fall, no longer sure she could cope with the vast differences in 1802 compared to the time she came from. *Oh, God, if only Charlie was here with me.*

She thought she knew what racism was back home. She had heard about racism all her life. Boy, she blew that call. She had never observed such blatant, overt racism in the future. She began to shake as a horrifying wave of realization swept over her: she only knew a tiny fraction of the racism that she could face here. How would 'normal people' treat her elsewhere in the United States and Great Britain of 1802? Had she made a horrible mistake in coming back in time to marry Charles?

They were all quiet the next morning. Rose and Kelly prepared a quick breakfast, with a pot of coffee boiled over the fire, and some jerky brought from the tribal village. As they gnawed on the tough meat and drank the hot beverage, they all began to relax a little and began making casual conversation again for the first time since the encounter with the planter the previous evening.

"It's only about fifty miles to Savannah." Running Bear gave her a little smile, his words were low and soft, a comfort compared to the voice of Winter Hawk.

Kelly glanced over at him, uncertain how to respond. "That will take us three or four days, right?"

He nodded. "Most likely, but we are close. The swamps and the river will slow us down some even though we are well out of the mountains. Soon we will find the shipping office and head to Belle Rose. Hopefully, your Charlie will still be there."

He paused for a minute before he spoke again. "His mother was killed by a settler when he was a boy. He witnessed it."

Kelly's throat spasmed with horror. "I'm surprised he offered to come with me."

Running Bear shook his head. "He didn't volunteer. The chief selected him to come because he is our best guide."

Kelly frowned. "Couldn't he refuse?"

Running Bear shook his head. "That is not our way. We do what the tribe expects of us. The tribe expects Winter Hawk to serve as your guide."

Kelly's Journal

I finally have a few minutes of privacy and decided to write down my thoughts. Believe me, my head is spinning.

This is tougher than I ever anticipated. Not just the time travel. Not just cooking over a campfire. Not just sleeping on the ground or coping with mosquitoes the size of Texas. Not even the entire latrine issue, which is beyond awful. Not just doing without things I took for granted all my life.

Not even waking up stiff and sore after we sleep on the hard ground night after interminable night.

It's the racism. Oh, I always knew racism existed. Dad often talked about racism. But to hear talk back home, nothing has changed in the way different races are treated in this country in the past 200 years.

Believe me, so much has changed. And then again, like Liz used to say, maybe nothing has changed at all.

The big difference is people don't try to hide their animosity towards people who look different here. They are very blatant about it. They don't mind calling you horrible, denigrating names I never heard anyone use back home.

Now I understand why Mrs. Winslow warned me that things would be hard here, even if I held myself out to be a Chinese princess. She's mixed, but she looks like a pretty, white woman. She warned me that here in the Southern United States where we are now traveling, she was viewed as mixed. Some people never viewed her as white. She was never good enough for many people. I thought she exaggerated.

She didn't.

They don't care if I am a princess. They only care that I look different. That my skin is not lily white, that my hair is not blonde, that my brown eyes have an 'almond' shape they find unsettling.

Dad always said white people fixate on the eyelids and epicanthal folds on the upper eyelids near the inner corner of the eye on Asians. It isn't really accurate to compare my eyes to almonds. I think white people have almond-shaped eyes. I don't view my eyes as almond-shaped. Fancy told me that in the late 1700s, poets wrote odes to the beautiful, exotic Asian women found in their travels to the Far East and their 'almond-shaped eyes'. Gosh, I wish everyone waxed poetic over my looks. At least I arrived here before the fear of the 'yellow peril' which will come later in this century. I would hate to see more racism demonstrated towards me based on my appearance than I already encounter.

We had a bad experience on our way to Savannah. A man threatened to shoot us because we had the audacity to stop on the edge of his property to set up camp to stay overnight. I lost my temper and blew up at the man. I guess I called him just about everything except a white man. Finally, one of my Cherokee guides had to shut me up with a hand over my mouth to keep us from getting shot as they hurriedly moved us off the man's land.

I am still stunned. I almost got us all shot because I dared to talk back to a white man. Well, Dad often said my smart mouth would get me in trouble.

None of us had much to say for days after that happened. The Cherokees think they are risking their lives for a crazy woman. I guess they are. I must have been crazy to attempt this cockamamie adventure.

How will I ever manage to fit into nineteenth century British society? How will Charles cope with his foreign wife, even if I am perceived in Great Britain as an 'exotic, Asian beauty' – assuming he still wants me when I get there? What will the other nobles think of his 'little bit of foreign baggage'?

Will he still love me?

Please, dear God, let him still love me.

Chapter 12
Charlie
Ireland 1802

It surprised Charlie there was a nip in the air when they reached Ireland. He had not realized how much cooler it would be at Cork than at Belle Rose in early September. He had to admit the cool air felt good.

Uncle Will sailed that ocean-worthy ship right up to the deep-water dock at Waterside. Uncle Will might be in his seventies now, but his Uncle Will was still spry and fit. He could still handle a tall ship like a young man.

Charlie felt the niggling of an old memory as they docked. He remembered they had been here before when he was very small, but was it possible he could remember Waterside from all those years ago? And then he saw the gardens, and he knew his memory was true. This was the first home he could remember. This was where his little sister, Dara, was born. Heck, this was where his Papa was born in 1730, seventy-two years ago.

Charlie's heart leapt as Uncle Will moored the ship. As he prepared to leave the ship, a tall, slender man about Uncle Will's age came hurrying to the dock. Charlie realized with a start that his grandfather had aged into a handsome older man. His strawberry blonde hair had turned platinum blonde but he still had a full head of hair. His eyes still burned the dark green with specks of gold in the sunshine that Charlie vividly remembered. He could see Marc's face awash with relief as he realized Will had come with a young man. Marc cast a cautious look at Will, who nodded.

"Yep, it's him."

As tears welled up in Marcus McCarron's eyes, Charles extended a hand to him. "Hello, Papa. I've missed you."

Suddenly, Marc could hold back those tears no longer as he grabbed his grandson into his arms for a bear hug. "Oh, lad, it's good to see you again after all these years."

The tears startled Charlie. He never expected his Papa to cry when he saw him. He stood stiff and unsure of himself at first, and then felt his bones melt in the warm embrace of the man he had loved for so much of his lifetime. He never knew his real dad, but Papa stepped up to the plate like a dad for him when he was little, especially after the hurricane in which it was believed that Kirk O'Malley died. Papa McCarron was the man he admired most in all the world except for Richard Winslow. The two of them comprised his ideal role model for a man. Of course, there was a healthy dollop of Will Selk in his ideal man, too, although he had not realized that until he met Uncle Will again on this trip.

As their embrace ended, Charlie glanced up as a tall, reed-thin, grey-haired woman rushed up to them. "Oh, my God, Charlie, we had given up hope you would ever come."

He reached out to hug Lily McCarron. "It's good to see you, Gramma. I have letters for everyone." He glanced towards the house beyond the gardens. "I have a packet of letters for Tamsin. How is she?"

Marc's face clouded. "She's well enough. She can talk again, and she never ceases complaining."

Lily swatted at Marc's arm. "Oh, behave yourself. She has been worrying herself sick about you. Fitz arrived a few weeks ago from London. She's about to drive him crazy."

"That old woman already drove me crazy," muttered Marc as he rolled his eyes.

Lily cut her eyes at Marc. "Behave yourself, old man. Of course, she will be disappointed Fancy did not come, too."

Charlie could feel his cheeks redden. "Bella married at Christmas last year. She's expecting a baby. Mom would not leave and come this far."

Lily laid a hand on his shoulder. "Oh, believe me, honey, I understand. Just be prepared when Tamsin fusses. In any event, you're here now. That will help tremendously, even if Fancy couldn't come."

As they entered the house, a thin woman with black hair beginning to turn grey arose unsteadily from a chair. Charlie recognized her by her blue eyes if nothing else. Otherwise, Tamsin Selk had aged more than he had expected, her face lined with worry. She paled and swooned as Charlie entered the room. "Oh, my land, Calvin..."

Fitz ran to grab his mother as she crumpled. She revived a few minutes later, apparently still a bit muddled about Charles' identity until Fitz managed to convince her that he was not Calvin, but his son.

"Mother, it's Fancy's lad, Charles. His father died at Yorktown, remember?"

She stroked a hand down his cheek. "Charles. Well, you are quite a handsome young blade. You look very much like your father did at your age. He was very handsome, too."

She looked around the room, desperation in her eyes. "Your Mama didn't come?"

Charlie shook his head. "No, Grandmama. Richard felt it would not be good for her. Her heart condition, you, know. But she sent you a passel of letters."

Her face crumpled. "Oh. Of course. I was just hoping maybe after all these years she would have come back to see me one more time..."

She turned away, so we could not see the tears as they spilled from her eyes.

Fitz rolled his eyes. "Now, Mother, there is no reason to get all blue deviled. You should be glad to hear that Fancy is still among the living."

Charlie finally cleared his throat. "Why did you think I was my father, Grandmama?"

She slowly turned back to me. "You look so much like Calvin did when he was young. He loved me first, you know. He wanted to marry me when Marc abandoned me and hightailed it to Indian Territory."

She wandered away to stare out the window.

"Tamsin, you know Calvin married Fancy," Marc began.

Lily laid a hand on his arm. "Not now, darling. She's been stressed enough today. Let it go."

He frowned. "But–"

"Let it go, Marc. Later." Lily remained adamant. "We don't need her to have another stroke."

One thing Charlie remembered from his childhood was that Grandma Lily meant what she said. Marc looked uncomfortable, but nodded, and bit his words back.

Finally, Tamsin turned back towards them again. "So, where's this passel of letters my daughter sent me? Humph. It's about time she wrote to me. She's been gone nigh on to twenty years now." She glanced down at Chico with a look of horror. "Oh, my land, what is that thing?"

"That 'thing' is a dog. He is a purebred wire-haired dachshund. Chico, sit pretty for the lady and speak."

Tamsin stared in shocked horror as the little dog sat up on his haunches and barked at her. She sniffed as if in disdain. She appeared unimpressed by the little dog.

Charlie pulled letters out for Tamsin as well as others for Will and Fitz. "Grandmama, Mother wrote to you many times. She kept a copy of each letter she ever wrote to you, because she knew the posts were so bad between New Spain – well, they call it Mexico now – and here. She figured that was why she never got letters from you."

Charles caught the quick wink from Uncle Will as Papa covered his mouth with his hand, pretending to cough.

Lily fought her own smile down, determined not to let Tamsin see it. She reached down to scratch the dog's ears. "Hello, Chico. What an adorable dog, Charles. See, Tammy, I told you she hadn't forgotten you. And don't forget, I brought you letters some years back when they lived in Indian territory with us. So, your Mama sent copies of all those letters she wrote over the years?"

He nodded. "Yes, ma'am, Gramma. And she sent drawings of everyone that Dad – Dr. Winslow, I mean – drew of all of us. We call him Dad. He's really the only Dad we ever knew. He likes to draw."

Charlie opened the satchel he carried from Texas and began to pull out the letters as well as the penciled drawings his dad made over 200 years in the future. The family all crowded around to peer at the pictures, and then to carefully pass the drawings from person to person. Charles passed out the letters from his mother to his relatives.

As Tamsin stared at the drawings, Charlie could see the little twitch in her facial muscle, which accompanied her partial paralysis. "They... they look good. Who is the boy?"

She pointed to Ronan. Charlie smiled. "That is our youngest brother, Ronan Roberts Winslow. I understand he looks a lot like Dad's father."

She looked confused by my words.

"I'm sorry. I call Richard 'Dad'. After all, he raised all of us. He is the only Dad I remember. He has been a great Dad to all of us."

She nodded, and resumed studying the pictures, a finger delicately tracing my mother's features. "She looks good."

"Yes, the climate in Texas agrees with her. She seems to be in fairly good health there. You know, uh, considering her heart condition and all."

Charles couldn't explain that Mom had heart surgery years ago or that she was fit as a Stradivarius. He chewed his lip as he next unrolled the oil painting Dad sent with him of the family. Dad even included Miguel standing next to Bella in her wedding gown, as well as himself in the picture. It was based off a wedding photo with everyone in it dressed in the clothing they wore at Bella's wedding. Dad even included Chico in the painting. As he explained to Tamsin who everyone was, Charlie noticed she carefully compared Bella's features in the painting to those of Mother. He cleared my throat. "Mom and Bella look a lot alike."

She nodded again. "Very much alike. Of course, Bella has my blue eyes. You have your Daddy's brown eyes. I'm surprised not one of you had black hair. It was so strong in the Selk family. So, you finally came home. It's about time, you young buck. You will need to go to London soon, to join the House of Lords and fulfill your destiny there. You could clean up and look every bit like two Bond Street Beaus, you and my Fitz. Sweetheart, you will have to take Charles shopping for some more fashionable clothing when you two get to London. We don't want him looking like some little country bumpkin from the Colonies."

"That's what Mom said. You will notice Mom's hair is lighter than Bella's hair. Mama's hair is strawberry blonde, or what Mom calls light auburn red. She says Bella and I have dark auburn hair."

She sniffed. "Humph. She got that red hair from Marcus."

Papa started to say something, but Lily laid a hand on his arm again and shot him 'a look'. "Probably so, Tammy, although it looks like Calvin's brown hair darkened theirs up from the shade of their mother's hair."

She shrugged. "I reckon."

"Well, we all need to visit for a while. I don't need to go running off to London today. We have plenty of time to catch up before Fitz and I go to London." Charles forced a smile.

Tamsin looked up from the letter she had opened and peered at him over her spectacles. "Hmm? Oh, of course. I believe I'll just go read my letters."

He sagged with relief once she left the room. "My God, she's exhausting."

"You haven't seen anything yet. She's always been like that," Marc muttered. "Always has to be the very center of all the attention."

"Now, Marc, that's not fair. I can remember a time when she most definitely would fade right into the background," Lily demurred.

He frowned as he shook his head. "She was the housekeeper at Belle Rose then. She was trained to be unobtrusive. But even then, she always wanted to get attention. Remember the blue dresses?"

"Your attention, darling," whispered Lily with a wink.

He sniffed in disgust. "I don't know why my damned brother had to go off and get himself killed all those years ago. He was the only man she ever thought was good enough for her."

Lily bit back her laughter. "Now, darling-"

He shook his head. "Nay, I'm serious. If she had loved me the way she loved Jay, she would have gone with me to Indian Territory in '59."

Lily's cheeks turned red as she struggled not to laugh. "And then I would never have found the man I love. Besides, you didn't love her."

His eyes softened as they fell to Lily standing beside him. He reached over and pulled her to him. "Nay, I never loved her. T'was you I was meant to love."

You found your once-in-a-blue-moon love, Charlie wanted to say, but he bit his tongue. *After all, was there really such a thing? And if so, where will I find mine now?*

•

Charlie's Journal

We made it to Ireland. Waterside is as beautiful as I remembered and then some. Your mother is one crazy old lady. She is damned difficult. Thank God for Gramma, Papa, Fitz, and Uncle Will. I will never for the life of me know how Fitz grew up to be so normal as he is with her for a mother.

I still feel pretty blue, but at least enough is going on here to distract me from my neverending pity party. Chico remains determined to entertain me. I don't know what I would do without the little fellow. He still sleeps curled up beside me every night. I think I'll mosey over to Ranscome Manor pretty soon. I can't stomach much more of Tamsin.

She is so ready for me to find a nice English girl and to settle down. She is horrified that Kelly is a foreigner from Asia. I pointed out she was a foreigner when she moved here, and she is mixed. You would have thought I had grown another head by the horrified look she gave me. "Oh, no. I was from the Colonies. I was born a British citizen."

Well, I guess she was at that. But, still, has she always been so difficult? So incredibly determined to put everyone else down? So damnably insane?

Papa says she was always difficult, but she is a lot worse since the stroke. Wouldn't it just figure that I had to come when she is at her worst?

I'm sorry this just seems like a bitch session about your mother. I figured you would understand better than anyone else I could talk with about her, unless it's Papa. Gramma says Papa and Grandmama fight like cat and dog. I think that is a generous analogy.

God knows I try not to talk poorly about her to Fitz. He has enough to handle, considering the cross-eyed bear who yokes him.

Give my love to everyone. Wish I could talk to you all. Wish I could see you, too. Tell Bella if the baby is a boy, she should name it after me. Carlos Vargas has a nice ring to it. I think they intended to name a girl Caridad, or something like that.

Did you ever hear from Kelly? I don't know why I'm asking. You can't write back to me. I miss her so much. I never dreamed it would hurt this badly to lose her, but then, I never dreamed I would lose her a second time, once she said she would come with me.

I sure wish I could hear from you guys. I am so lonesome for the sound of your voices. What I wouldn't give to hear one of Ronan's lame jokes about now, or to hear Bella pounding on those piano keys. What I wouldn't give for a time-traveling phone. If only…

Oh, well, like I said before, it's not like you can write me back anyway.

Love you more,

Charlie

Chapter 13
Kelly
1802

They reached Savannah four days after the 'incident'. Kelly located the Ranscome shipping office and after an hour's wait, she was ushered into the office of the shipping office director, the man in charge. Kelly presented the letters from Mrs. Winslow. The shipping office director looked startled, but quickly identified a ship headed northward the next day which could take Kelly and her Cherokee companions to Belle Rose. He put them up on the ship overnight. Kelly guessed the captain realized a 'Chinese princess' and three Cherokees accompanying her would have considerable difficulty finding a place to stay overnight otherwise.

Three days later, after stops in Charlestown and Wilmington, the ship pulled into the Chesapeake Bay and docked at Jamestown. They set out on horseback again towards Belle Rose. Winter Hawk figured it would be a forty-mile ride. As dusk fell the following evening, they finally reached the exquisite plantation named after its founder's wife, Belle Rose Selk.

Kelly had seen some pretty homes, but few places rival the beauty of the Belle Rose plantation in 1802. The fields planted with tobacco and cotton were impeccably maintained. The drive up to the home was shaded with oak trees, but it was the roses that flanked the plantation house that took her breath away. She had never seen such beautiful roses in all her life, and her dad always fancied himself to be an aficionado of roses.

It intrigued her that the field workers were both black and white. They sang in the fields, using the lines of the songs to keep their rhythm. Kelly heard laughter and joking among the workers, sounds she never expected to hear in a plantation field in Virginia. It was vastly different from the plantation outside Savannah. And then, she remembered with a start that Mrs. Winslow said her brother freed all his slaves in 1783. He paid wages to everyone working on the plantation. *Interesting. It might not be perfect, but it was a far sight more pleasant looking environment than the plantation where that fat little toad threatened to shoot me.*

An older black gentleman dressed in livery ran up as they pulled under the portico over the drive. "May I help you good people?"

Kelly nodded. "Yes, thank you, sir. My name is Kelly Nguyen. We are looking for the Belle Rose Plantation."

He nodded, as he held the horse while she dismounted. "Yes, ma'am, Miss Kelly, this is the Belle Rose. Let me help you down. Randy! Tell Miz Sassy we have company."

The younger man identified as Randy nodded and darted towards the front door. Minutes later, the door swung open, and a pretty, middle-aged woman rushed out, her eyes wide and her cheeks pink with excitement.

I hope I still look so good and have such a trim shape when I am her age, Kelly thought.

When she laid eyes on Kelly and her companions, a broad grin spread across Aunt Sassy's face.

"I told him you would come! Welcome to Belle Rose," Aunt Sassy shouted as she gathered Kelly into her arms.

For the first time in weeks, Kelly felt her tension and fears begin to ease from her body. "Is he still here, Mrs. Selk?"

She shook her head. "No, sweetheart, but please call me Aunt Sassy. His grandmother, Tamsin, had a stroke. My husband, Will, took him on to Ireland. I'm so glad you were able to come, Kelly. He loves you so much. It will be wonderful for him when you two are reunited."

She ushered them into the house, with Kelly's Cherokee companions looking more nervous by the minute. Finally, the man called Randy offered to take the Cherokees to the kitchen, while Mrs. Selk and Kelly talked.

Kelly sighed as she looked into a mirror. "Gosh, I'm sunburned. I thought with the hat and netting, not to mention sunblock, that I would not burn."

Aunt Sassy chuckled. "It will fade pretty quickly, sweetheart. I wouldn't worry about it."

Kelly shook her head. "I'm not worried about it. I just didn't want my skin to get any darker than it already is. I wasn't sure how it would go over in Britain."

"Oh, I wouldn't worry about it, Kelly. He won't care." Once they left the room, Aunt Sassy began her questions. "What happened? Why didn't you meet him as planned?"

Kelly sighed. "My dad figured out I was going to meet Charlie and locked me in my room. Can you imagine? I'm twenty-one years old, and he locked me in my room like I was a child. He took my phone away and I couldn't call Charlie and tell him what was going on. The next day, Dad let me go out with a friend, who helped me get to the airport. I flew to Chattanooga, and had Uber carry me to the trailhead."

Sassy frowned. "What's Uber?"

As Kelly explained about the transportation service of the future, Kelly could see recognition spread across Aunt Sassy's face. "Oh, kind of like a taxi service. How did you ever convince your dad to let you go out with a friend?"

Kelly could feel her cheeks redden. "Well, my dad wanted me to marry this man. He's Vietnamese American, like my family. Anyway, John knows I love Charlie, and he knew we – John and I - should never marry. He helped me get to the airport where I secured another ticket. Dad cancelled my first ticket to Atlanta when he figured out where I was going."

Sassy poured Kelly a glass of water, which she eagerly took from her and quickly gulped down. "Oh, thank you, Mrs. Selk. I must say it sure feels good to sit on something soft that is not moving. What a lovely room."

She laughed. "I remember that feeling. I rode here once some years ago from McCarron's Corner, too. But please, call me Aunt Sassy."

Kelly nodded. "That's right. Mrs. Winslow told me about that. Wow, that must have been some journey. We only had a portion of that ride, and I'm bone tired."

They talked for hours, as Kelly showed her photos on her phone and shared many stories about the future lives of the Winslow family. Finally, Kelly yawned. "Oh, I'm sorry."

Sassy looked alarmed. "Oh, my word, child, I am who should be sorry. I'll show you to your room. You would probably like to clean up and turn in."

Kelly grinned. "I have to admit that a bath sounds pretty good. Is there any place where the Cherokees could stay?"

She nodded. "Of course. I think they have already been taken to those quarters. Let's get you a hot bath and some dinner. I know you must be exhausted."

Kelly nodded. "I am. I sure wish Charles was still here. We could be married before we went on."

Sassy's face fell. "Oh, honey, I thought you realized..."

Kelly frowned. "Realized what, Aunt Sassy?"

Sassy began to blush and stammer. "Uh, honey, whites are not allowed to marry members of other races in Virginia. It could have proven problematic if Charles and you married before you came."

Kelly blanched. "Why? What do you mean?"

Sassy shrugged. "They call it miscegenation. They claim they want to keep the races pure. That's hogwash. Look around and you will see lots of mixed-race people. Heck fire, Fancy is mixed. She had to go to Bermuda to marry Calvin. When she married Kirk in Barbados, it was invalid because she is mixed. I love my life, but some things here are so backwards."

Kelly gulped. She could feel the blood drain from her face. She reached out to grab hold of the bed. "Will it be that in Great Britain, too?"

Sassy shook her head, but Kelly wasn't convinced.

"No, I'm serious, I need to know. Will he be allowed to marry me there?" Kelly couldn't help it. The fear reverberated in her voice.

Sassy pulled Kelly into her arms. "Oh, sweet girl, don't worry. Charles and you can marry in Great Britain. There are no miscegenation laws there against mixed marriages. With the tea trade between the Far East and here, men bring back beautiful Asian wives. But..."

"There will be racist attitudes about it?" Kelly whispered.

Sassy nodded. "Yes, I'm afraid so, my dear. The good part is Charles is a Duke and most people will be busy sucking up to his Grace and won't be overtly rude to your face."

Oh, great, thought Kelly with growing dismay. *I'll have to deal with a bunch of lying toadies who don't respect us. Was my father right? Am I setting myself up for a life of heartache? But I love Charles. How could I possibly spend my life with anyone else?*

She had dealt with racism before. She was graded down in her college entrance exams because 'Asians test too high.' It infuriated her, but she was still admitted to the college of her choice.

She grew up thinking it was her parents who were the racists. Dad often made disparaging comments at home about other races. It amazed her that he could control those outbursts at work but never tried to hide his disdain for other races at home.

She realized the Winslow's were probably the only white family with whom her dad ever socialized of his own volition. He commented a few times that they seemed to lack much of the stereotypical thinking he expected from Southern whites. She resisted the urge to tell him that they were mixed. She was not sure how he would have received that information. Probably not well.

Of course, she remembered one incident when Dad got crossways with Mrs. Winslow. He accused her of having white privilege and systemic racism. When Mrs. Winslow quit laughing, her Dad's face was beet red. Mrs. Winslow told him both Dr. Winslow and she were mixed. They might both look white, but they grew up in mixed families and they identified as persons of color. Mrs. Winslow quit laughing and her eyes narrowed as she leaned in towards Kelly's dad. "And you, sir, have no idea of the overt racial discrimination I have experienced many times throughout my life."

Kelly recalled her dad's laugh was short, terse, disbelieving. "Oh, really, madame? I cannot imagine a pretty, white woman such as yourself ever experienced racism. The idea is too ludicrous for me to give credence."

Dr. Winslow reached over and laid a hand on his wife's arm. "Let it go, sweetie."

She frowned, her shoulders still hunched as if ready for a fight. "But Richard-"

"Let it go. Col. Nguyen will never be able to comprehend what you endured as a child. And our lives are quite different here than in the past."

Kelly remembered the tension slowly ebbed out of Mrs. Winslow. "Maybe you're right, Richard."

Kelly now understood how much Mrs. Winslow must have suffered in the South since she was mixed.

The servants quickly filled the tin tub with hot bath water.

"Thank you so much." Kelly sighed with pleasure as she sank into the soothing heat. As she inhaled the lavender-scented fragrance, her worries began to drift away. She almost fell asleep in the tub, but finally lifted herself from the tub, dried off, slipped on a clean nightgown, and crawled into the inviting bed. "Like Scarlett said, 'tomorrow is another day.' I'll worry about all of it tomorrow."

However, she tossed and turned awhile before she was able to fall asleep. Once asleep, she was assailed by strange dreams. Her father's face would loom before her, gargantuan, as he screamed, "I told you that you could never fit in with those people!" Her mother stood to the side, sobbing that her daughter had brought shame and dishonor to their family. Her little sister cried that she would never see Kelly again.

And then Charles came riding up on a white steed. He swung down and knelt before her to slip the beautiful celadon jade and diamond ring on her finger. 'She will be my duchess, Col. Nguyen. There is nothing you can do to stop that. We are far beyond your grasping control." He bent to Kelly again, enveloped her into his arms, and kissed her.

It was late when she awoke the next morning. Kelly stretched, cat-like, as she fully awakened. It felt so good to be in a real bed after weeks of sleeping on the ground, especially after that luscious hot bath.

For the first time in weeks, Kelly felt hopeful. Optimistic. Excited about the grand adventure ahead of her. And most important, she felt renewed confidence that Charles would be thrilled – elated – that she managed to follow him. Maybe things wouldn't be so bad here in the nineteenth century after all. She sure hoped so.

She slipped off the four-poster bed and quickly rooted through her backpack for a clean *Ao Dai*. She pulled out the hairbrush and brushed her hair until it shone like liquid silk. Finally, she braided it into a long queue before she tossed it back over her shoulder and then hurried downstairs.

Sassy sat in a chair sewing as Kelly entered the room. "Oh, hello, sweetheart. Come here. I thought I could adjust this dress and it would probably fit you."

Kelly obediently walked over to Sassy, who arose from the chair and held a dress up to Kelly's shoulders. "Yes, I think it should just about fit you. I figure you need a few 'modern' looking dresses to look more like you fit into the early 19th century. Your ethnic outfits are beautiful, but they definitely scream 'foreigner!' Why don't you pull this gown on, and I can see if it needs any other alterations?"

Kelly grinned ear to ear as she nodded. She grabbed the dress and whirled around to fly back up the stairs and try on the beautiful gown. A few minutes later, she came back down with a frown on her face. "It doesn't fit right."

Sassy chuckled. "Well, you need the proper undergarments to make it fit correctly. Hmm... let's see. The sleeves are a good fit. The neckline fits well, and it doesn't show too much cleavage. And the hem is just right. We may need to tweak it a bit once you have some appropriate undergarments, but I think the dress will work. Mary Elena, you're about the same size as Kelly. Pull out a set of your new stays and a petticoat that she can try on with this dress."

Mary Elena nodded, grabbed Kelly's hand, and they ran back upstairs to Mary Elena's room. The pretty teen helped Kelly out of the Regency day dress, and quickly helped her don a shift, pantalettes, short stays, and a petticoat with a built-in bodice.

Kelly stared down at the pantalettes. They reminded her of loose capri pants. "Well, these are the most awkward panties I ever saw."

Mary Elena giggled. "You'll get used to them. Mama says she used to wear much smaller pantalettes in Texas like you had on. I think those look horribly uncomfortable. Anyway, Mama may say you don't need the short stays with that type of a petticoat, but we will let her decide. I like to wear a petticoat over my stays. I think it gives a smoother, more contemporary look, more in keeping with today's *beau monde*."

Kelly blinked. "*Beau monde?*"

Mary Elena laughed. "It means fashionable world. Mother isn't always up to date on today's fashions. She tries, but, well, you know how mothers are."

Once Mary Elena quit lacing the back of the pretty Regency gown, the two girls hurried back downstairs for Sassy to evaluate the look.

"Oh, yes, very nice, Kelly. I don't think you need both the short stays and the bodiced petticoat, but that is up to you. How does it feel?"

Kelly blushed. "It feels like I'm wearing a lot of clothing, Mrs. - I mean Aunt Sassy. However, it's all comfortable, and the dress is adorable."

Sassy nodded. "Yes, it's a pretty gown."

She finished a few extra stitches around the waistband, and then smiled. "That looks very nice. It is such a shame that Lady Washington passed away this summer. I would have loved for you to have had the opportunity to meet her."

"Did Charles get to meet her?" Kelly asked.

Sassy shook her head. "No, Lady Washington died in May before he arrived. I know she would have loved to have met Fancy's son and his fiancée. There, all done. Now, turn around and let me see the whole look."

Kelly slowly turned around, so Sassy could peruse the entire dress.

Sassy beamed with pride. "Oh, yes, that looks very nice, if I do say so myself. Let's go upstairs and see what Fancy sent with you. I can see if I need to alter anything else."

Kelly smiled. "She told me that several of the dresses she reworked for me used to be dresses you wore to reenactments at Williamsburg."

Sassy's eyebrows flew up. "Oh, wonderful!"

The women hurried up the stairs to Kelly's room, where she quickly pulled out the half dozen gowns Fancy had sent with her for her trip back in time. Tears welled up in Sassy's eyes as Kelly lifted a beautiful pink and white silk gown. "This is my favorite."

Aunt Sassy looked like she struggled to control the flood of emotions. She gently stroked the pink and white silk. "I always loved this gown. I wore this when Owen and I renewed our marriage vows at Williamsburg."

Kelly frowned. "Who was Owen?"

Sassy chuckled. "My first husband, Richard's father. He loved this dress. He kept a photo of me wearing it on his desk."

"Oh, I've seen that photo! Dr. Richard keeps it on his desk now. You don't mind me wearing it, do you?" Kelly began chewing her lip.

"Don't chew your lip. No, I don't mind at all. I've had five children since then, and about thirty years have elapsed since I could fit into that dress. I'm glad someone else will get to wear it. Pink is very becoming to you. Now, let's see what else Fancy sent. Oh, she sent the blue and silver court gown! That gown looks like it was made for a queen. I always loved the appliqué work on both the underskirt as well as the appliques on the overdress and train. That should come in very handy for the future wife of a Duke. You must wear this to Court sometime."

Kelly nodded. "That's what Fancy said. I thought I could wear it when I am introduced at Court."

"Excellent plan. This is a sweet little aqua dotted Swiss, and the puff sleeves are quite fashionable. I see she included a matching aqua ribbon to wear around the raised waist. Again, she selected gowns which look wonderful with your complexion. Of course, Fancy was always a fabulous dress designer and seamstress. Oh, I never saw the coral one before either. She must have made it specially for you, too. I am pleased she put modest necklines on the gowns. A navy day dress and a brown chintz print. Those are not gorgeous, but they will work, especially on the long ocean voyage. She added a couple of chemisettes and fichus you can wear under the dresses to give you the illusion of a high neckline. Those will come in very handy in England if you can't convince dressmakers to raise the necklines on the gowns for you. Very low necklines are all the rage right now. Now, if we can find you a riding habit, some hats, and a couple of pairs of shoes, you'll be set to take on Great Britain."

They played dress-up the rest of the morning, with Kelly trying on each gown, and Sassy altering each to her high standards. Finally, they completed the review of the gowns Kelly brought with her. As Kelly started to reach for her *Ao Dai*, Sassy stopped her.

"Put on one of the Regency gowns, Kelly. You need to get used to wearing them."

She frowned. "I don't want to mess them up."

Sassy made a 'tsk' sound. "Then put on the brown chintz. Let's get you accustomed to dressing like the prospective wife of a Duke and less like a 'foreigner.' Although I am sure you will want to wear your pretty Vietnamese outfits some of the time."

Kelly nodded. "They work really well on horseback."

Sassy laughed. "I imagine they do, with the slit sides and the pants underneath. You need to bring the pants down to me. I can line some with flannel for you so they will be warm enough to wear in the winter. It can get quite cold in Ireland and England. Hmmm… I may make myself some as well. I wish I had something like those twenty-five years ago when we rode here from McCarron's Corner. I wore my old jeans underneath my full skirts. I made a couple of divided skirts, too, but I still wore my jeans underneath as long as I could get away with it. I was expecting the twins then, and I refused to ride side saddle on that trip. I was afraid my skills at riding sidesaddle were inadequate to get me here in one piece. William thought that was funny, but he never fussed. Of course, he didn't know I was *enceinte* until we were about halfway here."

"*Enceinte?*"

She nodded. "Yes, it is French. It means 'expecting'. Women don't usually use the word 'pregnant' here. It's considered vulgar."

"Oh. Uh... your Will sounds like a good man."

Sassy nodded. "He's the best. I won the lottery with my Will. Now, we need to teach you how a respectable woman would act and talk in public in 1802, especially with men. For instance, you will always wear gloves and a hat in public. You won't address men by their given name. It will be Lord So-and-So or Mr. Whoever."

Kelly giggled. "That's what Fancy said. I've been wearing a hat and gloves."

"Very good. I'm amazed Fancy remembered that, since she left here nearly 20 years ago. However, she is a smart lady, and I am sure she read up on the subject."

Kelly shook her head. "No, ma'am, she says that even when she was here in the eighteenth century, it was inappropriate to address men by their given name, or to touch one unless you were betrothed or married. Do married couples really call each other Mr. and Mrs.?"

Sassy laughed. "Some do. Will and I have called each other by our first names as long as I can remember – unless he's calling me Little Bit. Hmm... I have an idea. Come with me. Let's go look at Mama Belle's closet. I bet we can find a couple of things we can remake into Regency gowns, replete with matching shoes and reticules." She frowned. "Shoes might be the hard part. Shoes are shaped differently now than when Mama Belle was alive."

The women hurried into another room, which looked like a large walk-in closet. Sassy began going through the exquisite gowns, and finally pulled out three.

"Here we go. The burgundy will be gorgeous for Christmas, and you might not even freeze to death in this luscious silk velvet. There is enough fabric from the full skirt that I can add long sleeves and maybe make a matching shawl or cape. The mauve polished cotton will do as soon as it is remade. The blue and white print is exquisite fabric. I remade it a few years ago, and I'll do it again for you now. And the white trimmed with the green. Well, the Irish are not supposed to wear green by order of the Crown, but then, you aren't Irish, are you? I think you can get away with it, even if your husband-to-be is a Duke from Ireland."

Kelly frowned. "Why aren't Irish supposed to wear green?"

Sassy shrugged. "It is the color of shamrocks and is supposed to encourage Irish nationalism. Yes, we can alter these easily before we get to Ireland."

Kelly blinked as her heart began pounding with excitement. "Are you going with me, Aunt Sassy?"

She nodded. "Yes, ma'am. Mary Elena and I are both going to be on the ship when it leaves. Mary Elena will stay in Boston with her sister, but I'm going on with you. She can help Rosa Linda with the baby when it arrives. We'll take an Abigail, too. Every single upper crust young lady needs one."

Kelly frowned. "What's an 'Abigail'? Oh, I know. Baylie said that is what Rose would be, my companion."

Sassy laughed. "Yes, that's it. An 'Abigail' is a ladies' maid who chaperones the young lady. Betty will be thrilled to have the opportunity to accompany us on this trip. My Will has been away from me for far too long. I'll go fetch my man back home. And this way, I will get to be with you when you are reunited with Charlie."

Kelly realized with a start she had forgotten to give Aunt Sassy the letters from Fancy and Richard. "Oh, I forgot to give you the letters they sent with me. Fancy said you asked about a couple of women you knew before you came here. I'm pretty sure they wrote to you about the ladies."

Sassy's eyes glowed with excitement as she grabbed the letters from Kelly. Sassy's eyes grew wide with surprise as photos of a beautiful home fell into her lap. "I swear the back of this house looks just like Elijiah and Rosa Linda's house on the Mystic River. Oh, my heavens, I think it is the same house! It looks like Bella moved into Rosa Linda's house in Medford. And look! It's the house that inspired the Grandfather's House poem. I guess Rosa Linda inherited Fancy's ability to write. Hmm. No, I guess it would be her daughter or her granddaughter. This house is gorgeous. Look at the kitchen! What I wouldn't give for that gas stove."

She peered over the photos for a few minutes before she resumed her letter, but minutes later, tears filled her eyes. "Oh, no! My best friend when I was growing up was a Chinese girl down the street. I wrote Fancy asking about her. She says Linda died a few years ago. Lung cancer."

She crumpled the letter as her hand clasped tightly around it just as the tears began to fall.

"She was so smart, so full of life. She was always the best student in all our classes. We ran around together all the time, to the mall, to the library, to the pool. We both loved to read. Every Friday we went to the mall to the Bookmobile to get an armload of books. I remember we read *The Good Earth* together. Afterwards, we asked her mother about the practice of foot binding. Her mother told us the Chinese used to bind women's feet, especially upper-class women. Her family were Christians and did not believe in foot binding. She thought it was a barbaric practice and described to us how it deformed and crippled a little girl's feet. She had known women in China who had their feet bound. She had some older relatives whose feet had been bound many years ago. Anyway, before my parents died in the car crash, we lived in a mid-century home in a neighborhood called Shearer Hills. Linda and I attended school together at Ridgeview Elementary from the first grade through the sixth. After my parents' death, my brother and I moved to live with our grandparents. They lived down the street from Trinity University. Their house is called Suarez House now. It's named after my grandparents. It used to be a much bigger ranchero when our family first moved to San Antonio in the 1730s. They owned the land Trinity was later built on. My great-grandfather had a rock quarry on part of the land and sold it to Trinity for a pittance. After our Abuelita died, and my brother and I graduated, we donated the remaining estate to the University with the proviso that students could live there if they received a Suarez housing scholarship. I think my grandfather always intended that the land would eventually go to Trinity. He taught foreign languages there for many years and dearly loved the University. I loved it, too."

"Bella lived at Suarez House while she went to Trinity," Kelly said.

Aunt Sassy smiled and reached over to squeeze Kelly's hand. "That's what Charlie said. Linda and I still saw each other often after Jim and I moved to live with our grandparents. My Abuelita realized we needed frequent contact with old friends. I remember eating at Linda's house lots of times. Her mom taught me how to cook a number of Chinese dishes, just as my Abuelita taught Linda how to cook various Mexican food. I could make lo mein and she could make tortillas and cheese enchiladas. I tried to set Linda up with a Hispanic friend once in high school, but she told me her parents would only let her date Chinese boys."

"Now, that sounds familiar," Kelly muttered.

"I figured it would. I remember her mom was a schoolteacher. I wanted to be a teacher when I grew up because Mrs. Chin inspired me. Mr. Chin was a pilot in China before the Communists took over. My Dad said he was a Flying Tiger. Dad said that was a big deal, because they fought the Communists who took over Mainland China. Mr. Chin would rarely talk about it. He talked to Dad about it some. My Dad had been in military intelligence. I remember Mr. Chin owned a grocery store after they moved to San Antonio. They did pretty well financially and put their all kids through college. Then, when we both graduated from high school, we went our different ways. I went to Trinity and Linda went to UT in Austin. I couldn't believe she wanted to go to such a big school. She couldn't believe I wanted to go to what she called a little piddly school down the street from our house. Her mom, my inspiration, obtained her master's degree in Education at Trinity. She urged me to go to Trinity because they had such outstanding history and education departments. After my graduation, I married Owen, and Linda married Tim. We stayed in touch a while, even though we moved to Boston, and they moved outside Dallas. Tim was a good man. He was a lot of fun to be around, and he loved gourmet food. Oh, that man loved crème brulee! Anyway, I earned my master's and then my Ph.D. in American History. Her husband went to seminary and became the pastor of an Episcopal Church. She had babies. Back then, I wasn't having babies. Owen didn't want more children. And to tell the truth, Rick was a handful when he was a teenager. We gradually lost touch with each other. But she was my age, she was my best friend for years, and now she's dead."

She pressed her hand to her mouth to stifle a sob.

Kelly cleared her throat. "I knew her daughter, Brandy. I met her in college. It was very sad when her mom died. We kind of bonded over that, because it was not too long after my brother died."

Sassy looked surprised by my words. "How did your brother die?"

"A car struck him while he walked across McCullough Avenue. He was apparently in a hurry to get home after school. I had been sick, and he was rushing to let his dog out. I remember I heard a lot of noise and a siren, like from an ambulance. A little later, my sister came in, but Bobby still wasn't home. A couple of hours later, Mom and Dad came in the house. Mom was crying. Dad told us Bobby had been hit by a car and died on the way to the hospital."

"Oh, my god, how awful. I am so fortunate that all my children have grown to adulthood and are healthy. I don't know how your Mom survived it."

"It was pretty hard for her. She came close to having a nervous breakdown. It was hard on all of us. Bobby was my twin, you know."

She looked horrified. "I did not know that. Jim is my twin. Oh, it would have killed me if anything had happened to Jim when we were growing up."

Kelly nodded. She paused and gulped hard before proceeding. "Yeah. Uh, well, I know they gave his dog away a couple of weeks later. Mother couldn't bear to look at poor Chico."

Aunt Sassy's eyes narrowed. "Chico? Isn't Charlie's dog named Chico?"

I nodded. "Yes, he adopted Chico after Mother took him to the shelter."

"I offered him one of my puppies. He laughed and said Chico was enough for him for now."

Kelly looked down at her feet to the puppies playing there with a ball. "One of these puppies? They're adorable. I love this little girl."

She bent over to scratch the cute puppy between her ears. The puppy seemed to smile up at Kelly and lovingly licked her fingers.

Aunt Sassy smiled. "Well, she is certainly quite taken with you."

Kelly dreaded for Aunt Sassy to read the next letter. She sighed with relief when Sassy folded the first letter and put it back into the envelope with the letter from Richard.

"Well, that's enough sadness for one day. I'll read the rest later."

Aunt Sassy sent a letter to the harbormaster when Kelly first arrived, to arrange for transportation to Ireland. That afternoon, they received a missive back from the gentleman, stating that a ship would be on standby whenever Mrs. Selk and her guests wanted to depart. Sassy squealed with excitement that they would soon be on their way to Ireland and beyond.

For the next few days, Kelly tried on dresses, Spencer jackets, pelisses, redingotes, shawls, fichus, shoes, gloves, hats, and jewelry. The shoes looked like the flat soled ballet slippers and mules that women would wear in the future. The mules were backless and had slight heels. Sassy also found Kelly some half-boots made of sturdy leather. Kelly would wear those on the trip to Ireland. Finally, they packed all the goodies in addition to the things Kelly brought with her, and they boarded the ship.

Four days later, they arrived in Boston Harbor. The ship cruised down the Mystic River to Elijiah's shipyard, where it would undergo some minor repairs while Aunt Sassy and Mary Elena visited with Rosa Linda.

They arrived just in time. Maybe it was the excitement of their arrival, but in any event, Rosa Linda went into labor early the next morning. After a short, uneventful labor (at least, that's what Aunt Sassy called it), a daughter was born who would be named Lydia Maria. This was their second child. A son named Paul had been born in 1800. A week later, the ship repairs were completed. Once Aunt Sassy was sure her daughter and granddaughter were thriving, they boarded the ship and left for Ireland.

In forty-two days, they would arrive at Waterside. Hopefully, Charles was still there.

Kelly's Diary

We finally arrived at Belle Rose Plantation. I am so relieved to meet such lovely people. Charlie's 'Aunt Gramma Sassy' is the most delightful woman. She wholeheartedly welcomed me into her heart and into her home. Better yet, she decided to accompany me to find Charles. I must admit I would be lost without her, especially since Rose has returned to the Cherokees.

Aunt Sassy still looks trim as a young woman. She swears she is fat as a hen, but I think she is beautiful. I hope I age so well.

Aunt Sassy cried when she learned her friend, Linda, died at age fifty-six. She folded the letter and put it away, unable to continue reading right then.

We left for Boston a few days later. Her daughter, Rosa Linda, was expecting her second child soon. She gave birth the day after we arrived. Mary Elena stayed with her older sister while we traveled in search of my Charles.

Aunt Sassy holds daily deportment classes for me. She is determined I will be a success. It is amazing how much more formal behavior is here than it was back home.

We are also continuing to sew. She has taught me basic stitchery, and now we are quilting petticoats and pants. She loves my Vietnamese outfits, but she knows I would freeze in the thin silks in England this winter. It is amazing how much warmer things are when lined with flannel and quilted. Aunt Sassy loves to do needlework, and embroiders everything as she quilts, resulting in true works of art, suitable for museums or the future. I can envision several of her outfits in the Smithsonian. She laughed when I told her that, but I swear Charles told me her wedding dress, which she remade from Will's mother's wedding dress, is in the Smithsonian. Perhaps someday my wedding dress will be there as well.

After we sew for a while, we take a break to practice dancing and deportment. Believe it or not, she even has a small pianoforte on the ship, and she is teaching me how to play it. I had a keyboard at home, so this is not totally alien to me. Bella would love the pianoforte even if my friend would probably laugh at my feeble attempts to play eighteenth and nineteenth century tunes. Aunt Sassy says I will be able to play a few popular tunes competently by the time we reach Ireland. I think I have Yankee Doodle down pat, but I'm not sure that it would be greatly appreciated in Great Britain!

Aunt Sassy wanted to stay a week with Rosa Linda before we would travel to Ireland. She hoped the baby would come while we were there. Sure enough, the baby girl was born the morning after we arrived. A week later when we left, Rosa Linda and baby Lydia Maria were doing well.

Now, we go to Ireland to find my love.

After the ship headed out into the Atlantic, Aunt Sassy finally pulled out the letters to finish reading them. She began the letter from Richard when she put her head down and sobbed. She managed to tell me between gasping sobs that her bestie at Trinity was a Hispanic girl who became a clinical child psychologist – one of the first Hispanic psychologists in the world. Sassy said, "I used to tell her that she studied rats, and I studied humans. She thought that was hilarious."

Aunt Sassy said Dr. Josie, as people called her, was widely known for her compassion for children, and that her friend positively influenced the lives of countless children. "When Richard was a teenager, I called Josie and got a referral to a psychologist for him. She referred us to Dr. Tanakawa. She was always kind-hearted yet had a fierce determination to advocate for children in need. She never hesitated to go to battle with teachers, administrators, and even parents if it helped a child. And what did I do? I wrote history books about Washington's spies."

I shook my head and pulled her to me. "No. You became one of Washington's spies. You're Madame X, for heaven's sake. You helped guarantee the United States won the American Revolution. You were important, Aunt Sassy. You still are. You helped formulate the Constitution, and Dr. Winslow says you contributed to the Federalist Papers even though you aren't named in them. You still are important to our country, not just to your family."

I squared my shoulders after a moment of hesitation. "You have to convince Alexander Hamilton not to duel with Aaron Burr. God knows we need Mr. Hamilton. I know he could never run for President since he was born in the Caribbean. But just imagine if he were on the Supreme Court someday. We need his legal genius. And God knows his family will need him very much in the years following his death."

She cupped my face with her hands. "Kelly, Alex could become the President. The Constitution states that to become the President, a person must be either a natural-born citizen or a citizen of the United States at the time of the Constitution's adoption. Hamilton was a citizen when the Constitution was adopted. I can tell you right now that the first seven U.S. Presidents will all have been born British citizens. Stop and think about it. This country did not exist before 1776 at the earliest. The British did not recognize the country until 1783. The Constitution was formed in 1787. Martin Van Buren will be the first U.S. president to be born an American citizen."

Kelly blinked. "Wow, I never thought of it that way. Well, that makes Hamilton's future death by Burr an even greater tragedy for our country."

Sassy nodded. "I agree. Do you have any idea how many times I have had a similar conversation with Alex and Eliza? She's my friend. My god, it almost killed her when their son, Phillip, died in that duel last year. Phillip was only nineteen years old then. He was younger than Charles and you are."

"I know. It horrifies me," she replied.

"Me, too. It eats at me that neither Will nor I can convince Alex there are more important things than 'honor.' My gosh, he was involved in the first sex scandal in our country, and he admitted to the deed. He wrote a pamphlet about it. Now, I did not think he was completely sane to have admitted it in writing, but that's Alex. I'm afraid our admonitions not to let 'honor' kill him as it killed Phillip have fallen unheeded. You and I did not grow up in the circumstances in which Alex Hamilton grew up. My god, he couldn't even go to school with other Christian children because he was a bastard. Add to that the fact that his mother died when he was a little child and his father totally abandoned him. You ask me, his father was the real bastard. Poor Alex. We don't begin to comprehend the factors that motivate him, that drive him, much less his concept of 'honor,' or why a man would be willing to die for it, especially when someone as low life and sleazy as Aaron Burr calls him a bastard and mocks his sexual indiscretion. God knows Burr has had his share of sexual indiscretions, not the least of which is a longstanding affair with a slave bought from India while he was married."

"I had heard about that before. Now, that's truly sleazy."

Aunt Sassy struggled not to laugh as she nodded. "Well, I won't argue with you on that. Will understands this whole 'honor' thing. Oh, Will would laugh it off if someone accused him of something, especially something he never did, but he understands Alex far better than I ever will. He has tried to explain it to me. I'm lucky my Will is secure in who he is, that he has never challenged anyone to a duel and has never been challenged. Tarleton may have come close with his all-consuming hatred of Will and me, but ...."

Her voice broke, and she paused before she continued. "But fortunately, it never came to blows between Tarleton and my William. Sadly, I don't think I have dissuaded Alex from his eventual duel with Burr. I'm not sure I could change that part of our history. Remember, usually I was telling His Excellency what to expect, to try to avoid changing history. I had to prod him to go to Yorktown, but if he had not gone there, we would have lost the war. I told him time and time again he did not want to try to change history because we did not know what would happen if we did. But you're right. We will need Hamilton's legal genius in the years to come. Alex has his faults, but he could be a wonderful President, or a fabulous SCOTUS justice. His death will be a terrible loss to not merely his family, but to our country. I fear his death will unhinge poor Eliza. She adores Alex, despite his faults. And yes, like I said, he has his faults, as we saw in the sex scandal involving Maria Reynolds. That entire fiasco would not have been nearly as significant if Alex had not made a big deal about Jefferson's relationship with sweet Sally Hemings. Sometimes, Alex does not know when to keep his mouth shut. That would have been an excellent time to keep quiet. Of course, Tom is not married, where Alex is married. The issue with Tom and Sally is that Sally is a slave under Tom's control. Believe me, Tom Jefferson was more than willing to throw Alex's affair right back in his face when Alex hinted that Jefferson was sexually involved with Sally. I think Tom would marry Sally if he had that option. Of course, he cannot free her because she is a dower slave, and even if he could free her, he cannot marry a person of color in Virginia, even if she is only 1/16 black. That is still more than a drop of black blood, so she is considered legally black in the South. They could marry many other places. Will went to Puerto Rico with his first wife because she was part black, and they could not marry here."

Kelly blinked. "I didn't know that."

Sassy nodded but did not pause in her discussion of the Jefferson – Hemings affair. "You know, Sally is the half-sister of Tom's deceased wife. She strongly resembles Martha, which is why I think Tom was attracted to her in the first place. He adored Martha."

"Wow. I didn't know any of those facts," said Kelly. "Well, I knew that Jefferson's wife and Hemings were related, but I didn't know the rest. They don't teach all that in history classes."

Sassy nodded, grim-faced. "Why does that not surprise me? Alex's pride is just one of his faults. Like I said, he has been known to philander, at least that one time with Maria Reynolds. It nearly killed dear Eliza when she learned about Mrs. Reynolds. I thought she would leave Alex. Eliza left for a few months, and went home to the Schuyler farm in upstate New York, but she returned to her Alex. She loves him with all her heart. He has no stauncher supporter."

I left her staring out over the waters deep in thought. I could tell she was lost in her thoughts about friends she had lost from her youth as well as friends she knew she would lose in the future. When she finally came in, she sighed and shook her head. "I don't understand it."

I frowned. "What don't you understand, Aunt Sassy?"

Tears filled her beautiful emerald-green eyes. "I don't understand why they still haven't found the cure for cancer by the twenty-first century. Rick invented a new heart valve and a minimally invasive surgical procedure to install it. He can do heart transplants, but they can't cure that horrible disease. I do not understand it."

"I agree. When I left, there was a new virus called COVID-19. I think the initials stand for 'CoronaVirus Infectious Disease 2019.' It was a horrible disease, and it killed hundreds of thousands of people in the United States, and more around the world. Miguel – that's Bella's husband – works in medical research in Boston. Gosh, I miss Bella so much. She was my best friend. Anyway, Miguel was on the team that created one of the vaccines for COVID-19. Miguel says another team was close to finishing a vaccine against cancer when I left. Apparently, they thought they had a breakthrough in developing a cure for cancer from the COVID-19 research. I hope Miguel is right."

I didn't tell her it almost killed me to think I would never know when Bella had her children or God forbid, when she died. Maybe it was better to always remember my best friend young and happily in love with Miguel. The last time I saw them was at their wedding and they were deliriously happy then.

Aunt Sassy lapsed into silence, unable to say anything else. We sat there as darkness fell around us, both lost in our own thoughts as I hugged her close. My puppy whimpered and crawled into my lap as we sat on the deck. I felt badly that I couldn't scratch Mimi's ears, but Aunt Sassy needed me more right then.

I had no other words to comfort this wonderful woman. All I could do was hold Aunt Sassy tight as she wept for her two oldest friends, both lost to cancer more than 200 years in the future.

Oh! I just realized I forgot to tell you the puppy came with me. Tell Bella I named my puppy Mimi, after her Skye. This one is part Skye and part Scotty. She is smaller than your Skyes, but she is so adorable. She is lying on my lap as I write. Aunt Sassy says she is the color of a wheaten Scottie.

Please give my love to Bella. I miss her so much. I think it has been harder to lose my best friend than to lose my family, although I do miss my Mom more than I ever dreamed possible. I'd say send Mom my love, but you don't need to have to deal with my Dad over that.

Chapter 14
Charles
Ireland 1802

Charlie could not get over how much he disliked his grandmother. How could this difficult, obdurate woman be related to his sweet mother? Could there be a more opinionated, hard-headed woman in all of Great Britain?

And maybe worst of all, she detested dogs. How could anyone hate dogs?

His cousin, Joe McCarron, left the day after they arrived. Joe said he would much prefer to be sailing around the world than to stay around his Aunt Tamsin, even though he loved being around Papa and Grandma McCarron. Tamsin Selk sent the man running for the wide-open seas after some nasty comments about his grandmother, Ginny Selk. Charlie sighed. He already missed Joe horribly. Hopefully, Joe would come back before too long. Maybe he would show up in London.

Charlie struggled to hold his tongue with Tamsin, but it was damned difficult. She insisted on criticizing his Mom every chance she got. He started to snap back at her a couple of times, but he would catch a glimpse of Lily's face, frozen in something akin to horror with that slight shake of her head he had learned was a warning not to do or say what he had planned. He would take a deep breath, count to thirty, and bite back his angry retorts.

He had to count to a hundred one time. He wasn't sure he could keep it up much longer, especially after she kicked at Chico last night. Chico let out a yelp of indignation and hurried to hide behind Charlie's legs.

"Oh, I'm sorry. I didn't mean to kick the dog. I stumbled."

Charlie might have believed her if she hadn't smirked, and then looked down at Chico with such scorn. It was all he could do to bite his tongue.

Fitz pulled him aside after her little dog kicking stunt and urged Charles to try to cope with her a little longer. "We'll be headed to London soon, and you'll be rid of her. Oh, she's my mother, and I love her, but I realize she is a difficult old Ace of Spades. Believe me, I know she can be quite demanding. It can prove to be very challenging to cope with her. But she means well."

Charles frowned and shrugged as he spread his hands. He had no idea what the expression meant. "Ace of Spades?"

Fitz laughed as if embarrassed. "It is slang. It means 'widow'. You could also say she is the Dowager Countess. My father died when I was very young, you know."

Charlie shook his head. "All I know is if she says anything else rude about my Mom, I'm liable to tell her what I think about a woman who abandoned her child to run away across the seas with a man she had only known a short while. Good God, Fitz, she left Mom at Belle Rose and they ran off to Ireland with Lily and Marc's baby! What kind of woman would do a thing like that?"

Fitz turned pale. "What? Are you sure? I-I-I never heard about that before. I know she left your mother at Belle Rose. She wanted to be sure it would be safe for a child before she brought her over."

Charlie shook his head, determined to set the record straight "Balderdash. They left Mom and brought Michael. They even tried to adopt Michael before Lily and Marc arrived here to get him back."

Fitz stood up abruptly, the color drained from his face. "B-but why would they have done that? I don't understand. Mother was expecting me when they came. They didn't need another son. And she always wanted Fancy here with us. She had me drawing pictures and writing to Fancy from the time I was very small."

"I realize it is cruel to speak poorly of the dead, but I think your dad convinced her to take Michael and leave Mother. Don't ask me why. You really didn't know?"

Charles knew exactly why Jay convinced Tamsin to take Michael instead of Mom, but he wasn't going to tell Fitz what his father's nefarious plot involved. Jay hoped to convince Josiah Selk to name Michael to be his heir, and Jay wanted to control the boy's estate until he reached his majority. No, some things did not need to be mentioned.

Fitz shook his head. "No, I had no idea. We wrote letters to Fancy all the time. I remember when Grandfather Selk passed away, we went to Virginia to try to bring Fancy back. Thomas Selk wouldn't let us see her. He insisted she didn't want to see us."

Charles snorted, the sound as rude as he intended. "Mom had scarlet fever. She nearly died then, like Grandpa Joe died from the same disease. The scarlet fever damaged her heart as it was. She never knew you guys came for years, much less that your Mother wanted to take her back to Ireland."

"Fancy told me that at Yorktown. I don't know why they didn't bring Fancy with them in the first place. I know Mother always regretted that decision bitterly."

Charles could see his uncle was upset and decided not to push it any further – for now. *But if Grandma Tamsin makes any more cracks about my Mom, she's going to find out why Mom has no desire to return to Ireland,* he thought. *And Fitz might learn why they wanted Michael and not Mom. It's always been such a rush to know Mom was the one who ultimately became the Duchess, and now I was Duke, when their plan was that they would adopt Michael and the title would go to him when he reached his majority. If they had waited, it might well have gone to Fitz instead of Mom and then on to me. If Jay had survived his stint at sea for three years, Grandpa Joe had promised Fitz would be his heir.*

And how could a woman who was one-fourth black be so blatantly racist? She even powdered her skin to appear lighter in complexion and brushed her hair until it hung nearly as straight as Kelly's hair. Tamsin made overtly racist comments about Blacks, Native Americans, and Asians, calling each by denigrating, politically incorrect names that made Charles cringe. His mother raised him to never use such terms about fellow human beings. She always said, 'we all bleed red.' Mom said use of such racially charged words insulted the user as much as the person being insulted because it showed the user to be 'a low person with poor morals.' God forbid, when Tamsin learned Kelly was Asian, he thought his grandmother was going to have another stroke.

"What do you mean, the girl's family are ... Asian? You mean Chinese? Oh, my land, Charles, you're a Duke. You can't marry some ... some ... little bit of foreign baggage! You ought to marry a nice English girl."

Charles tilted his head towards his grandmother, as if studying her. "Uncle Jay married you. You were a foreigner. And of mixed blood. If I am not mistaken, you are one-fourth black, Grandmama. Kelly is not 'some little bit of foreign baggage.' I am appalled you would call her that. Please do not refer to the woman I love with that vulgar language again."

She looked aghast. "No, I was not a foreigner. Virginia Colony was a part of Britain. I was a British citizen. How can you make such a comparison?"

He bit his tongue and resisted the urge to point out that since she was one-fourth black, she was considered a quadroon and she could not legally marry Jay in Virginia. He sure wasn't going to use the appalling term he heard planters use throughout the south to refer to blacks or to persons of color. *Let it go, Winslow*, he thought. He forced himself to smile. "You mean I should marry some sweet English girl with blonde hair and blue eyes?"

She nodded vigorously. "Yes, exactly. Someone who will fit in with the *ton*. Who will be accepted by *beau monde*, the upper crust. Not some … some …"

"Asian girl with slanted eyes, coal black hair and golden toned skin? Why, Grandmama, I never dreamed you were a racist."

She sniffed, annoyed with his comments. "That's not – what did you call me? A racist? I'm no such thing. I'm being realistic. I know how hard things were for me when I first came here. For your own Mama. She had to go to Bermuda to marry Calvin. They couldn't marry in Virginia because she was mixed, just like Marcus and I couldn't marry in Virginia because I'm mixed. That's why Jay and I married in New Haven. I want an easier life for you and your family. It won't be easy if you marry a girl who is of another race."

He blinked. He couldn't believe she raised the issue of her mixed blood any more than he could argue with her logic. He realized now more than when he left home the difficulties Kelly and he would have faced. His shoulders sagged. "Well, you'll likely get your way. Her family didn't let her accompany me. I miss her horribly, but…"

His voice broke.

Marc laid an arm across his shoulders. "Leave him alone, Tamsin. The lad has enough to deal with right now. He doesna' need to be searching for a bride right away. Give him time. My god, the lad is only twenty-one years old. He still must go to London to assume his position in the House of Lords. He'll meet appropriate girls in London during the next Season. He has plenty of time to find a proper bride."

She sniffed again. "If you say so, Marcus."

Charles rolled his eyes, unsure if he were more frustrated with Papa or Tamsin. 'Appropriate girls? A proper bride?' What were those cracks supposed to mean? Both seemed intent on marrying him off as soon as possible. He cleared my throat. "Maybe you could focus on finding *Fitz* a new wife and *Nicoletta* a new step-mother."

Both fell silent, as they cast nervous glances at each other.

"That's up to Fitz," Tamsin muttered with a nervous glance at her son.

"Well, he needs an heir as badly as I do. He's thirty-seven. I'm only twenty-one. Focus on the old guy. Poor little Nicoletta is the first one to tell you she needs a new Mama. That poor child talks all the time about wanting a new Mama. Let me have a little more time to find my bearings in all this. Who knows? Kelly might still show up."

"God forbid," Tamsin muttered.

Charles gave her a dirty look. "And then again, Kelly might never come, and I might well wind up looking for a different bride than the one I imagined. But give me some time, Grandmama. I don't need you pressuring me as soon as I arrive here to pick a bride any more than Fitz needs you pressuring him right now. We both deserve a little respect on this. We both lost the women we love. Give us both some space, some time to grieve, time to recuperate. We'll start looking for wives when we both get good and ready."

"Well said, Charles," said Fitz. "I quite agree, Mother. I still grieve for my Nicole. I never dreamed I would lose her in childbirth last year, nor that our son we both wanted so much would die with her. I'm quite sure Charles anticipated arriving here with the woman he loves. Give us both some time, Mother. We are both grieving for the women we loved and lost."

Surprisingly, she simply nodded. It further surprised me to see tears well up in her blue eyes – she does have gorgeous blue eyes – as she gingerly pressed her handkerchief to catch the new falling tears from her face.

Charles realized with a start that his eyes were leaking as well. He cleared his throat and turned to stare out at the exquisite gardens overlooking the bay. "I really should go over to Ranscome Manor and see what needs to be done there to put it in order."

Tamsin surprised him because she again held her sharp tongue and merely nodded as she pressed her handkerchief to her mouth. Charles wasn't sure if she did it to keep herself from saying something asinine, but whatever the reason, it pleased him she made no comment.

Papa Marc, Fitz and he walked outside into the beautiful gardens. "I remembered how she whined and cried when Mom said we would be moving to Ranscome Manor years ago."

Fitz gave Charles a sharp look. "That's not possible. You were too young. You could not possibly remember that."

Charles shook his head. "I remember a lot about Ireland when I was little. I remember jumping on Mom's bed on Christmas Day, and then Bella and I passed out presents to everyone."

Papa blinked in stunned disbelief. "But you were only a year old that day. Mayhap ye remember your Mam talking about it."

Lips narrowed, Charles shook his head again. "No, I remember specific things. I remember the way the parlor looked golden when the sun filtered in through the curtains. It still does. It made me smile when I saw it still looks like that when we arrived here. I even remember how excited everyone was when Dara was born. I remember Mom's bedroom was so pretty, with the robin's egg blue and pink. I remember the sensation of jumping all the way to the ceiling on that big feather bed, and then Kirk catching us mid-air. He would toss us back on the bed and tickle us until we laughed. I remember Kirk burned his hands while we were here. He had big blisters on them. They looked very painful. I liked Kirk. I guess I was the only one who liked him after Christmas Day."

"Hmm. You might be right about being the only one who liked Kirk after Christmas. I certainly remember the brouhaha when he presented your mother with the ring Richard earlier presented to her as an engagement ring. I thought we might have a killing right at the dining table." Marcus looked thoughtful.

Charles smiled. "She gave that ring back to Richard, and she put it on the day when she married him. She always wears it, unless she's in surgery with him."

He didn't mention that Kirk moved to Blue Ridge, where he subsequently married Melanie Henson. Some things were just too complicated to try to explain. Kirk becoming friends with Dad and ultimately marrying Dad's ex definitely fell into that category. Of course, it still would not be half as difficult to explain as time travel. Gramma and Papa understood time travel, having done it, but Charles doubted Tamsin and Fitz would ever buy such a 'far-fetched idea.'

The next morning, Charles loaded his things and moved over to Ranscome Manor. The Elizabethan manor house was much as he remembered it. Austere, enormous, and a bit cold. It needed fires lit in the fireplaces to warm up the enormous stone manor house, even if it was only September. Yet, he could see his mother's touch in every room. He entered the parlor and pulled off the dust cloths. Charles grinned as sunlight poured into the beautiful room. His Mother put up yellow gingham silk curtains which filled the room with liquid sunshine. He moved to the dining and pulled the dust cloths off the windows there next. The dining room was filled with an enormous Jacobean dining table, twelve matching chairs and a sideboard. Mom had decorated the table with burlap table runners. She stenciled yellow jonquils and blue irises by hand onto the burlap fabric. Yellow gingham silk trimmed the edges of the runners. The chair cushions were fashioned to match the table runners, with the same yellow gingham silk trim. More yellow gingham silk covered the windows in there as well. He smiled as he fingered the fabric. He vaguely remembered Kirk arguing with Mother that the burlap and yellow gingham would be far too casual for such a formal room. It pleased him to see his Mom's eye was correct and she had won the argument. The juxtaposition of the formal design and the casual accoutrements was delightfully charming. Only his Mom would have dared it, but she always had a flair with fabric and color most people lacked. Charles knew he would have to remember this trick at the Spring Haven estate in England and at the townhouse in London. The combination managed to make a mansion feel cozy and home-like.

Charles noticed the manor house could use additional wall coverings and rugs to help warm up the space. It needed some nice paintings on the walls, and fresh cut flowers on the tables. He started trying to look at the space with Mother's eyes to see what colors would brighten it and warm it up. Yes, Mother was on the right start with yellows and blues. He would need to remember to buy things with those colors to continue her plans in the parlor and dining room. He hoped he could find a pretty blue rug and a painting of irises in London. Those would complete the room beautifully.

Charles moved upstairs and quickly located the master bedroom. It was Mother and Kirk's room when they lived there, but now it would be his. He took a deep breath and squared his shoulders before entering it.

He walked to the window and pulled off the dust cloth and smiled. Mother loved the colors in the bedroom at Waterside, with the robin's egg blue and pink, but she realized that room was far too feminine for Kirk. She took the robin's egg blue, changed it to Wedgwood blue, and left the wood trim the natural color. She added crisp white sheets, and a coverlet of navy blue and white for a crisp, clean look pleasing to both Kirk and her. She appliqued a white mariner's cross on the coverlet. After all, she was married to a sailor then, and she owned a shipping line. Oops, he guessed Mom didn't really own the shipping line back then; he did. Charles could live with it 'as is,' at least until after he made his first trip to London. He might change the bed linens once he saw current styles in London. Charles knew he would buy fresh, new linen sheets. If he returned with a wife in tow, she might want new window treatments and bed coverings, but for now, the room felt like home and it would remain 'as is.'

His heart lurched as he opened his Mother's wardrobe. Her clothing still hung there, as if she might return at any moment. After all, they only meant to be gone a few months when they left forever. Charles pulled one of her silk gowns into his hands. He closed his eyes and inhaled, smiling as he smelled the scent of essence of roses she loved to wear still lingering on her clothing. *I'll have to let her know her presence is still here after all these years*, he thought as he caught myself rubbing the silken fabric against the side of his smooth-shaven cheek.

Suddenly, a little grey-haired woman dressed in navy and white livery came rushing into the room. She stopped, her face filled with shock, and sank into a deep curtsy. "My lord, I didna' ken ye were comin' today or I would have readied the house."

"I apologize. I'm Lord Ranscome and this little fellow is Chico. I should have looked about for you when I first came in. My grandmother was driving me batty over at Waterside and I decided it was time to come home to Ranscome Manor. It's a pleasure to meet you."

She flushed bright red. "I'm Mrs. Haskins, your Grace, your housekeeper."

Chico sat up and raised a paw to her. She chuckled as she regained her composure, clearly charmed by the little dog. Charlie bit back a grin, as he wished he had such success with women.

She bent over to shake Chico's paw. "How adorable! I'm pleased to make your acquaintance, milord Chico, and your Grace. Please, come back down to the parlor. I'll fix ye a nice, hot cup of tea and Ellie will air out the rooms for ye."

"I'll take you up on that cup of tea, and Chico might like a fresh bowl of water. Ellie is welcome to tidy things up to your satisfaction, but I think it looks great. I would really like to see the stables."

Her eyes softened. "Ah, you love animals. Aye, you're a true Ranscome indeed. Now, let's fetch ye that tea and perhaps a few biscuits, then Scottie will take ye out to the barns. He's the horse master. Ye'll find your horses are doing quite well."

The Ranscome stables have long been renowned for fine horseflesh. Charles knew Uncle Will bred and raced horses at Ranscome Downs, as did Grandpa Joe. Fifteen minutes later, his horse master, Scott MacGregor, commonly called Scottie, led Chico and Charles to the stables.

"How long have you been here, Scottie?"

"Nearly my life. My mother came to Waterside with Lady Meara long ago. My mother was only fourteen years old then. I was born there about 15 years later, in '38. My father became the Master of the Horses for Lord Selk here at Ranscome Manor when I was 2, after my mother died. He didn't want to remain at Waterside then. This is the only home I remember. Here, let me introduce you to your horses, milord."

Charles let out a low whistle of appreciation as Scottie and he entered the stables. They were impeccable. His Dad kept clean stables, but Charles would swear you could have eaten off the floors of the Ranscome Stables. As they walked down the row, Scottie introduced Charles to the various horses.

"Her name's Dolly. She's a pretty, wee thing. Mostly Arabian bloodlines. Ye'll see most of the horses here have at least a wee bit of Arabian blood. The bay is named Cass. He's more Arabian than thoroughbred. He's a fine stud. The big black across from him is -"

"My God, it's Cole," Charles said, his tone reverential as he entered the stall holding the gorgeous stallion, named Cole due to his coal black coat when he was young.

Scottie nodded, pleased Charles recognized Uncle Will's champion stud. "Aye, he is, indeed. He's still the king of these stables."

Chico sat down outside the stall as Charles ran his hands down Cole's face. It thrilled Charles as the old stud leaned into him. "I remember him when I was little. I thought he was the most gorgeous horse."

"Aye, and he still is. His sire was Eclipse, said to have been the fastest horse in the world. Cole was one of the last foals sired by Eclipse. He descends from the Godolphin Arabian, who was said to be headstrong and unloved by the stable staff. Like his grandsire, Eclipse was a bit surly tempered and not well loved among stable personnel or riders, but he was reputed to be the fastest horse in the world. In contrast, Mister Will swears Cole has always been a love. I think it has to do with the way they were raised. Cole was raised at Belle Rose and had a good start. He was always treated well by the people around him."

"I imagine he was treated well at Belle Rose. Mother says she remembers how gentle he was when she was a girl. She was afraid of some of the horses, but never Cole. That's actually surprising since he is so large."

"Aye, Cole he is a big boy, but he always had a soft spot for children. He's seventeen hands tall, big for a horse descended from the Turk. You have a good eye. He's starting to go grey now. You see it most around his eyes and on his muzzle. Of course, he's nearly thirty years old. I swear, I think he remembers you, lad."

Charles shook his head as he held a bit of apple on the flat of his hand for the old stallion to nibble. "I doubt he remembers me, unless it's my smell. I will admit I always have apples in my pockets when I come around the horses. I grabbed one in the kitchen before I came out here. Maybe he associates the scent of the apples with me. Maybe he just likes apples and can smell one on me. I sure remember him. Uncle Will looked so regal riding this stallion. I always wanted a horse like him some day."

His eyes narrowed. "Well, today may be your lucky day. Flossie is about to foal his get. You may have yourself a wee Cole yet."

About then, Uncle Will joined the men. "I thought I'd find you over here. I take it my sister was about to drive you mad at Waterside. Believe me, lad, I understand. She was getting on my last nerve, too. You know your father used to own Cole, don't you?"

It surprised Charles. His head whipped around to Uncle Will. "No, sir, I never heard that. Mother used to tell how handsome you looked when you would come to McCarron's Corner on him. I remember you looked regal on him. I didn't realize you got him from my father."

Will blushed. "Well, I didn't get him from Calvin. He got the stallion from me. He won the horse from me fair and square in a poker game. Then, when Tarleton came to Belle Rose in the summer of '81, he took Cole. Your Mama told me how your Daddy jerked Tarleton off that horse and beat the fire out of the damned man when Tarleton rode up to them on Cole at Yorktown. Cole must have been one of the few horses Tarleton didn't slaughter there. He killed about a thousand horses, according to your mother. Afterwards, we took Cole back to Belle Rose. The next year, I brought him over here to breed to some of the mares. He has gone back and forth, but he spent more time here than anywhere." Will shrugged. "I reckon he's yours, lad. Your dad won him fair and square all those years ago."

Charles felt his cheeks redden. "Uncle Will, he's only known Scottie and you for most of his life, and certainly for the past twenty years. He's your horse. I might try to get a service or two off him on the mares at Spring Haven before you take him home to Belle Rose."

Uncle Will looked stunned. "That would be wonderful, lad. I don't know how to thank you."

We walked on to another box stall where a pretty, chestnut mare stood munching on hay.

"This is Flossie. She's due any time now. This will be her third birth. I expect her to deliver tonight or tomorrow," said Scottie.

"She's a beauty, with that blaze like a lightning flash across her face and with her flaxen mane and tail. Mom would love her."

Scottie looked surprised. "Aye, as well she should. Your mam's mare was her grandmother. Flossie looks a lot like her mam, Genevieve, who also looked like your mam's mare. I think her name was Lightning."

"I think Mom got that mare from the Cherokees," I said.

Uncle Will nodded. "She did. They gave her that mare in 1779 before we came back to Belle Rose. You know, several braves wanted to marry your Mama."

Charles grinned. "Yes, Shadow Wolf told me. Of course, I remember something about Shadow Wolf wanting to marry Aunt Sassy, too. Scottie, you should take her food away this evening. And please muck out her stall before the birth."

Scottie looked surprised. "Ye sound like ye ken a thing or two about horses, lad."

He chuckled, self-conscious at the praise from the older man. "Well, I am a Selk, or my Mom was. I guess I get it honest. Plus, Mom and Dad – I call Dr. Winslow 'Dad,' after all, he raised me – always had horses. And I studied animal husbandry in college."

Scottie looked surprised. "Indeed? A college man. Your grandfather would be pleased to ken ye went to university and that ye understand horses. Aye, we'll let her have this bit of hay and then I'll move her to the foaling pen. Tis already spick and span, waiting for Her Ladyship to foal."

"You better move her now," Uncle Will said. "She's in labor."

Scottie and Charles quickly confirmed the mare was in labor and moved her to the foaling pen. Scottie sent his assistant to the house to notify Mrs. Haskins and Ellie why they had been detained there.

The foaling pen was a fenced area outside about 20 feet by 20 feet. The grassy surface was clean and ideal for the foaling of colts. Charles glanced at his watch as they led her into the foaling pen. Flossie walked around, and then rolled a time or two as she sought a comfortable position. Scottie quietly washed her private parts, teats and hindquarters with mild soap, and then rinsed her carefully. The men then settled down to watch her in her first phase of her labor. As they chatted, Scottie and Uncle Will both puffed on their pipes. Ellie, the downstairs maid, brought out a tray laden with tea and sandwiches for us. They thanked her and began eating their light supper as Flossie's labor progressed.

About two hours later, Flossie knelt down, her nostrils flared and her sides quivering, and her fetal membranes ruptured with a rush of fluids. Charles checked his watch again, but he felt pretty sure the mare had this well in control. "She seems to know what she's doing."

Scottie nodded. "She should. After all, she was not a virgin mare. It's her third birth."

Sure enough, less than twenty minutes later, she trembled, her sides heaved again, and then the colt's front feet appeared, followed by the head and the rest of its body. Thirty minutes later, the strong young foal was already up on his legs, nuzzling his mother's teats. Within the hour, she passed the placenta. Charles examined it and felt satisfied it was intact. The hole in it through which the foal emerged was the only damage to the placenta. By then, pretty Flossie was contentedly munching a bucket of oats and drinking fresh water from a clean bucket.

The colt was a beauty. Not quite a true black, he looked like he would be a very dark bay. Like his dam, he had a white mark shaped like a lightning bolt slash across his face. Will and Scottie laughed when Charles said he would name him Ranscome's Greased Lightning and would call him Slick.

"Why Slick?" asked Will as he struggled to control his laughter.

Charles shrugged. "I've seen lots of births. This was one of the easiest I ever saw. That boy was born slick as greased lightning. I gotta call him Slick. What else could I call him?"

The two men laughed so hard they fell together into a heap, but the name would stick. He would be Slick, Ranscome's Greased Lightning. He might not be coal black like his sire, but they could already tell he would be a beauty. His dam and he would accompany Charles to England when he would go first to Spring Haven and then on into London and to the House of Lords.

A foal will usually not wean for four to seven months. Charles waited a month to move Flossie and Slick to the Spring Haven estate in England. He wanted to take them both with him. He knew the colt needed his mother another five or six months. Cole came with them to service the Spring Haven mares. Hopefully, the old boy would go home to Uncle Will in a few months and would leave a couple of mares carrying his foals.

By the time they left Waterside to head to Spring Haven, Uncle Will and Fitz were both getting antsy to get away from Grandmama Tamsin's continual complaining at Waterside. Fitz accompanied Charles to Spring Haven when he left Ranscome Manor. Uncle Will planned to stay at Ranscome Manor for a month or so 'supervising the horses,' and then would come to England for the stallion. Charles couldn't blame either one for leaving Waterside. He reached that point weeks earlier, which was why he moved to Ranscome Manor. How Papa and Gramma McCarron could cope with her was beyond him. Charles urged them to go to England with them, but Gramma thought someone needed to stay with Tamsin since the others were leaving.

Tamsin cried when they left. Little Nicoletta stayed behind with her so she could remain with her tutors. The child adored Tamsin as well as Papa and Gramma. Charles figured his McCarron grandparents, the staff, and tutors would help keep the child centered and sane. He had personal doubts about Tamsin's grasp on sanity, but that may have been secondary to the stroke and based on information he obtained from his Mother's books. He never mentioned Mom's books to Tamsin. As far as he could tell, no one ever told Tamsin about the years of abuse Mother suffered while under Tom's control. He figured if they did, it would push Tamsin over the delicate edge into full-blown insanity. Lily agreed that Tamsin probably could not survive that information. If she did, she would probably never be in her 'right mind' again, although Charles was not sure Tamsin was in her 'right mind' while he was there. No matter how angry he became with Tamsin at times, no matter how badly he wanted to tell her about the abuse Mother needlessly suffered when she abandoned his Mom, he knew it would be a tragic mistake which Mom would want Charles to avoid if possible. For better or worse, Tamsin was her Mother.

Chapter 15
Kelly
1802

We arrived in Cork in early November. There was more than a decided chill in the air. It was downright cold. The ship sailed right up to the deep-water dock at Waterside. It is a gorgeous home. Unfortunately, it houses one of the most evil, racist bitches I ever met. Her name is Tamsin Selk Fitz Simmons, and she is Charles' maternal grandmother. I much prefer his grandfather, Marcus McCarron Fitz Simmons, who Charles calls 'Papa,' and his wife, Lily McCarron Fitz Simmons, who Charles calls 'Grandma.' Now, they are super nice people.

Tamsin welcomed Sassy with open arms. Me? Not so much. The scrawny old hag looked quite horrified as she snapped, "I reckon Charles' 'little Asian baggage' had to tag along after him, like a little puppy dog."

"I beg your pardon; did you call me 'Charles' little Asian baggage'?" I stood there, glaring in shock at the horrible woman, with my sleeping puppy in my arms. *Madam, I am no whore and I do not appreciate your denigration. And to say I tagged along after him 'like a little puppy dog'? Well, at least dogs are loyal and faithful, you old witch!* Her snotty comments definitely got the steam to start pouring out of my ears. I huffed up, ready to take on the mean old barracuda and tell her what I thought, starting with that 'baggage' comment.

Sassy laid her hand on my arm as I bristled. "Now, Tammy, calm down. Kelly is a beautiful young woman who is a princess in her country. Her father was initially worried about her coming this far away from her family, but he relented and allowed Kelly to come with her Abigail and with me as her chaperone. Calling her 'baggage' is unbecoming a woman of your position in the *bon ton*. Charles and Kelly love each other very much, as I am sure Charles has told you. Now, where is that young man? I know he will be eager to be reunited with Princess Nguyen Keiu Linh."

Tamsin let out the most unladylike snort I ever heard. "Princess? Surely you jest, Sassy. This bacon-faced abomination could not possibly be a Chinese princess. For starters, look at the size of her feet. Chinese noble women are well-known to have very small feet."

I rolled my eyes. "Oh, for the love of... Bacon-faced? Really? My face is moon shaped. It is considered a mark of beauty among my people. And I'm Vietnamese, not Chinese. Chinese bind the feet of their women to keep them subjugated to the men. My people have been ruled by great empresses over the centuries. Our women are equal to our men. We don't bind feet. Our women are subjugated to no one. Secondly, madam, judging from the look of your feet, *you* are in *no* position to criticize *my* size 5's."

I thought the hag's eyes were going to pop out of her scrawny face. "I beg your pardon, you little chit, what did you say to me?"

I shrugged. "Essentially, I said you're full of-"

Sassy slapped her hand over my mouth. "Now, ladies, settle down and be nice. No one needs to be slinging mud here today."

About then, Will walked back into the parlor. My God, he is one gorgeous old man! I hope Charles ages as well as his Uncle Will has - or as his Grandpa Marc for that matter. Both of those old dudes are drop dead gorgeous. Grandma Lily says that Uncle Will could be his late father's twin. She claims he looks more like his deceased father with each passing year. His hair is salt and pepper, originally black, now with a liberal amount of grey sprinkled through it. He wears a mustache, a bit unusual today but it sure works for him. His eyes are the most gorgeous shade of cerulean blue I ever saw. He looks enough like the handsome older guy who plays on Blue Bloods to be his double.

And like I said, Grampa Marc is no slouch in the looks department. He looks like Alexander Skarsgard aged into one incredibly handsome hunk of an older man. His hair turned pale platinum blonde with age, but his eyes are still deep forest green. He has laugh lines and crinkles around his eyes, but his skin is otherwise remarkably smooth for a 70-plus-year-old man.

Both Aunt Sassy and Grandma Lily say Charles looks very much like his biological father. The old hag agreed and admitted she would have sworn it was Calvin when Charles first came to Ireland 'if she hadn't known better.' Grandma Lily had to turn away and cover her mouth at that one. Later, Grandma Lily confided that Tamsin thought poor Charlie was his dead father when he first arrived – and worse, Tamsin thought Charlie came to sweep her off her feet! Considering that she walks with a cane, it wouldn't be hard to knock her off her feet, even if they are big as bricks. Grandma Lily says Papa Marc was simultaneously outraged and almost hysterical with laughter over her mistaking Charles for Lord Calvin. Uncle Will told me that he thought Fitz, Tamsin's son, would 'bust a gut laughing.' Knowing that, I can't wait to meet Fitz, who accompanied Charles to Spring Haven.

Tamsin grudgingly showed me to Fancy's old bedroom, a lovely, feminine room decorated in mauve and pale blue. She was not impressed in the least when I insisted on bringing the puppy with me. "That blasted, flea-bitten animal better not wet on my pretty Aubusson rug."

I glared at her as I hugged Mimi close to my chest. "She has no fleas, and she won't soil the rug. She's house trained. Aunt Sassy house trained Mimi before she gave the puppy to me."

I was actually stunned she put me up there instead of putting 'Charlie's foreign baggage' in the servants' quarters. In any event, Uncle Will announced at dinner that we would all be moving to Ranscome Manor the following morning.

Old Meanie, as I will call Tamsin privately, looked a bit shocked by his words. "But Sassy just got here."

"We'll be going on to England within a week or two," Uncle Will announced, his voice firm. "I've been away from home a long time. I'm sure the lads are doing a fine job running the plantation, but it would be nice if we could get home before Christmas, if that's possible. This way, Kelly can see Ranscome Manor before we go to England. She will have an opportunity to decide what she might want to replace when she arrives in London."

I noticed both Sassy and Lily struggled not to giggle. Marc somehow managed to keep the most innocent, angelic look on his face. Hmm. That old man must have some interesting stories to tell, maybe every bit as good as Sassy says Will has.

Old Meanie looked like she might have a fit of apoplexy the next morning as we prepared to leave. At the very least, she looked like she might 'cast up her accounts', which Sassy says means she would puke all over the place.

Aunt Sassy commented, "Tamsin, you look 'blue deviled.' Get over it."

I blinked and leaned over to her. "What does that mean?"

Aunt Sassy chuckled. "Later."

I took Mimi out for a bit of exercise so she could relieve herself before we headed to Ranscome Manor. Mimi is such a good girl. She ran to the grass, sniffed about for a minute, and then popped a squat to pee. After Mimi and I retired to my boudoir (that's fancy Regency talk for we went to my bedroom), Sassy explained that 'blue deviled' meant 'affected with the blue devils,' or in other words, she was 'low spirited.' I agreed that Tamsin looked 'blue deviled' when told we would be going to Ranscome Manor that morning. I guess she felt disappointed she could not bully me for very long.

After a hearty English breakfast that morning, we loaded into the Waterside carriages and traveled about thirty miles or so to Ranscome Manor. It is not as beautiful on the outside as Waterside. It is very austere and rather intimidating. The outside appeared a bit forbidding to me as we approached. It was built back in the 1500's when Elizabeth I was Queen. It looks very much like what I would expect from a Tudor manor house. It must have been a real statement house in its day. I soon learned it is quite lovely inside.

The formal Tudor gardens were being reworked as we approached by gardeners, who stopped and stared as the carriages pulled up in front.

"The young master left two weeks ago," one strikingly filthy fellow said as he scratched his ass.

Aunt Sassy struggled not to laugh. I simply stared with my mouth agape.

Will hopped down from the carriage and extended a hand. "I'm William Selk, young feller. We knew that the Duke left for his English properties two weeks back, but we wanted to stay here instead of at Waterside, with his fiancée, so she could see the place before she goes to meet Charles in England. That will help her know better what she might want to buy to spiffy up the place a bit."

"Excellent idea, Milord," said the ass-scratching miscreant.

Will shook his head. "Oh, no, sir, I'm no longer a lord. I'm just plain Captain Selk. I sail with the Ranscome line."

We entered the house, and as we began to unwrap our outerwear, a little pistol of a woman came hurrying from the kitchens. "Ah, Captain Selk, it's good to see you again. I thought you would have left by now."

"Mrs. Haskins, this is my wife, Sassy Selk and Princess Nguyen Keiu Linh, who is engaged to Lord Charles. She wanted to come over and tour the house before we go on to England, to see what she might want to buy to spiffy up the place when they go to London. Kelly, Mrs. Haskins is your housekeeper."

Mrs. Haskins' eyes widened in surprise. She rushed over to me and grabbed my hands. "Oh, Princess Kelly – I think that's how Lord Charles pronounces your name – he'll be thrilled you have arrived! He has been so despondent without you. I never saw a lad so blue deviled in all my life. Lord Fitz Simmons and he went on to Spring Haven with some horses."

I smiled and squeezed her hand. "Thank you, Mrs. Haskins. I am delighted to meet you. I hope you don't mind us showing up unexpectedly, and I hope you don't mind if I have a dog with me."

She shook her head. "Oh, no, your Grace – is it proper to call a Princess 'your Grace'? I'm just sorry Lord Charles already left. I know how excited he would be. He talked of you often. He missed you bitterly. However, it's your house, your Grace. The dog is yours? T'is more than welcome."

I beamed with joy and impulsively reached over to hug her. "You could not tell me anything that would make me happier. Yes, I was thrilled when my father relented and allowed me to come with Mrs. Selk and Betty as my Abigail. I looked forward to seeing this beautiful old manor house, and even more so, to making it a home for Charles and me."

Aunt Sassy looked rattled later that afternoon when Uncle Will rushed up in what she described as 'a state of high dudgeon.'

"That blasted pirate, Jolly Johnny English, attacked one of our ships off the coast of Inishmore. He took the ship and tossed the men overboard. If they couldn't swim, I reckon they drowned. Locals are still picking up bodies of the crewmen. I need to go over there."

"Oh, my lord, Will, be careful. You know he wants the Raptor," exclaimed Aunt Sassy.

"Well, he won't get her. I'll be back in a fortnight, and we'll go on to Spring Haven. With any luck, I'll catch the sorry dog and bring him to justice." Will sounded livid as he paced back and forth.

Sassy threw her arms around his neck. "You be careful. It would kill me..."

He bent to kiss her. "Don't you worry, Little Bit. I'm a tough old sea dog. I'll be fine."

She frowned. "William, listen to me -"

"I'll be fine. You go to town and buy some fabric to make this beautiful girl and you some more pretty things to wear in England. I'll be back before you know it."

He was gone for three weeks. Aunt Sassy sobbed as she clung to him when he finally returned. "I was so scared. You can't go off gallivanting after pirates like this again, William. You just can't. You are not a young buck anymore."

"Now, Sassy girl, you ain't telling me I'm getting old, are you?" He stood there, holding her in his arms, murmuring softly to her.

It was one of the sweetest scenes I had ever witnessed, and my Dad left to go to battle numerous times while I was growing up. I remember feeling cold terror after 9-11 when he was sent to Afghanistan. Of course, my parents were never overly affectionate in public, even though I know they cared about each other very much.

Mimi and I enjoyed our stay at Ranscome Manor. I loved to hike around the property. It amazed me to watch the gardeners work their magic as they restored the Elizabethan gardens. Mrs. Haskins beamed with approval as I planted an herb garden by the kitchen. We inventoried the things I needed to replace, discussed new colors for various rooms, and agreed I should buy new china and tableware in London. She agreed the house would benefit from lighter colors and a woman's touch, although I still love what Mrs. Winslow did twenty years ago in the parlor and dining room. Those burlap and silk table runners and seat cushions with the stenciled jonquils are too gorgeous to replace, as are the yellow silk curtains in the parlor and dining room. I just need to add some additional touches of blues and yellows to perk those rooms up some more. Aunt Sassy suggested I might look for some blue and white china. She says they import it from China as well as from Italy, Holland and Germany. Blue and white is quite popular. I might even manage to find some antique blue and white china from Vietnam. I want to look at Wedgwood china, too. It's a 'more modern' twist on the blue and white look. Aunt Sassy says it 'just' came out in the 1770's. I had to bite back laughter when she said that.

From the promontory overlooking the bay, I could see all the way to Cork. As a sense of calm and peace settled over me, I realized I could make a happy home here with Charles. We would be far enough from Old Meanie that I would not be constantly stressed out, and yet close enough that we could visit Lily and Marc if they stayed at Waterside. I hoped they would spend some of the time with us. Yes, I easily could envision life here with my Charles. If only he still wants me. Please, dear God, let him still want me when I get there.

We finally left for Spring Haven at the end of November.

Chapter 16
Charles
Spring Haven
November 1802

"Oh, bugger!"

Charles looked up from the hoof he was cleaning, surprised by the unexpected vulgarity from a feminine voice on his property. He grinned as he glanced down at Chico. The dog gave him a quizzical look and then yawned.

Charles had been at Spring Haven for less than a week and had not expected to see a beautiful young woman wearing an exquisite, Regency-styled, blue riding habit and riding helmet as she tried to repair a broken girth. The blue accented the blue of her eyes and flattered her blonde hair. The careful tailoring of the riding habit revealed she had a trim and shapely figure. She wore a linen chemisette beneath the dress to cover her décolletage. Her blonde hair was pulled back into a neat bun for her riding. Her riding helmet had a sheer veil attached to protect her complexion while riding out in the elements.

"May I help you, milady?" Charles remained knelt down where he held the hoof of the colt.

She looked askance. "Oh, dear heaven, I didn't know anyone was around. What a beautiful colt. Where did he come from?"

Charlie struggled not to laugh. "From Ranscome Manor, milady. In Ireland. He just arrived a few days ago with his dam and sire. Here, let me see if I can repair your girth."

"Oh, thank you ever so much. It's actually the girth strap. I suppose it wore through from use. I appreciate your assistance."

The pretty young woman stepped aside and pushed her veil back, pulled off her tan colored gloves, and began busying herself with the imaginary lint on her jacket as Charles repaired the girth. Once convinced the lint was removed, she gracefully slid her gloves back onto her slender hands.

A few minutes later, Charles turned to her. "I think that will get you home, milady. Unless, of course, you would prefer that the carriage take you home. I could lead the mare if you would prefer not to ride back home."

"No, that will not be necessary, my good man. May I have your name? I will be sure to have my father send word over to the house that you have been a great assistance."

He smiled at her. "Of course, milady. Please tell your father that I'm Lord Charles Hobbs."

She blinked, her hands stilled by his words. "I thought Lord Hobbs was the Earl of Spring Haven."

He nodded, as he tried to bite back laughter. "Yes, ma'am. I'm the Earl of Spring Haven and the Duke of Ranscome."

She turned pale at his words. "You jest. Please, tell me you're joking."

He shook his head and allowed a glimmer of a smile to show. "I'm most sorry, milady. I am not joking."

She threw her hands over her face. "Oh, dear God in Heaven, Father will never forgive me. Please, your Grace, forgive my rudeness. I can't believe I actually had a Duke repair my girth strap."

Charlie began laughing in earnest. "It's not a problem, milady. The only problem is that I don't know your name."

Her cheeks began to redden even more at his words. "Oh, dear me, I can be such a ninnyhammer at times. Please allow me to introduce myself. I'm Lady Annabelle Hays, from Meadow Glen. I was out riding when the girth strap broke."

"I beg your pardon? What is a 'ninnyhammer'?"

The young lady's flush deepened. "I can be such a chuckle-head. I am so sorry."

Charles struggled not to laugh at the poor girl's consternation. "Oh, please, don't put yourself down. You must be an excellent rider, or I would think you would have fallen when it snapped. It's a pleasure to meet you, Lady

Annabelle. I'll tell you what. Let me finish up here, and I will accompany you back home. I would hate for that girth strap to break again while you are riding. And that way, I can make my introductions to your father."

She smiled at him. "That would be quite lovely, your Grace. Thank you."

Annabelle accompanied Charles back to the house, where Scottie double checked the repair to the girth strap. "I'll just take the mare into the barn. I can punch a new hole in the strap right away, milady."

Scottie tipped his hat towards Lady Annabelle and then led the horses away.

As they entered the foyer of the manor house, Charles excused himself to run upstairs and make himself presentable. Chico followed along at his master's heels. Charles realized if Fitz saw the way he was clad, his uncle would have a bad case of the blue devils. He chuckled. The expression, 'blue devils', still made him laugh out loud whenever he heard it. Charles hurried upstairs to dress more appropriately for the visit to his neighboring lord.

Annabelle walked into the parlor, glanced in a mirror and straightened her riding helmet and jacket. She then began perusing the various portraits on the walls. As Annabelle stood admiring a painting of Charles' father, Fitz came rushing into the room, only to stop short as he realized a young woman stood there.

"Oh, I beg your pardon, milady, I did not realize we had company."

Annabelle turned and smiled at Fitz as her eyes looked him over. She casually smoothed her hair. "Oh, hello, I'm the unexpected company. I'm Lady Annabelle Hays. I live over at Meadow Glen. I was out riding and my girth strap broke. Lord Ranscome was kind enough to repair it. He wanted his horse master to double check it and ensure it is safe for me to ride the four miles home with it."

Fitz quickly attempted to straighten his hair and his cravat and then bowed to the beautiful young woman standing before him. "I'm Lord Winston Fitz Simmons, the Earl of Waterside, Lady Hays. It is a pleasure to meet you. Please, have a seat. Let me make sure the housekeeper knows you are here. I will ask her to prepare you a cup of tea while you await Scottie's determination on the girth strap. And then I'll go check on my errant nephew."

Annabelle curtsied. "Oh, is Lord Ranscome your nephew? You don't appear old enough to be his uncle."

Fitz laughed, suddenly very self-conscious. "Yes, Lady Hays, and thank you for the compliment. I am several years older than Charles. Please, allow me to go get that tea ordered, and to check on my nephew. Was he dressed appropriately this morning? He often goes out in a rather embarrassing state of undress in the mornings to check on that young colt of his."

She chuckled. "I will admit he was dressed a bit casually. A shirt, vest, trousers and boots. However, I cannot complain because he acted with utmost valor and assisted a lady in distress."

Fitz dimpled as he smiled. "Then I suspect all is forgiven. He's a good lad. He just came from Mexico, where he has lived for some years with his mother and stepfather. I suspect they are a bit more casual there, judging from his behavior at times."

"Oh, I'm not complaining. He was a perfect gentleman this morning, and a tremendous assistance to a damsel in distress." She smiled at the tall, dark haired, handsome man facing her.

"Very good. Now, if you'll excuse me..." He bowed again and turned with a flourish to go check on the tea and on Charles.

"My, my, they do grow them tall and handsome in this family." Annabelle's eyes lingered on Fitz's trim backside as it exited the parlor. "And such exquisite manners. I'm not at all sure which one is more attractive."

Fitz entertained Lady Annabelle in the parlor as Charles changed his clothes. Less than a half hour later, Charles bounded back downstairs nicely dressed. He wore buckskin breeches, freshly polished Hessian boots, a fresh, white linen, long-sleeved shirt and tan vest. His cravat was neatly tied and he wore a well-tailored black jacket. He smiled as he heard Fitz and Lady Annabelle laughing amiably over some story or joke which Fitz had apparently told her. *Probably telling her something foolish I did*, he thought with a wry smile. *He's always fussing about me behaving inappropriately.* After Charles, Annabelle, and Fitz each had a piping hot cup of tea and a fresh baked scone, Charles grabbed his black top hat and tan leather gloves.

"I'll take Lady Annabelle home."

Fitz frowned. "But-"

Charlie laughed and waved to his glowering uncle, ignoring Fitz as he muttered about 'lack of decorum' and 'inappropriate behavior.' The young couple went outside where the young footman quickly fetched their horses for them. Fitz stared after them in thin lipped silence from the doorway as they rode away.

Lady Annabelle struggled not to laugh. "Is he always like that?"

Charles blushed as he nodded. "Yes. I sometimes suspect poor Fitz thinks I was put on this earth solely to torment him. He often does not know what to think about me."

She chuckled as they rode along the creek bank. "He seems like a good man."

"Oh, he is a very good man. He was the Lieutenant Governor of Alberta after serving in our military. He's brave, intelligent, and a bit stuffy at times. I guess you have to be in order to become Lieutenant Governor of a province before you are thirty."

Lady Annabelle laughed, but her eyes narrowed speculatively as she glanced back towards Spring Haven.

They continued to chat as they rode the four miles over to Meadow Glen, a lovely Cotswold manor house built around the same time in the late seventeenth century as Spring Haven had been built. Upon arriving, a young footman clad in blue and grey livery ran up and took the horses. Charles quickly explained to the boy about the broken girth strap and showed him the repair before the boy led the horses away. Lady Annabelle led Charles into the house, threw open the door wide, tossed her hat and gloves to a table in the foyer, and called out for her father. Charles removed his hat and gloves yet held them to one side in his left hand.

"Father, Lord Hobbs met me on my ride and has come with me to meet you. Please come down and meet his Grace."

A few minutes later, a portly gentleman leaning heavily on a cane came hobbling down the stairs. "Ranscome? Oh, my heavens! Pardon me, your Grace, my gout is bothering me a bit today. For heaven's sake, Annabelle, take his Grace into the parlor. Elizabeth, fetch some tea and biscuits for us, and stoke up the fire a bit. It's unduly chilly in here. The Duke of Ranscome has come to call."

Charlie stifled the laughter threatening to spill from his throat as he extended his right hand to Lord Hays. "Oh, please, my lord, don't go to any bother. Lady Annabelle's girth strap broke. We repaired it, but I wanted to ensure she arrived home safe and sound."

Lord Hays looked alarmed as he shook Charlie's hand. "The girth strap broke? Were you jumping that blasted creek again? Good heavens, my girl, you could have been killed. Are you all right, my dear?"

"Oh, quite so, Father. Holly and I had just leapt over the creek separating the two properties when it broke."

Charles looked shocked. "I didn't realize you had just taken a jump, Lady Annabelle."

"Well, Lord Hobbs was absolutely wonderful. He came immediately to my assistance. His man checked his field repair before we rode over. He thought our horse master might want to replace the strap. I turned the horses over to the tiger when we arrived."

Charlie's brow wrinkled as he frowned. "The tiger? I didn't see a tiger outside. Why would anyone have a tiger? Those big cats are dangerous. I sure wouldn't hand my horse over to one."

Annabelle giggled. "Oh, Lord, Hobbs, you are so amusing. I suppose you don't use the expression in Ireland or New Spain. It's a new phrase, used for the young footmen outdoors. I think the expression may have come from nabobs returning home from India. Jamie is our tiger."

Charles could feel his cheeks redden. "Oh, I see. I didn't recall any striped cat out there, much, less a big one."

Lord Hays' laugh sounded like a seal barking. "Actually, there is a tiger striped tabby out there about to have kittens. I'm surprised she didn't sneak in with you two."

Charles looked down beneath Lord Hays' chair. "Do you mean this pretty girl?"

Annabelle looked horrified, her hands flying to her face in obvious dismay. "Oh, dear me, she is not supposed to come in. Come along, kitty, let's get you back outside."

"If she's about to have her kittens, she is probably looking for a warm and comfortable spot to have them. It's getting cold outside. Why can't the poor little thing stay in the house?" Charles asked.

Annabelle and Lord Hays looked shocked at his words. Finally, Annabelle forced a laugh. "Lord Hobbs, she's wild. She is a fabulous ratter, but she is a barn cat. She is not a house kitty."

Charlie's laugh sounded forced. "Well, even a barn cat deserves a comfortable place to give birth, but I'll take her out to the tiger. He can take her to the barn. Here, kitty, I guess I better take you outside."

Annabelle jumped up. "Oh, that's not necessary, your Grace-"

Charles shook his head. "But it is, my dear. Lord Hays, if you will excuse me, I will take Miss Tiger Stripes out to the tiger to carry her out to her barn. I think I'll accompany him out there to ensure she has a warm and dry place where she can have her babies."

"Of course, your Grace," gushed Lord Hays. "An excellent idea."

Annabelle cut her eyes at her father as she shook her father. "Really, Father? Is that necessary?" she whispered.

He smiled genially at her as he motioned her to follow Charles. "Go with his Grace, Annabelle, and make sure he finds a comfortable place for Miss Tiger Stripes to have her kittens."

She rolled her eyes and followed Charles. "Your Grace, allow me to accompany you."

Three days later, the cat gave birth. Annabelle looked surprised but enchanted as Charles sat on the barn floor right beside the cat as she birthed her kittens.

In the days that followed, Charlie often rode over to the Hays estate. His uncle accompanied him on at least half the trips. At first, Charlie came on the pretense of checking on Miss Tiger Stripes, as they dubbed the barn cat. However, soon, Annabelle and he began riding out together in the morning. With each new ride, her father beamed broader – although Fitz frowned more and more, often grumbling under his breath as he shook his head in disapproval.

One morning, Fitz remained at home grumbling as Charlie rode over to meet Annabelle alone. A short time later, she came out in a divided skirt instead of her usual riding habit. The skirt was wide cut and she had allowed the wide divided sections to hang over her boots. She topped the unusual skirt with a crisp white, linen shirt, a cravat, her blue tailored riding jacket, her tan gloves and a black helmet-shaped riding hat with a fine linen veil attached.

Charlie grinned. "Why, Lady Anne, how daring. What an unusual ensemble."

She looked askance. "Do you mind? I thought I would ride Father's Chelsea today. He needs exercise, and I never ride that horse side saddle. He can be quite a handful. I planned to ride astride."

Charles laughed. "No problem. I think it is quite sensible. You look very pretty. Blue is definitely your color. It brings out your eyes. I would swear they are the color of cornflowers. Here, let me hold Chelsea while you mount him."

She beamed at him as she handed the reins to him. He chuckled and knelt beside her as he held out a hand for her. After the slightest hesitation, she smiled and placed her foot in his cupped hand. "Thank you, Lord Charles."

He grinned up at her. "You know, you may call me Charles, milady."

She blinked, as if suddenly unsure of herself. "You wouldn't mind?"

He laughed, amused by her indecision. "Not at all, Anne. May I call you Anne?"

She still hesitated. "Yes, I suppose, but why do you call me Anne? My name is Annabelle."

"Beautiful name for a beautiful lady. However, my sister's name is Bella. This way, I differentiate between the two of you in my mind."

She smiled. "I see. Thank you... Charles."

He chuckled again as he boosted her onto the big bay gelding, and they rode out.

She was quiet when they returned to the house. After Charles left, she turned to her father.

"He calls me Anne."

His eyebrows shot up. "Oh, really? Why not Annabelle?"

"He says his sister is named Bella and this differentiates the two of us in his mind. Father, he doesn't call me Lady Anne. He calls me Anne."

His eyes narrowed. "Has that young buck been untoward with you?"

She shook her head. "Oh, no, not at all. He is an absolute gentleman. I swear he is a cut above other young men I've met. Of course, so is his uncle. Lord Fitz Simmons is more reserved, more how I expect a lord to behave. Do you think perhaps Lord Charles doesn't know it is inappropriate to address me so casually? He asked me to call him Charles."

Her father's brow wrinkled. "Well, he certainly hasn't spoken to me. Has he made any sort of an offer of proposal to you, my dear?"

She shook her head. "No, not at all. That's why I wondered if perhaps they don't use titles as much in New Spain. Like I said, his uncle is much more formal with me. I can't imagine Lord Fitz Simmons addressing me by my given name without an understanding."

Her father shook his head. "No, I think the Spanish are usually quite formal, although I think that they call New Spain 'Mexico' now. It declared its independence from Spain a few years ago. I can't imagine they don't call a pretty girl 'Senorita' before her given name there. Hmm..."

"Oh, now, Father, don't be like that. He's my friend. Nothing more."

He laughed. "Girl, you're a fool if you think that man is simply looking for friendship. He's looking for a Duchess. I'll tell you what. From now on, take the tiger with you when you go out riding if Lord Fitz Simmons does not tag along. If you ride over to go from there, ask his uncle to join you two. We don't want any miscommunications between you and his Grace like happened two years ago."

"Oh, Father." She frowned, as she stood tapping a foot nervously, as she twisted her gloves between her hands.

Lord Hays leaned towards his daughter and wagged a finger before her nose. "Listen, girl, do as I say. You had a bad season two years ago. You have stayed sequestered here on this blasted estate ever since, refusing to even go back to London again for a shopping excursion. You've become something of a bluestocking ever since. Annabelle, this is your golden opportunity. It's not every day that you bump into a Duke, much less a handsome, young, eligible Duke who clearly likes you. Mind your p's and q's, young lady. He'll make an offer for you yet."

Anne tried not to smile but could not keep the edges of her mouth from turning up. "Do you think so? I really do like him. I mean, I like them both. The uncle is quite charming as well."

He nodded. "Well, he's been very attentive. Lord knows the young man is over here every day, and it's not merely to see me or the cat. His uncle seems more settled, but he is older. He has been married before. I would expect him to behave more decorously, with more maturity behind each action. Mind your p's and q's, girl, and you might make the catch of the season, without having to endure another season."

Fitz was still furious when Charles returned to Spring Haven. As he began pacing back and forth as he scolded Charles again, Charles interrupted him. "I'm not a child, Fitz. You are not my parent. You do not need to be telling me how to interact with Anne."

Fitz stopped pacing and turned towards Charles. He looked aghast. "With Anne? Surely you don't call her by her given name. It …it's quite inappropriate, Charles. Surely you know it is not appropriate to address a young lady solely by her given name until you are married."

"Oh, hogwash, Fitz. Get over yourself. I swear, you can be so damned stuffy. Anyone would think you are twice your age."

Fitz let out a sigh of exasperation. "Oh, for heaven's sake… And you act as though you are dicked in the nob. I swear, boy, at times I doubt your mother taught you anything about proper etiquette."

Charlie bristled at his uncle's words. "Dicked in the—so you think I'm silly? No, I'm just not a fusty, old fashioned curmudgeon like you. You are the oldest thirty-eight-year-old man I ever met. You have lost your *joie de vivre*, your enthusiasm for life. Let it go, Fitz. Not your duck."

Fitz stared at Charles, flabbergasted. "Not my duck? What in the blazes does that mean? Where did you learn these bizarre phrases? Really, Charles, at times I wonder what kind of upbringing you had."

"Don't you dare criticize my upbringing. I had a stable upbringing with a loving and sane mother and a wonderful stepfather. We had a warm and loving home. But it's different where I grew up. People are not so stuffy, so ridiculously class conscious. They actually look to the character of the person, not merely their position in society."

"Oh, balderdash, Charles. And even if that could possibly be true, you live in Great Britain now. You must abide by the rules of British society. You are a blasted Duke. Start acting like one and not like a commoner."

Charlie glowered at his uncle for a minute before he forced himself to relax. "Perhaps you're right, Uncle Fitz. You may have to help me learn how to function more effectively in British society."

Fitz blinked. He had not expected the lad to capitulate so quickly. "I can do that."

Within the fortnight, the young couple were going back and forth between the two estates every day. Fitz often accompanied them 'for appearance's sake' but appeared increasingly unhappy about the way the relationship between the two young people seemed to be progressing. With each new visit, Lord Hays seemed more and more accepting and friendly towards Charles. With each new visit, Fitz seemed grumpier, more out of sorts. Charles and Anne completely dropped their titles in addressing each other while poor Fitz continued to frown and mutter beneath his breath about their inappropriate behavior.

Anne's eyes sparkled as she laughed. "Don't be such an old fussbudget, Lord Winston."

Fitz's cheeks reddened at her gentle scold. "I'm just trying to protect your reputation, Lady Annabelle."

She giggled each time he used her title and proper name. It seemed to have become a contest for her 'to push Fitz's buttons', as Charles put it. "I appreciate your concern, but it is not really yours to worry about."

Fitz reddened at her words, his lips thinning as he bit back an angry retort.

As Fitz continued to fuss at Charles that it was as if Charles and Anne had an understanding without an understanding, Lord Hays grew more sure by each passing day that an offer was forthcoming.

About two weeks later, Charles knocked on the door to Lord Hays' library one afternoon when Anne and he returned from riding. Fitz and he had argued again that morning about his 'inappropriate behaviors' with Anne. Charles decided it was time he cleared the air with Lord Hays.

"Lord Hays, may I have a moment of your time?"

Lord Henry Hays looked up from lighting his pipe, surprised by the serious tone in young Ranscome's voice. He stood up and motioned the Duke into his library. "Of course, Charles. Please, come in. Sit down over here by the fire. It is quite cold outside. And enough of this formality. Please, call me Henry."

Charles smiled. Almost. "Thank you, Henry. Yes, at home they call today 'Thanksgiving Day.' It's a day to give thanks for all our blessings."

"Oh, really? What a lovely idea. I like that. Perhaps we should incorporate that celebration as well."

Charlie nodded. "I agree. Lord Henry – I mean Henry, I am sure you have noticed that I am very fond of Anne."

Lord Henry smiled. "Yes, I must admit, I have noticed you two get along quite admirably."

Charles lowered himself to the edge of the chair as he began to worry at a fingernail. "Well, Henry, that's why I need to talk to you. You see, I am becoming quite fond of your daughter, but I'm not ready to make an offer. I think that is what you would call it. Fitz said that is what you call it."

Lord Henry looked askance. He ran a finger inside his cravat as if to loosen it. "Hmm. I see. May I inquire why not?"

Charles appeared embarrassed. "Well, you see, sir, I was engaged to a young woman in Mexico. We knew each other a long time and I loved her very much. But when I told her parents I was coming to Great Britain, they would not allow Kelly to accompany me. They said it was too far. Her mother could not bear to have her daughter leave and to never see her again. That was in May. I … I loved her very much."

Henry's wrinkled brow softened and he sat his pipe down. "I see."

Charles walked over to the window and he smiled as he waved to Anne. He squared his shoulders as he turned back to Lord Henry. "Well, you see, sir, I want to love my wife. I understand my father loved my mother very much. He died in her arms at Yorktown. Our family tells me that she grieved bitterly after he died. She has been fortunate enough to find love again with Dr. Winslow. They still love each other like they were newlyweds. I want to have a marriage like theirs."

Lord Henry nodded and picked up his pipe and he relit it before he took another draw from it. "And? I suppose there is an 'and' or we would be having a different conversation now."

Charles nodded. "Yes, sir. I care about your daughter. She is very special. I might be falling in love with her. But…"

Lord Henry sat his pipe down again. "You're not sure."

"I just need some time, sir. It's like my Kelly died. I expected to marry her for years, and now she's gone from my life. I'm grieving. Anne tells me you grieved when your wife died. And to tell the truth, I feel guilty even thinking about marrying another woman right now. About falling in love with another woman."

"I still do," Lord Henry answered, his voice soft. "That's why I never remarried. Ruth was the love of my life. We were also blessed. I knew her from childhood, and we loved each other when we wed. Of course, that's unusual in our strata of society."

"Then you understand my predicament. Please, sir, I don't mean to drag my feet. I don't mean to string Anne along. She is a wonderful young lady, and she deserves better than that. My Uncle Fitz is worried I'm stringing her along. He has fussed at me about it several times. He says I am behaving inappropriately with Anne. I certainly hope not. That is in no way my intention. I have only the utmost respect for Anne. I told Fitz I just need some time. If – well, when – I make an offer, I want to offer Anne my whole heart, not just a fraction of it. I don't want the shadow of the young woman I left in Mexico to ever taint any future we might have."

Lord Henry sat his pipe down again, arose, and walked over to the young man. "I understand completely, Charles. I appreciate your candor and honesty. If – when – you feel ready to move on, I would be most open to an offer for Annabelle's hand. What is more, I believe she would be most receptive. She is very fond of you. I will be so bold as to say I believe she might be falling in love with you."

Charles tried to smile. "Your daughter is a remarkable young woman. She's not merely beautiful, she is intelligent and kind. She loves animals. Chico loves her and I value my dog's opinion highly."

Lord Hays chuckled. He saw the little dog often tagged along with Charles.

Charles cleared his throat. "Well, my point is, Anne deserves a man who will love her with his whole heart. You understand, sir?"

Lord Henry patted Charles on the back. "Indeed, I do, my lad. And let me say, any young woman would be lucky indeed to have the wholehearted love of a man like you. I appreciate your confiding in me, Charles. Please, tell your Uncle Fitz I understand. And allow me to reiterate: if – when – you were to make an offer, it would be most heartily welcomed by me, and I believe by Annabelle as well. Nothing would make me happier than for her to find the kind of love I shared with her mother with a man like you."

· · ·

"I talked to her father," he said to Fitz that afternoon.

Fitz whirled around, his face grey with shock. "You made an offer for Lady Annabelle?"

Charlie shook his head. "No, no, but I told him about Kelly. I told him I care about Anne, but I want to love her with all my heart when I make an offer. He said he understood."

"Bloody hell – Charles, are you serious? I can't believe you did this. The old goat would do or say just about anything to have Lady Annabelle married to a handsome, young Duke. I don't know, Charles. I think you should have held off on any such conversation until you were ready to make an offer. Now they'll be expecting one, while it may never come."

Charlie frowned. "Oh, I don't think so, Fitz. He said he understood..."

Fitz shook his head. "He understands all right. He understands that there is an unofficial suggestion that an offer will be forthcoming. And I don't think you'll ever love her. Not the way Lady Annabelle deserves to be loved."

"Not the way – what do you mean by that crack?"

Fitz glowered at his nephew. "You know exactly what I meant by that. You should not have spoken to Lord Henry unless you were ready to offer for Lady Annabelle's hand in marriage. I swear, some days I think you don't have the good sense God gave a goose. If you had not spoken..."

His voice trailed off as he gazed out the window towards Meadow Glen, and then his shoulders sank as he rubbed a hand across his forehead. "Oh, well. You have spoken. But if you hurt that girl-"

"I won't hurt her. I promise."

"Hmm. Sometimes people get hurt when another person has no intention of inflicting pain upon them. If you hurt Lady Annabelle, let me warn you: there will be hell to pay. And not just from her father."

Charlie laughed and patted Fitz on the back. "Don't worry, old man."

Fitz shook his head. "I'm quite serious, Charles."

Charlie laughed again. "You worry too much."

"Not where Lady Annabelle is concerned," Fitz muttered under his breath.

Charlie frowned. "What did you say?"

Fitz looked dismayed as he realized he had uttered the words out loud. "Nothing. I was just thinking out loud."

But Charles' eyes remained narrowed as he studied his uncle. Finally, he spoke again. "If you say so."

Chapter 17
Charlie
Spring Haven, England
1802

Will finally got back to Ranscome Manor, full of stories about searching for the nefarious pirate and rescuing seamen from the treacherous seas off the coast of Ireland. A few days later, they boarded the Ranscome Raptor and headed to England. They landed at Bristol, where they rented a carriage to carry them on to Spring Haven. Three days after leaving Ireland, they finally arrived at the Cotswold manor house the first week in December.

It had been a long night for Charlie. One of the mares went into labor around midnight. It was her first birth, and Charlie now knew why there were jokes about Nervous Nellies. The mare was named Nellie and he had never been around such a skittish mare before, even when foaling for the first time. It was bad enough he was contemplating changing her name.

When Scottie realized Nellie was in labor, he put her into the foaling stall. It was too cold to put her in the outside foaling pen. He then hurried to the house, and awakened Charlie to tell him the mare was in labor. Charlie quickly grabbed a shirt and waistcoat and pulled on his pants and boots. Together, they rushed back out to the laboring mare as Charles pulled on his shirt and vest. Chico ran alongside his master, barking merrily as they hurried to the stables.

Poor Nellie did not know what to think or do. As her contractions intensified, she seemed increasingly terrified. However, the bigger problem was that once her membranes broke, Charlie realized she had a premature rupture of the chorioallantois. In such a delivery, the placenta partially or completely separates from the mare's endometrium prior to the delivery of the foal. This meant the foal would get little to no oxygen until it was delivered. The longer the time frame, the more dire the situation. If too much time elapsed, the foal would be stillborn.

"Milord, it's a red bag delivery." Scottie sounded horror stricken.

Charlie nodded as he glanced at his watch. Time was of the essence. "Indeed, it is, Scottie. Dammit. Well, let's get to work. We need to get this baby out of her as fast as possible."

Charlie jerked off his shirt and vest. He threw them across the room and they landed on a nail. He grabbed a pair of scissors and immediately ruptured the placenta. He then found the front feet of the foal and pulled. When he grunted with exertion, Scottie came to help. Once they got the foal's feet and head out of the dam, they pulled the foal down towards the mare's hocks. Neither man would do this in a normal foaling, but it was imperative that they get the foal out as quickly as possible if they were to save it, and perhaps to save the dam as well.

Within minutes, the foal slipped out. As soon as the foal was out, Charlie grabbed a piece of burlap and began to rub the foal's chest. "Dammit, she's not breathing."

"Then we need to lift the lass."

Since they did not have oxygen to administer, they had to do it old school. Scottie and Charlie lifted the foal upside down and continued rubbing the foal to stimulate her. The pretty foal soon gasped as she took in her first breath. Charlie felt relief, which quickly passed as he glanced back at his watch. Precious minutes had passed since the red bag first appeared. Hopefully, she would not be brain damaged from the lack of oxygen.

Charlie checked the placenta and saw there were no other tears than the one he cut to pull the foal out. Thank God he had not needed to perform a caesarean section. He had chloroform and could do one, although he was unsure what effect chloroform might have on a mare or her foal. Well, 46% of foals delivered via vaginal delivery after a red bag survived, and that was better than the 41% survival rate for c-section foals.

Scottie hurried to the house and asked Mrs. Cottington to fix them a pot of tea. He told her that they had some problems with the birth, and they would need to watch the foal for a bit. Mrs. Cottington quickly prepared the tea and brought it out to the men with some sandwiches. As the men sat drinking tea and eating their late-night supper, they talked horses and they fed tidbits of their leftover sandwiches to Chico. Then laughed as Chico barked for additional bites of roast beef even after he devoured all the scraps.

Scottie laughed. "That wee doggie is always hungry."

Charlie nodded as a grin crept across his face. "Especially when roast beef is involved."

Chico barked and the men howled with laughter.

Scottie told Charlie stories about Eclipse when he raced as a young horse as they sat by the mare and foal. "I never saw another horse as fast as Eclipse in my whole life. Why, there's no telling how fast that horse could run. He was a thing of beauty to watch as he ran. Now, mind you, he wasn't such a beauty himself. He had a downright ugly head, and the nastiest temper I ever saw in a horse. But running? He was sheer beauty on earth."

Charlie nodded. "That's what I have heard. Uncle Will said the horse could run faster than a scalded dog."

Scottie laughed. "Faster than a scalded dog, aye? I never heard that one before. I'll have to remember it. Yep, he could move like the wind. Once he started, the race was as good as finished, because he was going to the lead or die trying. Of course, I think he won every race he ever ran. They quit racing Eclipse when no one would race their horses against him. I think he ran his last race in '70."

"Eighteen starts, eighteen wins, as I recall. I think he was born in '64," said Charlie as he reached down to pat Chico.

Scottie nodded. "Aye. Cole was foaled in '74. Cole has lived nearly twice as long as his sire lived. Eclipse died when he was fifteen."

After a couple of hours, the little filly arose on shaky legs and wobbled over to her mother's teats. Within a minute or two, she began nursing.

"It almost seems you can see her strengthening as she nurses," marveled Scottie.

Charlie smiled as nodded. He reached down to scratch Chico's ears. "I agree. I think she's going to be okay, Scottie. I could be mistaken, but she's doing pretty good."

"Aye, milord, I don't think this one will be no dummy."

Charlie chuckled. "I think you are right, my friend."

Charlie decided it would be safe to leave the foal by mid-morning. His shirt and waistcoat still hung from a nail in the stables where he tossed them when he had to break the red bag. As he started for the house, he tied his shirt around his waist and swung the waistcoat back and forth on his hand. Chico trotted along by his side as Charlie trudged back to the house. Charlie realized he was in a daringly unacceptable state of 'undress'. Uncle Fitz would have a fit if he saw him like this. However, he was still soiled from helping the mare birth her baby, and he was too tired to pull the clothes back on. He would clean up in the house before he dressed properly for the day.

As he entered the kitchen, Mrs. Cottington 'tsked' at him reprovingly. "Look at yourself, coming in here nearly naked and covered in filth."

Charlie shrugged as he picked up a crispy piece of bacon. He yelped as she swatted at his hands. "Well, they do call morning wear 'undress.'"

"Aye, and you always push the rules of propriety. You have company waiting for you in the parlor. It's a good thing I brought you a set of proper clothing and a razor so you can wash up and change. Get yourself over to that wash basin, clean yourself up, get dressed, and get in there. My heavens, don't forget to shave. They've been waiting nigh on to an hour now."

Charlie frowned. "You should have sent for me."

She shook her head. "No. I told the young lady you were dealing with a difficult birth in the stables. She said they would wait. She's a force to reckon with, that young lady sure enough is, and she is a rare beauty. I ain't never seen no one what looks quite like that pretty girl. Now, you get cleaned up and get in there to your company."

Charlie chuckled. He hummed to himself as he quickly sponged off, shaved, and donned the fresh, clean clothing. After he finished tying his cravat and pulled on his vest and jacket, he presented himself for Mrs. Cottington's approval. She nodded and gave him a slight smile of approval as she straightened his cravat. "You'll do."

Charlie bit back the grin but bent over to kiss the cheek of the Spring Haven housekeeper. "Thank you for helping make me presentable for my company this morning."

"Oh, get on with you, silly lad! Kissing an old lady like me." Her cheeks blushed red with embarrassment and delight as he laughed. She shook her head and popped him on the arm with her dish towel.

Still humming, he exited the kitchen and walked into the parlor. Thank God Anne was a good sport. He figured many women would not have waited so long to go riding.

"Hello there!" he called out to the woman standing at the window overlooking the stables as he entered the parlor.

The lone figure turned slowly and allowed the hood to fall from covering her long dark hair as she finally faced him. "Hello yourself, handsome. How's the mare?"

Charlie stopped dead in his tracks for a moment, his heart racing. Was it possible? Was he dreaming? Could it truly be Kelly? And then without another thought, his heart pounding wildly, he rushed to her and pulled her into his arms. "I thought I lost you. I was sure I would never see you again."

Kelly stroked down the side of his cheek. "Never say never. I'm not some weak little flower of femininity. I am tenacious, if nothing else. Ask your Aunt Sassy. Gosh, you're a sight for sore eyes. You looked good enough to eat walking in from the barn with your shirt off, but I bet you were cold."

She sighed as she rubbed her hands up and down his arms even though they were now covered in a shirt and jacket.

"Nah, I was too tired to feel the cold. So, you saw me in my 'inappropriate state of undress,' huh? Mrs. Cottington gave me a proper 'what for' about my lack of clothing and lack of proper demeanor. Now I understand why." He chuckled and lowered his head to capture her lips with his.

As his lips met Kelly's, the front door flew open, and footsteps came rushing into the parlor. "Charles, I passed Scottie on the way here. He says that Nellie had her foal last night— oh my God!"

Anne threw her hands over her face in apparent shock.

Charles felt as if he had been punched in the belly. "Anne, let me explain. This is my Kelly-"

Anne stifled a sob as she wheeled around and rushed from the house.

As Anne rushed out the door, Fitz came down the stairs with Uncle Will and Aunt Sassy. Charlie still held Kelly in his arms. "What the bloody hell is going on here, Charles? Oh, sweet Jesus, who is this woman? What have you done? Why did Lady Annabelle rush out of here crying? If you've hurt her..."

Kelly took a deep breath and stepped towards Uncle Fitz. "Hello. I'm-"

Charlie stepped in front of her. "Fitz, this is Princess Nguyen Kieu Linh, my *fiancée*. Kelly, my love, this is my Uncle Fitz."

"Now you've gone and done it. I warned you not to hurt that girl. What the hell are you thinking? You cannot go around kissing young ladies to whom you are not married." Fitz appeared to be furious with his nephew.

Charles frowned, still hovering in a protective stance in front of Kelly. "Fitz, you are an old fuddy duddy. Stop your ranting. I love Kelly. She loves me. We are betrothed. We have been betrothed for years. You know that."

Fitz shook his head as he continued his rant. "I warned you that you were leading poor Lady Annabelle on for weeks. 'Oh, no, Uncle, Fitz,' you would say. 'I wouldn't do that. I'll never hurt her.' Well, dammit, you have hurt the dearest, sweetest young woman I ever met – well, other than my beloved Nicole, of course. Surely even a young blade like you can see that you hurt that young lady."

Aunt Sassy frowned, concern written across her face. She reached out and laid a hand on Fitz's arm. "Fitz, sweetheart, calm down. Charles didn't do anything purposefully to hurt Lady Annabelle. And may I add you are being a bit rude to poor Princess Kelly, who I have just brought thousands of miles so she can be reunited with Charles."

Fitz turned with a start to stare first at Aunt Sassy and then turned back to stare at Kelly, who clung to Charles as tears welled in her eyes.

"Charles, do you have an understanding with that young woman?" Kelly asked, her voice shaking with emotion.

Charlie shook his head. This was going all wrong. "No, no, of course not, Kelly. I … I …"

"You have been out riding with her every single day. You go to Meadow Glen three, four times a week, often staying for luncheon. Her father adores you. He thinks an offer is forthcoming." Fitz glared at Charles.

Charles gulped. This was not at all what he expected. What should be a happy reunion appeared to be turning into a fiasco. "But I told him about Kelly. I told him I still love my Kelly, that I wasn't ready to make an offer."

Kelly looked stricken. Her face paled as she began to tremble. "Oh, Charles, did you put it like that?"

Fitz nodded, his cheeks bright red with indignation. "He did indeed. The young fool told him he wasn't ready to offer, but if and when he did…"

Kelly took a deep breath and pushed back hard on Charles' chest. "Oh, Charlie, you big dope, you need to fix this."

Fitz shook his head as he paced back and forth before the others. "I don't think Charles can fix this, Princess Kelly. I swear, I've said it before, and I'll say it again: the lad does not have the good sense God gave a goose. Blast it, boy, I'll fix it myself."

Fitz muttered angrily under his breath as he grabbed his hat and gloves. He quickly donned both before he rushed out the door. He snatched the reins for his mount from the footman, swung up on his horse, while still ranting about Charlie. Charles stood in the doorway, staring after Fitz, unsure what he should do. He felt worse than he ever imagined possible by the time Fitz stormed out of the house after Anne.

Charlie's shoulders slumped and he sighed. "I feel lower than the slime beneath a slug's belly. I guess I should go over there, too. I've got some explaining to do."

Kelly walked up beside Charles and laid her hand on his shoulder. "No, Charles, don't go. Not today. If you go now, it will send the wrong message. A contradictory message. That girl thinks she is in love with you."

Aunt Sassy nodded as her coloring began to return to normal. "I agree. You wait until tomorrow. Besides, that girl only *thinks* she loves you. She loved the idea of loving you."

Charlie's eyes narrowed as he laid a hand over Kelly's. "What are you saying, Auntie?"

Sassy smiled and pointed after Fitz. "That's her Mr. Darcy."

Charlie's brow furrowed. "I don't understand. What do you mean?"

Sassy and Kelly both began to laugh. Finally, Kelly answered him. "Well, I get it. Jane Austin. Mr. Fitzwilliam Darcy. *Pride and Prejudice.* Remember?"

Charles's eyes widened as his heartbeat slowed. He grinned as he realized what they meant. "Her older curmudgeon. The man who was always correcting her."

"Bingo. By Jove, I think he's got it, Aunt Sass," chortled Kelly. She shook her head as she laughed.

Aunt Sassy nodded. Her eyes softened as she began to smile. "Darcy was the love of her life. I would make bank that Fitz will turn out to be the love of Anne's life. You let Fitz have some time alone with her today. We will all ride over tomorrow afternoon and talk to Lady Annabelle and her father."

"Well, I'll be hornswoggled. How on earth did I miss that?" Charlie shook his head, amazed the women had picked up on Fitz's apparent love of Anne, which he had never noticed.

Kelly laughed and reached up to kiss his cheek as her dark eyes twinkled. "You missed it because you can be an absolute goober at times. Hornswoggled? What does that mean?"

Will cleared his throat and finally spoke. "Harrumph. It's inappropriate to blaspheme in front of ladies. Hornswoggled is a substitute for a vulgarity men sometimes use. Yes, we will go over tomorrow and sort it all out with the young lady and her father. Hopefully, by then, Fitz will have made his feelings for Lady Annabelle known to them both. And who exactly is this Jane Austin? And who is Mr. Darcy? Is this *Pride and Prejudice* some ladies' book? I never heard of it."

Sassy laughed and hugged her husband. "You poor darling. I'm afraid we've done it to you again. Jane Austin is a young lady who writes romances. *Pride and Prejudice* will be her most popular novel. However, you never heard of it because it hasn't been published yet, darling."

He shook his head, frustrated by her reference to future events. "Well, no wonder I never heard of it, Little Bit. I have to admit, sometimes you still stun me when you know what will happen in the future."

Sassy laughed again and reached up to peck him on his cheek. "Don't you remember? I have the sight!"

Chapter 18
Lord Hays
1802

Annabelle never rode home so quickly before. She threw herself off her horse and tossed the reins to the tiger without looking to make sure he even caught them. She ran into the house, still struggling not to cry. She threw her hat and gloves towards the table in the foyer; both missed and slid to the floor. As she stood panting in the hallway, her hand pressed to her mouth, Lord Hays hurried over to his only child.

"Annabelle? What is wrong? Are you all right, my dear?"

She looked up, startled. "Oh, Father, I didn't see you there. Oh, it's horrible. She's here."

Lord Hays frowned. He sighed as he arose from his chair to hobble over to his daughter. "Who is here, dear? Slow down. Take a deep breath. Here, let's go sit on the settee. Elizabeth, fetch Lady Annabelle a cup of tea."

Anne shook her head as she paced about the room, twisting her hands nervously. "I don't think a cup of tea will fix this, Father. No offer will be forthcoming from Lord Charles."

Her words shocked him. "Why not? What happened, dearest?"

She glanced up at her father, her own shock still written across her lovely countenance. "The Mexican girl arrived. He still loves her."

Her words rattled Lord Hays. He could feel his cheeks redden at her unexpected pronouncement. "Well, um, harrumph! He always said he still loves her. That should come as no surprise to you, my dear."

Annabelle looked up at her father, the tears glistening in her eyes. "Well, it's a surprise that she is here. And, he kissed her, Father. I saw him holding her in an embrace, while he kissed her."

Lord Hays felt his face turn beet red. He reached out to Annabelle. "He ... he *kissed* her? In front of you? Well, that was a bit presumptuous."

"He didn't know I had come in. Oh, Father-" Her tears began coursing down her cheeks again as she leaned against her father.

Lord Hays gathered his daughter into his arms to console her as the door burst open again. He glanced up, expecting Charles. He knew surprise must be spreading across his countenance as Fitz rushed into the house. Fitz appeared to be in high dudgeon.

Fitz took a deep breath before he carefully sat his hat and gloves down on the table. He then strode over to Lady Annabelle, resolute determination written across his face. As he reached her, he suddenly looked unsure of himself, and gulped before he extended a tentative hand to her. "Are you all right?"

Annabelle took a ragged breath as she wiped the tears from her face. "I'll be alright. I'm still a bit rattled. I must admit I never saw that coming."

She tried to smile at Fitz. He bristled as tears welled in her eyes again and she pressed a hand against her lips.

"I warned him repeatedly he was behaving in an untoward manner with you. He was unsure of his feelings and yet led you to believe -"

Lord Hays interrupted Fitz. "Now, now, now, I wouldn't say that he misled us, Lord Fitz Simmons. We talked. I was quite aware he was still in love with the young lady from Mexico. You must admit he tends to wear his feelings on his sleeve."

"Perhaps. Sometimes," Fitz admitted with a frown.

Lord Hays could feel his anxiety begin to abate. He chuckled and patted Fitz on the back. "Don't be too hard on the lad. He's a young man, from another culture. He does not always understand the effect of his words or his actions."

Fitz's lips narrowed. He shook his head. "No, you're too easy on him, milord. I-I-I beg your pardon, Lord Hays, but I warned him repeatedly, and now he has upset Lady Annabelle. That, to my mind, is unforgivable. I-I-I would n-n-never-"

Fitz cut off his words and reddened as he realized what he was about to say. "I-I-I mean... if-if-if I had been in his position, I would n-never-"

Lord Hays laid a hand on Fitz's hand to try to calm him. "It's all right, son. I think I understand. You would never have treated Annabelle like this because you better understand societal expectations. Am I correct?"

Fitz gulped. He nodded as he looked into Lord Hays' eyes. "Yes, my Lord. I-I admire and respect Lady Annabelle greatly. Lady Annabelle is beautiful, amiable, intelligent, and cultured. She plays the pianoforte, sings admirably, enjoys drawing and loves to work in her gardens. She speaks several languages fluently. We discuss books sometimes in French. She is very well read. We have discussed literature on several occasions. She loves Voltaire as do I. It's quite enjoyable to discuss his writings in his language. Besides all this, she is possessed of a certain something in the way she walks and talks, in the tone of her voice, a certain *je ne sais quoi*. She is always very proper in speaking with other people, very lady-like. It is clear she is a cut above. To my mind, she is everything any gentleman should hope to be lucky enough to find in a prospective wife."

Annabelle stared at Fitz, as if stunned by his words.

Lord Hays tilted his head towards Fitz. He tried to bite back the smile tugging at the corners of his mouth. "Yes, I quite agree. And yet, your nephew is in love with another woman. What would you have done differently if you had been in his boots?"

Fitz looked from Lord Hays to Lady Annabelle. He straightened up and assumed a military stance. "I would already have offered for Lady Annabelle. We would have wedding plans in progress. And when Princess Kelly showed up, I would have introduced her to the woman I now love, the woman who filled the empty void in my heart. Lady Annabelle would most assuredly have never found me kissing another woman."

Lord Hays eyes narrowed as he studied the handsome younger man standing before him. "The woman you love, hmm?"

Annabelle stared at Fitz for a moment, her eyes narrowed suspiciously. "Speak for yourself, John Alden."

Fitz blinked, as if stunned by her comment. "I beg your pardon, I-I-I don't know what you mean, Lady Annabelle."

She shook her head. Lord Hays knew that look. The girl grew impatient. "Oh, come now, Lord Winston. You told me that your mother is from the

Colonies. I am sure you have heard the story of John Alden and Priscilla Mullins. I learned it in the classroom. It is a sweet story. Alden was a crew member on the Mayflower. Mullins was a passenger. He decided to stay in Plymouth Colony after they arrived in Massachusetts. Another man named Miles Standish wanted to court Miss Mullins, but he was too shy to ask her. He asked Mr. Alden to ask her if Standish could court her. John Alden did, and when he asked on behalf of his friend, she said, 'speak for yourself, John Alden.'"

Fitz paled at her words. Lord Hays noticed Fitz Simmons' hands began to tremble ever so slightly. "Wh-Wh-What are you saying, Lady Annabelle?"

She stared at him again before answering. "Speak for yourself, Winston Fitz Simmons. If you have an interest in courting me, spit it out. Don't speak on behalf of your nephew. I believe I am quite aware of his desires. He wishes to marry Princess Kelly. Speak for yourself."

Fitz swallowed hard. "Lady Annabelle, I had not spoken before because I thought Charles had intentions. However, having learned otherwise, I would like to say, I-I-I mean-"

"Speak for yourself, Winston Fitz Simmons. Spit it out," Annabelle said.

Lord Hays listened attentively. He felt proud of his daughter. The girl was not afraid to make her desires known to the man. *About time, m'girl,* he thought.

Fitz swallowed hard again and cleared his throat. "Then I would like to ask your father's permission and your permission to court you, milady. It would be my great honor-"

"Yes."

Both Lord Hays and Fitz blinked at the speed with which Annabelle answered Fitz.

"Yes, I would be most receptive to such a courtship with you... with one proviso."

"Wh-wh-what would that be, milady?" Fitz asked as he paled.

She smiled. "I didn't realize you stutter. I'm finding it rather endearing."

Fitz blushed. "I-I-I only do it when I am stressed. Wh-Wh-When things are very important to me."

Her face softened and she beamed up at him again. "When things are very important to you, hmm? I am glad to see you find this very important, Lord Winston. I find I rather enjoy being called Anne. I'm sorry, Father, but I was never fond of the name 'Annabelle'. If you will call me Anne, I will be most happy to be courted by you, Lord Winston."

He beamed at her. He stepped towards her, and for a moment it looked as though he might gather her into his arms. He appeared to remember himself and stepped back. "My family and friends call me Fitz. I-I would be honored if you would call me Fitz, also."

She laughed as a smile spread across her lovely face. "I would be delighted, milord."

Lord Hays could see Fitz cared deeply about Annabelle. More importantly, he realized his daughter had deep feelings for the handsome chap standing before them. He had never seen that level of admiration and excitement shine in her eyes regarding young Ranscome. He knew men and women could be friends. Ruth and he were dear friends before they fell in love and married. The foundation of friendship coupled with love gave them a strong marriage. It would appear Ranscome and Annabelle were never more than friends. Perhaps Fitz Simmons and Annabelle would have the kind of marriage someday which Ruth and he had years ago.

Well, well, well, thought Lord Hays. *An Earl was not a Duke, but Winston Fitz Simmons was still of the upper orders. Fitz Simmons attained the rank of Colonel in the military and served as Vice-Governor of the region of Quebec known as Ontario for five years before his wife died in childbirth. Young Fitz Simmons admirably managed Ranscome's properties for years while Ranscome was in Mexico, even while he was overseas with the military and in Canada. He was a well-established, well-educated, financially secure young man who reportedly had a beautiful, well-managed estate in Ireland. He was well-respected in the House of Lords by men on both sides of the aisle. And to top it all off, it appeared that he had strong feelings for Annabelle.* Lord Hays was not at all sure that the feelings Fitz Simmons held for Annabelle did not encompass far more than a mere *tendresse.* He would swear he already saw love shining in the eyes of Lord Winston Fitz Simmons.

Hmm. Most interesting, thought Lord Hays with a sly smile.

Anne picked up a basket and glanced coyly at Fitz. "Would you care to accompany me to the garden? I need to cut some flowers for the table."

Fitz bowed to her. "It would be my pleasure, Anna- I mean Lady Anne."

She dimpled as she smiled back at him, her blue eyes shining with excitement again. She curtseyed and they walked outside into the beautiful gardens. She held out a hand to Fitz. He hesitated only a moment before he smiled, reached over and took Anne's hand in his.

As the two young people walked hand in hand into the gardens to talk, Lord Hays had to admit Fitz was an excellent match for Annabelle for many reasons. He was tall, handsome, and quite striking in appearance with his black hair and blue eyes. They made an attractive couple, he with his dark looks and she with her blonde delicacy. Fitz was a bit older, settled, and had already seen some of the world. He also appeared to share the same moral code which Lord Hays possessed. Fitz had been married before, and loved his first wife dearly. Like Hays, he had a dearly beloved daughter from his first marriage. He apparently grieved when his wife died. However, many men married again after their wife died. He could not fault any man for that. He could relate to Fitz's deep emotions for his first wife – and his desire to move on now.

In sharp contrast, he remembered that Lord Calvin Hobbs played light and easy with the hearts of young women on numerous occasions. It had been Lord Hays' greatest concern about Charles. The lad might think his father loved his mother dearly, and Lord Hays would commend the Duchess Dowager for not speaking poorly of the dead. However, Lord Henry remembered more than one young lady in London who found herself with a 'twisted ankle' after Calvin Hobbs paid them court and then abruptly left the girls awaiting an offer. Years ago, rumors flew about that Lord Hobbs left more than one girl in a similar condition in the Colonies. Lord Hays suspected Hobbs made cuckolds of several the husbands of other women in London as well. *Calvin Hobbs was a regular bounder, that one was,* he thought. Lord Hays was willing to overlook the faults of Lord Calvin when Charles showed up, and was so sweetly attentive to Annabelle, especially when the young man was open and forthright with him about the girl who he was forced to leave behind in Mexico.

He smiled. Oh, yes indeed, Annabelle could do much worse than a match with a man the caliber of Lord Winston Fitz Simmons. Lord Fitz Simmons might very well be a better match for his daughter than Charles Hobbs would have been. After all, they came from the same background and had the same expectations about how people would act in society.

By the same token, his Grace and Princess Kelly came from the same background and had similar expectations about how people act in polite society. Hmmm. It would be interesting to watch those two in London and see how they fit in with the upper orders of the *ton* in the months ahead as the House of Lords reconvened.

When Annabelle and Fitz returned from the garden, he smiled and patted Fitz on the back. "You will stay to dine with us, won't you, Fitz?"

Fitz looked askance. "You wouldn't mind? I mean, I would love to join you two if it would not be an inconvenience."

Lord Hays noticed Anne reached over to touch Fitz's arm as she laughed. "Oh, Fitz, you will never be an inconvenience. Please stay for luncheon. I insist."

Lord Hays smiled. Yes, Fitz Simmons would do quite nicely. Someday, he would have to thank Mrs. Selk for bringing Princess Kelly to England.

Chapter 19
Kelly
1802

The next day, Charles, Kelly, Fitz, Sassy and Will rode over to Meadow Glen. Kelly quickly noticed that Fitz rushed to Lady Anne's side, to introduce her to his aunt, uncle, and Kelly.

Kelly approached slowly, pushed the veil back from her riding hat, and extended her hand to Anne. "I am so sorry we caused you distress yesterday. Charles and I have known each other for years. He asked me to marry him quite some time ago. I was heartbroken when my parents wouldn't allow me to accompany Charles to Great Britain. He left the end of May. By the end of July, my father was quite fed up with my crying and moping about like my world had ended, and he arranged for Aunt Sassy to come with me to Great Britain. I wrote to Charles that I was coming, but apparently, I arrived before the letters did. I am embarrassed you saw us yesterday. I wouldn't have hurt you for the world. Charles has said very positive things about you. I can see he thinks very highly about you. I hope we can make amends and become friends."

Anne hesitated just a moment. Kelly could see indecision written across the girl's face. Finally, Anne squared her shoulders, smiled and reached out to take Kelly's hand. "It is very sweet of you to come over here to apologize. I knew Charles loved a lady in Mexico with all his heart. He is an unusual chap, and it is exceptionally easy to talk with him. He must be thrilled you finally arrived. And besides, I think this worked out for the best."

Kelly's eyes widened as Lady Anne reached over to catch Fitz's hand. He stepped closer to her as he beamed down at the petite blonde. "Lady Anne has consented to allow me to court her."

Kelly beamed at them both. She glanced over to Aunt Sassy, who nodded with a little smile. Kelly felt thrilled Anne had found her Mr. Darcy. "That's wonderful. I am so happy for you both. Now, I understand there is a ball in London at Buckingham Palace on the 18th. I think it's called the King's Ball. It sounds very fancy. Charles must go to London to put his house in order and to prepare to assume his place in the House of Lords. I suspect Fitz and your father will be going as well. I say we all go to the ball together. I've never been to an event such as this before."

Lady Anne paled. "Nor have I. Oh, my heavens, you're talking about the King's Christmas Ball at the Palace. I haven't a thing I could wear. I haven't been to London in two years."

Kelly laughed and tossed her head. "I've never been to London in my whole life. I suspect we can find something quite lovely at this place called Floris on Jermyn Street, Lady Anne. Isn't that where you told me we should shop, Aunt Sassy?"

Sassy nodded, her eyes sparkling with excitement and a tad of mischief. "Oh, yes, indeed. I understand that it is the place for ladies of the *ton* to shop in London. They reportedly have the best *modistes* in town. Their head *modiste* came from Paris a few years ago. Please, come to London with us, Lady Anne."

Kelly nodded. She still clasped Anne's hand. "Yes, please come. I need as many allies as possible there when I am introduced to the King and Queen. I'm hoping you will be an ally. Lord knows I'm the odd one out and will look and feel quite out of place. I need as many friends there to support me as possible."

"I hope so as well," said Charles as he stepped up beside Kelly. "Believe me, we are two country mice who need some assistance in navigating the big city of London."

Anne blushed and squeezed Kelly's hand. "I've never been introduced to them either, Princess Kelly."

Kelly shook her head. "No, no more of that 'Princess Kelly' business. We are in Great Britain, not Vietnam. I'm just Kelly here – although I will use the title when I meet royalty. Mother stressed I should do that. Anne, I'm quite serious. If we are to be friends, and it looks like we may wind up relatives as well, you must call me Kelly. I brought some lovely things from home, and Aunt Sassy and I made some more, but a girl can never have too many dresses, especially when she is about to be introduced to royalty. So, let's all go to London and do some shopping. Then we can be, what is the phrase? Oh, yes, the pink of the *ton* at the ball."

Anne laughed as she looked at Charles. "I see why you love her. She is quite charming, and very persuasive. All right, I'll come—If I may do some shopping on Jermyn Street with Princess Kelly, Father."

"Of course, you may, my dear." Lord Hays beamed at his daughter. "I will count on Lady Sarah to help you select an appropriate ball gown."

Aunt Sassy looked shocked. "Lord Hays, I'm not a titled noblewoman. And no one ever calls me Sarah. Everyone calls me Sassy."

Uncle Will laughed. "After you know her awhile you will understand why we call her Sassy. Believe me, milord, she is my little bit of Texas Sass."

Kelly shook her head. "Uncle Will, you're being silly. Anne, you must go shopping with Aunt Sassy and me. Like I said, we're going to be good friends and it looks like we will be relatives as well. Ooh, would it mean I had to call you Aunt Anne if you marry Uncle Fitz?"

Everyone laughed except Fitz, whose cheeks flushed red with embarrassment as he ran a finger inside his cravat as if to loosen it a bit.

Lord Hays pounded Fitz on the back. "What's wrong, lad? Have you nothing to say?"

Fitz cleared his throat and tried to smile. "I think it's a wonderful idea. Let's all go to London, shop for some new clothes, and go to the King's Christmas Ball. No one wants to look like the country mouse who has come to the big city for an event of that magnitude. After all, it's not every day you are introduced to royalty, but then, it's not every day a man finds the woman of his dreams and she consents to be courted by you."

"Bravo, Uncle Fitz! Well said," replied Charles. "And perhaps you can help me gain a bit of the town bronze before the House of Lords resumes hearing matters."

Everyone laughed and nodded at that suggestion.

"That's a wonderful idea, Charles. This way, you will have two experienced Lords with you to help guide your way," said Aunt Sassy. "And Will has a bit of experience as well."

Lord Hays looked over at her quizzically. "Oh, really?"

Will cleared his throat. "I was the Duke of Ranscome before the War. I asked the Court to allow me to pass the title on to a relative since I planned to remain in Virginia, no matter who won. We have a thriving plantation there which was not entailed. Since Lord Calvin was married to my baby sister, the King and Calvin worked out an arrangement wherein their son would take the title. Until a son was born, Fancy held the title. It was quite unusual, and I'll never know quite how Calvin worked that magic. I do know the Ranscome title was originally given to a woman in 1580 after she saved Queen Elizabeth from an assassination attempt. Several women held the title through the years before it was enhanced first to Marquess and later to Duke. Old Calvin was a silver-tongued devil, if I ever knew one. He died shortly after he wangled that deal with the King. He was shot at Yorktown."

Everyone fell silent for a moment in respect for the memory of Charles' deceased father. Finally, Charles cleared his throat and spoke.

"Yes, if you gentlemen can help me gain the manners and culture expected of a duke in town, it would be a godsend."

For the next three days, the families ran back and forth between the two estates in preparation for the trip. With Aunt Sassy's assistance, Kelly and Anne reviewed each other's wardrobes to see which would be best to take to London. As the girls talked about clothes, they began to bond. They realized they both loved to ride and coaxed the men to go riding with them each morning. Anne laughed at Kelly's enthusiasm on the rides, and pronounced she wanted pants to go beneath her skirts like Kelly's. Aunt Sassy pulled out another swath of fabric, quickly cut it and stitched it up, and the next morning Anne wore pants beneath her riding habit like Kelly did.

"Oh, they are quite comfortable, and I feel much less at risk to reveal my undergarments or my lower limbs," chortled Anne.

Kelly nodded and bit back the grin at Anne's 'lower limbs' comment. "It is one thing I really love about Vietnamese clothing. The slit sides and the pants beneath the dress give a lot of freedom of movement lacking in British garb."

On Friday, Charles and Kelly rode into the little town of Bishop's Cleeve to talk with Rev. Tilton, the rector of St. Michael and All Angels Anglican Church. They noticed the countryside along the way was gorgeous with expansive views of the Cotswolds. They learned that the town was located in the Borough of Tewkesbury, Gloucestershire, about five miles north of Cheltenham. It was situated at the foot of Cleeve Hill, the highest point in the Cotswolds.

The village bordered Woodmancote on the east. The original land grant originated in the late eighth century when Aldred, sub-king of Hwicce, gave land to support a Minster church in the area dedicated to St. Michael and the Archangel. A century later, the land came into the hand of the Bishops of Worcester where it remained until the sixteenth century. In the seventeenth century, the Hobbs family obtained a sizable estate near the beautiful little village. "It's a pretty little town," Kelly marveled in a hushed voice.

Charles nodded, his eyes wide with wonder. "It certainly is. Bishop's Cleeve is a charming little village. It would be an attractive place to live if we didn't have Spring Haven."

She giggled. "But you do have Spring Haven, and it is just a few miles from here. What a gorgeous old church."

"Here, let me help you down." Charlie helped Kelly dismount from her horse. He took her hand, and they walked into the parish office where they found Rev. Tilton, the vicar of the elegant old church. "Hello, Reverend, could Lady Kelly and I talk with you for a few minutes? I'm Lord Charles Hobbs."

Rev. Tilton jumped up from seat and hurried over to the couple. "Lord Hobbs, I believe you are the Earl of Spring Haven."

Kelly nodded and struggled to bite back a saucy grin. "He is also the Duke of Ranscome, Reverend."

She smothered a laugh as the vicar's face showed surprise. "Oh, my heavens, I didn't realize you are also the Duke of Ranscome, your Grace. Please, come in and have a seat."

"This is a beautiful church. I don't think either of us know the history of St. Michael's," Kelly said as she flashed her most engaging smile at the vicar.

The reverend beamed. "Please allow me to tell you about it. Parts of our church are over 900 years old. This was originally a monastic settlement in Anglo-Saxon days. Later, after the Norman Conquest, the main body of our church was built to be a Catholic facility. The St. Michael's bell tower is the oldest in-use bell tower in Great Britain. There are nine bells. Eight are rung for regular services and special occasions. The ninth bell is a little sanctus bell, which is rung at various points in a Holy Communion service. Parts of the original frescos still remain on the walls in the church today. The Delabere family expanded the church in the 1700s."

Charles brow wrinkled. "I think my father was related to the Delabere family."

"Quite so, milord. I believe your grandmother was a Delabere. She had three older brothers, but none of them had children who survived. When she gave birth to sons, the eldest inherited Spring Haven."

Charles looked surprised. "Oh, I didn't realize that. Was my father the eldest son?"

The rector shook his head. "Oh, no, milord. His two elder brothers both died from consumption. I imagine your father survived because he moved to Bermuda. I understand it is a warmer climate."

Charles nodded. "It is a very mild and temperate climate."

The vicar smiled as he eagerly nodded. "They had an older sister who later moved to Bermuda to live with your father after her husband died."

"I think Mother had mentioned that my Father's older sister lived at Spring Haven in Bermuda with them when they first married. Mother did not have a lot of information about Father's history, except that he owned the estate in Bermuda and the one here," Charles mused.

"I would love to see the frescoes, the church, and the bell tower. You must show us around sometime," Kelly said, using her most persuasive tone.

"Of course, milady. It would be my pleasure to show you around right now if you have the time. As I said, the Delabere family expanded the church in the last century to better accommodate our growing congregation. I think it is quite beautiful."

Charles nodded as he looked around the elegant old church. "I agree."

After Rev. Tilton showed Charles and Kelly around the church, Charles broached the subject of their marriage. "Lady Kelly and I were engaged in Mexico before I returned to Great Britain. We planned to marry before we came, but her mother became increasingly blue-deviled, and decided she could not bear to have her daughter move so far from home and to never see Kelly again. Fortunately, Kelly and her father were able to persuade Lady Nguyen to allow Kelly to come on with my Aunt so we could marry here. I would like to arrange a ceremony which would culminate with those eight bells being rung for a special occasion."

The rector smiled. "What a sweet story. So, we need to plan a wedding. Hmmm... I see I have several days still available in June."

Kelly could feel her cheeks pale. She shook her head. "Reverend, could we possibly be married sooner than that? Perhaps before the end of the year?"

Reverend Tilton looked a bit shocked. "May I inquire why you two young people are in such a hurry to marry?"

Kelly pasted her most engaging smile on her face. "In my family's culture, it is considered unlucky to marry in one's twenty-second year. I turn twenty-two on December 31st. I arrived in Britain a few days ago. If it is at all possible to get the banns read and schedule it, we would love to be married before my birthday. I realize the date will not affect our luck. We already found our luck when we found each other. But my Mother requested we marry before my birthday if possible. She can't be here. It seems the least I can do is marry before my birthday and be able to let her know we did as she requested."

"And my birthday is Christmas," interjected Charles. "That's when I turn twenty-two."

The minister's face softened as Kelly recounted her story. "Oh, I see, my dear. I must say I was concerned at first you would say there were other 'exigent circumstances' as to why you wished to marry so quickly."

Kelly felt her cheeks redden. "Oh, my heavens, no, sir. Charles is not that kind of man, nor am I a woman who would have engaged in conjugal intimacies before we married. Neither of us were raised like that. We both come from fine, upstanding Christian homes."

"Very good. I can read the banns tomorrow, on the fifth, and on the twelfth, and on the nineteenth. With no problems, we could get you two young people married on the morning of the twenty-third... no, let's say the twenty-fourth. I realize it is Christmas Eve, but it is also a Friday. Many people will be coming to church that morning for Christmas Eve services. I am sure you want to invite the congregation to attend your nuptials. How would that work for you two young people?"

Charles and Kelly grinned at each other and nodded to the minister. "That would be wonderful, sir. And that way, I can report to my mother we were married before either of us turned twenty-two, on Christmas Eve."

After they departed the church, Charles turned to grin at Kelly. "We wouldn't have engaged in intimate relations before we married?"

Kelly shook her head as she felt her cheeks heat with color. "Oh, hush. We wouldn't in 1802. Now, behave yourself."

Charles laughed as he helped her mount her horse. They rode on to Meadow Glen and shared their news with Anne and Lord Henry before they returned to Spring Haven.

Fitz frowned as he tapped a finger against his forehead "If you hold the wedding on Christmas Eve, we will have to travel to London for the ball and then return here for the wedding. Why are you rushing into this?"

Charles began explaining the Vietnamese tradition as Scottie rushed into the house. He politely tipped his hat to them before he spoke. "Your Grace, I need you to come to the pasture. The men found summat ye need to see."

Will, Charles and Fitz all looked at each other and frowned before the three jumped up and raced after Scottie. When they reached the pasture, Scottie bent down and pointed towards the newly turned soil. "Ye see, milord, we wuz turning the earth over for a new planting, when we found this. It looks like tiles were beneath the soil. What could it be?"

Charlie bent down and ran a finger over the ancient tiles as Kelly and Sassy caught up with the men. "Aunt Sassy, you're the historian. What do you think?"

Sassy gasped as she held her side. "Oh, my heaven, it looks like an old Roman mosaic. How far does it extend, Scottie?"

The workers paced out the area to which the tiles extended. Sassy became increasingly excited. "I swear these are old Roman tiles. This must have been a Roman villa. The Cotswolds are full of old Roman finds. Will, isn't there an Office of Antiquities in London?"

Will nodded. "I think so, Little Bit."

"Yes, there is. The men need to quit their excavations. This could be a very important discovery." Fitz's eyes sparkled with excitement.

Charlie nodded in enthusiastic agreement as he nibbled on a thumb nail. "Quite so. Carefully mark the perimeters with stakes, Scottie. Brush the soil off the tiles with great care. We mustn't damage the tiles. This could be one of the most important Roman discoveries in the Cotswolds."

Uncle Fitz cleared his throat. "While I doubt it will be more important than those at Chedworth, this could certainly be significant. Scottie, don't let the men dig there anymore. Lord Hobbs has plenty of acreage so they can plant the hay elsewhere."

"Aye, sir."

"Keep the animals off that plot and shoot anyone that comes nosing around without my express permission," Charles continued.

Scottie looked shocked. His mouth fell agape as he blinked rapidly while trying to ascertain whether Charles was serious. "Milord, I'm not going to be shooting no high falootin' lords. I'd wind up hung."

"Of course, you won't be shooting anyone, Scottie. Charles, he's telling you the truth. Scottie would be hung if he shot someone like that, and God forbid if he shot a nobleman. You just need to send a letter back if you authorize anyone to view the tiles." Uncle Will frowned as he shook his head.

"Quite so," Fitz agreed. "Let's not get poor Scottie hung over bits of old glass in a field."

Charles frowned as he glanced from face to face. "Okay, but this find could be very valuable. I don't want thieves to try to steal the mosaic floor from a third century Roman villa."

Kelly placed a hand on his shoulder. "It will be okay, babe. Only we know about it. No one will come nosing around without your knowledge."

Charles stared at the ancient tiles as he stood chewing his lip before he answered. "Maybe so."

That evening, Charles drafted a missive to advise the Office of Antiquities of the discovery. Aunt Sassy sketched out drawings of the tiles, with approximate sizes of the area involved in the pasture. Charles kept a copy of the letter and the sketches for their records.

"I will hand deliver the letter and drawings to the Office of Antiquities when we arrive in London. They will get it quicker that way than if I mail it," Charles mused.

The next morning, Rev. Tilton read the banns for the first time to announce their wedding. He told the congregation they were all invited to the nuptials, which were planned for December 24th just after the morning services, and a reception would be held afterwards. The congregation murmured in excitement.

Kelly and he slipped back out to the site of the Roman villa that afternoon to photograph the tiles.

"I'll send the photos to Mom. She will be very excited," said Charles. "This might even inspire another novel for her."

Kelly smiled. "I imagine she will be delighted. Just imagine. Your father never knew these were here. Didn't he collect antiques?"

Charles nodded. "Mother said he did. He had a lot of first edition books at the Spring Haven house in Bermuda which were damaged in the hurricane."

"Well, this should more than make up for the loss of the books," said Kelly as she squeezed his hand.

He shrugged. "I don't know. Mother said he had a copy of Romeo and Juliet and a couple of other really old books."

Kelly looked shocked. "First edition Shakespeare? Wow."

That evening, the Hays family joined Fitz, Uncle Will and Aunt Sassy, Charles and Kelly at Spring Haven for dinner. After ham, mashed potatoes, salmagundi, and an excellent assortment of wines, the men retired to the library for cigars, whiskey and cards, while the ladies went upstairs to finish their packing.

"Sweetheart, you might want to wear this at the King's Christmas Ball." Aunt Sassy smiled as she pulled out the family coronet and handed it to Kelly.

Kelly opened her eyes wide with surprise. "Aunt Sassy, that may be the most beautiful piece of jewelry I ever saw. Will women be wearing things like this at that ball? Don't you want to wear it?"

Sassy shook her head. "No, you should wear it. Charles' grandfather, Lord Josiah Selk, bought it for his wife, Belle Rose, long ago on their honeymoon to Paris. Can you imagine the opulence of Paris in the 1720's? It must have been an incredible time. The plantation is named after Mama Belle. The coronet is crafted of pink tourmaline and aquamarines. It was fit for a duchess when they bought it. At that time, he was simply the third son, with no expectation he would ever inherit the title. Jo was elevated in title first to Marquess when his brother died, and later to a Duke. Will says their dad was quite flummoxed when he was made a Duke. Tom then inherited the title from his father, and when Tom died at Saratoga, Will became the Duke. I wore it a few times at grand balls. I wore it once at the Governor's Winter Ball in Philadelphia during the War. General and Lady Washington were there, and Gov. Arnold and his wife sponsored the ball. It took place before Arnold turned traitor. Of course, Will was the Duke then. When Will relinquished his title and Fancy became the Duchess, I gave the coronet to Fancy. When Fancy moved west with Richard, she left the coronet at

McCarron's Corner. When Marcus and Lily came to Belle Rose the next time, they returned the coronet to me. I held it in safekeeping until Charles would return someday. Since you are both here, it should be for his bride."

Kelly felt dismayed. "But Aunt Sassy, I'm not his wife yet."

Aunt Sassy smiled. "You will be his wife on Christmas Eve. You are his fiancée. You should wear it to the King's Christmas Ball. I think it will be quite appropriate. Anne, is there a family coronet you can wear?"

Anne nodded as her eyes began to sparkle with excitement. "Yes, Father bought it for Mother years ago. It hasn't been worn since she died."

"Well, Lord Hays better fetch it out of the safe because you need to wear it at the King's Christmas Ball," said Aunt Sassy with a saucy grin.

"And for your wedding," Kelly interjected, her eyes twinkling.

Anne blushed and looked downward. "Fitz hasn't asked for my hand yet."

Aunt Sassy smiled, her eyes softening with affection. "He will, my dear. And he is a wonderful man. I think he is absolutely perfect for you."

Anne beamed at Aunt Sassy. "So, do I. I must admit, I am quite fond of Charles, but in a different way. Perhaps more like the brother I never had. Charles never made my heart pound with excitement as he approached the way Fitz does. It was more like, oh, look, it's Charles coming. And I was always a bit embarrassed about the way we met."

Kelly tilted her head as she studied Anne's reddened face. "Okay, we haven't heard this story. Tell us."

The red on Anne's cheeks deepened. "It's quite embarrassing. I was out at the edge of the two properties, and I had just taken a jump over the creek when my girth strap broke. It frightened me when the saddle began slipping when the horse and I were mid-air jumping across the creek. I said something decidedly vulgar. Charles heard me and came to my aid. I was very embarrassed to have been caught uttering a vulgarity, especially when I realized Charles is a Duke."

Kelly and Sassy laughed. Finally, Aunt Sassy spoke. "What did you say?"

Kelly was surprised that poor Anne's face could turn any deeper red but it did. "I, um, I would rather not say, Aunt Sassy."

Sassy grinned and leaned closer to Kelly. "Oh, come on. We're all girls here. Spill the beans."

Anne's cheeks were still bright red, but she lifted her head. "Fine, if you insist. I said, 'oh, bugger.' Just like that. It quite startled me when the girth strap broke. I thought I was miles away from the house or anyone who could assist me. I was rather horrified to realize Charles was close enough that he overheard me."

Aunt Sassy began laughing hysterically. "I bet you were horrified."

Kelly frowned. She knew a look of uncertainty must be all over her face. "What does 'bugger' mean?"

Aunt Sassy bent over and whispered, "To put it as nicely as possible, it means 'anal intercourse.' Anne, what did he do?"

"He was quite the gentleman. He inquired if I required assistance, but he never mentioned the word I uttered," she responded, prim as a schoolteacher.

Kelly nodded. It sounded like the man she loved. "That's because he's a good man. But let's be honest: Charles never had your heart the way Fitz does."

Anne's cheeks had almost resumed their normal color. At Kelly's comment, she blushed again. "I must admit, there are times when Fitz enters a room, and my heart quickens so fast it frightens me. It makes me feel quite giddy. I become a bit bashful and I trip over my words as I try to speak with him. I didn't understand it when we first met. I do now."

Aunt Sassy smiled. "Yes, he's a wonderful man. I bet he asks for your hand in London. He is quite taken with you."

Anne gave Aunt Sassy a quick, eager smile. "Do you think so?"

Aunt Sassy nodded. "I certainly do. Now, let's get this packing finished."

Finally, the two households loaded their luggage onto the carriages and they headed to London. Kelly's puppy sat quietly on her lap or by her feet, although she sometimes chewed on a toy. The girls sat beside each other playing with the puppy with Aunt Sassy across from them as she did needlework. Chico alternated between riding between the girls or on the saddle with Charles from where he would bark with excitement and enthusiasm. Mimi would occasionally join with him in barking at people passing by the carriage. The young men rode horseback while Uncle Will and Lord Hays rode together in the Hays carriage. After a night on the road at an inn, they arrived in London late the next evening. Fitz stayed with Lord Hays and Anne to help them get settled into their townhouse while Charles and the others went on to the Spring Haven townhome. After the Hays family were settled into their townhouse, Fitz went on to his own townhouse a few blocks away.

The following day, Fitz and Charles headed to the Office of Antiquities with the letter and drawings of the newly discovered tiles. Aunt Sassy and Kelly picked up Anne in the Ranscome carriage and the ladies headed downtown to shop. Aunt Sassy knew most upper class, wealthy women shopped at *modistes*, such as Floris, located on upscale Jermyn Street. Women could pick the fabric for their purchases, and be fitted for undergarments, gowns, gloves, shoes, and even hats and parasols. The *modiste* shops offered the whole package. It was the original one stop shop.

"Hello, I am Mrs. Sarah Selk. This is Princess Nguyen Kieu Linh, from Vietnam, and Lady Anne Hays, daughter of Lord Henry Hays, Earl of Meadow Glen, from the Cotswolds. We call the Princess 'Princess Kelly' because her name is difficult to pronounce in English. She is engaged to my nephew, Lord Hobbs. We will be needing some assistance in selecting gowns and accessories for the King's Christmas Ball."

"Ooh, Lord Hobbs is right handsome. I done seen him before down on Bond Street," gushed one young *modiste*. "He sure enough looks like a real Corinthian."

The head *modiste* cast a baleful eye at her protégé. "You saw him."

The girl nodded. "That's what I said."

"No, you said 'I done seen him.' We must use proper English in this shop. You saw him."

The girl blushed. "Oh, yes, of course, mistress. I'm sorry. But he is quite handsome."

Kelly bit back laughter. "The young lady is correct. Lord Hobbs is quite the Corinthian."

The smiling *modistes* quickly ushered the three women into a private area to make their selections. The head *modiste* assured them that they could finish creation of all purchases before the date of the ball. She then brought in bolts of fabric from which they could make their selections as the assistants began helping the women undress to measure each of them for their new garments.

"Oh, my heavens, how does a person ever decide which to select with so much beautiful fabric?" lamented Anne as a *modiste* helped her out of her gown to take her measurements.

"Don't worry, Lady Anne. That's what we are here to do. We will be most happy to assist you in your selections. With your fair coloring, and unmarried status, I would recommend light colors and whites for you," said the head *modiste*.

Kelly nodded. "I quite agree. However, no muslin, please. It's far too cold to consider wearing such a light garment."

The *modistes l*ooked startled by her words. "Are you sure? The white muslin gown is the most fashionable item right now. It's straight from Paris."

The three women nodded. Aunt Sassy spoke for them. "Yes, Kelly is quite right. It is far too cold out to wear something as light as muslin. I don't care how stylish it is in Paris. Perhaps a layer of muslin or some other sheer fabric over white velvet or silk. I would not want either girl to catch her death of pneumonia for the sake of fashion. It will be far too cold to wear muslin here in London until at least March. I suggest you show us silks, velvets, and maybe pretty brocades. The girls might wear white velvet now and you will start a new trend for winter. White velvet trimmed with white fox around the neckline would be quite gorgeous. It's always best to be on the leading edge of fashion."

The head *modiste* smiled. "Quite so, madam. Girls, fetch the silks and velvets."

Kelly already knew she had a gorgeous court gown, but fully intended to wear her pink *Ao Dai* which Fancy Winslow had made Kelly for the Ball at which she would be introduced to King George and Queen Charlotte. Fancy crafted a beautiful ombre pink silk *Ao Dai* embellished with a beaded phoenix on the front. The long sleeves trailed to the ground like some medieval dresses had done, and the court train extended five feet behind the gown. It had a high neckline typical of traditional Vietnamese gowns. A long raspberry pink scarf would drape from the front of her throat, over her shoulders, and flow down her back over the train. She showed it to Charles, who agreed it would be perfect for the introduction of the Vietnamese Princess to the British King and Queen. They knew it would be unlike any other gown at the ball.

Kelly whispered to the *modiste*, "I already have a new gown for the ball, but can a girl ever have too many dresses?"

The young woman giggled. "Not at all, my lady."

Kelly would save the beautiful blue and silver court gown Fancy sent with her for another event at Court. Nonetheless, she made fabric selections for several gowns, two riding habits, and another beautiful court gown. It would be made in much the same style as the one Fancy sent with her, but in different colors, with a creamy white velvet under dress and a bronze-colored silk net overdress. She had them make another in white velvet, trimmed in ermine around the hood and the long sleeves.

"The net is quite fashionable, milady," urged the seamstress.

"Yes, I think both gowns will be exquisite. The design for the white velvet should be very dramatic. Neither new court gown needs to be ready before this ball. I would like to have them in January. Now, let's select fabric for some other gowns, also. I don't need them immediately, but I will need more gowns. I really need a couple of stylish riding habits, maybe one in blue and another in some other acceptable color. Mine is quite outdated in style. Please prepare the ball gowns for Mrs. Selk and Lady Hays first."

The young woman looked impressed. "You're a good friend and a good person. Not every woman would be so generous. They are fortunate."

Kelly blushed, embarrassed by the woman's compliments. "Thank you. I try to be a good friend."

With much prodding from the *modistes* as well as from the other two women, Anne finally selected a lovely sky-blue silk taffeta with a nice hand which would be covered with white lace. It would have a modest, square neckline and puff sleeves. The *modiste* assisting her pointed out Anne could have the under-sleeves removed when the temperature warmed up. Sky-blue ribbon and pearls would decorate the neckline, and a sky-blue ribbon would accent the raised waistline of the gown. Two more rows of ribbon and pearls would decorate the bottom of the gown just above the hemline. The exquisite, handmade lace would extend beyond the back of the gown to form a court train. It was elegant enough for an introduction to the monarch and was still youthful enough for a girl only nineteen years old like Anne to wear for the formal event. The *modiste* would make a coordinating shawl she could wear over her shoulders and arms if needed. Matching ribbons trimmed with pearls would be thread through her blonde curls the night of the ball, and she would top her hairdo with the family coronet.

"It's gorgeous, Anne. It will look stunning on you. Of course, you have such beautiful skin." Kelly sounded wistful.

Anne looked around at Kelly in surprise. "Why, thank you, Kelly, but you have beautiful skin, as well."

Kelly blushed. "Mine is so much darker than yours. The color of your skin is what we call 'snow' in Vietnam."

Anne snorted. "Your skin is a beautiful golden shade. Mine is white as snow, and burns horribly in the sun."

Kelly looked stunned. "Huh. I always wanted skin white as snow. My mother has skin like that. Her name is Tuan, which means snow in Vietnamese. My complexion is more like my father's. I could never understand why anyone would want skin the color of mine."

Aunt Sassy frowned. "Oh, pish. Both of you have gorgeous skin, you silly girls. Wait until you are my age and have wrinkles."

With some additional prodding, Sassy and Kelly convinced Anne to also order several day gowns and two additional evening gowns. Kelly bit back a grin as she overheard Anne whispering to the *modiste* about fabrics for a possible wedding gown.

"Oh, there's no 'possible' about it. The man adores you. He's courting you now. I promise you, an offer for your hand in marriage is forthcoming from Lord Winston Fitz Simmons."

The head *modiste* looked impressed. "The Earl of Waterside? Oh, my dear, that would be quite a catch."

Anne laughed as her face reddened. "Yes, indeed, and beyond that, he is the most wonderful man. Sweet, kind, loving, intelligent, and an excellent manager of his estates. I might want a dress in white muslin for my wedding – IF he asks me. But I am not the only one with a prospective wedding. Kelly is engaged to marry the Duke of Ranscome."

The three *modistes* all gasped with excitement and began talking at once.

"We must select the fabric and style immediately, milady!"

"When are the nuptials?"

"Is he handsome? Is he young?"

"Is he rich?"

Kelly laughed at their excitement. "Yes, he is handsome, young, and quite rich. The wedding is set for Christmas Eve. I brought a wedding dress from home to wear. My mother made it for me. She is an excellent seamstress, and it is an exquisite oriental design."

The *modistes* all looked keenly disappointed. "Oh, what a pity."

"I will bring it in, and we can see if it needs any alterations. I lost some weight on the trip. You could also help me find the right shoes and accessories for it. You will find it is quite different in style and color from the gowns commonly worn in Great Britain." Kelly chuckled as she contemplated the impact the Vietnamese-styled wedding gown would have on the French head *modiste.*

Sassy shook her head. "Not really. While I generally hear that our high waisted, flowing gowns emulate the classical Greek styles, I have also heard they emulate Oriental styles."

The *modiste's* eyes narrowed and she nodded in agreement. "Actually, milady, the Oriental look is quite popular. I look forward to seeing what we might need to tweak it a bit and perhaps give it a mixture of Oriental and English style."

Kelly beamed with excitement. It was beginning to look more each day like everything would work out perfectly for their wedding. "The gown is red with gold embroidery and beadwork. There is a matching overcoat. It is a beautiful gown, and I love it even more because my mother made it for me."

Sassy smiled broadly as she viewed the numerous fabric bolts. Her eyes lit up with enthusiasm as she selected a rose-colored silk matelassé fabric. The *modiste* would make the ball gown with a low square neckline, puff sleeves with detachable long under-sleeves and tight-fitting cuffs. She planned to wear it without the under sleeves for the ball. Several rows of ruching accented the hemline. It would be cut lower than the gowns for the younger women, who balked at the popular, more revealing neckline. Sassy also ordered new undergarments, long gloves, shoes, and two hats as well as three other day dresses before they left.

"I wish Fancy was here to see all the fabrics. She would be in heaven," Sassy said as she fingered a swatch of aqua silk.

Kelly nodded. "I thought the same thing. Can you imagine her reaction to all these beautiful fabrics?" She smiled at the *modiste.* "Lady Fancy is Lord Charles' mother. She loves to sew, and she has a real eye for combining fabrics. Hmm. Maybe I should buy some fabric to send to her."

Sassy's eyes twinkled as she nodded. "I think that is a wonderful idea. Since she lives in Mexico, perhaps the *modiste* would be so kind as to send a pattern with the fabric you select."

"Of course, madame," the *modiste* quickly replied.

Kelly and Anne also selected hats, shoes, gloves, and new undergarments for their new gowns. They also ordered opera-length gloves to wear at the ball.

After they left the elegant shop, they located the tea shop one of the *modistes* recommended, where they had a light luncheon. As they exited the tea shop, a shadow loomed over the women. Anne looked up, paled, and stepped back in apparent shocked distress. "You. What are you doing here?"

"Why, Lady Annabelle, is that any way to speak to an old friend?"

The tall, dapper, middle-aged man had salt-and-pepper hair with a white streak in the front. He bowed low over her hand, but Anne snatched it from his cloying grasp. "You're not my friend. You proved that two years ago. Get away from me, Col. Darlington. And stay away from me."

Aunt Sassy appeared shocked. She stepped between Anne and the dashing man. "You will depart immediately, Col. Darlington. You heard Lady Annabelle. You are not welcome around any of us. That goes for your cousin, too."

He turned to give a slight bow to Aunt Sassy, all smiles and sleaze. "I beg your pardon, madam, I do not believe I have had the opportunity to make your acquaintance."

"Good," she muttered under her breath.

Kelly raised her chin. "She is the aunt of both the Duke of Ranscome and the Earl of Waterside. You heard the ladies. Your presence is not wanted here. Begone. Now. Begone!"

He looked askance as Kelly motioned for him to leave with her hand. He bowed. "Then I will take my leave. Fair Lady Annabelle, it was never my intention to hurt you-"

"Liar," she snarled. "You and I both know exactly what you intended. You hoped to force my hand into marriage. You failed. Get away from me and stay away. Or you will be sorry."

"And what would you do, sweeting?" He leaned in to caress a curl. "I had forgotten you are so beautiful."

"I'm warning you, don't touch me again, Brice Darlington. Your charms are lost to me. I am on to your wicked ways," snapped Anne, her hands shaking with a combination of terror and rage.

Kelly noticed Anne struggled to keep the tremor of fear out of her voice. She placed a protective arm around her friend's shoulders. "Don't pay any attention to him. He's not worth your concern."

"Come, girls, let's go home. There is no need for us to interact with this churlish riff raff," snapped Aunt Sassy.

As they climbed into the carriage, Col. Brice Darlington bowed with a flourish. Anne shuddered.

Once safely ensconced in the carriage and on their way, Kelly could hold her tongue no longer. "How do you know that horrid man? There is something not quite right about him."

Anne gulped, and then straightened up. "He is the man who tried to ruin me two years ago. He is the reason I had not returned to London since then."

Aunt Sassy's eyes narrowed as she looked back at Darlington, still staring after the coach. "Don't worry, sweetheart. He won't hurt you again."

"I-I told Fitz about him. I didn't want him to meet him and learn from the scoundrel what he tried." Anne struggled to hold back tears as she sat trembling in the carriage.

Aunt Sassy stared at the man who stood still watching the carriage depart. "Fitz already knew about that man. Darlington has a less than stellar reputation in our family."

Anne paled. "Oh, really? Why?"

"He and his cousin kidnapped Charles' mother years ago. Charles was just a baby, but Fitz assisted us to locate Fancy and bring her home."

Anne's eyes were wide as saucers. "Oh, dear God."

Kelly paled as well. "You mean that was one of the men..."

Aunt Sassy nodded. "I most certainly do, and his cousin is now in Parliament. They are a sorry couple of bounders if I ever met any. Will, Fitz and Richard had to 'have a talk' with Darlington years ago after Fancy was kidnapped. That was when he admitted what his nefarious cousin had done with Fancy and where we could find her. Believe me, if they have to 'talk' to him again, Brice Darlington will sorely regret that he did not heed their warnings twenty years ago."

Chapter 20
The King's Christmas Ball
Kelly
1802

The evening for the King's Christmas Ball finally arrived. The women all worked together to style each other's hair and assist in dressing. Aunt Sassy pulled out a jewelry case of fabulous jewels to ensure each wore something special with her gown. Since Anne's coronet was decorated with diamonds and pearls, she wore a dainty diamond pendant extended from a pearl choker, with pearl earrings.

"I feel overdressed," fussed Anne as she fretted with her hair..

"Tsk, you look quite lovely. Trust me, Anne, you are appropriately clad for this event," said Aunt Sassy.

Kelly wore the Selk coronet clad in pink tourmaline and aquamarines and a pair of Sassy's pink tourmaline earrings with her pink gown. "I feel rather overdressed, too, like Anne said."

Aunt Sassy gave a sharp shake to her head. "No. You are a princess about to meet the monarch of Great Britain and his consort. It is imperative that you look like a princess tonight, Kelly. You need to wear the coronet."

Kelly took a deep breath and nodded. "Okay, Aunt Sassy. I'll trust you on this."

Sassy chose a beautiful parure of rubies which Will gave to her some years before for Christmas. She pinned the matching brooch to a wide ribbon and thread it through her hair with the brooch in front above her forehead. She rarely had an opportunity to wear the elegant ensemble in Virginia. Two feathers extended above her head to give her a look viewed by the *ton* as "oriental."

The men dressed in black formal wear with tailcoats, crisp white shirts, stiff cravats, and elegant silk brocade waistcoats, as dictated by the court. They appeared awestruck as the women came down the stairs at the Ranscome townhome. Finally, Lord Hays began clapping. The other men quickly joined him in applauding the three beautiful women as they descended the stairs, one blonde with blue eyes, one a brunette with green eyes, and one with coal black hair and eyes dark as the night.

The night had turned bitterly cold. The men helped the women into their warmest coats for the ride by carriage to the Ball.

Charles was excited because he received a letter from the Office of Antiquities. "Their letter said they will send a team of archeologists out to review the tiles right after Christmas."

"That's wonderful, Charles. Did they say what day they might come?" asked Kelly.

He shook his head. "They seemed interested but did not give me a specific date. I think they need to determine when they can get a team out there. After all, it's a two-day ride to Spring Haven, and it is almost Christmas."

Kelly nodded. "That makes sense. I hadn't thought about the trip. Oh, look, we are pulling up to the *porte-cochere* now."

Once they arrived, the men helped each lady down and into the palace.

Kelly gasped and threw one hand up to her mouth. She had never seen anything quite so extravagant before. They entered from the second floor, where they removed their cloaks and coats and checked them in, and then proceeded to the doorman. After they gave him their names, he announced each couple as they walked down a long, curved stairway which ended near the dais for the King and Queen. They were supposed to approach the monarch, where the men would bow, the women would make a low curtsey, and they would make brief pleasantries with the British ruler and Queen Charlotte for a minute or two before the next couple would come down the stairs to do the same.

Uncle Will and Aunt Sassy went down first. Uncle Will bowed to the King. To Kelly's surprise, the King arose and grabbed Uncle Will into a hug.

"It's good to see you again after all these years, Lord William. I have missed your wit. Have you returned to stay in Great Britain?" asked King George, excitement in his voice.

Uncle Will thumped the king on the back like they were old friends. "No, your Majesty, I'm here visiting kinfolk and they asked us to accompany them tonight. If I may, allow me to introduce my beautiful wife, Sarah Selk."

Aunt Sassy bent into a low curtsey. Upon arising, she smiled at the monarch. "King George, I am thrilled and honored to be able to meet you at last. Queen Charlotte, what a beautiful gown. You look stunning."

The two women chatted about fashion as Charles and Kelly slowly descended the stairs. As they reached the thrones, Charles bowed first, and then Kelly bowed low with her hands folded in front of her chest in the Vietnamese manner.

Charles cleared his throat. "Your majesty, I am thrilled and honored to finally meet you. My mother regaled me with stories of you throughout my life. May I introduce to the Queen and you my beautiful fiancée, Princess Nguyen Kieu Linh. The Princess's family are from Vietnam, south of China."

The king reached out a hand first to Charles and then to Kelly. "I'm pleased to meet you both. Charlotte, my dear, I think we have found tonight's Incomparable."

"I quite agree, my dear," responded the Queen with a ready smile.

Kelly could feel her cheeks heating as they turned red. "Thank you very much, your Majesties. However, Queen Charlotte, you look the very height of fashion in your exquisite gown. And your hair is beautiful. I wish I could coax such lovely curls into my hair."

King George looked perplexed. "Young Ranscome, I am not sure I can say your fiancée's name correctly."

"Most people simply pronounce my name 'Kelly,' your Majesty," Kelly interjected.

He smiled. "Ah, yes, much simpler, Princess Kelly. Now, tell me exactly where this Vietnam is located."

She beamed at him, eager to tell about the country her family came from. "It is directly south of China. It was part of China many years ago. It became a separate country about six hundred years ago. My family came to New Spain from an area known as the Bay of Tonkin and the Tonkin Peninsula."

"Your gown is exquisite, my dear," said Queen Charlotte.

"Thank you, your Majesty. Charles' mother made it for me to bring with me. It is in the style that the women of my country wear, and it is called an *Ao Dai*. However, you will note that I also wear the Ranscome coronet tonight. My fiancé thrilled me when he inquired if I would like to wear it. We felt the combination of the *Ao Dai*, and the coronet demonstrated a melding of our two cultures."

"We are hoping to be married soon, if it pleases Your Majesty," added Charles.

The King nodded. "Of course, your Grace, of course. But tell me, how did a family from Vietnam come to live in New Spain? I understand that is where you met Lord Charles."

Kelly smiled and nodded. "Yes, your Majesty. My father is Chinese. He was sent as an ambassador from the Emperor of China to the Martial King Nguyen Phuc Khoat in the City of Phu Xuan, in Vietnam. While there, he met the daughter of one of the counselors to the Nguyen Lord, and they fell in love. They could marry with two provisos: one, that no daughter would ever have to submit to having her feet bound, as is the custom in China, and second, that the eldest daughter would return at age sixteen to Beijing to marry a son of the Emperor."

The King looked puzzled. "And how did that get you to New Spain, my dear?"

She laughed. "Well, your Majesty, when my older sister was born, the Emperor of China wanted my father to return to Beijing and turn her over to the care of his first wife. My mother became hysterical. She refused to turn her baby over to the Chinese. She knew they would insist on binding Tuan's feet so she would have golden lotuses. The Chinese believe a woman should ideally have feet no more than three inches long."

Queen Charlotte frowned. "I don't understand. How on earth can they manage that?"

"With foot binding, your Majesty. It's a horrible practice. They begin binding the feet when the girl is very young. They begin by forcing the baby's toes to bend beneath the foot. Later, they break the arch to further bend the foot into the three-inch-long ideal called the golden lotus."

Queen Charlotte appeared horrified. "Oh, my heavens, how absolutely appalling! I cannot imagine the pain the poor girls undergo."

Kelly nodded, excited the queen comprehended the inherent tortuous abuse of foot binding. "I quite agree. My parents refused to send my sister, so they concocted a plan to flee Vietnam. They boarded a ship which was supposed to take them north to China. Instead, it took them south first to Australia, and then on to California. In California, they made their way to Texas, which is in the northern part of Nuevo Espana, called Mexico. I was born in San Antonio de Bexar, the town where Charles and I later met in Nuevo Espana."

The king nodded. "Fascinating. And how did you meet young Ranscome?"

She smiled again as she glanced at Charles, love shining in her eyes. "We met over a dog, your Majesty."

The King's eyebrows shot upwards. "A dog? Do explain."

She laughed, charmed by the King's attentive questions. "Lord Charles is very fond of animals. One day, he found a little, abandoned dog. As he gathered the dog up to take him home, I happened upon them. I was very impressed with his kindness to animals. We were introduced and became very good friends. From friendship grew love. Over a year ago, he asked me to marry him. I am very honored to be the future Duchess of Ranscome, and to be marrying such a charming, handsome, intelligent and kind young man as Lord Charles."

"Well said, my dear!" responded King George. "Your Grace, I would like to introduce you to someone who wanted to meet you tonight. Lord Charles Ranscome Hobbs, I believe you were named after General Charles Cornwallis."

General Cornwallis stepped forward to greet Charles and Kelly. "M'god, you look enough like your father that I would have thought you were Lord Calvin when we were young men. I am delighted to finally meet you, milord."

Charles grabbed Cornwallis's hand. "General, I will be sure to write to my mother and tell her I met you this evening. She has often talked fondly about you and how you worked diligently to protect her at Yorktown, sir."

Cornwallis's cheeks reddened. "Your mother is very kind. She is a remarkable woman. She organized the women to butcher the slaughtered horses so we would have enough meat. She worked without ceasing in the hospital tent with our wounded. She worked so hard that she fainted at one point."

"I never heard about that," Charles murmured, his eyes wide with surprise.

Cornwallis nodded. "And then when I was sick with typhus, she took the articles of surrender to General Washington. She is a most amazing, courageous and formidable woman."

Charles smiled, his eyes shining with pride at the General's description of his mother's valiant behavior at Yorktown. "She certainly is, and then some."

They moved aside so that Lord Hays and Lady Anne could make their introductions to the King and Queen. Anne stood pale and trembling as Lord Hays introduced his terrified daughter to the monarch and his wife. She sank into a low curtsey as Fitz came bounding down the stairs immediately after them.

"Lord Winston Fitz Simmons, the Earl of Waterside," intoned the doorman with a frown.

Kelly struggled to bite back a chuckle. It was obvious the doorman was unaccustomed to people moving down the stairs prematurely.

The King arched his brows again, but his face softened as Fitz approached Lord Hays and Anne and took both of Anne's hands into his to help her up before he turned to bow to King George and Queen Charlotte. "Your Majesties, I am fortunate enough to be able to say I have been given permission to court Lady Anne. However, with my liege's permission..."

He paused as he awaited a nod from the King. The King smiled and nodded, his eyes twinkling with excitement.

Fitz dropped to one knee in front of Anne. "Then your Majesties, Lord Hays, I would like to take this beautiful moment to ask Lady Anne to become my bride."

People nearby in the ballroom gasped.

Gen. Cornwallis pointed to Fitz kneeling before Anne. "Oh, look, Lord Charles. Isn't Lord Fitz Simmons related to you?"

Charles nodded, his eyes alight with excitement. "Yes, milord, he's my uncle. Let's watch."

Kelly tugged on Charlie's sleeve. "I knew Fitz would ask her to marry him tonight. How exciting!"

The King nodded again to Fitz as did Lord Hays. Fitz smiled and then proceeded. "Lady Annabelle, whom I know prefers to be called Lady Anne, would you do me the very great honor of marrying me?"

Anne's eyes were sparkling with excitement and unshed tears. "Of course, Lord Winston. It would be my great honor."

Winston Fitz Simmons pulled a ring out of his inner coat pocket and slid it onto Anne's trembling finger.

"Oh, Fitz, it's a love ring, with a tiara on top. It's quite beautiful," whispered Anne. "And now I will always wear a tiara of my own."

He squeezed her hand as he beamed at her. "I hoped you would like it. This little love ring has 'all the bells and whistles', as Charles put it. The symbolic pairing of a diamond and ruby, the Fede hands, a jeweled crown and the three bands are joined to make one. Hidden inside is a tiny, engraved inscription that says *'Gage D'Amitie.'* I believe that means 'a token of love.' I found it when Lord Ranscome and I went shopping last week. I did not simply purchase new clothing for tonight. I bought you a ring. I hope you like it."

"Well, go ahead, Lord Fitz Simmons. Kiss the girl," coaxed the King.

"Yes, kiss her, Lord Fitz Simmons," echoed Queen Charlotte, her cheeks bright pink with excitement.

The couple looked surprised by his words. Fitz recovered first, chuckled, and then pulled Anne into his arms for a lingering kiss.

Anne appeared glassy eyed as the kiss ended. As a finger traced across her lips, she smiled. "Well, I guess I can't say I've never been kissed any longer."

"Bravo!" The King and Queen both began the clapping. Soon, many of the people in the ballroom clapped for the happy couple.

It was later while the couples were getting cups of punch that the problem arose when General Tarleton, now a Baron, and Col. Darlington approached.

Fitz instantly bristled. He knew Darlington tried to force himself on Anne two years earlier. Anne's reputation was unfairly tarnished when she refused to marry the scoundrel who tried to ruin her. Fitz also remembered the part both men played in the kidnapping of his sister years before. He slipped an arm around Anne's waist. Darlington looked at him in surprise, and Fitz nodded towards Darlington. Anne gasped and slid closer to Fitz. Fitz bent over and kissed her cheek. "Don't worry, my love. He will never get another opportunity to harm you."

Charles bristled as well. He did not know Anne's story, but he knew what happened to Aunt Sassy and to his mother. He pulled Kelly close to his side and whispered, "Don't let those bastards near you, Kelly."

Silent, she nodded as she inched closer behind Charles.

Aunt Sassy gasped in horror at the sight of Tarleton and began to shake. Uncle Will pushed Aunt Sassy behind him, to protect her from Tarleton. She clung to the back of his jacket as she trembled with fear. She knew Will would kill that sorry bastard right there in the palace, in front of the King, before he would ever let Tarleton dare touch her again.

Darlington approached Anne and reached to touch a curl hanging over her shoulder. "Why, darling, you look absolutely good enough to eat."

Anne shuddered and shrunk back from Darlington's grasp. "I already asked you not to touch me."

Fitz slapped Darlington's hand from where it lingered poised in the air as if it were about to touch Anne again. "I don't believe you were invited to touch Lady Anne."

Darlington's brows raised. "Lady Anne is it? And who are you?"

Fitz almost smiled. "Lord Winston Fitz Simmons, Earl of Waterside, her fiancé. You might recall we had a conversation some years ago about my sister, Francesca Hobbs, who was then the Duchess of Ranscome."

Darlington paled and stepped back. "Oh, quite so, my Lord. I didn't recognize you. I apologize. I did not realize you were in a relationship with Lady Hays."

"It doesn't matter if you recognized Lord Fitz Simmons or not. Just keep your filthy paws to yourself," said Charles, his lips narrowed in rage.

"And what is it to you, young buck?" interjected Gen. Tarleton, his voice low as he stepped forward, menacing in his demeanor.

"I'm the Duke of Ranscome. It is 'to me' because of what you bastards did to my mother and my Aunt twenty years ago. You are not fit to be in polite company. You both need to leave immediately."

Tarleton arched a brow at Charles as he stepped closer to Charles, apparently intending to intimidate him. "Indeed? And what if I choose not to do so?"

Charles' cold smile did not touch his eyes as he stepped closer to Tarleton. He reached over to finger the label on Tarleton's coat and gave it the slightest tug towards him. Even though Kelly could see he had regained his control, his anger still rang in every word. "I would be more than happy to release copies of the statements of the twelve women and the federal conviction for rape from Philadelphia to the King and to Parliament. How would that do for starters?"

"You sorry little bastard," snarled Tarleton, as he paled and stepped back from Charles. He wiped his lapels as if to remove imaginary dirt. "You wouldn't dare."

Charles shook his head and then chuckled. "I'm not a bastard. I'm quite legitimate. You must be thinking of someone else who *you* sired. And believe me: I would dare."

"I ought to challenge you to a duel..." Tarleton snarled as hot pink spots bloomed on his cheeks.

Charles chuckled and smiled. "Is that a challenge, General Tarleton?"

Kelly gasped. "Darling, don't-"

"Yes, I believe it is," snapped Tarleton, as his face grew redder with each passing second. "No one is going to besmirch my sterling reputation."

Charles laughed. "Your *sterling* reputation? Perhaps you mean your *honor*? Ha! No, you did that all by yourself. No one helped you. You even wrote in your memoirs how you had sex with 20,000 women in the Colonies. Men of *sterling* character do not brag of their conquests. Fine, I accept your challenge. I believe that means *I* have the right to determine how the duel will be fought?"

"Oh, dear God, Charles, no!" interjected Kelly as she began to shake. *He cannot be doing this. Please God, don't let my Charles get killed fighting a duel!*

For the first time, Tarleton looked askance. "Yes, if you insist."

Charles laughed, the corners of his eyes crinkling with amusement. "Oh, yes, I wouldn't dream of not fulfilling your little fantasy duel. Then I accept your challenge with the understanding that we will fight at a place to be designated by Gentleman John Jackson. The method will be Mixed Martial Arts."

Tarleton looked confused. "I beg your pardon, what is your choice of weapon?"

"Our bodies. Mixed Martial Arts. It incorporates Western and Eastern methods of fighting. I will find out tomorrow when it will be convenient for us to conduct the fight. Still want to duel, old man?"

Tarleton's face reddened. "You impertinent young blade, I'll show you 'old man.' Fine. You want a boxing demonstration? I'll be happy to give you one. Arrange the time and date. I will be there."

Charles smiled. "Let me clarify that I did not challenge you to a boxing match. I challenged you to a Mixed Martial Arts match. It is comprised of elements from Boxing, which originated in Rome, Wrestling, which originated in Greece, and Jiu Jitsu, which originated in the Far East."

Kelly nodded. "I believe that is correct, your Grace."

Tarleton paled. He huffed up and began muttering something unintelligible before he turned abruptly to leave.

Kelly's eyes were wide with stunned surprise. "You just got that middle-aged man to agree to a MMA fight with you under the supervision of Gentleman John? Oh, my god, Charles, you will obliterate him."

Uncle Will frowned. "What's MMA?"

Charles smirked. "Mixed Martial Arts. It combines skills from Europe, Asia and South America into a rough and tumble sport that is also called cage fighting."

Uncle Will appeared shocked. "My god, you got Tarleton to agree to a cage fight?"

Charles nodded and began to laugh. "I don't think he understands fully what he agreed to do, Uncle Will. I plan to totally humiliate the pompous ass. There are reasons my Dad taught me to fight like a tiger. He knew I would eventually return here and would need superior skills of self-defense. I have trained at MMA since I was a small child."

Aunt Sassy looked confused. "You are actually going to duel him at Gentleman John's? I think Mr. Jackson will require you to abide by his boxing regulations."

Charles laughed. "We will see. If John Jackson won't authorize it, I guess we will be going out of town to find a spot where we can 'duke it out.' Have no fear, Aunt Sassy. I shall win this match for Anne, Mom and you."

Chapter 21
Charlie
London 1802

The next day, Charlie found his way to Gentleman John's establishment. The two men retired to Jackson's office, where Charles explained the situation to Mr. Jackson, who burst into laughter as Charlie explained how he trapped Tarleton into the 'duel'.

"Of course, I'll help you set up the fight. Tarleton always struck me as a cocky braggart. Now, show me what you can do."

Charlie took off his jacket, vest, cravat, and shirt, to fight Gentleman John. As they both climbed into the ring, Gentleman John paused with a frown.

"Do you know my rules?"

Charlie shook his head. "Not really. I know Boxing rules and Wrestling rules from the United States, but I do what is called 'Mixed Martial Arts' fighting. I learned it in the New World. May I show you?"

John Jackson's eyes crinkled with amusement as he laughed. "Certainly, but I warn you, I can block you and beat you. I have an exceptional reach with my arms. Allow me go over the rules of the sport of boxing. First, if a man goes down and cannot continue after a count to thirty, the fight is over. Hitting a downed man and grasping below the waist are both prohibited. Head butting, hair pulling, eye gouging, scratching, biting, kicking, hitting a man while he is down are also prohibited. There is no hitting below the belt, no holding the ropes, and no using resin, stones or hard objects in the hands. Those are all illegal."

Charlie frowned as he pondered Jackson's words. "Wow. No kicking? That is an essential skill in mixed martial arts."

Jackson shook his head. "No, absolutely not in boxing. Is it allowed in your mixed martial arts?"

Charles nodded, eager to explain his sport to Jackson. "Yes, it is. I have exceptional leg reach, and I pack a mean punch."

Jackson tilted his head to study the young buck standing before him. "Hmm. Show me."

Charles grinned and then kicked hard and strong into Jackson's abdomen, one, two, three times. As Jackson tried to catch his breath, Charlie began his assault on Jackson with his fists. As Jackson collapsed to the floor, Charlie dropped and wrapped Jackson into a clinch hold.

"Stop! My lord, I never experienced anything like that before in my life. You must teach me this new method," gasped Jackson after Charles freed him from the clinch hold.

"It is far more aggressive fighting than your style of Boxing. It is not 'gentlemanly' in style. It is designed to win a battle against an opponent, in the ring or in an alleyway. It includes stand up, striking styles like Boxing and grappling skills like Wrestling. The inclusion of the leg kicks comes from the Far East and gives a man greater reach than from the arms alone. When you add the clinches and chokes, it makes a man very strong in a fight. Dad and I used to fight in matches back home. My stepfather is an outstanding Mixed Martial Arts fighter. So is Kelly's father. Kelly is my fiance. Her real name is Princess Keiu Linh, but everyone calls her Kelly. It's simpler to pronounce."

"I can understand why," gasped Mr. Jackson, who still struggled to catch his breath. "Would you be averse to limiting your fight to strikes and punches for the duel?"

Charlie frowned as his foot thrummed on the floor in nervous agitation. "I challenged him to a MMA fight. He accepted. I expected to be able to abide by MMA rules."

Jackson laughed as he shook a finger at Charles. "Ah, milord, but no one here, including Tarleton, knows those rules."

Charles frowned as he began to chew his lip. "What if I write the rules out for you?"

Jackson laughed again. "I'm glad you're here, milord. You'll keep me on my toes. Yes, I would like you to write out the rules for this sport. I think you could get away with a limited number of kicks if I explain at the beginning of the fight that they are allowed in your mixed martial arts style of fighting, to which he agreed to fight. I could then read the rules of the Mixed Martial Arts fight aloud for the spectators and participants. You might demonstrate a few kicks before the duel commences. I do not think you could incorporate the clinch holds and chokes in this fight, although I would like to be able to explain those are usually included. We could even demonstrate them before the fight commences. Those are strictly against the Broughton boxing rules. Of course, kicking is forbidden, also, but it is more accepted than choking. I think by sharing the rules of the game with him just before the fight, he might forfeit."

"Really?" Charles asked as he rolled his shoulders and a grin began to play on his lips.

Jackson nodded. "Of course, this fight will have to be taken out of the city, where rules can be looser. However, you do not want to be deemed ungentlemanly, much less a poor sport. I would suggest you show him the kicks, and I will say kicks are allowed, but to be used sparingly."

"Well, that takes a lot of the fun out of the fight," grumbled Charles as his lips curled into a frown.

John Jackson laughed, the corners of his eyes again crinkling with amusement. "You don't want to be called a poor sport."

"The man is an abuser of women. He has no respect for women. I want to win. I want to rub his nose in the dirt when I win."

Jackson quit laughing at the seriousness of Charles's voice. He nodded. "Hmm, I have heard similar complaints about him before. He has a rather unsavory reputation."

"So why do you think he would abide by the rules in the first place?"

Jackson sighed and he shook his head. "Good point. Well, if he doesn't abide by the rules, you may proceed full force with your Mixed Martial Arts. Now, tell me more about this method of fighting."

Charlie nodded, eager to explain the sport he loved to Jackson. "There are basically three fighting styles which a mixed martial arts fighter learns and trains in order to be successful. Striking fighting styles, such as in Boxing, as you instruct, teach a man how to strike with his fists and arms when on his feet. Dad always says that is the place to begin. Of course, we wear gloves when we strike, and don't strike with our bare knuckles."

Jackson's eyes lit up with excitement. "Oh, really?"

Charlie nodded. "Yes. Gloves allow you to use different body posture. I will bring my gloves next time to demonstrate how they are used. Next in mixed martial arts are takedowns, and protection from takedowns, which you learn from Wrestling. Dad said Wrestling is the oldest competition fighting sport other than Boxing that we still have. It goes back to the Greeks. He said Boxing goes back to the Romans."

Quite so," replied Gentleman John. "However, I believe the Egyptians and Babylonians wrestled, also."

"I had forgotten that. The third method of mixed martial arts are the submissions, which come largely from Asian martial arts, such as Jiu Jitsu. The idea is you get your opponent down on the mat and force him to submit. You can get him to the mat by striking until he falls, by kicking him until he falls, or by using other grappling-like holds from wrestling. That includes clinches and chokes, which I can teach you. Of course, you said I have to avoid those in this fight."

"Unless he starts fighting dirty. Then you may proceed as you wish."

Charles grinned. "Very good. I'm pretty sure he'll fight dirty. You have to possess all three kinds of skills to excel in the sport of Mixed Martial Arts."

Charlie avoided mentioning other types of martial arts. Those would be hard to explain in 1802, but he could use the skills he had learned from those varieties if Tarleton would throw even one dirty punch or kick.

Jackson's eyes narrowed as he thought about Charles' words. "Hmm. I see. Now you will need to explain what each of those involve."

"Sure. Let me demonstrate for you a primer on Mixed Martial Arts fighting."

For the next hour, Charlie went over basic moves from each of the three groups with Jackson. By the end of their time, Jackson was throwing strong kicks and punches as Charlie had demonstrated but had not mastered takedowns or forcing submissions.

"This is fun. It is a hard workout, but it is invigorating and quite challenging," gasped Jackson.

"You'll get the hang of it the next time we spar," Charlie encouraged him. "It takes time to become proficient at this. I started learning it when I was about three years old. Let's face it, Jackson: I have almost two decades of experience."

"I can see you are quite experienced. I look forward to decades of learning with you, Lord Ranscome. I hope we can spar again soon. I will locate a place for the fight and will notify both of you when I have it arranged. And I must add that these new skills will render him putty in your hands. He is a decent boxer, but he definitely lacks your reach and strength. However, you must remember to lean back and keep your arm extended for maximum force while punching with bare knuckles."

"We will be going back to Spring Haven Tuesday for a week. Princess Kieu Linh and I are getting married on Christmas Eve. We can return on the 27th."

"Jolly good. Try to squeeze in another round with me before you leave. I might purposefully suggest that Tarleton observe us sparring. Let me urge you to practice slugging a punching bag bare knuckled. You will want to hit strikes with your fists as often as possible. I realize you are accustomed to the other methods, but if you can stick to boxing for this, it will be in your best interests."

Charlie looked surprised. "You really think so?"

Mr. Jackson nodded. "Oh, yes. As I said before, we don't want anyone to think you cheated when you use a different skill than he knows. It's an ungentlemanly thing to do. Since you are accustomed to fighting with gloves, a novel idea, I must admit, you should toughen up those hands a bit. Use the punching bag daily for an hour. You might also soak your hands in vinegar."

"Those are both great ideas, but believe me, Tarleton can fight dirty. I expect he will fight dirty. I would be surprised if he stuck to the rules. Thank you, Mr. Jackson."

Jackson smiled. "Yes, I know his reputation. Rest assured if he begins his shenanigans, you can go at him with the full fury of your Mixed Martial Arts. Do bring your gloves to our sparring matches. I may want to encourage the men to begin wearing them."

"I can bring a spare pair for you to wear, sir."

Jackson nodded. "Excellent, milord. I must say, I really want to learn this new sport of yours. And be sure to send a messenger to me when you return. I will try to schedule the fight for some time that week."

Charles laughed. "My soon-to-be-wife's birthday is on New Year's Eve. She might prefer the fight not occur on her birthday."

Jackson laughed. "Right-o. Then I will see if I can schedule it for the first or second week in January, if that is better. Timing always depends upon where I can locate an appropriate spot for the fight. Plus, by setting it then, we can spar some more when you return to London. You must be in tiptop form before this fight, you know."

"That sounds wonderful. I promise to spar at home with my uncles until we return. Thank you again, Mr. Jackson."

Charlie was humming the tune to an old Kung Fu song when he came back into the townhouse. Kelly looked up from her book and smiled as Aunt Sassy groaned and covered her ears.

"Did you get everything worked out okay?" Kelly asked as he bent to kiss her.

"Perfectly. Aunt Sassy, does my singing offend you?"

Aunt Sassy shook her head. "Of course, not Charles. Hmph. And they say my singing is bad."

Kelly laughed. "It's okay, Aunt Sassy. I'll sing it at the fight."

Aunt Sassy looked horrified. "Kelly, darling, women don't attend fights or duels. This is both. You can't be there. Besides, they don't do music at duels. It's considered poor form."

Kelly laughed, her eyes sparkling with mischief. "You wanna bet? Watch me."

She stood up and began singing the song as Charles acted it out.

Aunt Sassy shook her head. "Charles, dear, you will never beat him like that. Maybe you should simply sing, and your voice would run him off."

Charlie laughed and walked over to hug her. "Don't worry, Aunt Sass. I've got this one."

Aunt Sassy frowned at her nephew. "Charles, don't be a fool. William, I think you need to go over the rules of dueling with Charles."

Uncle Will nodded. It appeared he struggled not to laugh. "I believe you are correct, Little Bit. I will be sure to do that well before the fight."

Charlie had a second sparring session with Gentleman John the following morning. Jackson worked with him on rapid handwork. He left Gentleman John several copies of the rules for Mixed Martial Arts fights which he had written out for Gentleman John before he left the gym.

"Jolly good, your Grace. Would you mind if I gave a copy of these rules to Lord Tarleton?"

Charles laughed. "No, I thought you might do that. Let me know how he reacts."

"Indeed, I shall, and heartiest congratulations on your forthcoming nuptials, your Grace."

The two families left to return to Spring Haven the next morning. Once back at Spring Haven, Charlie began daily sparring sessions with Uncle Will and Fitz. Charlie soon realized Uncle Will was pretty tough for an old guy, and suspected Uncle Will had engaged in cage fighting in the past. Fitz was tough as nails in the boxing ring, also.

Charlie also began slugging the punching bag hung in the stables with a renewed ferocity. He hung up a striking bag he brought from home and began working on improving the speed of his rapid strikes. Charlie intended to make sure his hands would be tough enough and his strikes fast enough for bare knuckle fighting when he took on Tarleton.

Kelly stood by with a stopwatch to time his number of strikes per minute as he improved. She also sparred some with him "to stay in shape," even though she had trained in martial arts since she was a toddler.

Chapter 22
The Wedding
Kelly
1802

"I swear this must be the prettiest wedding I ever saw," sniffled Aunt Sassy.

Uncle Will laughed. "I disagree, my love. I think our wedding was the prettiest. As I recall, it was attended by both Pres. Washington and Pres. Jefferson. And while she is a lovely bride, I believe you were prettier."

She laughed. "You always were a sweet-talking devil, Will Selk. We married years before either gentleman was President, even though they both attended it. And yes, ours was a very pretty wedding."

It was a cold morning, and snow began to fall just before sunrise. As the parishioners entered the church for the wedding, the grounds were covered in white. People hurried inside, clapping their hands together to warm up before taking seats in the beautiful little church which had been decorated with hot house orchids, holly greenery and holly berries. Large red bows decorated the ends of each pew. Braziers were set about to warm the church, but most people kept their coats on due to the cold. Some parishioners draped quilts over the laps of their families for extra warmth as they settled onto the pews. As people settled into their seats, Will and Fitz slipped into the sacristy to join Rev. Tilton and Charles for a prayer. Afterwards, Uncle Will slipped away as the minister, Charles and Fitz walked to the front of the church while the organist began playing Pachelbel's Canon in D. Aunt Sassy hugged and kissed Kelly. Aunt Sassy would go sit with Uncle Will at the front of the church.

Anne squeezed Kelly's hand, and then started down the aisle ahead of Kelly. Kelly had learned young girls were usually bridesmaids in England, but she didn't know any little girls. She asked her friend, just as she would have done back home. Anne seemed surprised but pleased to be asked to serve as her bridesmaid.

Kelly took a big breath to help calm herself before she started down the aisle. As a girl, she always imagined her father would be holding her arm as she made a walk like this, but Daddy was far away. Uncle Will offered to walk her down the aisle, but she had come this far on her own. She was on her own now, for better or worse. As the organist continued to play, the congregation let out a collective gasp as she walked forward, her head held high, wearing the wedding gown and overcoat her mother sewed and embroidered for her.

Aunt Sassy had marveled at the exquisite work on the *Ao Nhat Binh* wedding gown and matching coat. Both were crafted of red silk, lavishly embroidered with golden phoenixes. Thousands of gold beads accented the embroidery, and more embroidery, beadwork and gold lace trimmed long trains on both the gown and coat. The long gown and matching coat were both made with long, full sleeves. Aunt Sassy insisted on lining the overcoat with red wool flannel for warmth. The wedding gown had a high mandarin collar. The overcoat was cut lower in a 'v' to show off the neckline of the gown while still covering the phoenixes on the gown beneath the coat. She was glad both had long sleeves for the warmth. The long sleeves also covered up the bruises on her arms from sparring with Charlie. The *Ao Nhat Binh* covered wide cut matching red trousers, also lined in flannel for warmth. With the wide-cut pants, it appeared that Kelly wore a long gown over a matching red petticoat, more in the style of the West.

Kelly also wore a beautiful Vietnamese-styled, red bridal *khan dong* headpiece decorated with fresh orchids which matched those in her bouquet. Aunt Sassy wanted Kelly to don the Ranscome coronet again for the wedding, but Kelly insisted she would wear the headpiece Fancy Winslow made to coordinate with her wedding ensemble which her mother had made. It was a royal pain to get it to Britain without crushing it. Kelly knew it would be special to wear something both of their mothers made for her wedding. She wore red embroidered slippers from Floris on her feet. The slippers were just barely warm enough with wool stockings covered with silk ones. She could still feel the cold seeping through the thin soles of the shoes. The cream-colored silk stockings were embroidered with a gold phoenix on the ankle of each leg.

Kelly thought it would be one of the last times she would wear Vietnamese-styled clothing, although Charles insisted that he wanted a painting of them dressed in their wedding finery. From now on, she was determined: she was a member of the upper crust of Regency England and she would dress accordingly. However, she figured she would continue to wear her Vietnamese-styled pants beneath her dresses, especially in early morning "undress," during the cold English winter and when riding.

Her hair was styled parted in the middle, with sections braided and pulled to the back, where it was coiled high on her crown. The rest of her long hair hung straight down her back like a sheath of black silk. She wore no jewelry other than the white jade earrings her grandmother gave her years ago and which she grabbed as she was leaving the house that last day. She carried a bouquet of orchids also graciously given to her from Lord Hays' hothouse.

The music ended as Kelly joined hands with Charles. Rev. Tilton cleared his throat. "I believe that most of you know that Princess Kieu Linh is from Vietnam. She tells me that her mother made this incredible ensemble for her to wear at her wedding. It is the traditional garb of a Vietnamese noblewoman of the Nguyen Lords to wear at her nuptials. By the way, they tell me that the color, red, symbolizes good luck for the bride. Princess Kieu Linh also tells me the Vietnamese believe it unlucky for a bride to marry in her twenty-second year. Princess Kieu Linh will turn twenty-two on December 31st, and the young couple wanted to avoid any potentially bad luck by marrying during that year. Consequently, we are having their nuptials today, as we also celebrate the birth of our Savior."

The congregation murmured approval.

Rev. Tilton smiled and continued. "I believe the young couple have some things they wish to say to each other before they exchange their vows."

Charlie smiled at Kelly. He took a deep breath. "You look absolutely beautiful. It's amazing that a man like me is marrying such a beautiful, intelligent, thoughtful and loving person like you. I thank God every day that he brought you into my life, and that your family relented and allowed you come join me in Great Britain. You have renewed and strengthened my belief in God. I believe wholeheartedly that God created me for you, and you for me. You know, I did not know there were words to the Canon in D until Rev.

Tilton showed them to me. The words say what I feel. 'You are my life, my best chance to live free. You are my eyes when I watch the sun setting over the sea. You are my lungs when the cool breeze blows softly to me. You are my ears when I listen to the Canon in D.'"

The congregation sighed as Charlie paused to catch his breath. He looked surprised as Kelly felt her eyes fill with moisture. He smiled and squeezed Kelly's hand before he continued. "I touch your hands and I grow strong. I look down at your lovely face and I hold the world in your embrace."

Kelly blinked back the tears threatening to fall. *He's paraphrasing the words to Younger Than Springtime,* she thought. *The song about an American man in love with a Vietnamese girl.*

Charles took a deep breath and began speaking again. "Kelly, we met on a blue moon. I knew then that you were something special. Just as blue moons are rare, and only occur on the second full moon of a month, so is finding a love like we share. It is unusual for a Duke from Great Britain and a Princess from Vietnam to fall in love in Nuevo Espana of all places, and yet somehow, the Good Lord had a plan. He let us meet there and fall in love. You are my 'once in a blue moon' love, Princess Nguyen Kieu Linh, and I thank God he brought you to me."

Kelly beamed at Charles. As she blinked back tears of joy, she responded. "Oh, Charles, my love, the Canon in D is my favorite song, and now you realize why I love it so much. 'My happiness you were, you are, and always will be. When you laugh, when you sing, when you cry and when you dream, when you are near or when you are far, you always will be, always were, and always are, *mi Cario,* my soul mate.'"

She paused to collect herself lest she begin to cry. "Give me just a moment. No one shall ever say I shed tears on my wedding day, other than tears of joy, but I would prefer not to shed any tears at all until after the ceremony. The first time I saw you, I knew that there was something different about you, Charles Ranscome Hobbs. Something special in your love for animals, your desire to ensure all animals have loving, caring homes. You have this fire inside you that is always burning. You motivate me. You inspire me. I admire your tenacity, your enthusiasm, your athleticism, and your competitiveness. I love your desire to seek the most out of life. I love that you give far more than you take. With you, I feel like I am living with my arms stretched wide open, embracing the world every minute, whether we are running errands or riding across the moors, or reaching for the sky on the tallest mountains. With you, I can do anything. How could I not have convinced my parents to let me follow you to Great Britain? How could I not have come? This is my destiny. You are my destiny. 'My sweetest sweet, my dearest dear, my only trust and hope after God. You are always my freedom from my fears. So deep and long my love for you, so strong and lasting, so real and true.' Yes, you and I met on that blue moon long ago. Just as blue moons are rare, so is love like ours rare. You are my 'once in a blue moon' love. I was willing to go to the ends of the earth to claim you as my own. I thank God he brought you to me. But after today, I am Princess Nguyen Kieu Linh no more; now I am Lady Kelly Hobbs, your Duchess."

"Oh, the dear girl! What a wonderful young lady our Duke has chosen!" gasped one elderly spinster on the front row, who began to cry into her handkerchief. The other women nodded in agreement as they sniffed into their hankies, as they struggled not to shed tears of their own.

Rev. Tilton then proceeded with the standard wedding service from the Book of Common Prayer. As they completed exchanging their vows, Charles slipped the jade and diamond ring on Kelly's ring finger which his father gave his mother years earlier in a little Anglican church overlooking the Atlantic Ocean in Bermuda.

Rev. Tilton then intoned, "I now pronounce you man and wife. Your Grace, you may kiss your bride."

Charles beamed down at his new bride and after the slightest hesitation, dipped his head to claim her lips with his own. The congregation sighed as they kissed. As their kiss ended, both beamed at the congregation before they hurried out of the church towards the parish hall as the organist pounded out the recessional.

Everyone followed them into the parish hall for the reception. Aunt Sassy and Anne had outdone themselves decorating the parish hall in addition to the church early that morning with holly and orchids. Breakfast was waiting to be served to the parishioners, who eagerly accepted plates of the poached eggs, biscuits, slices of ham, and slices of bacon. Pots of hot chocolate and hot tea were both available.

Before everyone began eating, Fitz tapped a knife on a crystal wine glass. "I have been asked to say a few words."

Charles groaned. "Oh, no! What will he say?"

Kelly smiled. "Don't worry, darling. Your Uncle Fitz loves you. I'm sure his toast will be lovely."

Fitz smiled over at Kelly and winked. "I have been asked to say something to the young couple today. As you know, I am Lord Ranscome's uncle. I was present when Lady Kelly arrived. It is clear from the moment she arrived that they are very much in love. I know they will always appreciate how much Aunt Sassy went through to bring Lady Kelly here from America. Charles, I am delighted you have returned to assume your duties to the Crown and to your estates. Let me assure you all that he made my life easier by his return. Charles, I have seen you in Ireland and here, and I am impressed with your dealings with the animals, the land, and the people who work your lands. I am quite sure you will not only be a wonderful husband and father, but you will be a marvelous lord overseeing your lands, and an asset in the House of Lords."

Parishioners clapped, encouraged by his words.

Fitz smiled. "Lady Kelly, I was quite surprised when you first arrived. It amazed me that a beautiful young lady such as you would have undertaken such a perilous adventure, even for love. Your arrival has been such a blessing to all of us. I am so glad you came into my nephew's life. You have brought him so much happiness, so much joy. I thought I had seen a well-rounded young man before your arrival. I was wrong. I saw half a man before. Now, he is whole. You complete him. You held the other half of his soul. As Aunt Sassy says, you are his twin flame." He turned to the parishioners gathered in the hall and raised his tea cup. "And now, I say let us lift our cups in a toast to this charming young couple. Long may they live in joy and happiness!"

The parishioners raised their cups and joined in the cheer. "Here, here!"

Charlie bent to kiss Kelly's cheek. "At least he didn't wish us a dozen children."

She grinned as she stroked Charlie's smooth-shaven skin. "Thank God! But hopefully, our years of joy and happiness will include healthy, happy children."

As the plates were cleared, a large wedding cake was brought out. Charlie and Kelly giggled. Neither had ever seen a wedding cake made of fruitcake and dusted with powdered sugar before, but the housekeeper assured them this was a typical wedding cake. Charlie and Kelly cut the cake and began serving slices to the waiting crowd. Later, the parishioners followed Charlie and Kelly outside to pelt them with bird seed and laughter as they entered the Ranscome carriage to leave.

As the carriage pulled away, Anne began to cry. Fitz pulls Anne into his arms. "Don't cry, darling. Please don't cry."

Anne struggled not to cry and smiled up at Fitz. "They are not tears of sadness. 'You are my once in a blue moon love,' she said. 'I was willing to follow you to the ends of the earth to claim you as my own.' Don't you understand, Fitz? Beyond all hopes and more than any girlish dreams I now believe in fate. You are *my* destiny. You're *my* 'once in a blue moon' love. I never would have followed Charles to the ends of the earth. I care about Charles, but not like that. But you? That is an entirely different matter."

Fitz pulled her close to his heart. "Oh, my darling, I never dreamed I could love like this again. When do you want to have our wedding?"

Anne smiled. "Just say when, Winston Fitz Simmons. Tomorrow, next week, next month, whenever you want. When I was younger, I memorized the Book of Ruth. My father has often said how much Mother was like Ruth. Her name was Ruth, you know. In it, Ruth says, 'Whither thou goest, my love, I will go. Whither thou lodgest, I will lodge. Thy people shall be my people, and thy God, my God.' I would never have followed Charles to the ends of the world. Obviously, Kelly would. However, I would follow you wherever you want to go. Ireland, Canada, wherever, Fitz. Whither thou goest, I will go. You are my destiny, just as Charles is Kelly's destiny. You are my once in a lifetime love, Winston Fitz Simmons, just as Charles is Kelly's."

"Oh, my darling... propriety be damned." Fitz kissed her as the Ranscome carriage passed from sight. "Oh, my heavens, I better talk to your father about a date we might wed."

Anne laughed. "I already told you, darling. Whenever you want. Do you want your mother and your daughter to be able to come here?"

Fitz grimaced. He laughed, but his laugh sounded forced and hollow. "Would you mind if my Mother came? She can be very difficult, but I know she would love to attend. Lord knows you are everything she could have hoped for me to find in a wife and stepmother for Nicole. It would be the easiest way, if she could bring Nicole. I would like you to meet Nicole before the wedding, and for her to attend our wedding."

"Didn't you hear me, Fitz? Whatever you want, milord. Perhaps we should write to your mother. However, if she is going to come from Ireland with Nicole, we might want to plan a spring wedding, once the weather is a bit nicer. Crossing the Irish Sea can be a bit unsettling in the winter. And I agree. Nicole should have the opportunity to meet me before our wedding. Perhaps she can be my bridesmaid."

Fitz beamed at her. "What a wonderful idea. I think Nicole would like that."

"Come on, Henry, it's time we leave," said Uncle Will.

Henry Hays nodded. "I think you're right, William. Now, as we planned earlier, let's all retire to Meadow Glen. Give the newlyweds the rest of the day and the night alone. Fitz, did you bring your things?"

Fitz nodded. "Yes, Lord Henry. We all did."

Henry Hays smiled. "Then let's depart. We will see them tomorrow for Christmas dinner. And you two lovebirds try to contain yourselves. There will be other people in the carriage."

Uncle Will, Aunt Sassy and Lord Henry laughed as Fitz and Anne blushed with embarrassment, but Fitz hugged her close again.

"I think she should sit by me." Aunt Sass flashed a sly grin.

"Oh, no, let them sit together. We might even bundle them together tonight," replied Lord Henry with a wink at Fitz.

Fitz and Anne both blushed deeper red as the older adults continued to laugh.

Chapter 23
Kelly
Their Wedding Night

Charles and Kelly kissed all the way back to Spring Haven. They caressed each other as they continued kissing while they walked up to the manor house. Kelly giggled as Charles swung her up into his arms at the door. "After all, I have to carry my bride across the threshold."

Scottie stuck his head out of the kitchen door when he heard the disturbance, and grinned when he saw the young lovers struggling in the door as they continued to kiss. Scottie chuckled and slipped back into the kitchen.

Finally, Charles swung Kelly down long enough to shrug out of his overcoat, and to toss his hat and gloves on top of the heavy winter coat.

Kelly slipped out of her heavy Kinsale cloak and tossed it into the pile as well. She turned around and began to tug her fur-lined gloves off her hands. "She slowly slipped her mask down and removed her gloves…"

She arched her brows at him suggestively.

Charles laughed as he swung Kelly up into his arms again to make traversing the stairs simpler. "Where did you get that line?"

After her initial shocked shriek, she began giggling again, wrapped her arms around Charles' neck, and snuggled close to him as he mounted the stairs. "It was in some romance novel that came out during Covid19."

"You crack me up, Mrs. Winslow."

She shook her head as she grinned. "I think the proper title is Lady Hobbs, milord."

He laughed so hard he had to stop to make sure he didn't drop her. "I think you are correct, Lady Hobbs."

He stopped climbing the stairs and bent over to kiss her again.

Once they entered the master suite, he sat her feet on the floor. They fell upon each other as if they were starving.

"I love you so much." Kelly stroked his face.

"I love you more." He pulled her close for another kiss.

She pushed back and shook her head. "That might be debatable after all I went through to get here to be with you."

She kissed him again savagely, as if she were afraid that he might escape her grasp if she did not cling tightly to him.

Kelly knew she was starved for Charles' touch. It had been far too long since they were last intimate together. Before her father found the picture Bella took of them at the beach in Galveston, she slipped away from her college in Waco to drive over to College Station twice a month to see him. The photo pictured them lying in the surf, her back to Charlie's broad, well-muscled, and tanned chest, as she tilted her head up to meet his kiss. Bella wanted to snap the picture of them in the embrace posed like that because they looked so much like a photo she had seen of France Nguyen and Lawrence Harvey from an old movie. Bella snapped the picture one afternoon as the waves gently crashed over their bodies, catching the seductive pose of the two young lovers. They were both clothed in swim wear, but Kelly admitted their swimsuits were not what you noticed about the photo. You noticed Charles' hand reaching across her bosom to hold her about where she figured her heart was in her body, his hip lying atop her own. You noticed her eyes closed in passion, her lips swollen from kisses, and their lips about to touch again.

It was Kelly's favorite picture of them, and she cherished it before her father found it and destroyed the photo in a fit of anger. Her dad would never know that Bella mailed her another copy of the picture while she was in Georgia, before she came to find Charlie. Her father would never know they were intimate before marriage, although he suspected that Charles and she spent that Labor Day weekend together, making love. He also would never know Labor Day was not the first weekend they spent together in each other's arms.

She hoped Charlie would never know her father beat her when he found the photo. After Dad's initial storm of rage, he grabbed a thick, leather belt and lashed her repeatedly across her back and shoulders. When her mother realized Kelly's skin was broken and bleeding, she begged her husband to stop. He finally stopped when he, too, realized the skin on Kelly's back was broken and bled where the metal prong of the buckle gouged cuts into her back. He threw the belt across the room as he yelled obscenities at Kelly before he stormed out of her room.

Kelly lay on her bedroom floor sobbing for hours from the horror and loss of the man she loved more than from the painful beating, for it was that night her father told her she would marry a Vietnamese man and she would never marry Charles. That hurt worse than any blow from a belt could cut. "You will never be alone with that damned man again!"

Her mother convinced her dad to go to the Winslow's for Thanksgiving dinner because it would give everyone a chance to settle on last minute plans for Bella's forthcoming wedding. If both their mothers had not insisted, the Nguyen family would not have joined the Vargas family at the Winslow's for Thanksgiving dinner. Kelly had not seen Charles since Labor Day, although he still called her every evening and wrote to her often at her college dorm. She told him her college classes that semester were too hard and she needed to stay at her university to study. He offered to come there, as he had done in the past, but she couldn't bear to face him and tell him about the incident with her father. It was too humiliating. *I should have told him Dad found the picture, and what happened,* she thought. *I just couldn't bear to tell him.*

I couldn't bear to let him see my back. I was afraid if he saw it, he would confront Dad.

No, I have to be honest with myself. I knew he would confront Dad.

She had no choice in the matter when Charlie proposed at Thanksgiving. If he had asked her any other time, she could have explained what happened. They could have eloped. But with her father glowering at her at Thanksgiving, and with her mother's look of terror, she knew she had to tell Charles that her father expected her to marry a Vietnamese man. She could not explain that her dad found the picture or his fury over his mere suspicion that his daughter had engaged in sexual intimacies with Charles. It broke her heart to utter those words to the man she loved, to tell him that she could not marry him, but she feared her father would become so enraged he might otherwise beat her right there at the Winslow house. She wanted to explain all that to him after Bella's wedding, but Charles was desperate to leave and would not wait to talk.

When she was growing up, sexual activity among teens was the norm, yet Charles had been her only lover. He was the only boy she ever desired. She would always believe she had been his one and only. Once they met that Saturday at the shelter, they had little time for anyone else in their lives.

At first, her father wholeheartedly approved of her working at the shelter. But as she spoke less about the animals and more about Charles, her father voiced concern about their relationship. Kelly told him numerous times that 'Charlie was just a friend.' Dad frowned when they went to proms together, but bit back angry words as Kelly's mother would speak to him in soothing terms in their native language.

Kelly forced the unwelcome thoughts of her father from her mind as Charles began carefully helping her undress from her formal wedding attire. She sighed as he rained kisses from her lips down to her belly after he slipped the gown over her head and carefully laid it over a chair. He untied her garters, eased her stockings down her legs. She giggled as he tickled her toes.

"This is silly. I could have undressed myself," she protested as she continued to giggle.

He shook his head. "Nope. You get to undress me next. But first, I get to undress you and adore your beautiful body."

Her eyes widened in surprise. "Ooh, really? Well then, continue your adoration, my love."

He stood behind her as he gently lifted the fine lawn shift over her head, and then stopped with a sharp intake of breath. Kelly began to tremble as Charles traced the faint scars from the beating her father inflicted on her after their Labor Day trip.

"Jesus Christ, this is why you never came back to College Station after Labor Day," he whispered. "The sorry bastard beat you."

She twisted around and caught his face between her hands. "He found the photo Bella took. He was pretty upset. He lost his temper. 'Baggage' might have been the nicest thing he called me that night. I think that is why it upset me so much when your Grandmama called me 'baggage.'"

"She called you what?" Charlie looked horrified.

She nodded. "Baggage. I admit Dad beat me worse that time than he ever beat me before. But darling, like Gramma Lily would say, it was long, long time long ago in a galaxy far, far away. It's over. He can never hurt us again. I'm here now. I'm your wife. Kiss me."

He hesitated for a moment, and then he pulled her to him with an unexpected fierceness as he began to kiss her again. "Oh, my god, Kelly, I almost lost you."

She trembled at his touch as his hands roved lovingly over her body. "But you didn't. Now it's my turn. Let me undress you."

She slid his cutaway dress coat off and tossed it to the chair holding her wedding gown and the beautifully embroidered coat. With a teasing smile, she unbuttoned his waist coat and slipped it from his arms before she untied his cravat from the intricate knot and tossed both aside. With a flirtatious grin, she unbuttoned his cuffs and the button at the neck of his shirt before she pulled his shirt over his head. She grinned up at him and then swept her tongue down his taut belly. "Yep. You still look good enough to eat."

She bent to unfasten his pants. "Gosh, there's a lot of buttons and hooks."

She finally got the pants unfastened and slid the trousers and underpants off. She then knelt to pull his Hessians off. She giggled as she fell backwards when the first boot slid off. She grinned and threw her hair back from her face. She pulled the second boot off and then slowly slid his stockings and garters off his legs. "It's amusing to me that they call men's knee high socks 'stockings' and their underpants 'pantaloons'."

He grinned. "Yeah, they call them pantaloons. They look pretty much like boxers to me."

Finally, Kelly lowered herself to engulf his member in her mouth.

Charles groaned. In his wildest dreams, he never imagined she would take the lead tonight and start like this. He should have remembered she often began their lovemaking this way. He shuddered as he lay back against the pillows. He wound his fingers into her beautiful, long hair as she loved his organ with her tongue. Finally, he pushed her back, rolled over on top of her, and plunged deep inside her tight sheath.

It had been sixteen months since they were last intimate together. Charles purposefully stayed away from Kelly's room after she arrived at Spring Haven to avoid any negative talk among the staff about her. He knew the servants talked between houses and he did not want any negative comments about the woman he would marry and who would become his Duchess. There had already been some talk that she followed him here from New Spain, even though she came with Aunt Sassy and an Abigail. Thank God he would not be forced to stay away from her again.

Within minutes, the young couple shuddered together as they reached their first orgasms. They snuggled close together, whispering words of love to one another before Charles began kissing Kelly again.

She grinned. "You ready again? So soon?"

"Oh, most definitely." He bent to suckle her nipple, causing her to gasp.

They took longer the second time. Touching, caressing, tasting, until their passions fully were stoked so they could ride together to another wave of thunderous orgasms.

This is what I needed. This is where I longed to be, with the man I love, to be back in his arms. This makes the whole interminable trip worthwhile. My Charles. Forever mine.

Finally, Charles fell asleep nestled against the woman he loved, with her long hair still entwined between his fingers.

Kelly smiled as her hand smoothed his unruly curls. *How did I get so lucky? How did I ever manage to marry the man I love so much?*

Oh, yes. I claimed him as mine. I wouldn't back down. I didn't cower in fear this time. I didn't let Dad keep me from Charles. I didn't let him force me to marry Johnny Tran. When Charles had already left, I didn't slink home like a whipped dog. I stayed the course. I stuck it out through some damned tough times. Because life with this wonderful man is my destiny.

She fell asleep smiling, her fingers entwined with his.

Chapter 24
Christmas
Charlie
1802

"Wake up, Sleeping Beauty! It's time to rise and shine."

Kelly whimpered and tried to pull the quilt over her head. "Five more minutes."

Charlie laughed as he began to tickle her. "No more 'five minutes,' Lady Hobbs. You have already had an hour worth of 'five more minutes.' We need to get moving or we won't get to the Hays house in time for luncheon."

Kelly pouted and slapped Charles's hands away from tickling her and pulled the quilt over her head. "You know I hate to be tickled."

Charles pulled the quilt away from her face and trailed kisses to her lips. "Better?"

She sighed and pulled him to her for a deep, lingering kiss. "Much. Do we have time?"

He moaned. "For you, Lady Hobbs? Always."

She giggled as she pulled him back down to her in the bed.

A half hour later, Kelly felt warm and Christmas-y in her red and green tartan gown with a sheer woolen camisette at her neckline. She laughed to see Charles wore a red and green matching waistcoat beneath his black coat and overcoat.

"Well, don't you look dashing." She began re-tying the knot on his stiffly starched white cravat.

He winced. "I hate tying those blasted things. Thank you."

She finished the elaborate knot and grinned at him. "The blasted thing? My heavens, my lord, you are beginning to sound British."

"Enough of that talk, wench, or I'll show you 'British.'" Charles wrapped her Kinsale cloak around her as they hurried through the snow to the carriage. They arrived shortly before time for Christmas dinner. They both laughed at the good-natured teasing about their wedding night.

Anne grew red-faced with embarrassment. "Will they tease us like this the day after we marry, Fitz?"

Fitz chuckled and caressed her hand. "Probably, my love, unless we leave right away to go on a honeymoon. Just do like Kelly is doing. Laugh and ignore it. People will tire quickly enough when you do not respond."

Anne shook her head, appalled by the ribald jokes.

The Hays' housekeeper, Elizabeth, announced dinner was ready to be served, and everyone seated themselves around the large dining table. "There is a pot of tea and there are bottles of port available on the side table."

Moments later, they all inhaled rapturously as she brought in the roasted duckling and sat it in the middle of the table. As Lord Hays prepared to carve the bird, Elizabeth brought in an assortment of other dishes and artistically placed them around the table and on the sideboard.

After dinner, the guests all enjoyed an assortment of Christmas candies and pies. The men then retired to Lord Hays' library for cigars and port and the ladies retired to Anne's rooms to ogle her Christmas presents from her father and from Fitz.

"Oh, Anne, this is beautiful! Wherever did he find this?" asked Kelly as she fingered a pearl necklace with a mother of pearl cameo clasp. "I would wear it with the cameo showing."

Anne nodded. "I quite agree. I understand that cameos will be quite the thing this next year. I mentioned that at dinner one night with Fitz, and the darling man went out the next day and bought this for my Christmas present. What did Charles give you?"

Kelly held up her wrist. "They must have gone shopping together. He gave me this bracelet, with four cameos around the wrist. I understand that they can come apart and the cameos can be attached to a ribbon around my waist on my gowns. I think it is quite lovely."

"Ooh, in Wedgwood blue. Quite lovely!" cooed Anne. "You will need a muslin gown with a blue sash for the spring so you can put the cameos on the sash."

"My idea exactly. I thought I could wear it to your wedding," said Kelly.

"You girls are not the only ones who received cameos. Uncle Will gave me this beautiful brooch. I think I may wear it on a ribbon around my neck or attached to my sash." Aunt Sassy held up the beautiful cameo brooch Uncle Will gave her that morning.

"We will look like the cameo sisters!' exclaimed Kelly.

Shortly after, Charles, Kelly, Sassy and Will returned to Spring Haven. After they got settled in, they exchanged their gifts. Charles and Kelly were thrilled with the new bed linens Sassy and Will bought them. Sassy and Will seemed thrilled with the silver tray Charles and Kelly gave them. They then began opening packages from Charles' family. Sassy seemed thrilled to receive copies of Fancy's books, and disposable cameras with which she could take pictures to send back to Fancy. Will appeared thrilled with models of steam engines and instructions how to build them.

Finally, Charles opened a package from Elizabeth. He began laughing hysterically.

"Oh my god, I can't believe she sent this."

"What is it?" asked Aunt Sassy.

"Well, it's a family joke. You see, I used to hang a pair of panty hose over a hook on the fireplace at Christmas. I said all I wanted was for Santa to fill the pantyhose. What they say about Santa checking the list twice must be true because every Christmas morning, although all the rest of our stockings were overflowed, my poor pantyhose hung sadly empty."

Will frowned. "What are pantyhose?"

Charles chuckled. "Pantyhose are stockings that pull on like panties, and are attached to panties."

Will nodded. "And... what are panties?"

Charles turned red and began muttering. "Uh... well... you see..."

Sassy laughed. "Pantalettes, darling."

Will's cheeks reddened, too. "Oh. I see. Unmentionables. Please continue, Charles."

"Well, a couple of years ago, Liz decided to cook my goose, as that old saying goes. She got Kirk to go with her. They put on sunglasses, and went in search of an inflatable love doll. They don't sell those things at Wal-Mart. I understand they had to go to an adult bookstore in downtown Atlanta."

Will frowned again, looking stressed. "Okay, I'll bite. What is an adult bookstore?"

All the others laughed. Charles, again red-faced with embarrassment, explained. "It is a place where they sell books and other things that adult men enjoy using to pleasure themselves."

Will turned beet red but said nothing in reply.

Charles choked back his laughter to continue his story. "Kirk took her, and I heard she was there an hour saying things like, 'What does this do? You're kidding me! Who would buy that?' I would bet you Kirk was pretty embarrassed by then, too."

"You reckon?" asked Uncle Will with a wry smile.

Charles struggled to bite back his laughter. "Finally, Liz told the clerk that she wanted to buy me a standard, uncomplicated inflatable love doll. One that could also substitute as a passenger in my truck so I could use the carpool lane during rush hour. Love dolls come in many different models. Liz said the top-of-the-line model could do things she would bet that I had only seen in a textbook on animal husbandry."

Charles noticed Uncle Will looked a bit green around the gills but continued his story.

"Do I dare ask for additional clarification of 'what exactly is this love doll' thing?"

"Uh... like I said before, it's a life-sized doll used to help a man pleasure himself."

Uncle Will looked horrified. "Good lord, why do I keep asking him that question? All he says is 'it's used to help a man pleasure himself. I reckon I should have asked 'what is a truck.'"

Charlie nodded as he bit back laughter. "A truck is a vehicle we use for transportation, like a wagon with a motor. It has a back section that is open and in which you can haul stuff. Mine had a trailer hitch so I could haul horses in a horse trailer with it. Anyway, to get back to the story, Liz settled for a model called 'Lovable Louise.' It was at the bottom of the price scale. Liz was in college and wanted to purchase the cheapest model. On Christmas Eve, with the help of an old bicycle pump, Louise came to life. Bella was in on the plan and stood guard as Liz filled the dangling pantyhose with Louise's pliant legs and bottom. They told me later that they went to bed giggling about the prank. The next morning, it stunned me, but I must admit I was rather thrilled. Santa left a present in my stocking that amazed me, but left poor little Chico confused. The poor dog would bark, start to walk away, then come back, growl at the doll and bark some more."

Aunt Sassy and Kelly were laughing so hard they fell together. Will looked increasingly puzzled. "Uh... okay, why was the dog barking at it?"

Kelly and Sassy burst into peals of laughter. Aunt Sassy finally answered for Charlie. "Darling, it's a life-sized doll. The dog probably wondered why it was in a pair of panty hose stuck on the mantle."

Charles struggled not to laugh. "We all agreed that Louise should remain in her panty hose so the rest of the family could admire her throughout our traditional Christmas dinner. Mom insisted that Liz put some clothes on Louise, so my sister fetched a scanty camisole and slipped it over Louise's head. Mom had a good friend who was quite a bit older than Mom. Mom invited Mrs. Olson to Christmas dinner. Mrs. Olson noticed Louise the moment she walked in the door. She said, 'What on earth is that?'

"I explained, 'It's a doll.'"

"'Who would play with something like that?' I swear, Mrs. Olson spat those words out."

"Well, I had several candidates in mind, but I kept my mouth shut. Anyway, Mrs. Olson frowned. 'Where are her clothes?'"

Uncle Will looked ready to explode. "You mean the dad blasted thing was naked?"

Charlie nodded. "She nearly was. All she had on was this scanty camisole top and the panty hose. I said, 'Boy, that turkey sure smells nice, Mom,' and I tried to steer Mrs. Olson into the dining room. But that old gal was relentless. 'Why doesn't she have any teeth?'"

Uncle Will hung his head in his hands and shook his head. "Oh, for the love of... My lord, I don't know what this world is coming to."

Aunt Sassy and Kelly burst into peals of laughter. Charlie tried to stifle his laughter. "Again, I could have answered, but why would I? It was Christmas and no one wanted to ride in the back of the ambulance saying, 'Hang on, Mrs. Olson! Hang on!'"

"But you'll tell this vile story to me? In front of your bride and your Aunt Sassy, on Christmas Day?" asked Uncle Will. "That is just plain rude, Charles."

Aunt Sassy wiped tears of laughter from her face. "Oh, hush up, Will. I want to hear the rest of the story."

Uncle Will shook his head in disgust, but he remained silent.

"Mr. Withers was a delightful old man with poor eyesight who accompanied Mrs. Olson that Christmas. He was about 5'2", bald as an egg, and starting to go deaf. Mr. Withers sidled up to me and said, 'Hey, son, who is the scantily clad gal over by the fireplace?'"

"I told him her name was Louise. A few minutes later, I noticed Mr. Withers hobbled over to the mantel, where he began talking to Louise. Not just talking but flirting. It was then that I realized this might be Mr. Withers' only Christmas with us. Senile dementia was affecting him and his awareness of reality in a bad way. Anyway, the dinner was going well with the usual small talk about who had died, who was dying, and who should be killed, you know, classic Christmas chatter, when Louise made a noise that sounded a lot like Dad in the bathroom the first thing in the morning. I guess the correct phrase would be she sounded like she had a bad case of the vapors."

Uncle Will spit his tea. He wiped his chin and glared at Charles.

Aunt Sassy laughed until she cried. "Please, Charles, continue."

"Louise lurched from the panty hose, flew around the room twice, and fell in a heap in front of the sofa. The dog screamed. I passed cranberry sauce through my nose. Mr. Withers ran across the room, fell to his knees, and began trying to administer mouth to mouth resuscitation to poor Louise. Ronan fell backwards in his chair and spilled his tea all over himself. It looked like he had wet his pants. Mrs. Olson threw down her napkin and stomped out of the room. Mom ran after her. Poor Mrs. Olson went outside and sat in the car until Mr. Withers was ready to leave. It was indeed a Christmas to treasure and remember."

Uncle Will looked stunned, and just shook his head. He finally managed to speak. "You people are crazy." He scratched his head. "Wait a minute. Who in the blazes is Ronan?"

"He's our youngest brother, Uncle Will. He was born after Mom married Dr. Winslow."

"Oh, yeah, now I remember." Will looked embarrassed to have forgotten the name of one of Fancy's children.

Charlie bit back a laugh. "Later in the evening, Ronan and I conducted a thorough examination and found the cause of Louise's collapse. We discovered Louise had suffered from a hot ember to the back of her right thigh. Fortunately, thanks to a wonderful product called Gorilla Tape, we restored her to perfect condition."

"I don't even want to know what Gorilla Tape is," muttered Uncle Will with an air of resignation.

Kelly and Aunt Sassy burst into new peals of laughter.

"Mr. Withers is probably heartbroken she's gone," snickered Kelly as she winked at Charlie.

Aunt Sassy then snorted some cranberry sauce through her nose. She laid her head down on her crossed arms and laughed until she cried for the second time.

Poor Uncle Will still looked dumbfounded as he sat there shaking his head. "They are all certifiably crazy. I should look for an asylum for them all. Oh, heck, maybe I'm the one in need of an asylum. After all, I married into this family."

Charlie decided it would not be a good moment to remind Will that his mother was Will's sister. It would be best to simply put Louise away, to be a relic from the far distant future, never to be used again in this era.

Chapter 25
Charles
Late December 1802

The following week, Charles received a response from the Department of Antiquities, expressing great interest in the Roman tiles found in the pasture. "We appreciate that you immediately stopped work on the pasture upon discovering the tiles. Please do not disturb the tile work. A team of archeologists will be coming out shortly to evaluate the tiles and commence excavations."

Charles and Kelly were delighted. They rode out to the pasture to carefully look around for other evidence of old relics and to mark the perimeters for the archeological crew.

"Charles, look at this," Kelly called out as she bent down.

Charles frowned. He bent down beside Kelly and stared at a depression under a tumbled pile of rocks. "What do you think it is?"

She shrugged. "Heck, it beats me. I don't know. Archeology was my major, but I never worked on a Roman dig like this one."

"Well, it looks like it might not just be a hole in the ground. We definitely want to show it to the archeologists when they come out here," Charles said, his brows furrowed together.

Kelly's eyes widened in surprise. "Oh, babe, do you think it might go down to some sort of subterranean room? How exciting!"

"I know they found a subterranean room where Roman soldiers reportedly worshipped Mithras. Archeologists have found some subterranean sepulchers, too. Who knows what it might be? It might be nothing more than a hole down to a rat's nest. We'll let the experts decide. They would probably be horrified if we started digging it up and disturbed an important relic."

Kelly nodded. "I guess you're right. We must be sure to show them this."

Charlie grinned. "Absolutely. Now, do you want to go practice boxing with me?"

Kelly laughed as she leaned over to hug her husband. "Sure, but I think Will or Fitz are better sparring mates for you."

Charlie crossed his arms and shook his head. "I don't know. You're tough as nails, Lady Hobbs."

They rode back to the stables and turned the horses back over to the footman before changing their clothes to return to the stables to begin their practice. At first, Kelly stood by with a stopwatch to time Charlie hitting the punching bag as quickly as possible.

"You're timing is getting better, and your punches look stronger. Keep it up."

Charlie winced. "My hands hurt, your Grace. My knuckles are getting tougher, but I could use a break. Could we please go inside a few minutes? I want something to drink."

Kelly laughed. "Let me see your hands. They may be sore but they are not bleeding. Come on, you big goof. Let's get a drink, rest a few minutes, and then you are back out here, slugging away."

Fifteen minutes later, Charlie returned to the stables with Uncle Will in tow. Will rubbed some horse liniment on Charlie's hands, which stopped the aching.

Charlie blinked in surprise. "Wow, that stuff feels like Ben Gay."

Uncle Will's brow wrinkled as he frowned. "What's that? Or dare I ask?"

Charlie laughed out loud. Uncle Will might never recuperate from the Louise Story on Christmas Day. "It's a liniment people use 'back home' for aches and pains. This feels a lot like it. It really helped, Uncle Will."

Will shrugged. "It's probably about the same thing. Now, let's get down to business and figure out what this thing is."

They sparred a half hour, at the end of which both men were exhausted. They walked into the manor house together, sweaty, bruised, and still talking about their training session.

"How did it go?" Kelly looked up from her needlework and smiled as they entered the parlor.

"Pretty good. This young man of yours wields a mean punch. Tarleton better look out." Uncle Will smirked at the idea of Tarleton beaten to a bloody pulp.

Kelly smiled as she looked back to her embroidery. "Hmph, I could have told you that in the first place. Charles, look what Aunt Sassy taught me how to do. Isn't it beautiful?"

He looked over her shoulder. "It sure is, Kell. Your embroidery is quite lovely. Hmm. Yellow jonquils and blue irises. It makes me think of the ones Mom made at Ranscome Manor, but it has a decidedly Asian flair. What are you making?"

"It's going to be a table runner. I thought I would send it to your mom one of these days with a letter. I know she loves jonquils and blue irises. Aunt Sassy and I thought she would appreciate my spin on the design. At least, I'll send it to her if I ever manage to finish this." She shrugged as she grinned at her husband.

When Fitz came back from Meadow Glen, Charles pulled out the letter from the Department of Antiquities. Everyone bubbled with excitement.

"That's wonderful!" Fitz pounded Charles on the back.

Charles nodded, brimming with excitement. "And today, Kelly and I went back out to the pasture to walk the area again. Kelly, tell them what we found."

Kelly blushed. "Well, we both found it, but it's just a hole beneath some old rocks."

Uncle Will looked stunned. "My god, girl, that could lead down to something amazing."

She shrugged. "Or it could be nothing more than a rat's hole."

Fitz nodded, his own excitement showing. "Oh, I doubt that, Kelly. I quite agree with Uncle Will. Charles, take us back out there and show Uncle Will and me what you discovered."

The three men walked back out to the pasture with Scottie. Charlie quickly showed them the fallen rocks nearly covering the hole.

"It could just be a rat nest." Charles began chewing on his thumbnail.

"Aye, but it could be summat else. I saw a hole like this over near Cirencester once. It led down to a Roman burial site. This could be summat like that, milord." Scottie's excitement rang clear in his voice.

Charles grinned. "I guess just about anything would be better than a rat nest."

Scottie shook his head. "I dinna ken, milord. Badgers are right nasty, too."

The men all laughed. "You got me there, Scottie. Badgers are pretty nasty. Uncle Will, do you think it might be anything beyond a natural hole?"

Uncle Will bent low to examine the opening. "I sure wish we had a light we could shine down there. I reckon a candle wouldn't work. We would probably get burned before we could figure out what is down there, but I swear I see some steps downward."

Fitz bent down to peer into the hole, too. "Hmm. It does look like something might be there, Uncle Will. I wonder if we could see down in it if we had a lantern or a torch?"

"We could try," Uncle Will suggested. "Hmm. We might try a long pipe."

Charles shook his head. "I think we'll wait for the experts. I would hate for us to be tampering with it and damage something."

Will looked at him sharply. "You think we could damage something down there with a lantern? How?"

Charles laughed, suddenly self-conscious. "We might set something on fire, or maybe a rat might run in our faces. Oh, heck, I don't know, Uncle Will. Let's get a lantern and something to make a torch and see if we can discern anything down there."

The men straightened up, dusted the dirt off their hands and clothes, and quickly hurried to find a lantern and something to make a torch before they returned to the site. Will lay flat on the ground holding the lantern as first Charlie and then Fitz peered into the dark hole.

"I can't see a blasted thing." Fitz's disgust dripped from his words.

"Neither can I. Uncle Will, you have a sailor's eye. See what you can make out," urged Charles.

"Well, give me a few minutes. I'll put a patch over one eye, and let my eye adjust to the dark. After a few minutes, I'll remove it and I'll be able to see better in the dark."

Will passed the lantern to Fitz and peered deep into the dark chasm. "Well, I always carry my spyglass with me, just in case I might need it. Hmm. I think I can see something, but I can't quite make out what it is."

"Let's try the torch." Charles urged Uncle Will as his heart pounded wildly in his chest.

Fitz lit the torch and handed it to Charles. Charles carefully extended the torch into the hole.

Uncle Will bent back down and flipped the patch off from the shielded eye to peer inside with his spyglass and gasped. "You aren't going to believe this."

Charles handed the torch to Will and took the spyglass from Uncle Will. He then bent down to peer into the hole. "Wow. Absolutely incredible."

Fitz shoved Charles out of the way, grabbed the spyglass and peered down the hole. "Merciful heavens, it's a big room."

The men all started talking at once. Finally, Charles said, "This could be a great find."

Fitz nodded, his eyes shining with enthusiasm. "Who knows what could be down there? It could be another Temple of Mithras."

"Or sepulchers, like we thought initially," said Will, his eyes sparkling.

Charles stood up and dusted off his hands again. "It could be anything. Let's rope off this area, too. I'll write to the Department of Antiquities again and urge them to get a team out here as quickly as possible."

Uncle Will arose as he nodded. He shoved the sailor's patch into his pocket and dusted the dirt off his hands, too. "I think that is a mighty fine idea, lad."

"We're due to return to London in a day or two. I can hand deliver another letter to the Department of Antiquities like I did the first one," mused Charles.

Will nodded again and patted Charles on the back. "Another excellent idea, son. I just wish we had some way to get an accurate picture of the area and what we can see down the hole."

Charles gave Uncle Will a sharp look. "That really would be wonderful. It's a shame we don't have anything like that."

Charles had to bite back laughter as Will nodded, somber and quiet. Charles knew his uncle had seen his little penlight before. Fitz had no idea such an item would ever be invented. If Fitz wasn't there, Charles would fish the little light out of his waistcoat pocket and would use it. *Oh, well, we can come back later without Fitz.*

The men were still talking with great excitement when they returned to Spring Haven. They continued talking as they ate dinner and completed packing to return to London the next day.

Later, after supper, Charles and Kelly went back to the hole. Kelly laid flat on her belly and peered in the hole with the little penlight Charlie brought back in time. "Honey, I think you guys are right. It looks like there is a room down there. I swear I can see tile mosaics."

She moved over so Charles could peer down the hole as well. He let out a low whistle. "Good lord, those mosaics are impressive. I wonder what on earth it is?"

Kelly shrugged. "I haven't a clue, but we will find out once the team of archeologists come out and start digging. Just remember, archeologists currently use some primitive archeological techniques. You will need to watch them every minute to make sure they don't destroy as much as they find."

He nodded. "I agree. At least we both took some archeology classes in college."

She laughed. "As I recall, you took those classes as a reprieve from science classes for vet school. I majored in archeology."

He joined her laughing. "Who would have thought an archeology degree would really have paid off like this?"

She nodded. "I wanted to be an archeologist, but figured I would be working in North Georgia on Cherokee digs while you ran a vet clinic. I never dreamed I would work on a dig in the Cotswolds on an ancient Roman discovery."

The next morning, they headed to London. Once there, Charles took his new missive to the Department of Antiquities. This time, he was greeted with enthusiasm and ushered immediately into the director's office.

The director leapt to his feet as Charles entered his office. "Your Grace, please come in and have a seat. Milord, we are extremely excited about your tiles. We are organizing a team to come to your estate as soon as the snows ease up."

Charlie smiled. He began to relax as he crossed his legs, with one arm draped casually over the arms of the comfortable chair. He held the packet of new information for the director in one hand, with his other hand laying in his lap. "It's not snowing there any longer, although it snowed at Christmas. The snow melted off by the time we left to come to town. However, I have another issue."

He smiled again as he handed the new missive to the director, who grabbed the packet and eagerly began to read. He looked over his spectacles at Charles.

"You found a mound of tumbled rocks with a hole? And it appears to lead down into a subterranean room?" The director sounded dumbfounded.

Charles nodded, as he grinned at the Director. "Yes, sir. I think the melting snow washed a bit of the dirt away to reveal the opening. We tried to look into the hole with a small torch. The hole appears to open down into a subterranean chamber. I would swear we could see reflections of tile down there. I hope it is not just wishful thinking."

The director stared at him, his mouth agape. Finally, he cleared his throat and leaned forward as he replied, eagerness in his voice. "I am astounded. Of course, there have been some wonderful old Roman finds in that area. We will move the date up for your investigation. I trust you will be staying in London to attend the House of Lords?"

Charles nodded. "Yes, sir, I will be at the Ranscome townhouse. However, if need be, my wife or my uncle, William Selk, could meet the team at the estate."

"Very good, your Grace. I will arrange a more extensive team than I thought we would need initially and get it scheduled to come to Spring Haven. I will apprise you of the dates as soon as possible."

Charles stood up and extended his hand. "Thank you very much, Director. We look forward to working with you and will do everything we can to facilitate your research at Spring Haven."

"Jolly good, your Grace." The Director arose and beamed as he shook Charles' hand.

Charles, Fitz and Uncle Will next went to Gentleman John's gym, where they conferred privately with Mr. Jackson. "Your Grace, I tentatively scheduled the fight for January 15th. That is a Saturday. I thought it would work well since Parliament will be in session. We can hold it just out of town, or if you will be in the Cotswolds then, we could hold it at Swindon or just outside of Oxford."

"Since we will already be back in London, let's plan it for somewhere near the outskirts of London," suggested Charles.

"I've arranged boxing matches at Henley-on-Thames before. Would that suit?"

Charles nodded and grinned. "It sounds good to me. Get me the particulars so we can notify Tarleton where and when it will be."

"I'll take care of that, milord, unless you prefer for your second to attend to those details."

"Just include me in the loop," interjected Fitz as he stepped into the office. "I'm Charles's second. Oh, and allow me to introduce myself. I'm Lord Winston Fitz Simmons, the Earl of Waterside. Tarleton insulted my sister and our aunt, also. I'm Charles' uncle."

"Oh, of course, milord. I'll be happy to include you in all communications." Gentleman Jackson nodded.

"So, I'm assuming the final destination will be at Henley-on-Thames on January 15th, and the fight will commence at 7 a.m.?" asked Uncle Will.

Jackson nodded again. "Yes, it will commence at 7 a.m. Now, let's see how you have progressed since last we boxed, your Grace."

Charles pulled off his jacket, waistcoat, cravat, and shirt to enter the ring with Mr. Jackson. Soon, the two men squared off and began exchanging blows. After fifteen minutes, they took a break so Jackson could critique Charles' form and make suggestions. As both began drinking tankards of port, Jackson grinned.

"You're tougher than I expected. Your hands are doing quite admirably. I urge most men to lean back while punching, but you are so quick and you have such fast recovery that I think you will do fine with your current form."

"Thank you, sir. We have worked hard on my speed," replied Charles as he flexed his hands.

Fitz rubbed his jaw. "Oh, believe me, he has worked equally hard on his prowess. I would hate to be the recipient of any harder blows from Charles."

Uncle Will joined the men and nodded in agreement. "Quite so. The lad pulls a mean punch."

"Then I suggest you gentlemen carry on. Your Grace, Gen. Tarleton is expected shortly. Would you like to be giving a demonstration of your mixed martial arts when he arrives?"

Charles grinned ear to ear. "Nothing could please me more."

About ten minutes later, Tarleton and Darlington entered the gym. Tarleton strolled over to Jackson's office, barely noticing the crowd watching the match in progress.

"Mr. Jackson, have you determined when the boxing fight between Lord Hobbs and I shall take place?"

Jackson looked up from his desk and smiled. "Ah, General, I was just writing to you. The fight between his Grace and you shall commence at 7 a.m. on the morning of January 15th at Henley-on-Thames. But it is not

233

scheduled to be a boxing match. I believe you agreed to a mixed martial arts contest."

Tarleton scowled in impatience and waved a hand in the air. "Whatever you want to call it. My heavens, there is a lot of noise in the gymnasium this morning. Who is fighting?"

Jackson smiled and leaned back into his chair "Lord Hobbs is sparring with Lord Fitz Simmons, his second. I believe they are utilizing this mixed martial arts which he chose to use at your fight."

Tarleton paled as he blinked. "Oh, really? Well, let's go have a look-see."

Jackson came around his desk and patted Tarleton on the back. "Excellent idea, General. You will find it is a bit different from boxing, although also it incorporates many boxing techniques."

They walked out to the boxing ring, where the crowd parted for Jackson and Tarleton. As they approached the side of the ring, Fitz fell back against the ropes as blood sprayed from his nose. He threw his hands up into the air.

"Charles, I asked you not to strike my nose again. You've bloodied it thrice in the past week alone."

"Sorry, Uncle Fitz. I'll try to avoid your nose. I can't have Lady Anne get angry again that I damaged your handsome face."

Fitz shook his head in disgust. "Oh, for the love of … Bring it on, pup."

Charles laughed, wheeled around, landed a drop kick and knocked Fitz to the ground. "Pup, huh?"

Fitz got up, wiped the blood from his nose, and assumed a boxing stance again. "I should have said 'arse'."

Tarleton walked up beside his cousin, ashen-faced. " My God, is this mixed martial arts?"

Darlington nodded as he chewed a fingernail. "I'm afraid so. He's damned good at either sport. He's lethal at this one. You aren't really going to fight him, are you?"

Tarleton watched the fight in silence for a few minutes before speaking again. "Dammit. There's no way I could beat him in an honest fight."

Chapter 26
Charles and Kelly
January 1803

The days flew by as Charles and Kelly became accustomed to married life in London. Kelly ordered new curtains and bed linens for the town house and selected new silver and china. Charles continued to work out at Gentleman John's gymnasium each day after attending sessions at the House of Lords.

On Tuesday before the fight, Charles received word that the Department of Antiquities was sending a team to Spring Haven that Thursday. He frowned as he nervously tapped his foot. "But the House of Lords is in session."

Kelly laughed and laid a hand on his. "No problem, darling. I'll return to Spring Haven. I can show the archeologists to the site."

Charles frowned. "But what if they won't pay adequate attention to you because you are a woman?"

Kelly frowned and started to protest just as Uncle Will cleared his throat. "How about I accompany Kelly to Spring Haven? If we leave Tuesday, we will be there before they arrive, and together we can show them what we found."

Kelly's shoulders relaxed as she unclenched her fists. She forced a smile and nodded. "I think that is a great idea. That way, they won't dismiss my comments as mere foolishness from a woman."

Charles continued to frown as he chewed his lip. "I hate to miss their arrival and commencement of the investigation, but I guess that is the best we can do. I would appreciate it if you would accompany Kelly to go out to Spring Haven to meet the team, Uncle Will. She probably knows as much if not more about archeology than they do, but I agree that they might be disrespectful to her. I would hate to have to kill them."

Will nodded and struggled not to laugh. He gave Charles a crisp salute. "I'll come to Henley-on-Thames Friday evening, so we will be there bright and early the next morning. I can make some reservations for us at the inn on the way to Spring Haven to make sure we have enough beds for the three of us Friday night."

Kelly's face lit up. "I want to go, too!"

Uncle Will frowned at her. "Kelly, you know good and well you are not going to be allowed to attend that fight. You stay at the house and supervise the archeologists as they commence their digging. I'll take care of the lads."

Kelly pouted. "Sometimes you are no fun, Uncle Will."

The men laughed as Kelly continued to frown.

Kelly, Aunt Sassy and Uncle Will left to return to Spring Haven in the Ranscome carriage Tuesday morning. They arrived before the archeological team. Kelly ensured they had adequate food for everyone for at least two weeks. The staff bustled about preparing rooms for everyone due to arrive with the archeological team.

Once the team arrived on Thursday, Uncle Will and Kelly showed the team the tiles and the suspicious hole. "Her Grace found it. Lord Ranscome and I agree with her that it appears to lead down to something."

Initially skeptical about the hole, the archeologists soon became excited as they carefully began to excavate and found steps leading down into a tiled subterranean room.

"I told you there were tiles down there, Uncle Will," Kelly whispered.

He nodded as he lit his pipe. "Yep, you sure did, Kelly girl. Sir, please proceed carefully with that shovel. There are valuable Roman antiquities all around here."

The man tipped his hat to Uncle Will. "Yes, sir, Captain Selk."

The team continued excavating. Uncle Will left late Friday afternoon to meet Charles, Fitz and Jackson at Henley-on-Thames.

"You take care of him, Uncle Will. Don't let that horrid man hurt my Charles." Kelly felt like she might cry. She hugged Uncle Will tightly as she struggled to contain her emotions.

Will laughed and patted her on the back. "Don't let that horrid man hurt Charles? Honey, Charles is gonna wipe that man up off the mat. Tarleton hasn't a chance."

She frowned again. "Tarleton hasn't a chance if he fights clean. I know that man's reputation. He is a dirty fighter."

Will looked thoughtful as he puffed on his pipe. "Girl, I reckon I know that better than just about anyone around except my Little Bit. You girls stay safe way out here. We'll be headed here right after the fight."

Kelly nodded. "We'll be fine. Don't worry."

"It will be fine, William. If Tarleton shows up, I'll shoot him." Sassy looked determined, her lips thinned into a nervous yet resolute line.

Will looked shocked. "Darlin', I don't think he'll show up here, but if he does, just hogtie him and wait for us. I don't want you to get in trouble for shooting a lord."

Sassy nodded, but said nothing else. Kelly noticed Aunt Sassy's lips were still in a tight line.

As he rode away, Kelly spoke. "Would you really shoot him?"

Sassy nodded. "In a New York minute. The man is pure evil. Why?"

Kelly smiled. "I was hoping you would say that. Of course, I guess it would be better if the Duchess had to shoot him in self-defense."

Sassy nodded again as her eyes narrowed thoughtfully. "My thoughts exactly. You know, hungry hogs can devour a body in about ten minutes."

Kelly grinned and winked at Sassy. "I look forward to seeing that one of these days."

The men were glad to see each other again at Henley-on-Thames. Uncle Will caught Charles and Fitz up to date on the excavations under way at Spring Haven. He assured Charles that the girls, as he called Sassy and Kelly, were fine and would be safe until the men arrived Saturday afternoon.

Charles frowned. He felt uneasy that Aunt Sassy and Kelly were alone at the estate. "I hope so. Kelly said something about Tarleton playing dirty. I keep worrying he will pull some stunt."

Will chuckled as he lit his pipe. "Keep your guard up. If the sorry weasel pulls anything, it will be when he is fighting you. The women will be fine at Spring Haven."

Charles stared out towards Spring Haven. He wanted to remind Uncle Will that both Aunt Sassy and Mom were alone when Tarleton attacked them on previous occasions. "I hope you're right, Uncle Will, 'cause I would have to kill that sorry bastard if he hurt my Kelly or if he hurt my Aunt Sassy again."

"You would have to get in line behind me, son," said Uncle Will, his voice soft yet menacing.

Early Saturday morning, Kelly went out to check on Nellie and her foal. She slipped out of the manor house wearing a quilted cotton *Ao Dai*, in case she had to wrangle the damned mare into the stall again. She was pleased to see both were doing well in the pasture. As she started back towards the house, arms suddenly grabbed her around the waist.

Kelly trained in martial arts since she was a small child. Without thinking, she tightened her core muscles, collected her strength into the pit of her belly, and threw the weight of her legs upward. She would have flown over his shoulders if he had not held a tight grip on her. As he lost his grip on her, she focused her strength to bring her legs back down to earth. She then tucked her right arm close to her body so she could pull his head down as she went toward the ground. As her feet reached the ground, she threw the man over her shoulder. He landed with a thud, and groaned. Before he could recover, Kelly grabbed a hay rake and whacked him on the head several times before she jumped on top of him. He paled as she pulled a knife from her boot, and slid the bare blade of it to his throat.

"Well, this is an interesting turn of events, " she commented calmly.

"How the bloody hell did you do that, you little Chinese whore?" snarled the man, rattled to be on the bad end of the knife.

She smiled. "Chinese whore, hmm? Those are fighting words, Tarleton. My God, you really must be stupid to spout nonsense like that while I am holding a knife to your throat. I'm not Chinese, and I'm not a whore. You may address me as 'your Grace.' And by the way, if I told you how I did it, I'd have to kill you. Of course, I may kill you anyway. The better question is, aren't you supposed to be at a fight at Henley-on-Thames about now?"

Tarleton glowered at her but refused to comment.

"Mr. Tarleton? Are you sure you don't want to answer me?"

"Fu—" he began.

She pressed the knife into the tender flesh at the base of his throat. She smiled as a line of red bubbled from the thin cut. "Now, that isn't very nice, Mr. Tarleton. Are you really sure you don't want to politely answer my question?"

About then, Scottie came running into the stables. "What the blazes is going on here? Oh, sweet Holy Jesus, your Grace, are you alright?"

She nodded as she held the knife to Tarleton's throat. "I'm fine, Scottie. I'm guessing the General decided he didn't want to fight Charles, and thought I would be easy picking. The General is thinking about now that he should have taken his chances with Charles this morning. Right, General?"

"Shut up, you stupid Chinese bitch. What kind of lady knows how to fight like that? You disgust me."

She chuckled as she pressed the knife closer into his flesh. "Yeah, like I said, I'm not Chinese. I can tell I disgust you enough that you were going to rape me, you sorry little rat bastard. Scottie, fetch some rope."

Scottie blinked. He began to tremble. "Milady, I canna hang the man, no matter how low a scoundrel he may be."

She nodded. Her lips thinned in impatience. "I understand that, Scottie. Fetch the rope. Tie his hands together."

Scottie looked uncertain but finally nodded. "Aye, your Grace."

Once Tarleton's hands were securely tied, Kelly removed the kerchief from around her hair to gag Tarleton. She then tied his feet together and then smiled again. "Well, if he's not going to talk nicely and only wants to call me ugly names, he can just be quiet. Scottie, go fetch Mrs. Selk. She might like to see this."

Scottie hesitated for a moment. "Uh, your Grace-"

"Go get Mrs. Selk right now, Mr. MacGregor. I won't ask again."

Scottie flinched at the tone of her voice. He nodded and touched his hand to his hat. "Aye, your Grace."

Minutes later, Aunt Sassy ran out to the barn with Scottie. She stopped and gasped as she realized Tarleton lay tied up on the barn floor. He glared at Kelly, and then at Sassy, unable to speak due to the gag in his mouth.

"Oh, my word, Charles will kill him."

Kelly laughed. "Charles may not have to kill him. I may kill him first. Wouldn't that be sweet, Tarleton? To be killed by a little China gal who pitched you like you were a sack of taters?"

She bent over and began to cut his clothing off him.

"Your Grace, are you goin' to strip the man naked." Scottie sounded horrified.

Kelly smiled again. "Almost. Not quite. I'll leave his small clothes on. I understand he likes to be naked around women he doesn't know. Well, this is close enough to naked for my taste. Scottie, help me hoist him up on the hay pulley."

Scottie rushed over to help Kelley lift the rope holding Tarleton's hands onto the barn pulley. She directed Scottie to hoist Tarleton just off the ground. Tarleton grunted as he was lifted inches off the floor.

"Now, tie him off there, Scottie. Aunt Sassy, could you hum the tune to 'Kung Fu Fighting' for us?"

"Uh, Kelly, honey, you know I'm tone-deaf, " Aunt Sassy kept glancing nervously at Tarleton. "Uh…. What are you going to do to him?"

Kelly walked over near the punching back and picked up Charles's Muay Thai gloves. As she slipped them on, she flexed her hands. She looked from Tarleton and back to Aunt Sassy. "Why, I'm going to give him a lesson in mixed martial arts. I think it's long overdue."

Kelly began talking to Tarleton. "I'll be kung fu fighting. You'll see that I'm fast as lightning. Just be warned. It might be a little bit frightening to watch this little 'China gal' fight with expert timing."

About then, Kelly lashed out with her first blows, her fists hitting soundly into Tarleton's belly. She backed off to dance on the balls of her feet as he gasped for air.

"Having fun, General? Or is this not quite the fun you had in mind when you came to Spring Haven this morning?" She flashed her sweetest smile at him.

He glared at her, unable to speak.

"Aw, poor baby, it must be tough to have someone beating on you, and you are not able to do a thing about it, " she said as she spun around as she prepared for her next attack.

Aunt Sassy's eyes grew wide as Kelly launched into the kick. Kelly jumped into the air before her feet pummeled Tarleton's face. Blood poured out of his broken nose before Kelly landed back on her feet. Aunt Sassy stood trembling, her hands covering her own face.

"You okay, Sassy?" Kelly continued to dance on the balls of her feet.

Sassy shook her head and kept her face covered. "I think I might throw up."

"Oh, hang on, Aunt Sassy. He has it coming, and then some." Kelly smiled and sang the next verse. "I heard what he did to Fancy and you as well as to other women in the Colonies. The man is an animal. He called me a little Chinese whore. Well, he can think of me as a funky China gal from funky Chinatown. I'm chopping him up, and I'm chopping him down."

Tarleton cringed as she made chopping motions with her hands.

Kelly laughed and resumed talking to him. "I'll display the ancient Chinese art. I sure know my part from a feint to a slip and a kick from my hip."

She kicked again, this time striking Tarleton's ribs.

He groaned as blood trickled from his mouth.

Kelly smiled again. "Hmm. I broke some of his ribs that time. Oh, here I am kung fu fighting…"

Aunt Sassy continued to stare, her mouth agape. She appeared unsure whether she was horrified, appalled or delighted.

Kelly laughed. "Having fun yet, Tarleton? Or are you still shocked the 'little China gal' got the drop on you? I reckon it's a little bit frightening to see a 'little China gal' fighting with expert timing."

He glared at her. As tears of fury and pain began to run down his face, she smiled. "You know, Aunt Sassy, my Dad was worried I would have to face racism when I married Charles, but this pathetic excuse for a man is the only overt racist I have encountered here in Britain. It would just figure this piece of pig offal would be the racist my Dad always warned me about. I have to admit, I wish my Dad could see me now."

Kelly wheeled about, launched into the air again and kicked Tarleton square in the chest.

"You see, General, this is why my Dad taught me martial arts. To be able to protect myself from racist rapists like you. Because nobody makes this baby girl sit in the corner."

Aunt Sassy struggled not to laugh at the Dirty Dancing reference. "Did you really say that?"

Kelly nodded. "One of my favorite lines ever."

About then, Kelly smiled towards the entrance to the barn. "Oh, hi, Charlie. You back so soon? Now, do we get to feed him to the pigs? Or can I kill him first?"

Charles looked grim. "I have come here to chew bubblegum and to kick ass, Tarleton, and I'm all out of bubblegum. Kelly, let me take a crack at him."

She sighed in frustration. "Well, don't go easy on him. He called me a Chinese whore."

Charlie's eyes narrowed. "Did you call her Grace a whore?"

He ripped the gag out of Tarleton's mouth.

Tarleton spat blood. "She is a whore. Why else would you marry that slant-eyed baggage?"

Charlie smiled. "Oh, them's fighting words, Kemo Sabe."

"Where do you lunatics get these insane comments?" Tarleton snarled.

"From lunatics," snapped Charles.

Aunt Sassy nodded. "In Texas."

"He hasn't learned his lesson yet, babe." Kelly's grin looked smug.

Charlie smiled again, but it did not reach his eyes. "Well, good, then I will break him like a Kit Kat bar."

Kelly began to sway back and forth, snapping her fingers. "Do it, Charlie. Break me off a piece of that Kit Kat bar."

Aunt Sassy covered her face again. "I can't watch." She peeked through her fingers. "What are you going to do to him?"

"I told you, Aunt Sassy, I'm going to break the smarmy little weasel. It's time for his comeuppance for his eff-uppence. Kelly, give me my gloves."

Kelly grinned as she peeled the martial arts gloves off and handed them to Charles.

Sassy's eyes widened. "Are ... are you going to ... to discipline him?"

"Oh, no, Sass. The discipline will be my job once Charles is finished breaking him." Will's voice was soft and low but filled with anger. "And believe me: that man will never hurt another woman as long as he lives."

Chapter 27
Epilogue
Fancy
The Present

"Mail's here, Mom!" Ronan dropped the heavy envelope on the table in the foyer.

I wiped my hands with the corner of my apron and walked to the stack of mail. I frowned as I lifted the heavy envelope. "You went to Suarez House today?"

Ronan nodded while he continued chewing the fresh baked cookie I just took out of the oven. "Yes, ma'am. I passed right by there on my way from Trinity. I walked Shannon to the door, and the housemother said you had a package."

I grabbed the envelope and ripped it open. I gasped as letters, journals, and pictures fell out into my hands. "Oh, look, Charlie and Kelly sent us pictures!"

We sat down side by side at the table to read the letters and look at the pictures. "Look, Mom, he sent sketches of Kelly and him in their wedding finery. They have Chico and what looks like a little Skye puppy with them. But who is this guy?"

I gasped as I carefully took the sketch from Ronan. "It's my brother, Fitz! It looks like Fitz got married again. The little girl must be his daughter, Nicole. Oh, my gosh, he included drawings of Daddy, Lily, Will, Sassy... even my mother. She looks so frail. They all look so old."

"Yeah, Charlie says she looks frail but she's still tough as nails. Look, Mom, they found Gramma Meara's next diary! You will have enough about her to write a book. Hmm. What are these?"

I gasped as he held up what appeared to be ancient earrings. "Oh, my heavens, those look like they could be Roman. I hope they tell me how they got those earrings in one of these letters."

"Cool Mom. Hey, did you see this picture?" He dangled a picture in front of me.

I leaned over Ronan to see the picture and gasped as fresh tears welled up in my eyes. "It's dated January 1804. Oh, my heavens, Kelly had twin boys. They named them Richard Ranscome Winslow Hobbs and Marcus McCarron Hobbs."

Ronan grinned. "Well, she was a twin, Mom. I guess this means Charlie has his heir and his spare?"

I nodded as I swiped at a tear leaking from one of my eyes. "It looks like it. Gosh, I wish I could hold those baby boys."

Ronan hugged me and pecked a kiss on my cheek. "Looks like he really went back to fulfill his destiny, Mom. But who knows? Maybe someday we'll see them again."

I smiled at my youngest child, and tousled his unruly auburn curls. "It sure looks like he found his destiny in the past with the woman he loves. And yes, who knows, Ronan? Maybe we will see them again some day."

Ronan grinned. I was still crying, but my youngest child knew my happy tears when he saw them. "Are you going to tell her mom where they went? That they got married before their twenty-second birthdays? Or about the twins?"

I stared at the drawing of Kelly and the boys a minute before I answered. I finally turned and grinned at Ronan. "I could make a copy of the artwork of Kelly and Charles in their wedding clothes and of Kelly and the twins for her. What do you think?"

His face lit up with teenage devilment. "Maybe someday, Mom."

I fist bumped him as we both laughed. "Yes. Maybe someday."

About the Author

Sharon K. Middleton is a fourth generation Texan. Her first relative to the Colonies came in 1742 as a 12-year-old Irish indentured servant. Her great-grandmother immigrated from Mexico in the 1890s. Sharon is a graduate of Trinity University, Texas A&M, and South Texas College of Law. She is an attorney licensed to practice in Texas. She enjoys writing, quilting, showing and raising Skye terriers. She loves the wilds of North Georgia and hopes to retire there soon.

Note from the Author

Word-of-mouth is crucial for any author to succeed. If you enjoyed *The McCarron's Destiny*, please leave a review online—anywhere you are able. Even if it's just a sentence or two. It would make all the difference and would be very much appreciated.

Thanks!
Sharon K. Middleton

We hope you enjoyed reading this title from:

BLACK ⬥ ROSE
writing™

www.blackrosewriting.com

Subscribe to our mailing list – *The Rosevine* – and receive **FREE** books, daily deals, and stay current with news about upcoming releases and our hottest authors.
Scan the QR code below to sign up.

Already a subscriber? Please accept a sincere thank you for being a fan of Black Rose Writing authors.

View other Black Rose Writing titles at
www.blackrosewriting.com/books and use promo code
PRINT to receive a **20% discount** when purchasing.

CPSIA information can be obtained
at www.ICGtesting.com
Printed in the USA
LVHW040249081021
699881LV00005B/20